"The greatest hero in Texas never dreamed winning a raffle would net him a dead horse, a thrice-widowed beauty, two sons, a spicy-mouthed mother-in-law and redemption for his troubled soul. *The Wedding Raffle* was a hoot!"

—Yvonne Zalinski, Paperback Outlet

"I absolutely loved Honor's story. Something for everyone. Heroes aplenty. Is Rafe Malone going to have his own story too? I'm looking forward to selling the start of this 'Texas' series. Hope they come out fast. Women love them."

—Sharon Harbough, Munchkin Books

"A delightful love story—the plot is charming. The characters have an outstanding sense of humor. Exceptional Western romance."

—Joan Lutz, The Book Rack

"Now this was a good, good book. Thrills, chills, danger and an all-conquering love. Not to mention the rigged raffles! Geralyn—good job. I have a new favorite book for my keeper shelf. . . . It was even better than *Bad Luck Wedding Dress.*"

—Merry Cutler, Annie's Book Shop

"I really enjoyed this story. It was a great way to spend a hot summer's day under the shade tree. Complex characters, snappy dialogue, real emotions."

—Holly Deems, The Book Rack

Books by Geralyn Dawson

The Wedding Raffle
The Wedding Ransom

Published by POCKET BOOKS

"How Many Men
Have You Known, Maggie?"

Silence stretched, long and black like the tunnel behind them. When she finally opened her eyes, the fear had disappeared. Instead, Rafe saw sorrow and embarrassment, and it cut him to the quick.

"None," she said flatly. "It's one reason I've been flirting with you, Malone. Most women my age are married with children, but not me. I have overprotective pirates for guardians, and one way or another, they've scared off every man who ever came near me."

Rafe knew he should keep his mouth shut. He knew he should remove her from his lap and put some distance between them. Instead, he dipped his head and whispered, "No, darlin', not every man."

Then he kissed her.

And she kissed him back.

Her lips moved against his, hotly, passionately. Desperately. The slightest of whimpers emerged from the back of her throat, and the sound of it rippled through him.

He wanted her. Oh, how he wanted her. He broke off the kiss and looked at her. A shimmering look in her eyes—sweet and needful and asking for the obvious, but also something more.

And Rafe knew without a doubt that in this place, this moment, Mary Margaret St. John was his for the taking.

GERALYN DAWSON

THE WEDDING RANSOM

POCKET STAR BOOKS

New York   London   Toronto   Sydney   Tokyo   Singapore

An *Original* Publication of POCKET BOOKS

 A Pocket Star Book published by
POCKET BOOKS, a division of Simon & Schuster Inc.
1230 Avenue of the Americas, New York, NY 10020

Copyright © 1997 by Geralyn Dawson Williams

ISBN: 0-671-00127-2

First Pocket Books printing February 1998

10 9 8 7 6 5 4 3 2 1

POCKET STAR BOOKS and colophon are registered trademarks of Simon & Schuster Inc.

Front cover illustration by Lina Levy

Printed in the U.S.A.

Writing is like a chocolate stain.
Sometimes it's hard to get out.

—John Patrick Williams
Seventh-Grade Honors English

This one is for you, John.
You understand your mother so well.

THE WEDDING RANSOM

➤ **1** ⬅

Republic of Texas, 1845

The bite of razor-sharp steel against his jugular jerked Rafe Malone from the oblivion of sleep. Beneath the warmth of the springtime sun he lay frozen, his eyes closed, his senses as sharp as the blade at his throat. Quiet breaths, distinctive scents, and the shifting of shadows relayed the information that three men, possibly four, surrounded him. The thrill of danger coursed through his blood. Here, with death but a slash away, he felt more alive than he had in years.

It was all Rafe could do to keep from grinning.

A sting of pain stroked across his neck and Rafe opened his eyes. Sunlight blinded him at first, then four figures came into focus. *Good Lord.* He blinked and looked again. Pirates? Gray-haired pirates? On his central Texas ranch? A laugh slid past the cutlass threatening his throat.

"Did you hear that, Ben?" growled the man holding the blade. He lifted a finger and traced the old, ugly scar running across his cheekbone, then tugged at his silver hoop earring. "He cackled at us. I have my

1

blade at his throat and he laughs. That's proof enough for me."

The tallest of the men nodded, the diamond stud in his right ear twinkling in the afternoon sunlight. Wrinkles framed the intelligent blue eyes studying Rafe from beneath bushy salt-and-pepper brows. Clothed in a flowing white shirt and close-fitting breeches, he stood in a spread-legged stance, his hands braced upon his hips. He could have been standing on a ship's deck instead of a field of green grass beside a shallow creek. "Aye, Gus," he said in a voice ringing with command. "I heard it. I guess we all know what that means."

"No!" A third man loomed over Rafe, fierce dark eyes glaring from beneath the red bandanna tied around his head. He was short and stocky, and with his meaty fists clenched and nostrils flaring, he looked mean as an old range bull. "It's not enough. Go ahead and stick him, Gus. See what happens then."

"I'll tell you what'll happen then, Snake," said the fourth man in a raspy, gravelly voice. "He'll bleed." He hunkered down beside Rafe and smoothly confiscated the pistol at the prone man's hip. "I told you Snake would want to slice him up. He hasn't killed a man in months. You know what the smell of blood does to him."

A maniacal chuckle issued from bloodthirsty Snake's mouth.

Rafe's attention shifted from pirate to pirate, observing their solemn nods, trying unsuccessfully to figure out where this conversation was leading. The fourth buccaneer tilted his head, and his horseshoe-shaped sapphire earring captured Rafe's notice. Expensive little trinkets, these fellows wore.

And interesting old scars they sported, too. Rafe winced at the ring encircling the fourth pirate's neck. At some point in his life, this fellow had been hanged. Rafe swallowed instinctively, having come close to a similar fate once himself.

Guess this teaches me to take an afternoon nap, he thought, as a gentle puff of cedar-scented wind stirred the bushes around him. After being up the better part of last night helping Dapple Annie bring her foal into the world, he had only wanted a little bit of shut-eye. When he'd stretched out on a comfy bed of clover and succumbed to the lure of sleep, all had been quiet and peaceful around the Lone Star Ranch.

Having his sleep interrupted wasn't exactly unexpected. Life on the central Texas horse farm in springtime did tend to run from one crisis to another. But pirates? The very idea of it struck him dumb. His spread lay a good three hundred miles west of the coast. Damn near thirty years had passed since Jean Laffite said *au revoir* to Galveston Island. Who were these men? Why the hell were they here?

Did they honestly intend to kill him?

The one with the diamond in his ear, Ben, appeared to be the leader. Gus-with-the-cutlass looked to him and asked, "What do you want me to do, Captain?"

Rafe concluded it might be to his benefit to interrupt the answer. He lifted a hand and pushed the blade away from his neck, taking care not to betray any pain as the cutlass sliced into his palm. Propping himself up on his elbows, his fingers in position to reach for the knife in his trouser pocket, he drawled, "Why don't you boys try heading southeast? Y'all are obviously lost." He jerked his head to the right. "The Gulf of Mexico is thataway."

Cutlass Gus, Snake, and rope-ringed fourth man whipped their heads toward Ben. The captain slowly, solemnly nodded.

What happened next made Rafe shake his head in wonder. Gus blew a sigh of what sounded like relief as he sheathed his cutlass. The fourth pirate grinned and held out his hand, wriggling his fingers toward Snake who muttered, "Well, clam it."

Clam it? Rafe silently repeated. What kind of a curse was that for a bloodthirsty pirate?

3

The trio of heavy gold hoops in Snake's left ear clinked against one another as he yanked off his bandanna. He reached inside the cloth and removed a wad of bills.

Prepared for a more lethal weapon than cash, Rafe let out the breath he'd been holding.

Snake shoved the money toward the fourth man. "I can't believe you actually won the bet, Lucky Nichols. You never win anything. You are the most *un*lucky man alive."

The fourth man, Lucky Nichols, kissed the bills, then gleefully stuck them in his vest pocket, along with Rafe's gun. "This is a sign that my luck is changing, I can feel it."

Snake snorted and reached out a hand to flick a bug off Lucky's shoulder. "What you're feeling is a caterpillar crawling up your back. Our bets financed my bad habits for the past thirty-two years, and I don't see that changing. This was a fluke."

"This outcome was predetermined," interjected the captain, his blue eyes gleaming with amusement. "I warned you not to bet him, Snake. A band of washed-up old cutthroats like us never stood a chance of frightening the likes of Gentleman Rafe Malone."

Rafe wondered if the Republic of Texas had put in a mental hospital down the road in Bastrop and neglected to guard the gates. Sitting all the way up, he demanded, "What the hell is going on?"

The leader bowed his head. "I beg your pardon, Mr. Malone. I believe introductions are in order. I am Captain Benjamin Scovall. With me are my colleagues, Gus Thomas—"

Cutlass Gus saluted.

"—Snake MacKenzie"

He folded his arms and scowled.

"—and Lucky Nichols."

Lucky gave his earring a twist and nodded while Captain Ben continued. "We were attracted by your exemplary reputation, Mr. Malone, but since you've been out of the . . . business for some time now, a test of your courage was deemed appropriate."

"So you dressed for a costume ball and put a knife to my neck?"

Ben fingered the billowing blouse he wore and shrugged. "Our dress is no costume, but the garb of our youth. It can be intimidating, don't you agree?"

"Yeah, but not all of us could get into his old clothes," Gus said, looking pointedly at Snake Mac-Kenzie's protruding belly.

The short man turned a glare on his companion that widened Rafe's eyes. *A look like that could scare the ugly off a buzzard.* "I am pleased to say you passed our test," Ben continued. "You are a brave one, Gentleman Rafe Malone."

"He's a cocky blighter," Snake added unhappily.

Rafe gazed around the ragtag group. What was it the captain had said? Exemplary reputation? Somehow he didn't think the ol' swashbuckler was talking about the horse-breeding business Rafe had established with his old friend Luke Prescott. Four years had passed since Rafe had last committed an illegal act. Four years since Luke Prescott tracked him to his east Texas hideout dangling an amnesty from the government in exchange for a little help with a particularly vicious band of murderers.

Rafe rolled to his feet and casually brushed the dirt from his trousers. "Like you said, I'm out of the business. I gave up thieving years ago, so if you're here looking for the *gentleman* in Rafe Malone you've wasted your time. I'm plain old Rafe, now."

"You're not a gentleman?" Frowning, Snake Mac-Kenzie folded his arms. "Maggie will want a gentleman."

"I'm not a *thief,*" Rafe replied, eyeing each of the four older men in turn. "Not anymore. I have a deal with the Texas Rangers. The people of Texas get to keep their money, and I get to keep my neck out of a noose." After a moment's pause, he added, "Who's Maggie?"

"Mary Margaret St. John," Ben explained. "She's our granddaughter."

Rafe quirked a brow. Four grandfathers?

Snake MacKenzie snorted. "I thought this fellow was a gentleman. It's why I agreed to this plan."

"It doesn't matter whether he's a gentleman or not," Lucky said, a threat obvious in his voice. "He's not getting anywhere near our Maggie."

"You're dreaming, Lucky." Gus shook his head sadly. "You are all dreaming. I've been trying to tell you that for some time now. Whether we like it or not, Maggie is a woman full-grown. For all our trying to mold her into a gentle lady, she is her father's daughter, curse his black soul. She'll be wanting herself a man before long." He jerked his head toward Rafe. "Mark my words, she'll take one look at the shoulders on this fellow and swoon. He's just the type to attract her. She'll like his attitude as much as she likes his looks. And we all know how he'll react once he gets a look at our Maggie."

Snake MacKenzie moved like a twenty-year-old as he reached over and grabbed Gus's cutlass from its scabbard. Before Rafe could react, the blade was back at his neck. MacKenzie spoke through gritted teeth. "Touch even a hair on her head and you'll lose your own, Malone. Understand?"

"Put the weapon away, Snake," Ben instructed. "By all accounts, Mr. Malone is an intelligent man. Knowing Mary Margaret is under our protection, he'll not trifle with her."

Gus rubbed the scar on his cheek. "I'm telling you, he's not the one we need to worry about. It's that little gal of ours. By sending her to that fancy school, we tried to mold her into something she's not. We have quashed her spirit for too many years. Have any of you taken a good look at her lately? Did you listen to her in the courtroom? Our little Maggie is all grown up. She's going to want a man!"

"Well I don't want a woman," Rafe snapped, backing away from the cutlass.

"You want a man!" Lucky exclaimed, an expression of alarm flickering across his face.

Rafe lost his patience. "What I *want* is the opportunity to enjoy an uninterrupted nap on my own land. Alone! And you can damn well rest assured that if I were in the mood for a woman, she sure as hell wouldn't be the female offspring of a band of over-the-hill buccaneers!"

MacKenzie's complexion flushed red. "Are you saying our Maggie isn't good enough for you? I'll have you know she's the prettiest, sweetest, most gentle and loving girl in Texas. In all of America, for that matter. Maybe even the entire world. It doesn't matter that the lass is our granddaughter. You won't be able to resist her. You will try to take her to your bed and then I'll have to kill you." He turned to Ben and heaved a sigh. "This won't work. We may as well go home. He'll die before he steals our treasure back for us."

Rafe dropped his head back, his eyes shut. "I'm dreaming, that's what this is. I'm really asleep and having a nightmare."

The chuckle began softly, then swelled to a full-bodied guffaw. Ben Scovall laughed for a full minute before regaining control. "I haven't been so entertained since we took that troupe of actors captive off the coast of Trinidad." He clapped Rafe on the shoulder. "Relax, son. Allow me to explain why we have come."

Rafe's wasn't in the mood to relax. That had ended when a blade pricked his skin. But surprisingly, neither was he of a mind to throw these intruders off his property. In the midst of MacKenzie's diatribe a few moments ago, he had said something that caught Rafe's attention. The pirate had spoken a word—two words, actually—that appealed to the side of Rafe he'd stifled for a long time now: "steal" and "treasure."

Damn, but at times he missed the life.

For the past four years, Rafe had lived on the right side of the law. But prior to that, he had been unarguably the most successful thief in Texas. He'd stolen almost everything under the sun—horses, guns, cash. Anything of value. He'd learned his craft young, stealing food to survive, clothes to wear, all the necessities an orphan required to stay alive. He'd taken a hiatus from thievery during those years the Prescotts took him in and treated him like their own, but after the Texas Revolution—after the debacle following the battle of San Jacinto—Rafe's outlook on life changed. He'd been betrayed by men in power—the officers of the Army of the Republic of Texas—based on the ugly, false accusations of his half brother Nick Callahan. As a result, he went back to stealing with a vengeance, until his best friend, Texas Ranger Luke Prescott, worked a deal to get him amnesty for his crimes. An amnesty subject to revocation should Gentleman Rafe Malone ever again take to stealing in Texas.

Rafe wouldn't break his word to Luke for any price, but he was a curious man by nature. The mystery and ramblings of these old men appealed to that long-unappeased part of him that craved adventure. What would it hurt to listen to them?

He scooped his hat from the ground and placed it on his head, eyeing Lucky, Gus, and Snake MacKenzie before fixing his gaze on Ben. "Why don't y'all come on up to the house. I have some decent whiskey, or maybe rum."

"Do you have any wine?" MacKenzie asked. "Bordeaux, preferably. It's heading on to four o'clock. Time for our dose of Lake Bliss water. We've found it mixes best with Bordeaux."

Lake Bliss water? Rafe didn't think he even wanted to ask. "I'll see what I can do," he said dryly.

The visitors walked their horses as Rafe led them toward the log dwelling a short distance away. Built in the two-room dogtrot style common in Texas, the house was small but comfortable. Rafe had lived here for a little over two years. The curtains on the window and cushions on the chairs made it a bit fancy for a bachelor's abode, in Rafe's opinion. His views hadn't mattered squat once Luke's wife Honor had taken it to mind to spruce the place up.

When Rafe and Luke had decided to go in as partners on a horse-breeding business, the Prescotts had sold their old place, Duvall Farms, and bought the land adjacent to his. They had built a large new home on the other side of the hill from Rafe's, which was handy because the Winning Ticket Ranch had a damn fine cook.

Honor liked to mother—a good thing considering she now had four children and an elderly mother-in-law to tend—and she'd taken Rafe on as a project. Other than the matchmaking, he mostly enjoyed the attention. If the pirates gave the bows and ruffles on his frilly yellow gingham window curtains a second glance, he didn't care. Rafe was nothing if not confident in his manhood.

Lucky Nichols admired the roses decorating the cabin's front wall, but as they walked indoors it was Snake MacKenzie who truly surprised Rafe by saying, "Lookie there, Gus. Malone has kitchen curtains just like mine."

Rafe also had a kitchen table large enough to accommodate the entire Prescott family when they came to call, so he gestured for the men to take a seat, then rummaged around a stack of storage crates until he found a dusty bottle of port. "This will have to do," he said, pouring a round for the pirates. Having sworn off liquor for the most part himself, he filled his own glass with cider. "So," he said, taking a seat. "You fellas want to tell me what this is all about?"

Lucky stood and tugged a small flat bottle from his back pocket. He pulled out the cork with a pop. "This is what it's about."

Rafe lifted the clear glass flask and eyed the cloudy liquid inside. Bringing it to his nose, he sniffed. And grimaced. *Rotten eggs.* "That smells worse than turned buttermilk."

"But it can make an old man feel like a young buck," Gus said.

"Or give a sick girl relief from her pain," Ben added in a quiet, solemn voice.

The pirates shared a look that had the hairs on Rafe's neck standing at attention. Then Gus snorted and reached into his shirt. Pulling out a broadside, he tossed it onto the table.

"Hotel Bliss?" Rafe read aloud.

"The finest spa west of Saratoga, New York," Lucky said, beaming. "Our curative waters will doctor all sorts of ills, and our mud baths will not only ease your aches, they'll make your skin soft as a newborn's behind."

Glancing at the old pirate's leathery skin, Rafe swallowed a pithy remark and read from the broadside. "'Located in the beautiful Big Thicket of deep east Texas. Romantic dance parties. Picnics and buggy races.' A billiard saloon?"

Snake MacKenzie linked his fingers over his belly and leaned back in his chair. "The hotel is closed at the moment, but that's only a temporary setback. You see, the lass is looking to attract visitors on holiday, not simply those in need of medical miracles. On account of what she went through herself, it's real important to her that sick folk get to rub shoulders with healthy folk every chance they get."

On account of what she went through? Rafe was intrigued. He'd always been a curious sort, and the more the pirates talked, the more he wanted to know about Maggie St. John. What was this about a court-room? And of course, he hadn't forgotten the treas-ure, either.

"Help me out, here, fellas. I'm having trouble making the connection between bottled water and a health spa, Mary Margaret St. John, and waking from my afternoon nap to a Caribbean toothpick against my throat. In other words, where does treasure come into it?"

"Why don't you tell him, Ben?" Gus said. "It's your idea. You're the one who figured out how we're gonna save Maggie."

Ben poured a long splash of the bottled water into his glass of port, obviously gathering his thoughts. "I am afraid my friends got ahead of themselves in explaining our purpose for approaching you. What they mentioned—the spa, the water, even Mary Margaret—are our personal motives for making this trip and do not concern you." He reached for the saddlebags he'd carried with him into the house and tossed open the flap.

Rafe's gaze fixed on the canvas bag Scovall with-drew. Ben tossed it onto the center of the table, and the old familiar *chink* as it landed sent Rafe's heart beating double time. Coins. Gold coins? At Ben's go-ahead nod, he reached for the pouch and confirmed his suspicion. Old gold coins. "Spanish doubloons."

"Aye. A mere sampling of the pirate booty we collected over the years. The value of that bag is approximately three thousand of today's dollars. We have at least a hundred times that amount in gold, jewels, and other riches hidden away."

A shiver raced up Rafe's spine. He'd been poor too long—a thief too long—not to react to that kind of figure.

Ben Scovall smiled at him knowingly. "We chose our treasure hoard carefully, Mr. Malone, and for many years we have been able to access it whenever necessary. That, I'm afraid, has changed. And that is why we have come to you."

Rafe thought of what MacKenzie had said earlier about stealing their treasure back for them. "So you're hoping I'll steal back what someone else stole from you after you stole it from the owners in the first place."

Gus snapped gnarled fingers. "The man is quick, too."

"And you're out of luck," Rafe replied. He shoved back his chair and stood. "Sorry, fellas, but if I'm caught stealing in the Republic of Texas, the rangers will revoke my pardon and put a noose around my neck. I'm not the man for this job."

"The impatience of youth," Ben said with a sigh. "Sit back down, Malone. I think you are the man for this job, and if you will allow me to finish my explanation, I believe you will agree. The situation is not as simple as you think. This mission does involve danger, true. But unless the Texas Rangers have international jurisdiction, landing in a Texas prison is not one of those hazards. Tell me, Mr. Malone, do you consider yourself an adventurous man?"

Rafe set down his glass of cider with a thud. "Are you telling me your treasure isn't hidden in Texas?"

"Not even in the United States. Think about it. We are willing to negotiate a substantial fee for your services and at the same time we are offering a . . . holiday of adventure, one might describe it."

Adventure. Rafe twisted his wrist, swirling the cider in his glass as yearning filled him despite his better sense. He tried to hide it behind a sarcastic drawl. "So, other than a treasure hunt, what could I look forward to on this . . . holiday of adventure?"

"Could be some fighting," Lucky said, his eyes gleaming.

Ben gave him a disapproving stare. "Only if your skills are rusty, Mr. Malone, and I seriously doubt that is the case. You should be able to elude the difficult individuals who have taken up residence in the area. It is true that a successful conclusion of this task will require the use of stealth, cunning, and superior physical strength, but you, of course, possess all three."

Gus nudged Lucky with an elbow. His scar twisted on his cheek as he spoke softly from the side of his mouth. "Never heard the captain flatter a man before. He's almost as slick at that as he is with the ladies."

When Ben didn't react, Rafe wondered if the pirate captain wasn't a little hard of hearing. "Why don't you elaborate some on these 'difficult individuals.'"

Lucky, Gus, and MacKenzie shared a grimace, then looked toward their captain to reply. "It is an out-of-the-way part of the world," Ben said. "Being a Texan, you undoubtedly know such spots often attract a . . . scruffier element of society who tends to settle in among the natives. In this case, it is the descendants of those who settled the region with Captain Laffite after he left Texas years ago. The natives are—"

"Yucatecs," Rafe interrupted, aware of the pirate king's destination after deserting Galveston over thirty years earlier. "They're also embroiled in a war, if I'm not mistaken. You hid your treasure in a jungle?"

Ben cocked his head and smiled. "We hid it in one of the most beautiful places on earth. Consider it, Malone. You will be gone six weeks. Two months at the very most. Think of turquoise water and unspoiled beaches. Riches beyond belief."

"You might as well throw in the other lure," Gus interrupted. "A beautiful woman to look at. Toss in a little rum, and life just doesn't get any better."

"Woman!" Snake MacKenzie slammed his fist down onto the table. "She is not going. Especially not with a man like this one. Besides, this is no pleasure cruise. What if the lass gets sick again? No, I simply won't hear of it!"

"Hearing has nothing to do with it," Gus said, his

voice brimming with sorrow. "It'll take physical force to prevent Maggie from going. We may be mean sonofabitches on the high seas, but not a one of us has what it takes to raise a hand against our Maggie. Nope, we won't be able to stop her from tagging along."

Rafe glanced around the table. The woebegone expression on Lucky's face suggested he agreed with Gus. Rafe couldn't read a thing on Ben Scovall's countenance.

"She's been angling to go ever since we brought it up, you know it," Gus continued. "You're gonna have to let it go, Snake. Let *her* go. She's twenty-five years old. It's amazing we've been able to put this moment off as long as we have. We've done our best by Maggie, and we have to trust her to choose what she needs. If that means a bit of adventure with Malone here before she settles down with a good man, then we have to accept it."

Good man, Rafe thought, offended. *What the hell am I, a prized pig?*

"I'll be damned if I accept it." MacKenzie glared at Rafe. "I'll cut off his jewels first!"

Instinctively, Rafe pressed his thighs together.

"You won't hurt him, Snake. I have dibs on that." Lucky rubbed a hand across his jaw. "I hate saying it, but Gus is right about some of it. Maggie is getting more difficult to handle by the day. The longer she's home with us, the less of a hold all that gentility she learned in school has on her. She's reverting to the old ways. All the schooling in the world can't overcome the years of living with the likes of us."

"I need another drink." MacKenzie banged his glass on the table. He closed his eyes and hung his head. "Whiskey this time, please."

As Rafe rose to retrieve the bottle, Ben spoke in a placating tone. "It is possible we are worrying overmuch. Chances are Mary Margaret won't have the slightest interest in making the trip. After all, she is devoted to making Hotel Bliss a success. That is where all her energies lie."

"I'm not worried where her energies lie. It's where her body lies that has me shiverin' in my shoes." MacKenzie tossed back the drink Rafe had provided him and signaled for another.

"Now, Snake, don't think so negatively." Lucky twisted his earring three times. "I think Ben is right. Even though the hotel is temporarily closed, Maggie still has a lot of work to keep her busy. I don't believe she'll want to make the trip this time." He looked at Gus. "I'll bet you twenty dollars she wants to stay home."

"Done." Gus nodded.

MacKenzie groaned and clutched his head with both hands. "Now you've done it, Nichols. She's bound to want to go if you made a bet she wouldn't."

Rafe poured the drink, watching him, watching his companions. All four of them appeared shaken by Lucky Nichols's bet. Slowly, Rafe grinned. These petrified old pirates were entertaining as sin. What the hell. A call to adventure. A woman he most definitely wanted to meet. It was the best offer he'd had all day.

He flipped his chair around and straddled it. "So, men, let's talk treasure. Where exactly is it? How much of it comes to me as my fee? And . . . " He paused, giving Snake MacKenzie a baiting look. "When do I get to meet your granddaughter?"

In her first-floor bedroom at Hotel Bliss, an ache in Maggie St. John's right leg woke her from a fitful sleep. Wincing, she threw back the bedcovers and sat up, gingerly touching her knee. Swollen and hot. She gritted her teeth. She must have overdone it yesterday when she'd climbed across the roof to patch shingles stripped away by high winds during a recent storm. Or maybe she shouldn't have run that second mile-and-a-half lap around the lake.

She flexed her leg, and along with the pain, anger flared inside her. She whispered one of her papa's favorite curses. Maggie was all too familiar with this sort of pain, but she hadn't had a spell in months. She had hoped this bit of trouble was gone for good.

"I don't have time to be sick," she whispered. Her grandfathers needed her to care for them, now. *They* were the sickly ones, whether they wanted to admit it or not. Poor Papa Gus, for example. Some mornings he was so stove up he could barely move from his bed.

This can't happen to me. Not now. Not on top of all the other trouble. Maggie drew a deep breath, attempting to calm her rising temper. And if beneath her anger lay a sliver of fear, she refused to admit it.

Light from a full moon and countless stars beamed through the open window and illuminated her bedroom with a soft, silvery radiance. Lifting her watch from the nightstand, she saw that dawn was but a short time away. Maggie listened to the night, soaking in its tranquility, until the distant sound of a masculine snore from the guest rooms upstairs destroyed any chance of regaining her peace.

She scowled and dragged her hands through her hair, finger-combing the long curls. The devil take that cursed Barlow Hill, the paunch-bellied, sourbreathed bounder who threatened all she held dear. The man who'd used lawyers to steal Hotel Bliss. For a moment she damned her conscience and wished she'd not forbidden her grandfathers their revenge. It would be oh-so-convenient if Barlow Hill were to die.

As much as she regretted the fact, Maggie couldn't let them do it. Her papas had gone out of their way to see her raised a lady and too many of the lessons had stuck. She couldn't condone killing the man, no matter how attractive the idea sounded.

Upstairs, Hill's snore all but rattled the rafters, and Maggie wanted away from him, out of the hotel this minute. She rose, cautiously resting her weight on her sore knee, biting her lower lip against the pain. She whispered another invective, grabbed her wrapper from the foot of her bed, and slipped it on. Barefoot, she left her bedroom and limped quietly through the darkened hotel, headed for the summer kitchen.

Built separately from the three-story, fourteenguest-room hotel building, the kitchen was her Papa Snake's domain. A pot charmer of extraordinary skill, Snake took it as a personal affront that the cooking lessons he gave his adopted granddaughter had never quite taken. He'd thrown in the soupspoon, so to speak, the day he'd hung the sign that read: Where There's Smoke, Maggie's Cooking.

Maggie smiled at the memory as she turned the spigot of a large earthenware urn and filled a tin cup with water. Not just any water, but special water. Curative water. Lake Bliss water.

She carried her drink toward the table and chairs that sat beneath the kitchen window and took a seat. Bringing her cup to her mouth, she sniffed the water's slightly sulfuric fragrance before downing it in a three-swallow gulp. She shuddered. Her mouth puckered. She gently massaged her knee and waited for the water to do its work.

Maggie believed in the powers of Lake Bliss water. Daily doses of the liquid had effectively given her back her life. Orphaned at the age of four and unofficially adopted by the four seafaring friends of her late father, she had spent her childhood climbing ship's rigging during sea voyages and running the sparkling beaches of the Caribbean island where they lived when not aboard ship. When swollen joints first began to plague her at the age of thirteen, the forced inactivity of chronic illness had hurt her spirit as much as the pain plagued her body. Local physicians failed to offer a remedy, so her papas had taken her from city to city across the world, seeking answers and searching for a cure. One doctor after another had told them no treatment existed and that Maggie could expect to be crippled by the age of twenty. Unwilling to accept such a diagnosis, her grandfathers had broadened their inquiry, pursuing every avenue of potential aid no matter how unusual it seemed. Papa Ben had been the one to hear about the small lake in Texas whose waters appeared to possess healing properties.

Her first sight of the lake on that long ago morning had made an indelible impression on Maggie. To this day, she recalled the thrill that ran through her when she spied the ribbons of steam rising from emerald waters surrounded by the towering trees of the Big

Thicket. She'd smiled at the pink-and-white beauty of dogwood blossoms splashed along the bank. She'd closed her eyes and absorbed the soulful note of the mourning dove's coo. She'd sighed with pleasure as she whiffed the bite of cedar-scented air.

Something about the place, some intangible essence, struck the heart of the well-traveled girl. To her, this little piece of Texas was as beautiful as the turquoise waters and sugar sand beaches of the Caribbean. For Maggie, it felt like coming home.

They'd built a log cabin along the 130-acre lake's south bank in March of her sixteenth year. By August, following daily doses of water and therapeutic mud baths, her pain had all but disappeared. After much planning, debate, and discussion, Maggie and her landlocked pirate papas left the place Maggie had christened Lake Bliss, taking a year's supply of bottled water with them. Before leaving Texas, they tracked down the owner of the Lake Bliss land and purchased the area from him. Or so they had thought.

In the shadowed darkness of the moonlit kitchen, Maggie grimaced and cursed the careless mistake made so many years ago that caused them such grief today. Land speculation ran rampant in Texas, then and now. The title they had purchased had not been a clear one, a fact they'd recently discovered when Barlow Hill, rot his soul, sued them for ownership of Hotel Bliss and won.

Restless, she rose, wincing as much from the ache in her heart as that in her leg. Between the water and the exercise moving provided, the soreness in her knee had eased. Now she felt sickly in another manner entirely. Thinking about Barlow Hill had made her both nervous and nauseous. What she needed now was something calming and comforting. What she needed now was a little more Bliss.

Maggie decided to head down to the bathhouse and indulge in a mud treatment. In all of her twenty-five years, she'd never discovered anything quite so soothing as a nice long soak in the naturally heated mud of Lake Bliss.

The hotel boasted both a ladies' and a gentlemen's bathhouse. Papa Ben had designed and erected the three-sided structures at the spot where the hot spring bubbled up from the earth before flowing out to form the lake. The bathhouses allowed open access to the water, while at the same time providing privacy and creature comforts for bathers. Before litigation closed the hotel, a half-dozen employees worked in the bathhouses ministering to the guests. Now, Maggie was the lone woman on the premises, the only woman around to partake of the recuperative pleasures of the bath. "Just like the old days," she said softly as she exited the kitchen and walked the gravel path toward the lake.

Above her, heaven shone in a million fading stars as the eastern sky took on a rosy glow. Maggie smiled at the beauty of the sight and repeated a silent prayer that they would defeat Barlow Hill, and that she would remain at Lake Bliss to watch a thousand more dawns like this one.

This was her home, the home she'd fought so hard to gain. It was the place that made her grandfathers' declining years happy ones. Leaving it would break her heart.

Maggie sighed, and hinges creaked as she pulled open the bathhouse door and slipped inside. She crossed to one of the pegs lining the wall, shrugged off her robe, and hung it up. She removed the gold chain and small key-shaped charm from around her neck and looped it around a second peg. Then, assured of privacy by both the walls and the time of the morning, she pulled her nightgown up and off.

Cool night air chilled her naked skin and she shivered as she covered the necklace with her gown. Turning, she walked to the edge of the spring, extended pointed toes, and tested the water's temperature. "Aah," she said with a sigh as heat lapped at her skin. For a moment, she debated whether to choose the hot spring or a soak in the six-by-ten-foot log-lined pool filled with mud. *Definitely the mud tonight,* she thought. Her weary body would appreciate it, and by noon, the ache in her knee would be nothing but a bad memory.

She slipped into the thick warm pool and sank into mud up to her shoulders. Taking a seat upon a submerged ledge made from cemented rock, she leaned her head back, gazed out over the lake, and gave herself up to the pleasure of the moment. Stretching out her legs, she felt for the opposite ledge and purred, "You're a lucky woman, Maggie St. John. This is true Bliss."

Her right foot brushed something. Something solid. Something . . . hard.

A raspy male voice emerged from the shadows. "No, ma'am. It's not bliss quite yet. But you're darn sure in the neighborhood."

At thirty-four, Rafe Malone wasn't a stranger to naked women. A good number of husbands and lovers might justifiably accuse him of being more familiar than he had any right to be. But in all of his amorous adventures, Rafe had never faced a situation quite like this one. Being naked in a tubful of mud with the adopted granddaughter of four elderly, over-protective, homicidal pirates was a first, even for him.

As his words died in the air, the woman gasped and clutched her arms to her breasts before sinking to her neck in the mud. Rafe anticipated her scream before it ever left her mouth, but the thick ooze sucked at him, slowing him down as he lunged for her. She got out a loud, shrill squeal right before he clamped his hand across her mouth.

"Hush now, honey," he cautioned, his free hand snaking around her waist. He pulled her against him and murmured into her ear. "Wake any of those fossilized pirates and I'm liable to lose my neck. I may be here at their invitation, but that hasn't stopped them from promising to kill me if I dared to touch you."

She fought him like a slippery hellcat, and Rafe hardly had time to notice the feel of her bare curves against his skin. He muttered a curse as she landed a hard jab with her elbow on his thigh, entirely too close to sensitive areas. "Please, Miss St. John," he ground out. "I don't aim to hurt you, and I'd be obliged if you'd return the favor. If you'll promise to keep it to a whisper, I'll let you go. I'd just as soon not face your grandfathers under these circumstances."

His words must have finally worked through to her mind, because slowly she stilled. With gentle hands, Rafe turned her around to face him. He gazed solemnly into wide, frightened eyes. "Don't be afraid, all right? If I let you go, promise you'll be quiet?"

Slowly she nodded. Rafe released her, and she scrambled to the opposite side of the pool.

The fear faded from her features, replaced by an angry glare that gleamed like cat's eyes in the night. He saw that he'd managed to deposit a handful of mud in her mouth. "Sorry about that," he said, grimacing. The mud emitted a slight but distinctive odor of sulfur, and he hated to imagine its taste.

Maggie St. John twisted around and grabbed at the pile of clothing lying on the ground beside the pool, inadvertently giving Rafe a glimpse of mud-slicked breasts in the process. He drew an appreciative breath, and when she wiped off her tongue with his shirt, he wished she'd used his skin instead.

Her harsh whisper whipped across the space separating them. "My grandfathers have returned? You're the thief?"

Good. She was thinking. Maybe she wouldn't bring the buccaneers' wrath down upon him. Rafe cleared his throat. "I'm sorry, I should have given you my name right off. Yes, I'm Rafe Malone. I rode in with the pirates about three hours ago."

Turning away from him, she yanked on his shirt. Rafe heard her angry mumbles. "Never heard them come home. A man in my mud bath. They should have woken me up." She tossed an accusing glare over her shoulder. "My grandfathers' invitation to Hotel Bliss didn't include an offer for you to share my bath. Please leave, Mr. Malone."

Rafe considered it. Briefly. "I could do that, but I won't. I'm not through soaking yet."

"Fine. Then I'll go. If you'll just turn your back . . ."

The rascal in Rafe couldn't resist grinning. "I could do that, too, but I won't."

"But I'm not dressed."

"Yeah," he replied. He licked his lips. "I know."

Her expression steamed, filling with such outrage that Rafe wouldn't have been surprised to see the mud begin to boil. Swallowing a laugh, he said, "I have some questions, Miss St. John, and this looks like the perfect opportunity to ask them. Your modesty makes you a captive audience, so to speak."

Her eyes narrowed, glinting like light on a bowie knife. "You are no gentleman, Rafe Malone."

"Sure, I am. That's what they call me, you know. Gentleman Rafe Malone—on account of the polite way I treated the folks I robbed during my highwayman days."

She gave a loud, unladylike snort. "Times have changed, haven't they?"

Rafe couldn't hold back soft laughter. "I've been looking forward to meeting you, Miss Maggie. The buccaneers never stopped talking about you."

"All those tired old stories, I'll bet." Maggie closed her eyes, losing some of her starch at the mention of the old men.

Rafe didn't answer at once, his mind busy recalling

the tales the pirates had related. As much as they'd seemed to enjoy yammering on about their Maggie, they hadn't liked answering Rafe's questions. He'd all but pulled teeth to learn that the woman's parents were dead, and he never did get a straight story about how she came to live with the freebooters. The old men flatly refused to talk about it. Rafe thought that was strange.

Of course, some of the things they had bragged about were pretty damned peculiar, too. "Did you really scar the cheek of an English earl?"

She shrugged. "A girl doesn't grow up with grandfathers such as mine without learning to carry and wield a knife when necessary. The man deserved it. He was entirely too free with his hands."

Rafe touched his face with a muddy finger. At least he knew she carried no concealed weapons at the moment. He recalled the image of her full, high breasts and thought, *No, her weapons are all out in plain view.*

Maggie's voice softened, and despite the sting in her words, her love for the pirates rang loud and clear. "Pay them no mind, Malone. My grandfathers don't always tell the truth, especially when they speak about me." Petulantly, she added, "I guess they wore out their tongues so much talking *about* me that they couldn't bother to talk *to* me when they came home."

"Actually, they did more worrying about you than storytelling," Rafe told her. "When one of them finished fretting on about you, another started right in. Each one of the old men peeked in your room to check on you right after we arrived. The boy who works for y'all told them you'd felt poorly and bedded down early. That really got the old men flustered, almost as much as hearing you'd stayed here at the hotel instead of going to the boy's home like you'd promised you would."

She groaned softly. "I never actually promised I'd stay at the Liptons'. I swear I'm going to wash Billy

Lipton's big mouth out with the strongest dose of Bliss water I can find. He had no business telling them any of that. I was tired, that's all. I replaced some shingles on the roof yesterday and that's hard work. Now they'll baby me for a month."

In the increasing light of dawn, Rafe studied Maggie St. John intently. During the trip from the hill country, he'd gathered from different things the corsairs had said that she suffered from an illness of a sort. Outwardly—and it had been Rafe's good luck to see quite a lot in that respect—the woman appeared to be the picture of health. If Gus was right and she intended to tag along on the treasure hunt, then Rafe needed to know the true state of her well-being. Abruptly, he said, "They told me you're sickly."

Her head came up and her shoulders squared as she visibly bristled. She rose from the mud, his shirt clinging to her breasts like a second skin. Damn, but the woman was put together nice.

"I am *not* sickly," she protested. "It's my grandfathers who need worrying about. Lucky's old shoulder wound still pains him, and Ben's breathing troubles scare me half to death. I do wish he'd leave off with the tobacco. I don't see how that can be good for him. Why I—" She broke off suddenly and tossed Rafe another glare. "Why am I defending myself to you? You should be asleep like the others, not invading my bath. This is so embarrassing. I'm surprised I didn't swoon."

Rafe shook his head. "Nah, you don't strike me as a swooner." Rafe was good at reading people, and he could tell this woman possessed strength to go along with her beauty. And she *was* beautiful. Maggie St. John was exquisite.

Dawn had slowly painted their surroundings with light, treating Rafe to a clearer picture of the woman with whom he shared the bathhouse. She wore her fiery reddish gold hair piled high on her head. Disheveled tendrils escaped to spiral invitingly beside her flushed, high-boned cheeks. Rafe marveled at her eyes. They were a brilliant blend of blues and greens framed by long, curling lashes. A dusting of freckles bridged her thin, straight nose and her mouth . . . good Lord, her mouth was rosy and ripe and damned kissable.

Maggie St. John. She was a true pirate's prize. No wonder the buccaneers defended her so ardently. Rafe forgot all about the questions he'd intended to ask, as his voice dropped to a husky rumble. "My life has been a tad tame of late, Miss St. John. I'm looking for adventure."

She rolled her eyes. "In my bath?"

Rafe's gaze fastened on her lips. "It wasn't what I started out to do, but now that you bring it up, it seems like an excellent place to begin. A moonlit dawn, a beautiful woman. She's all but naked. I am naked."

She plastered herself against the wall. "You're not wearing bathing attire?"

"Only the natural kind. Just like you." Amusement played at the corners of Rafe's mouth as he feigned an affronted tone. "You didn't notice when I grabbed hold of you? Shoot, woman. You've struck a blow to my masculine pride." He flicked at the surface of the mud with his finger and clicked his tongue. "Reckon I'll have to make up for it. Now, where was I? We're alone, it's still officially nighttime, and your grand-fathers—"

"Will kill you if you touch me."

"I know," Rafe replied. "They've warned me at least a hundred times. That adds to the excitement, don't you see? The forbidden is always more tempting than what is ours for the taking. Add that thrill on top of what we can give each other and, well, we can have ourselves a right fine adventure. What do you say, Miss Maggie?" He lowered his voice to an intimate purr. "Care to go adventuring with me?"

Rafe didn't know what reaction he expected from

her at his blatant attempt at seduction, but the one he got surprised him. Pressed back against the timbered wall of the pool, she spurted a laugh. "I can't believe this. My grandfathers have brought home a lothario. If you're not as bold as black on a bride."

"Now, Miss Maggie."

She cocked her head and studied him. "No, that's not it after all, is it? Judging by your reputation, Malone, you are not a fool. Your sense of humor might be a bit misplaced, but you're not stupid. That wasn't a serious proposition."

Yeah, it was, Rafe thought. Halfway serious, anyway. He certainly wouldn't have refused her if she'd accepted.

Rafe leaned back against the wall and frowned at her, his masculine pride pricked. She didn't have to act as if the idea was totally preposterous. Why, he knew plenty of women who would be tickled spitless to have him sharing their tubful of mud under similar circumstances. "You figure it out however you like, lady. I'm not in a habit of explaining myself. And just in case you're thinking of getting snippy on me again, remember that you are the one in the wrong here. *You* walked in on me. *You* took your clothes off in front of me. You can't blame a man for his natural reaction."

Wariness flashed in those stunning eyes. Bravado filled her voice as she replied, "Maybe not, but I can blame a man for being in the ladies' bathhouse."

"This is the ladies'?"

Maggie nodded.

"Well, how was I suppose to know that?" Rafe flung his arm toward the wall, slinging drops of mud. "It's not painted pink, is it? I didn't see a sign in the dark."

By now he'd worked up a good mad, a natural reaction when affronted male pride is combined with sexual frustration—a state from which he'd suffered to one degree or another ever since Miss Maggie hung her robe on the wall peg. "All I know is I had trouble sleeping and I thought I'd avail myself of the amenities those four senior sea dogs yammered on about since they interrupted my siesta days ago. They invited me to use the facilities any time I liked. And I *did* like. The mud proved as pleasant as they promised. I was happily relaxed—just about to drift off, in fact—when you showed up."

"Drift off to the Gulf of Mexico, I wish," she muttered beneath her breath.

Rafe heard her. "Drift off to *sleep*. I'm a guest here, you know. You should be concerned that the lack of lumber in the hotel walls makes it damned near impossible to rest when someone is sawing down a forest of logs in the room next to you."

"That's Barlow Hill," Maggie said with a grimace.

She was, Rafe realized, unafraid of his outburst. She probably reacted to him just like she did to those harmless old marauders. That pissed him off even more.

"Believe me," Maggie continued, "I'd give anything if he weren't upstairs snoring." She turned her stare toward the lake. "Everything has gotten so complicated."

Her unexpected revelation took the heat from Rafe's anger. Who was Barlow Hill? The pirates had never mentioned him.

A myriad of emotions played across her face. Bitterness colored her tone as she said, "We need your help, Gentleman Rafe Malone. I'm sorry your sleep was interrupted, and I apologize for disturbing your peace." She paused before adding, "Next time, though, speak up if I walk in on you. All right?"

Damn, I like her spirit, Rafe thought, a slow grin breaking across his face. Bowed but not broken. The pirates had told Rafe little of why they wanted him to recover their treasure, and he'd assumed they wanted the money for the usual reasons anyone wanted money. Now he wasn't so certain. Who the hell was this Barlow person? He started to ask, but then he hesitated. At this particular moment in time, all he really wanted to think about was the captivating woman sharing a mud bath with him.

In the last half hour, Rafe's interest in the happenings at Hotel Bliss had escalated. His interest in Maggie St. John had shot off the map.

"Honey," he said in a soothing drawl. "When you walked in that door, I couldn't have talked if I tried. It took all my effort just to breathe. I was getting ready to go rinse off in the lake when you walked in and whipped off your clothes. With the moon being full, it wasn't all that dark." He paused, remembering, and added, "You sure are a beautiful woman, Mary Margaret St. John."

He could see her mouth working, but no sound emerged. Tension built between them, and Rafe wanted nothing more than to close the distance separating them and take her in his arms. He might have done it, too, had not a voice sounded from the bathhouse door. "Maggie? You in here, sweetheart?"

"Papa Snake?" Maggie jumped and Rafe slid noiselessly into the concealing shadows, with a dozen of Snake MacKenzie's more innovative threats flashing through his mind.

Maggie's voice croaked. "Papa Snake? When did you get back?"

"Thank God." Relief sighed in the old freebooter's voice. He stepped inside the structure, but like a gentleman, kept his back turned toward the pool. "Glad I am to hear you speak up. I thought I heard you squeal a few minutes ago so I went to check on you. It took five years off my life when I discovered you weren't in bed. Why are you down here in the middle of the night? Are you hurting, Maggie? What's wrong? What are you doing in the mud?"

"I'm fine, Papa, and it's not the middle of the night. I'm taking a mud bath. You know how I enjoy coming down here this time of morning. I'm sorry you worried, but you needn't have. Why don't you wait for me outside? I'll get out and get dressed. We'll talk."

"Are you sure you feel all right?" Snake called. "You're not hurting? Billy said you were sick."

"Billy talks too much. I was tired, Papa. That's all. I had a good night's sleep and now I'm fine. I promise. Go on and let me rinse off. I'll meet you—"

"No, no. Stay where you are and enjoy your bath. I'm plumb whipped myself. We got in real late, and I think I'll catch a few more winks. I don't expect the others up anytime too soon. We'll wait and all talk together later. One thing, though, in case you're worrying. Our trip was a success. Rafe Malone came back to Bliss with us."

Maggie peered into the shadows toward Rafe. "Well, I have absolutely nothing to worry about then, do I? Go on back to bed, Papa Snake."

"All right, Maggie. I'll see you a little later."

For a full minute after the pirate's departure, neither of them spoke. Then Rafe asked, "Why didn't you give me away?"

She shrugged. "Like I said before. We need you. Had Papa Snake discovered us like this, he'd have been hard-pressed not to kill you, or at least carry out one of his more creative threats."

"Did he really sew some fella's lips together just for kissing you?"

"No, of course not. I've never in my life seen Snake touch a needle."

Rafe slowly stood, debating whether to pick up where they'd left off or wait for another time to learn the taste of Maggie St. John. He took a step out of the shadows toward her, and she flattened herself against the wall of the pool.

"That was Lucky," she said. "Sewing is one of his special talents. He did a lot of work with sails."

Rafe stopped abruptly. Forgetting where he was, Rafe rubbed his fingers across his lips and tasted mud. "Bleh." He glanced toward the open lake and acknowledged that the moment had passed. His questions could wait, and so could he. He'd have the lady where he wanted her another time. Another time soon.

Placing his hands on the ground beside the pool, he pushed himself up and out of the mud. From the corner of his eyes he saw Maggie look away, but as he stood next **to** the clear water spring with his bare backside to her, he sensed her gaze upon him. Rafe indulged in a little preening, rolling his shoulders and flexing his back before he hopped down into the warm water. "I'm going to take a lap across the lake. You might use the opportunity to finish up here."

Her voice sounded strangled. "Yes. Of course."

Rafe stretched out to swim, but she halted him with a question. "Mr. Malone? About Barlow Hill. Have my grandfathers explained exactly why they wanted to hire you? Have they told you why we can't anger Mr. Hill?"

"I know nothing about Hill. All I do know is that your grandfathers want me to steal their treasure." He gave her a wink and added, "Now I get to decide which one."

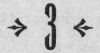

The man could model for a Greek god statue.

Maggie wasn't thinking of her Papa Lucky when she watched him take position over the leather and feather-filled ball later that morning. She was thinking about Rafe Malone. When Lucky drew back his wooden club, she pictured the thief's broad shoulders. As the stick swung down and connected with the sphere, she recalled the sensation of hard, sculpted muscle surrounding her. While following the trajectory of the small ball through the air, she remembered the wickedness of his smile. As it landed in a clearing some hundred and forty yards away, Maggie envisioned the flash of firm buttocks as he dove beneath the waters of Lake Bliss.

"Nice one," Papa Gus observed.

Very nice, Maggie thought, her mind still on that last image she'd had of Rafe Malone earlier that morning. Embarrassed heat warmed her cheeks, and Maggie forced her attention back to the game. Her Papa Ben had lined up over his ball.

The game they played was a bastardized version of a sport introduced to Snake MacKenzie in Scotland years before. When an unfortunate accidental murder sent him fleeing for survival, he brought with him to the sailing life a love for the game called golf and a dozen of the very expensive leather balls, items he'd stolen along with a substantial amount of cash from the not-so-dearly departed. In time, he'd passed along his passion for the sport to the other grandfathers, and once they'd settled at Lake Bliss, the men had gone about establishing a three-hole course along a rolling meadow just west of the hotel.

The competition often turned ugly, and Maggie had started going along with them to intervene when tempers exploded and fists flew. Somewhere along the way she'd caught a fever for the game herself. Now she was as proficient with a club as the papas and had initiated an argument a time or two herself while on the course.

Ben took his shot, and it was Maggie's turn. She eyed her target, a grassy patch some hundred yards away, then addressed the ball. With a slow, controlled movement, she drew back the club. At the top of her backswing, a loud voice boomed from directly behind her.

"Here you are!" Rafe Malone exclaimed. "I've been looking all over for y'all. A stranger rode in. Some blubber belly came out of a room upstairs to greet him, then started hollering for Miss St. John."

Maggie sliced her shot right. Way right. Into the lake right. Gus gleefully observed, "Bad luck, Maggie-mine. I'm afraid that penalty stroke will make it impossible for you to beat me."

Maggie rounded on Rafe. "You fool! I'm going to skewer you. I'll slit your gullet from stem to stern. I'll—"

"Whoa there, Mary Margaret." Ben put a restraining hand on her arm. "Allow me to introduce you to the gentleman before you inadvertently ruin our chance to save Bliss. This is Rafe Malone. If you kill him, we all have more trouble than a soggy ball.

Malone, this is our granddaughter, Mary Margaret St. John."

Malone tipped his hat. "I'm pleased to make your acquaintance, ma'am."

Maggie tried to reel in her temper and was only partially successful. She nodded abruptly and said, "Malone. You made me miss my shot."

"Now, Maggie," Gus chided. "You were the one holding the club."

Lucky sneered. "Quit being smug, Gus. You can't beat her fair and square." Glancing at Ben, he added, "I say we give her a free shot."

"No!" Gus braced his hands on his hips. "That's against the rules!"

"What rules?" Snake asked. He took a practice swing with his club. "We make them up ourselves and change them whenever we want. I'm with Lucky. I say we have this new rule: the lass gets a redo whenever Rafe Malone shouts while she's swinging."

"If I may make a suggestion," Rafe interjected, twirling his black felt hat on one finger. "Add the words 'the club at the ball' to your rule, would you please? The way she's looking at me, I'm afraid she'll think 'fist at my face' is acceptable."

"Perceptive, aren't you, Malone?" Maggie drawled.

Ben offered Rafe an apologetic look. "This family tends to take our games seriously." Turning to the other men, he added his opinion about the proposed rule change.

While the pirates argued, Maggie twirled her club between her fingers and eyed Rafe Malone. Curse the man. He was just as appealing with his clothes on. Washed free of mud and dressed in buckskin pants and a blue cotton shirt, he stood a good two inches taller than Ben, who at six feet was the tallest of the papas. Sunlight reflected glints of red in Malone's dark auburn hair. His eyes were a deep alligator green and glinted with a knowing amusement that put her on the defensive.

She raked him up and down with a doubtful gaze. "So, Rafe Malone. The thief. Tell me, are you any good?"

He folded his arms and grinned wickedly. "I could steal your shadow if I were so inclined."

"You don't suffer from a lack of self-confidence, do you, Mr. Malone?"

"That would be stupid. I may have one or two shortcomings, ma'am, but stupidity isn't one of them."

"What is?"

"I'm a tad bit hardheaded at times. For instance, if someone tells me I can't have something, I tend to take that as a personal challenge. I've simply got to have it."

He winked and Maggie felt its effect clear to her toes. She reacted defensively. "I didn't want you here. You weren't my choice for the job."

"Oh, yeah?" He had the nerve to look amused. "Who was?"

"I wanted the bravest man in Texas. I wanted Luke Prescott."

That wiped the satisfaction right off his face. "Well, I don't think his wife would agree to that, Miss St. John," Rafe snapped back, glowering at her.

"I meant that I wanted to hire him to retrieve our treasure. He's strong and courageous."

"And I'm . . . ?"

"Impertinent."

Lucky took a break from bickering with the other grandfathers to caution, "Maggie, I think you should mind the words coming from your mouth."

"Aye," Snake added. "Keep it up and we'll be living back on the boat again."

She looked at her papas. "Well it's true. Luke Prescott is a hero. Rafe Malone is a thief. What's to keep him from stealing our treasure from us once he's recovered it?"

"My word," Rafe said flatly.

Maggie heard a wealth of meaning in his tone of voice. Surprised, she faced him. This was a different Rafe Malone from the rogue who'd flirted with her last night or the fool who'd interrupted her backswing. This man appeared taller and broader. He was coldly furious. This Rafe Malone was dangerous.

His gaze captured hers, his eyes narrowed and hard. "I'll say this once, lady, so listen up. My word is my most valuable possession. I never, *ever* break it."

She swallowed hard and fought the urge to take a step backward. This matter was too important. Her papas' health and happiness was at stake. "And do we have it, Mr. Malone? Do you give your word we can trust you with our treasure?"

The light in his eyes changed, softened. A lopsided grin stole across his face and he drawled, "Well now, Miss Maggie, I reckon that depends on your definition of treasure. If you're talking about the chest they have stashed in the Caribbean, then yes, I've given your grandfathers my word they can trust me with that."

Maggie frowned. What other treasure existed to define? Her fingers stole to the necklace her papas had given her years before as she considered the question, then quickly dismissed it. The only prize that mattered was the one they would use to save Hotel Bliss. "All right, then. I guess that question is settled."

She nodded once, then turned to her papas. Snatching a golf ball from Lucky's hand, she slid it inside the pocket of her skirt. "This is no way to relax and recover from your trip. I'm declaring the game over. Papa Gus wins this one fair and square."

The four grandfathers burst into debate. Maggie folded her arms and shook her head. Seeing they couldn't sway her from her position, the papas adopted such hangdog expressions that Maggie almost checked the ground to see if they were dragging tails. She sighed and kissed each one in turn on the cheek, giving Gus a second, congratulatory buss.

"Now, since Mr. Malone has joined us, why don't we use this opportunity to discuss the upcoming trip in relative privacy. Our 'guest' has become quite a nuisance about interrupting private conversations."

"Barlow Hill, the blighter," said Gus.

"The bounder," said Lucky.

"The bastard," said Snake.

"The blackguard," said Ben.

Malone shook his head in amazement. "I take it Barlow Hill is the blubber belly? Who is he to you?"

The papas shared a look, then Ben gestured toward a shady spot a short distance away. "Mary Margaret is right. Why don't we sit a spell and go over the plan. Malone needs to know how to deal with that dimwit Hill."

"The devil." Lucky sneered.

"The demon." Gus spat.

"The dastard." Snake snorted.

Sunlight sparkled off the diamond in Ben's ear as he headed for the shade. Lucky, Snake, and Gus fell in behind Ben. Maggie started to follow them, but Rafe stopped her with a question. "You did hear me say this paragon of evil is looking for you?"

"Yes. He can wait. Barlow Hill isn't going anywhere anytime soon, blast the bad luck. Come along, Malone. You've been saying you have questions. Answer time has arrived."

The buccaneers explained to Rafe that sitting and storytelling was as much a part of their golf game as playing. They'd built benches at intervals all along their short course to accommodate such activity. The men all took what appeared to be their customary seats while Maggie plopped down on the grass.

Rafe sent Snake a measured look as he stretched out beside her. Snake's brows dipped menacingly and his gray eyes flashed, but he held his tongue. Gus smirked while Lucky pulled a flask from his back pocket and passed it around. "Bliss water," he warned when it came to Rafe. He declined the offer and passed it along to Maggie. She took a sip, shuddered, and returned the bottle to Lucky.

Ben said, "We told you we want you to rescue our treasure, but we declined to provide the details as to why. After speaking with Mary Margaret earlier this morning and learning that during our absence our enemy has taken up residence among us, I have decided it is best you understand our motives. We cannot afford to alienate Hotel Bliss's only guest, Mr. Malone. Difficult though it is, we—and I mean every one of us—must be nice to the rat, Barlow Hill."

"The weasel."

"The mole."

"The polecat."

Rafe slowly shook his head at the pirates' reaction to the man's name. Did they do this every time Hill's name was mentioned?

Ben frowned fiercely and continued. "He has stolen our home right out from beneath our feet. You see, Malone, we purchased the Lake Bliss property years ago from the family who originally homesteaded the land. We've lived here off and on for years. Once Mary Margaret finished school, we decided to settle permanently on our land. We built the hotel and opened it up to visitors, offering our guests access to the same healthful waters and treatments we have long enjoyed."

"That's when the trouble started," Gus broke in, stroking the scar on his cheek with an index finger.

Snake nodded, his trio of earrings swaying with the motion. "The vermin saw how well we were doing and decided he wanted a piece of it—the whole piece. Took us to court, he did."

"We should have killed him the first time we saw him," Lucky declared in his raspy voice. "Instead, we cured him. A week's worth of mud baths and Bliss tonic three times a day completely rid him of that twitch. First time I ever wished Lake Bliss was filled with something other than miracle water."

As one, the marauders sighed sorrowfully and passed around the flask once again. Maggie skipped it this time. She looked at Rafe and said, "He claimed we didn't have clear title to the land. He produced a lien on the property from years ago. The court awarded Lake Bliss and all its improvements to Barlow Hill."

"The cockroach."

"The termite."

"The weevil."

"The dung beetle."

Rafe's gaze swept the righteous pirates, and he fought a smile. The crotchety old men managed to appear both fierce and almost . . . cuddly, too. *Yeah, Malone, like grizzly bears are cuddly.*

He knew without a doubt who was responsible for the softness in the pirates. One beautiful, intriguing woman with sea green eyes, old-gold hair, and a smile that could light the night.

Rafe sprawled lazily across the ground, his legs stretched out in front of him and crossed at the ankles, his torso propped on his elbows. The heady scent of magnolia blossoms drifted on the breeze, and he felt a strong urge to shift around and lay his head in Maggie's lap. But it was too nice a day to die, so he forced his mind back to the business at hand. "So, if the cockroach won the lawsuit, why are you still living here?"

Ben answered. "We pleaded hardship with the judge. He took pity on us and said we could have nine months to vacate the premises. More than three of them have already passed."

"Hardship? What hardship?" Rafe's brows arched as Maggie's eyes shot daggers at her grandfathers. The woman obviously didn't want them talking.

Gus didn't catch her look, or if he did, he ignored it. "Hardship on account of Maggie's rheumatism and her need for Lake Bliss water."

"Rheumatism?" Rafe sat all the way up. He pinned Maggie with his stare. "How can you have rheumatism? You're young. And besides, you said you'd repaired the roof. You couldn't climb around on the roof if you had rheumatism."

"You repaired the roof!" Lucky shouted.

Mackenzie shoved to his feet, his hand gripping the hilt of the dagger at his waist. "And how did Malone learn about it? When has he been talking to our Maggie? Has he touched you, lass?"

Maggie bounded to her feet. "Papa Snake, you calm down. Mr. Malone didn't have to talk to me to learn what I've been doing the last few days. Yes, Papa Lucky, I repaired the roof, and I won't be scolded for doing work that needed doing. If we're going to own Hotel Bliss, then we are obliged to keep it up. I wasn't about to let the spring rains ruin the upstairs walls."

Bracing her hands on her hips, she turned her glower on Rafe. "I am not sickly. I'm as healthy a person as you'll ever meet. It's true that when I was younger I suffered spells of rheumatism. They came as flare-ups, occasional attacks much like Papa Ben's malaria. But I've outgrown it. I haven't been bothered by it in years. I won't have it talked about by any of you." She fired a glare around at all the men. "Does everyone understand?"

She didn't give them a chance to reply. "Now, if we're through discussing my personal business, I'd like to return to important matters." She waited until each of her grandfathers nodded their acquiescence before turning to Rafe. He held her gaze for a long minute, silently conveying the message that the conversation was postponed, not finished.

Regally, she took a seat on the ground. Rafe had the distinct impression that she almost stuck her tongue out at him. He gave her his wickedest wink, then spoke to Ben. "She mentioned owning the hotel. I gather this is how you intend to use your treasure?"

Ben reached into his pocket and removed his pipe. "Yes. We convinced Barlow Hill, the viper—"

"The varmint."

"The villain."

"The vermin."

"—To agree to sell the property back to us. He set an outrageous price and we agreed to it. We went so far as to have a legal contract drawn up spelling out the particulars. He has no idea we'll be able to meet it."

"From your mouth to the Mayan gods' ears," Gus grumbled.

"And then to the judge who will oversee the lawsuit," Maggie added. "You can bet he won't give up without a fight. That's one reason it's so important that we remain nice and friendly to the man. Surprise is a powerful weapon. We need to wield it when its power will be most effective—when we have the cash in our hands."

"We'll be able to meet it as long as Malone has better luck than Lucky and I did when we headed down there to fetch it," Gus said.

Lucky frowned. "The first mistake was sending me to begin with. I'm full of luck—all bad."

Nobody bothered to argue with him. Instead, Gus said to Rafe, "We're running out of time. The rat's moving into the hotel only rams that truth home harder. We have fewer than six months left. It doesn't leave much room for error."

"It doesn't leave *any* room," Snake added glumly. "If Malone fails we won't have time to send anyone else."

Rafe sat up straight. Lucky Nichols had no way of knowing that his words had touched Rafe's most sensitive nerve, a nerve born during the war for Texas's independence almost a decade ago. The setting of a failure that had changed the course of Rafe Malone's life. He met the gazes of each of the others in turn, then flatly stated, "I won't fail."

At first no one reacted to his grim confidence. A long moment passed before Gus slammed his fist into his palm, Lucky broke out in a crooked-toothed smile, Snake folded his arms and smirked, and Ben acknowledged Rafe with a nod, his blue eyes twinkling.

Maggie St. John beamed and said, "Excellent! So, when do we set sail?"

The subsequent argument dragged on for hours. Rafe hadn't seen such down-and-dirty fighting for years. When it was done, the victor kissed each vanquished combatant on his cheek. Each combatant except for Rafe, that is. To him she offered a smug, victorious smile.

He decided then and there he'd have his kiss, and soon.

Not on the cheek, either.

Carrying a tea tray, Maggie paused outside the door to the suite of rooms Barlow Hill had usurped upon his arrival at Hotel Bliss. On the tray sat a pot of coffee and a plate of molasses cookies baked by her own hand. Hill wanted refreshments for two, and Maggie was pleased to provide them.

She eyed the sweets' burned edges and smiled. For the first time in memory, Papa Snake had crowed with pride when viewing the results of Maggie's baking. In fact, he had declared she should do all the cooking for Mr. Hill while her papas saw to the final preparations for their trip. A week of Cuisine Maggie probably wouldn't kill the man, and a little bit of subversive activity was good for morale. Gus had even expressed the belief that enough of Maggie's cooking might cause Hill to reconsider his decision to live at Hotel Bliss.

It doesn't hurt to hope, Maggie told herself as she knocked on the door.

"Enter."

Maggie pasted on a false smile and pushed the door open.

"Ah, Miss St. John," Hill said from his seat behind Papa Ben's large mahogany desk. He climbed laboriously to his feet. "Finally. I've been looking for you the better part of the day."

Actually, he'd sent Malone and the papas with his various summons. Far be it from Barlow Hill to make the effort to search for her himself.

The other occupant of the room also stood and Hill motioned to him now. "I want to introduce you to our visitor. Mr. Graham Knight is the architect overseeing the construction of my personal home here at Lake Bliss. Knight, may I present the most beautiful lady in Texas, Hotel Bliss's hostess, Miss Mary Margaret St. John."

Befitting her finishing school education, Maggie outwardly glided right along with the social amenities. Inwardly she wondered what Hill was up to. He'd always treated her politely, even during the trial. Now, though, he acted as if she were queen of the castle.

She poured coffee for each of the men beneath Hill's watchful eye. When she returned the silver server to the tray, she saw him nod with what appeared to be satisfaction. What in heaven's name was going on? The situation grew even more strange when she turned to leave.

"Maggie, dear," Hill said, stopping her. "If you have a moment, I'd like you to look at the plans I have had drawn up." He wiggled a finger at the architect who spread a set of blueprints over the desk.

Maggie's eyes narrowed. Had Hill found a subtle way to get back at her for her cooking? Did he have any way of knowing how much she hated the idea of his building a home at her beloved Lake Bliss?

She approached the house plans with a sour taste in her mouth. When she saw what he had planned, nausea swam in her stomach. It was perfect. A dream house. Three stories high, gables and verandas, and literally dozens of windows. Maggie couldn't hold back her sigh of envy.

"It's magnificent." The words dragged from her mouth. "You've done an excellent job, Mr. Knight. It will be the showcase home in Texas."

Barlow Hill preened. "I quite agree. Knight has done a superb job, using my ideas, of course. I plan to build on the far side of the lake from the hotel. We'll construct a dock, and I plan to put a rowboat and possibly a small sailboat on the water. Eventually we may add other amenities to those you have already established at the spa. I envision an English country home atmosphere. What do you think of my idea, Maggie dear?"

Maggie dear? She wished he wouldn't call her that. She backed away from the desk. "It's a fine idea, Mr. Hill," she said. "Now, if you'll excuse me, my grandfather needs my help."

"No." The word shot from Hill's mouth like a bullet. "I have a matter to discuss with you." He speared the architect with a look. "If you'll excuse us?"

"Certainly, certainly," said Mr. Knight, rising from his chair. "I need to be on my way if I'm to make it into town before dark." He looked at Maggie and added graciously, "Thank you for the cookies, ma'am. They were quite . . ." He faltered just an instant before adding, "Delicious."

As the visitor departed, Maggie inched closer to the door. Hill frowned, shook his head, and gestured toward the chair Mr. Knight had vacated. Maggie took a seat on the horsehair sofa near the doorway. Hill smiled smugly and sat down beside her. "Maggie," he said, leaning toward her. "Maggie, my dear."

Good Lord, Maggie thought. Tell me he's not batting his eyelashes. He was so close that she could smell on his breath the onions he'd had at noon.

"While our case was before the court, I watched you closely. You impressed me. I recognized loyalty and integrity in your character. I admired your tenaciousness, your spirit, and your mettle. And through it all, faced with losing the home that appeared to mean so much to you, you never lost your poise, grace, and refinement. That impressed me. And of course, your beauty captivated me."

Oh, no. Oh, heavens, no. Maggie pressed back against the cushion wishing the sofa could swallow her whole. "Mr. Hill, I appreciate your kindness, but I really must be going." She tried to stand. "My grandfathers—"

"Can wait. I am building my manor house, Maggie, my dear. Such a home needs a lady in residence. My home will not be complete until I live there with my wife."

She forced a breath past the lump in her throat. "Well, um, how nice. I am certain your lady will love it here."

"I am too. Because, you see, she already does."

Maggie's stomach dropped to her feet. "Uh, Mr. Hill."

"Barlow, please."

"I couldn't," she replied to more than the use of his Christian name.

"You must. Think of how nicely it all works out. It's true I would have preferred to establish my residence in New York, but my funds stretch further here in Texas. However, I have high hopes that in the not-too-distant future one of my investments will pay off and allow me to relocate, but until then, Bliss will be my home. As it is yours. I didn't enjoy the thought of evicting you, my dear. This solution means I'll not be obliged to do it. And with you as my lady of the manor, I wouldn't think of forcing your grandfathers to leave the spa. They will spend their declining years living at Hotel Bliss. It is a perfect solution for all of us. Don't you agree? The house should be finished by fall. We'll marry then." He lifted his teacup in a toast. "You, Mary Margaret St. John, will make a beautiful bride."

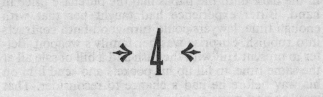

Maggie couldn't speak. She could hardly draw a breath. Marriage? Marriage to the very man who had stolen her home away from her? How could he even think she'd consider it? Barlow Hill was nutty as a pecan pie.

Or was he? The question slithered through Maggie's consciousness. What if he hadn't agreed to sell the hotel? What if she didn't have the treasure to fall back on? What if, God forbid, he refused to honor their contract once they presented him with the money? What if a court found in his favor yet again? How far would she be willing to go to ensure that the papas didn't lose their home, their health?

As far as marriage to Barlow Hill?

"I don't know what to say, sir," she finally managed. "This is so sudden." A sudden threat, to be precise. Maggie didn't cotton to threats one little bit. But as much as she'd like to tell him to take his proposal and sink it in a mud bath, Maggie realized she had a narrow path to tread. She must refuse him without offending him or raising his suspicions.

Despite his having signed a contract agreeing to the

sale of the hotel, Maggie knew it was best to keep him in the dark until the papas had the purchase price in hand. Bitter experience had taught her that with enough time, lawyers could turn good-faith contracts into rubbish. Surprise was her family's weapon. Better to present Hill with the cash and a bill of sale all at the same time, to fill up his pockets and send him on his way before he had a chance to reconsider. That was the best route to take.

In the meantime, she'd need to buy time. The question remained, what was the best way to do it?

She pushed to her feet. "We hardly know one another. Please, sir, don't take this wrong, but wouldn't you prefer marriage to a woman who . . . well . . . who has had the opportunity to develop . . . uh . . . feelings for you?"

Feelings other than hatred, she silently added. His offer to allow the papas to stay at Hotel Bliss if she married him—it was blackmail pure and simple.

He dismissed her objection with a wave of his hand. "I have no doubt we'll suit just fine. And now that my house plans are finalized, we shall have more time together. We will spend the next few weeks getting to know one another better."

No, they wouldn't. The trip. Gratitude for the upcoming journey washed over Maggie like a sea swell. In that moment she could almost taste the salty tang of freedom on the cigar-stained air here in Barlow Hill's suite.

She affected an air of distress. "Oh, dear, I'm afraid that won't be possible, Mr. Hill. I mean, Barlow. With the hotel temporarily closed, I have planned a holiday of sorts. I'll be away from Lake Bliss for a time."

"You're leaving?"

"Yes. In a few days."

"Where do you intend to go?"

"New Orleans," she replied, lying instinctively, because information was power and Barlow Hill already had enough of that.

"New Orleans?" He shook his head. "No, that won't do at all. You'll be gone weeks. You must change your plans. I had thought we would host a betrothal ball. I want it held before the summer heat comes. Much more comfortable that way."

Betrothal ball! She hadn't even said she'd marry the slug.

She could go ahead and lie to him, tell him yes, but her tongue refused to form the words. Maggie needed a diversion, a way to sidestep the question. She seized on the first possibility that popped into her head. "Tell me, Barlow, if I were to accept your proposal, would you wish us to have a formal wedding? Would I require a special gown? I could shop for one while I'm in New Orleans. That is one of the main reasons I'm taking the trip, you see. I'm in desperate need of new, more fashionable dresses. I feel it's important to keep up appearances, don't you agree?"

He blew out a heavy onion-scented sigh. As his brows furrowed in thought, he pursed his pale, fleshy lips.

Hidden in the folds of her skirt, Maggie crossed her fingers as she flashed him a smile—a first for her.

Finally, Hill nodded. "Yes, I shall want you to wear a special gown when we marry. Our wedding should be the premier social event of the year. We must begin preparations immediately. I'll put your grandfathers to work sprucing up the hotel today."

Her grandfathers. Maggie closed her eyes, dread seeping through her. No, that wouldn't do. That wouldn't do at all. If her papas learned that Barlow Hill thought to marry her, they'd have a fit and take a fillet knife to him. No, her papas couldn't learn about this. No one could. "It must be a secret."

"Pardon me?"

"The wedding," Maggie said, making it up as she went along. "We should keep it a secret. Like the wedding between the earl of Bellingham and Lady Millicent Cavanaugh in London. Society thought they'd been invited to a ball and the wedding was a surprise. No other event of the Season topped it. Papa Ben told me all about it."

Hill's eyes widened, then narrowed in thought. "Hmm. I've never heard of such a thing."

That's because the story was all a lie. A falsehood that Maggie hoped would appeal to Barlow Hill's excessive vanity. "We could say it was a reopening celebration for Hotel Bliss. It would certainly be a first for Texas society, and being first is always good, don't you think?"

"Yes. Yes, I do." Hill nodded decisively. "Of course, your grandfathers—"

"Must not know!" Maggie insisted. "They don't keep secrets worth beans. Why, telling my papas would be like announcing the wedding in the newspapers. Take my word on this, Barlow." Her voice rang with sincerity as she added, "It's best they know nothing about any wedding."

Hill's brow dipped as he frowned over the question. Finally, he said, "Very well. We shall keep news of the wedding between the two of us for now. However, in private I will expect you to treat me with the respect due one's betrothed."

Maggie's smile went a bit sickly at that. She could only imagine what he meant by that, and her imaginings didn't bode well. *I'll simply have to do my best never to be alone with the mullet.*

"As the event draws near," Hill continued, "we may be forced to bring others in on the secret. For now, however, I shall provide you with a list of items to acquire in New Orleans." After a moment's pause, he added, "You are not traveling alone, I trust? I didn't approve of your relations taking off and leaving you here alone with but a boy for protection."

Maggie managed, just barely, to hide what she thought of that remark. Keeping her smile pasted on, she shook her head. "Snake and Gus plan to accompany me. Ben and Lucky will come with us as far as Galveston. Papa Ben received notice that an order he placed over a year ago has arrived from Europe, so they'll see us off before returning to Bliss with the supplies."

"And the stranger?"

"What stranger?"

"The man who returned with your guardians to Lake Bliss. This Malone character. I have only just met the fellow, but something about him grates like chalk on a slate. The name seems familiar, too, although I have not been able to place it. In any case, I would not approve of your traveling with him."

Finally she had reason to be pleased with her grandfathers' choice to retrieve the treasure. Maggie met Barlow Hill's gaze and lied. "I won't be traveling with Mr. Malone. He's here on business. He's a horse breeder. You've probably heard of the Lone Star Ranch? Mr. Malone is interested in my Papa Lucky's quarter-miler. I doubt his visit will last long."

She edged toward the door and added, "Now if you'll excuse me, I promised Snake I'd help him roll out piecrusts for dinner."

Maggie pretended not to hear Hill's objection as she slipped from the room and pulled the door closed behind her. Taking a step toward the stairs, her knees suddenly went watery, and she grabbed for the banister to steady herself. By nature, Maggie was strong during a crisis, but the minute it was over she fell apart. She fought to hold off such a reaction now.

Marriage to Barlow Hill. What a horrific thought. But at least she'd managed to think on her feet and soothe the fool without ruining her own game. At least, that's what she hoped had just happened. Drawing a deep breath, she made her way downstairs and out the back door, instinctively seeking the company of one of her grandfathers.

Sunshine toasted her face and chased some of the

chill from her bones as she glanced toward the corral where Lucky was busy making certain the horses were ready to make the upcoming trip. She couldn't go to Papa Lucky. He would take one look at her and know something was wrong. Then he'd decide to make it better, and end up making it worse.

Maggie gazed toward the garden looking for Ben. Upon retiring from the sea, the pirate captain had discovered he possessed a green thumb. He enjoyed digging and pruning and weeding and had made it his habit to spend part of the afternoon in the garden each day. During the golf game earlier that morning, he'd declared his intention to harvest a supply of ready vegetables to send along on the voyage. Maggie knew if she went to Ben and he sensed her troubles, he wouldn't erupt like an angry volcano. But he would fret something fierce. That wouldn't be good for his health. Those breathing troubles he'd suffered upon occasion worried her.

No. She turned away from the garden. As the head of their unique little family, Papa Ben had enough trouble on his mind already. He didn't need to concern himself with Barlow Hill's nutty plan.

Fearing Hill might follow her to the kitchen should she choose to visit Snake, Maggie decided to look for Gus. He probably was the best choice, anyway. Gus was the type to offer her his support without forcing her to explain her mood. Earlier this morning he'd indicated his intention to lay in a stash of Bliss water for the trip, so Maggie headed for the lake.

Papa Gus habitually filled the tonic bottles at a spot across the lake from the hotel where the water was at its deepest. Scanning the dock, she confirmed that the rowboat was missing, then she veered off toward the path that followed along the bank of the lake. She made her way toward the spot where she expected to find her grandfather.

Maggie walked slowly, consciously babying her

knee after a misplaced step twisted her leg and reminded her of last night's flare-up. She admitted she might have acted precipitously by joining her papas in their golf game this morning, but when they mentioned it, she couldn't say no. Maggie hated to allow the cursed rheumatism to limit her in any way. She found it easier to deal with the physical aches than the blows to her spirit caused by forced limitation of her activities. Besides, one little spell didn't mean she was bound to have another bout of the disease. And that's all last night was—one little spell. She wouldn't think of it any other way.

The afternoon's warm and muggy air closed in on her, adding to her tension. Days such as this often brought thunderstorms before dark. Maggie glanced above her, searching for threatening clouds but thankfully finding only a wide expanse of pale blue. Even though a nice violent roar of wind and rain would suit her mood, today she'd just as soon stay dry.

Shadows swallowed her as the path disappeared into the woods lining the shore. Oaks, maples, and bald cypress trees towered above her, and from their canopy of branches she heard the high-pitched squeal of hatchlings and the scold of a mother mockingbird standing guard at her nest.

Maggie drank in the peace of the thicket. With every step, stress seemed to roll off her shoulders in waves. As much as she loved the ocean, the kiss of wind upon her face, and lap of waves against her ankles, she preferred to wrap herself in the sweet, fragrant blanket of the forest. The Lake Bliss forest, in particular. Papa Ben called her a nester, and she guessed he was correct. She figured it was a typical reaction to living so much of her life at the mercy of the tradewinds.

Twenty minutes of leisurely walking brought Maggie to the rolling bluffs that comprised a little more than half of the Lake Bliss shoreline. The forest and the exercise had worked their magic on her. By the time she reached the sharply sloped trail leading down the tawny, weatherworn crag to water's edge, she sought companionship more than comfort. And to make her feel even better, her knee didn't hurt one little bit.

Reaching the bottom of the path, Maggie spied the flat-surface boulder where Gus sometimes sat to dip his bottles. She didn't see the rowboat at its normal mooring beside the rock. Looking closer, she spotted signs in the gravel and brush that someone had recently made his way along the narrow ledge that rimmed the water. Had Papa Gus followed the trail around the bend? If so, where was the rowboat? Why wasn't it tied to the rotting stump as usual? Maggie worried the question as she followed the path toward the point where the shoreline made a bend.

A voice not her grandfather's caused her to halt suddenly.

"Hell, I could have made a mistake like that myself." Rafe Malone's matter-of-fact tone echoed off the steep wall of the bluff. "You said you aren't hurt. No harm done."

Maggie's eyes went wide, and her first instinct was to rush forward. But the rule to look before leaping drummed into her since childhood gave her pause. Suspicion glided like a water moccasin through her mind.

What was Rafe Malone doing out here away from the hotel? The last she'd heard he was to meet with Papa Ben to study the maps of the Yucatán coast. Why was he out here a few scant hours after he was told about the treasure?

Had he lied this morning about his trustworthiness? Was he meeting someone? A partner from his old gang, perhaps? Someone he had recruited to steal the treasure from her papas once they'd recovered it? Rafe Malone was a thief and likely a liar. They'd be fools to trust him. Why hadn't her grandfathers listened to her? Her grandfathers. Oh, Lord. Where was Gus? Had Malone done something to Gus?

Cursing the fact she didn't carry a weapon, Maggie cast her gaze around her, searching for something, anything she could use. As she stooped to lift a plate-sized rock off the ground, she heard a most welcome string of curses.

"No harm to anything but my pride," Papa Gus griped.

Relief drenched Maggie. She released a breath she hadn't been aware of holding and shook her head at her own foolishness. What had gotten into her? It wasn't like her to jump the gun like that. What had made her so quick to expect the worst of Rafe Malone?

That wicked grin of his, most likely, she decided. That and perhaps the aftereffects of her encounter with slimy Barlow Hill. Maggie started forward ready to confess her foolishness, but her grandfather's next words stopped her.

"I don't want anyone to know about this. Especially my Maggins. I'll have your word on it this minute, Malone."

"But, Gus, you needn't—"

"Your word, Malone. I've gone from being the most surefooted sailor on at least five of the seven seas to dunking my ass in Lake Bliss. It's a long way for a man to fall."

"Nah, five foot at the most. Look, Gus, you're making a big deal out of nothing."

"Nothing?" He laughed dejectedly. "It's not nothing that my eyes are going on me. I'm a piss-poor judge of distance anymore, Malone. And I never used to get dizzy in the head."

Maggie's eyes widened at the defeat in his tone. Gus didn't talk this way. It worried her; it frightened her. She stealthily eased her head around the bramble blocking her view and peered at her grandfather. His gnarled fingers held the branch of a willow, mooring him to the shore as he floated neck deep in the green-tinted water, embarrassment painting a slash of red across his face.

Maggie couldn't see Rafe Malone from where she stood, but she heard his words clearly. "If you think you're bad off, you should see my pa. How old are you, Gus? Sixty-one? Sixty-two?"

"Sixty-nine come August."

"Well, I'll be dipped. Never would have pegged you for that old. My pa is sixty. Damn near a decade younger than you. He's been falling over things for at least five years now. And he's getting soft in the head. What I'd give for him to have his mind back all sharp like yours."

After a long pause in the conversation, Gus said, "Reckon I'm like a broken-backed rattler. I still have a little bite left in me. Only saving grace in all of this is that none of the others were here to see me. The men would give me ever-loving grief, and Maggie, well, she'd get all fretful. Worrying is bad for her health; she'll sometimes have a spell if she gets to stewing too much. Now, I never did get your word to keep quiet. Say it, then help me out of here, boy."

"You have my word."

Ducking back behind the bush, Maggie heard water splashing and the rustle of brush.

"You sure you'll be all right?" Malone asked. "That's a nasty tear in your shirt."

"Didn't even break the skin. Now back off, boy, and keep your hands to yourself. I'm telling you I'm fine! I'll not be needing you for a walking cane. In fact, I think I'm in the mood to hike back to the hotel. It'll give me time to dry out before the others can get an eyeful. If you want to help, you can fill the bottles and row the boat back to the hotel for me."

Maggie took brisk but careful steps back toward the boulder. There she paused. From the sounds of it, Papa Gus wouldn't want her to see him this way at all.

Glancing around, she spied a leafy holly and dashed behind it just as Gus lumbered into sight.

"No barnacles on me yet," he grumbled as he passed her hiding place, his expression set with determination. "Plenty of spring in my step. Can sail rings around men half my age. I'll be a cracked-shell crustacean before I let the years win."

That's the way to talk, Papa Gus, Maggie thought as she blinked away the sudden tears flooding her eyes. She knew her grandfathers wouldn't live forever, but she wasn't prepared to lose any of them anytime soon. She stared unseeing at the path where he'd disappeared, her mind lost in fears of the future and memories of the past.

"You can come out now."

Rafe's voice startled Maggie, and she jerked her head up and back. The man was naked again! Half-naked, anyway. He wore only a pair of snug buckskin trousers.

Heat from a blush stained her cheeks, and she attempted to turn around. A fierce tug at her scalp was the first indication she'd caught her hair in a bramble bush behind her. "Son of a blowfish," Maggie muttered beneath her breath.

To her embarrassment, Malone laughed. "Why, Miss St. John, I am appalled. Such language from a lady."

She closed her eyes. Just her luck the man had hearing good enough to hear the sun rise.

"Of course," Malone continued, "it took me a few hours in your grandfathers' company to realize y'all have your own particular way of cussin'. I must say I've wondered about it."

He could just keep on wondering. Maggie didn't feel like explaining that her papas had cleaned up their speech when she, at five years of age, had spoken a particularly vulgar curse during a moment of frustration. Instead, while she lifted her hands to her hair to work it free of the thorns, wincing as the movement yanked at her scalp, she asked, "How did you know I was here?"

"You were about as quiet as a running buffalo. Bet it comes in handy that all your grandfathers are hard of hearing." Malone clicked his tongue and added, "Hold still, Maggie. You're gonna get yourself tangled even worse."

His shadow blocked the sun as he moved close. The scent of sandalwood soap made her want to lean forward.

When he touched her, she froze. His fingers worked gently, slowly freeing her hair strand by strand. As the seconds dragged by, Maggie felt a fluttering in the pit of her stomach. To her dismay, she realized it wasn't fear or apprehension causing the reaction, but rather something just as elemental.

Rafe spoke in a low, husky drawl. "This calls to mind a story a friend of mine tells about helping untangle a lady from a bramble patch a few years back. The incident caused him no end of trouble. I gotta say being with you like this makes me appreciate the tale in a whole new light."

He massaged her scalp where a tangle had pulled, and Maggie's eyelids grew heavy. She wanted to purr. She cleared her throat instead. "What happened?"

Malone chuckled. "To Katie and Branch? Shoot, a person could write a book about those two. I guess the shortest way to tell the story is that he married her."

Maggie opened her eyes and immediately snapped them shut. Rafe Malone's bare chest was mere inches away.

He continued. "You remind me a bit of Katie Kincaid, actually. You're both strong, outspoken women. You both have a temper." He paused a moment, the pitch of his voice deepening as he added, "And you, Maggie St. John, are heartstoppingly beautiful all dressed up in briars."

His compliment stole into her heart and warmed

her like the Caribbean sun. *Strong. What a wonderful word.*

He freed the last tangled strand from the thorns and smoothed it back away from her face. His fingers lingered in her hair. "Spun silk. Gold with a hint of red, just like a west Texas sunset. You be more careful with it, Miss Maggie. It's too pretty to leave behind on brambles."

Placing his hand beneath her elbow, he helped her move out and away from the bushes, but he didn't release her. Awareness stretched between them, and Maggie fought to remember all the reasons why she didn't trust this man. He was a rascal. A seducer. A thief.

My word is my most valuable possession.

"You lied."

"No, ma'am." His voice wrapped around her like a velvet ribbon. "West Texas sunsets are oftentimes gold as your pirates' doubloons with a hint of red for excitement. And if your hair isn't silky, then I'm not the most talented thief in Texas."

And Rafe Malone *was* the most talented thief in Texas. She wondered if his talents extended to stealing women's hearts.

The thought was enough to break the hold he had on her. She scooted past him and stepped back to the boulder. "I wasn't talking about me. I heard what you said about your father to Papa Gus, yet when you spoke to me this morning you claimed to me to be an orphan."

He shrugged. "Now there's a lesson for you, Miss Maggie. Eavesdropping has its place. The problem is sometimes you hear things you'd rather not have heard. Gotta be prepared to take the bad along with the good."

He was right and Maggie knew it, and that riled her anger. "Put your shirt on, Malone," she groused. "I've seen more of you naked than I have clothed."

"A few minutes earlier and you'd have seen even

more of me naked," he fired back with a wicked grin. "Your Gus had me diving for the bottom of Lake Bliss searching for something one of the others lost a while back."

Maggie nodded, grateful to have something to think about other than Malone's bare chest. "Papa Lucky's lucky dagger. He was using it to cut line last year and dropped it into the lake." While she spoke, Rafe grabbed his shirt off a nearby bush and slipped it on. Maggie doggedly crushed a quiver of disappointment that he'd honored her request to dress. "Could you reach the bottom?"

"Easily. The water wasn't twelve feet deep. It took some doing, but I finally found the knife. Actually, I don't think the dagger was the entire reason he wanted me to dive. I got the feeling it might be a test of sorts."

The man was perceptive, she'd give him that. Gus had told her the path to the treasure required some diving. Obviously her grandfather had thought to put Malone through his paces while taking advantage of the opportunity to hunt for Papa Lucky's lost weapon. Its retrieval would make her papas happy, she knew. Especially on the eve of the trip. Not long ago, Maggie had heard Lucky blame the cave-in that blocked easy access to the treasure on a turn of bad luck that began with the loss of the knife. "I know my grandfather appreciated your help."

He watched her expectantly. Maggie remained silent.

A rustling in the bushes nearby caused a blue heron to take flight and she observed its ungainly effort to gain the air. That was when she finally spied the rowboat secured to the bank some thirty yards up the lake. "I'll take care of the bottles for Papa Gus if you want to head back to the hotel," she said, offering Rafe an encouraging smile.

He shook his head. "We'd best stick together. No

telling what that rustle was a minute ago. Maybe a bear, you think?"

"It sounded more like a squirrel to me."

But Rafe Malone was not to be dissuaded. He followed her along the path toward the boat and stood beside her as she knelt, favoring her bad knee, atop a dusty rock beside the crate of empty bottles. Removing one, she dipped it into the lake. Air bubbled to the surface as water rushed into the container. When it was full she set it carefully inside the crate and grabbed another bottle. She filled three more before she found the nerve to ask, "So whom did you lie to, me or my grandfather?"

Rafe sprawled beside her and plucked a cork from a small box inside the crate. "You mean about my family?"

"Yes."

Taking one of the filled bottles, he inserted the cork with a firm slam of his fist. "Look, Maggie, the man misjudged his step and took a plunge in the lake. It embarrassed him. His pride was hurting. All I did was ease it a bit."

"That's the only reason?"

"Yeah." He cocked his head and inquired, "What other reason could I have?"

Maggie couldn't imagine.

She filled four more bottles with Lake Bliss water and wondered if it could be true. Had he lied to Papa Gus solely to spare her grandfather's ego? Handing him a bottle to be corked, she lifted her gaze to his. Malone's eyes glittered like sunshine on water and she stared mesmerized into the light.

And Maggie believed him. Darned if she didn't believe him. One little lie made her wonder if she hadn't been too hard on the man. What was the old saying? *A lie told in kindness doesn't count against you.* What Rafe Malone had done, what he'd said to Papa Gus, *had* been an act of kindness. In fact, it sounded just like something her grandfathers would do.

The similarities between Rafe Malone and her papas struck Maggie like a fist. All five of them were rascals, rogues capable of charming peas from their pods. They were dangerous, adventurous, appealing men. Honest in their dishonesty. Honorable.

My word is my most valuable possession.

Maggie inhaled a deep breath. And Rafe Malone was kind, just like her papas. Was that why she was drawn to him? Had her grandfathers brought home a younger version of themselves?

Was Rafe Malone Maggie's kind of pirate?

"What do you mean, you don't have a ship?" Five days after leaving Lake Bliss, the question exploded from Rafe's mouth as his gaze settled on the impossibly small sailing vessel docked at the end of a Galveston pier. The forty-five-foot sloop bobbed gently in the muddy bay waters, the name *Buccaneer's Bliss* a golden arch across its bow. Bliss, ha. Nightmare was more like it.

Rafe drew a slow breath, filling his lungs with salty air, and turned to his companions. "I'd just as soon not sail anywhere in that. It looks like one decent-sized wave will swamp it." Shaking his head, he gazed back at the boat. *"Buccaneer's Bliss.* You should call it the *Leaky Teaky.* I can't believe you don't have a ship. What kind of pirates are you?"

"Retired pirates." Snake's droll brogue rolled across the salty morning air like breakers on the beach. "We traded in the *Mary Margaret* for rocking chairs once we realized the barkentine wouldn't fit on Lake Bliss. Now, grab your bag and stow it. We sail in the morning with the tide."

Rafe stood his ground, his frown fixed on the boat, while Gus scowled and folded his arms. "What's the matter with you, Malone? Do you actually think we'd take chances with our Maggie's safety?" He gave

Snake a sidelong glance and said, "The fella may be brave, but I question whether he has any smarts."

"I'm wondering about how brave he is," Snake replied. "The boy sounds like he's afraid to sail with us."

"I'm smart enough to be afraid to put to sea in that rickety old tub," Rafe fired back, his voice rising like the caws of the sea birds perched on the yardarms of the *Buccaneer's Bliss.* "I signed up for adventure, not suicide."

A feminine laugh drifted from behind him. "Whine, whine, whine. You sound just like my children."

Recognizing the voice, Rafe whirled around in surprise. "Honor?" He had just enough time to grin before the brown-eyed beauty, Mrs. Luke Prescott, threw herself into his arms and kissed him.

"Rafe Malone, am I glad to see you!" she said.

"That doesn't mean you have to kiss him, Sunshine. Malone, get your hands off my wife." Luke Prescott ambled up the pier holding a bundle of blue-eyed, blond-haired one-and-a-half-year-old feminine energy in each arm.

Rafe gave Honor Prescott an extra hug for her husband's benefit before releasing her so he could swoop one of her daughters from Luke's arms. He smelled talc and lemon candy and happiness. "Kimmy, my love," he said, giving the child a tickle kiss on the neck.

"Me, too!" cried the child in her father's arms.

Tess wasn't about to let her sister have all the fun, so Rafe relieved his partner of his other daughter and nuzzled her into giggles also. Rafe was laughing, too, when he looked past Luke and said, "Hey, Micah. Jason. Fancy new hats y'all are sporting, boys."

Micah tipped his hat and grinned. "Nana bought them for us yesterday at the dry goods." Turning to Luke, he asked, "Pa, is it all right if we go on back down the pier a ways and watch that fella playing the game with seashells some more. I really think he was cheating somehow. I want to see if I can catch him." At Luke's nod, the boys scampered away.

Well aware that the pirates were observing the reunion with avid interest, Rafe kept his tone casual as he glanced at the man he considered his brother and observed, "Smart boy, that Micah. Y'all traveled a far piece to do some shopping and spy out a confidence game."

Luke cocked his head to one side and his tone was droll. "It was a spur-of-the-moment decision."

"It was my fault." Honor reached into her handbag and removed a folded piece of paper Rafe recognized as the brief note he'd left for Luke, tacked to the door of his cabin. "You know me," she said, her smile not quite reaching her eyes as she fanned her face with the makeshift fan. "I get these wild ideas and off I go. Sometimes I even forget to mention them to my family ahead of time."

Rafe bit his lower lip in chagrin. As much as he envied Luke his happy marriage, Rafe was happy not to have to deal with Honor's temperament on a daily basis. The woman wielded guilt like a rapier. He offered her his most charming, get-me-out-of-trouble smile, but she wasn't falling for it. Even worse, she appropriated little Tess from his arms.

Gus nudged Snake in the side. "She reminds me of our Maggie."

"That she does," the burly pirate replied. His amusement transformed to pain, however, when Miss Kimberly Prescott took a shine to his earrings. Quick as lightning, she leaned away from Rafe and made a grab for the gold hoops, snagging two of them. "Yeow!" Snake roared.

The baby laughed. Luke Prescott cursed. Honor winced in embarrassment, and Rafe thanked his lucky stars little Kimmy took the heat off him by courting her mother's displeasure. Once he'd managed to untangle Kimmy's fingers and Snake's ear, he said, "Now that your daughter has said hello, I reckon I should introduce you to my companions. Captain and Mrs. Luke Prescott, allow me to introduce Mr. Gus Thomas and Mr. Snake MacKenzie."

Honor shoved little Tess at her husband, then led Snake to a nearby bench where she dabbed her handkerchief against his bleeding ear, her apologies coming fast and furious. Gus took a look at the twins squirming in Luke's and Rafe's arms and followed Honor and Lucky.

"What the hell are you doing here, Luke?" Rafe asked, keeping his voice low.

"That's my question, Malone. I was just shaking hands on a deal to sell two geldings to a ranger captain fresh from the Indian wars when Micah came running into the stables yelling that Uncle Rafe had been accosted by pirates."

"Micah was there? I never saw him."

"He wanted to see Dapple Annie's foal. He wasn't armed—he didn't think to bring his corsair's cutlass with him—so he figured the best way to help was to get me. Captain Ross and I galloped hell-bent for leather to your place, and all I find is a note saying you'd met some new friends and gone off adventuring for a couple of months."

"Now wait a minute," Rafe said, affronted. "I also said in that note that I put Rusty in charge of the Lone Star and that if you needed to contact me you could send word by way of Miss Alice's Gentleman's Club in Galveston." He paused, then snapped his fingers. "Shoot. I forgot all about going by the whorehouse."

Tess started squirming in earnest, and Luke bent over and set her on her feet. Luke did the same with Kimberly, and as the toddlers took off down the pier, the two men each grabbed a hand to keep the girls safely at their sides. Luke continued, "I decided right off you needed checking on, but Honor wouldn't hear of my going alone." For the first time, a note of accusation crept into his voice. "You worried her, Rafe."

"I apologize, Luke, and I'll apologize to Honor, too. I never intended for her to fret."

Luke sighed. "She wouldn't have if it hadn't been for Micah seeing a sword at your throat. What's the story, Rafe? Who are those people?"

In brief, succinct sentences Rafe repeated the tale of the events that had brought him to the Galveston pier. When he finished, Luke slowly shook his head. "Hell, Rafe. Why doesn't this surprise me? I knew you'd find horse ranching a little tame eventually, but I didn't think it would be this soon. You must have been thinking of moving on anyway for you to have gone along with this."

"I admit the West has been calling out to me some. Texas is getting downright civilized these days. But I didn't go looking for this escapade, you know. They came to me."

"You didn't have to go with them. There's a lot of work on a horse ranch this time of year."

"Rusty's a good man. He'll see the work gets done. Besides, it's to be a short trip, so I'll be back soon. Look, Luke, I've never been to the Caribbean before. I thought this would be a good chance to see that part of the world." He glanced back toward the *Buccaneer's Bliss* and added wryly, "At least, that's what I thought before I got a load of the *Leaky Teaky*. Now I'm not so sure."

Luke's laugh rumbled up from deep inside his chest. "Treasure to steal, a beautiful woman to enjoy, and a holiday from the Lone Star during the season of the year that means a lot of lost sleep—maybe I should go with you."

"Did I say the lady was beautiful?"

"With your luck, would she be anything else?"

Rafe's mouth tilted in a slow grin. "She's as pretty as a west Texas sunset, and you can't come because

I'm not sharing. For one thing, Honor would kill us both."

"Yeah, she would, wouldn't she?" Luke duplicated Rafe's smile. "Reckon I'll just have to suffer and do without a little taste of your good fortune."

Rafe glanced over his shoulder to where Luke's exquisite wife was holding court to the four Lake Bliss pirates. "Some suffering," he dryly drawled.

Luke laughed and clapped him on the shoulder. He lifted his daughter back into his arms and asked, "So, where is she? When do I get to meet Miss Mary Margaret St. John?"

The elderly woman held the bottle of Lake Bliss water up in front of the mercantile window and frowned. "And you say this will cure my rheumatism?"

"Not cure it, I'm afraid," Maggie replied. "But chances are it will ease your pain. The story I told you is true, Mrs. Best. Once I started taking daily doses of Lake Bliss water, my rheumatism disappeared for the most part."

Luella Best smiled at Maggie. "You are a sweet girl, Miss St. John. I knew it the first moment I saw you. My Rafe wouldn't have grinned at you the way he did if you weren't sweet."

Maggie fumbled the bolt of fabric she'd been considering for a new bathing sarong and it thudded to the floor. "Your Rafe? You know Mr. Malone? You saw us together?"

"Yes, earlier. We've been waiting for him for days. I tell you we were all happy to see him arrive on the ferry this afternoon."

"We? Who is we?"

"The Prescotts, of course."

"Luke Prescott?"

"And his wife and children. I'm Honor Prescott's mother-in-law, her second husband's mother. The boys, Micah and Jason, are my grandsons, although I consider the twins just as much my granddaughters even if we're not blood related. We're all family, you know."

No, Maggie hadn't known. She'd had no idea this woman was in any way connected to Rafe's partner Luke Prescott. She'd introduced herself to Luella Best in the mercantile because she'd noticed the pained steps the woman took as she entered the mercantile. "Does Rafe know you're in Galveston?"

"Likely by now he does. Luke and the others were headed to see him when they dropped me off here. I wanted to check you over."

"Oh." She didn't have the slightest clue of what else to say. That didn't matter, because Luella had plenty of questions to ask. She appropriated a stool from behind the counter, settled herself down, and proceeded to conduct an interrogation worthy of any Texas Ranger on the hunt for facts. After fifteen minutes, Luella knew everything about Maggie that was of any interest and a number of things that weren't interesting at all.

"Now where was it you first saw women wearing these bathing sarongs?" she asked, holding up a length of the bright floral cotton Maggie had chosen.

"Tahiti."

Luella clicked her tongue as her gaze measured Maggie's curves. "That Rafe sure does lead a charmed life. I know he will simply love this trip."

"Tell me a little about him, Luella," she asked, figuring the woman owed her some data in return.

"What would you like to know about my favorite rascal?"

The first question poured from her mouth like water from a dipper. "Does he have a lady friend back home?"

"No, not at the moment. I'm afraid he spent too long pining over his lost love, Elizabeth Perkins. They knew one another as children, and then once he settled in Bastrop he took up with her for a time."

Luella wrinkled her nose. "He's better off without her. Elizabeth is a silly twit. She chose Jasper Worrell over Rafe. She claimed she couldn't abide being married to a man of his tainted reputation."

"He still loves her?" Maggie asked, her throat surprisingly tight.

"No, and in truth, I don't believe he ever did. Not true love, anyway. I think he's still looking for it. Of course, he does enjoy the looking. You won't find a more accomplished rogue in the republic. Yet at the same time, Rafe is a gentleman about it. He likes women, Miss St. John, but he doesn't use them, which is more than one can say about many men. I think he wanted to love Elizabeth, and he convinced himself he did. He's been slower to take up with the ladies since then." She sent Maggie a sly look and added, "He's probably about due. The woman who casts her net and lands him will be one lucky lady, that's for certain."

Heat stained Maggie's cheeks and she looked away. "I'm not fishing, ma'am. My stringer is full at the moment. The four men in my life fill it up nicely. Between my papas and the spa, I have a very busy life."

"Yes, I intended to ask more about these sailors." Luella leaned forward, her eyes alight with interest. "I noticed them earlier. Quite manly specimens. Tell me, Maggie dear, the gentleman with the fascinating blue eyes is named Ben, you say?"

→ 5 ←

Despite the early hour, the entire Prescott contingent stood at the end of the Galveston pier as the *Buccaneer's Bliss* slipped her mooring and sailed out into the bay. Excitement thrummed in Rafe's blood. He smelled the brine in the air, heard the creak of wood and lap of water against the hull, and grinned. Adventure. It heated his body like a drug.

He glanced at the woman standing at his side and saw from the sparkle in her brilliant blue eyes that she felt it, too. He didn't analyze why he felt compelled to catch her hand in his as he tipped his hat in salute to Luke and his family.

"I liked them," Maggie said softly, waving and blowing kisses back to the twins. "The boys are so sweet to their little sisters, and Honor couldn't have been any more gracious. And Luella is a hoot."

Rafe's smile turned wry. "That's a diplomatic way to put it. A time or two last night I thought she might pose a threat to our little adventure."

"How's that?"

"Gus acted ready to run off with her."

Maggie gave a long-suffering sigh. "Lucky was just

as bad. Did you see him when she asked him about the scar around his neck? I've heard him tell the story of how he came by his nickname—how he was hanged by a rival pirate captain for freeing a female captive and how the other papas saved him—but he's never bragged about it before. Last night he puffed up so much I thought he'd burst his buttons."

Rafe's gaze fastened on Luella Best as she stood beneath a ruffled lime green parasol, waving a lacy handkerchief in farewell. "Luella has a way with men."

So did Maggie, but Rafe didn't think it prudent to mention it. Not under the present circumstances. Ever since yesterday afternoon, the woman had acted peculiar around him. Mighty peculiar.

Maggie St. John was flirting with him.

He hadn't recognized it for what it was right off. He'd sensed something strange once Luella and Maggie met up with the others down by the boat, but it had taken Luke's knowing look and an elbow in the ribs during dinner last night at the Tremont Hotel for him to put a name to Maggie's behavior. Rafe's excuse for being so slow was that this woman didn't flirt like other women of his acquaintance, and Rafe had been acquainted with plenty of other women.

The buccaneer's granddaughter didn't bat her eyelashes. She didn't simper or sweet-talk. She didn't swish her fanny. No, what Mary Margaret St. John had done starting yesterday afternoon and continuing on to this morning was touch him. Often. Too often.

But not often enough.

The sails flapped overhead as Rafe dropped her hand and put some distance between them. "And what did you think of my good friend Luke? Do you still wish he was the one making this trip instead of me?"

She folded her arms, cocked her head to one side, and gave her lips a considering purse. "Well . . ."

It bothered Rafe that she didn't automatically say no. He shot her a sharp look, then relaxed as she met his gaze with a teasing twinkle in her eyes.

"I've decided you're the right man for the job, Mr. Malone."

Damned if something about that didn't sit well, either.

Rafe turned his attention to the fishing skiff hauling in its nets off the starboard bow. He would have gone to Gus and Snake with an offer of help, but they had made a point of ordering the "landlubber" to stay out of their way until the *Buccaneer's Bliss* had safely navigated the sandbars spitting across Galveston Bay.

As the boat moved out into the bay, Rafe absently watched the large flocks of diving white gulls feeding on wide areas of jumping shrimp. Something was pushing the shrimp to the surface, and the occasional splash and roll confirmed the feast was being shared by predators both above and below the waters.

The boil in the water mirrored his own thoughts as his mind returned to Maggie and her confounded flirting. Her behavior had him tied in knots. Since showing up with Luella yesterday, she'd taken every opportunity to bestow friendly brushes of the hand and teasing nudges with her shoulder. If he said something that made her laugh, she'd reached over and squeezed his hand.

It was the damnedest thing. Rafe had always been a toucher, but he was accustomed to being the one who reached out, not the other way around. He found it disconcerting and distracting.

Arousing.

His gaze drifted over the woman who'd now joined her papas, adding an educated-sounding opinion to their argument over perceived inadequacies in the current map of Galveston Bay. While they debated facts, sandbars, and tides, Rafe considered Maggie.

She'd turned the tables on him. Flirting was his

forte. She wasn't suppose to do it back at him. Not when it marked such a change in her behavior. Rafe wanted to know why. He had the sneaking suspicion the woman was laying a trap for him, and he was too distracted by lust to figure out how.

She knew she got to him, too, the little witch. He could see it in her eyes. Maggie St. John's sea blue eyes had wicked twinkles down pat, and since Rafe was the champion of wicked twinkles, he knew exactly how they looked.

Shoot, in a contest she might even beat him.

The question of why bristly Miss Maggie had turned into a flirt had nagged him like a gnat half the night. The other half he'd spent dreaming of a fall of hair the color of old gold stroking his bare chest as her mouth made good on the promise in her eyes.

Rafe didn't think she'd fallen for his manly charms as Gus had predicted that first day in the meadow at the Lone Star. If that were the case she'd have started flirting sooner. After all, the first time they met she'd seen a helluva lot more than the breadth of his shoulders; she'd gotten a gander at the whole damned package. That hadn't done the trick. It hadn't done much for Rafe's pride, either, come to think of it.

The *Buccaneer's Bliss* rounded Galveston Island and headed out into open sea. As Rafe watched the Texas coast fade into the horizon, he tried to regain his earlier sense of excitement and adventure. Here he was on the ocean for the first time in his life, with water all around him, the blue sky above as big as that over west Texas. He joined the pirates for a lesson in critical aspects of sail trim and listened to stories of the king of the pirates, Jean Laffite, and how he'd ruled the island back in the twenties.

But all the while, thoughts of Maggie St. John haunted his mind. The woman had a method to her madness. Rafe was an intelligent man; he'd figure out what it was in time.

The lady in question emerged onto the deck and Rafe damned near swallowed his tongue. She'd changed her clothes. She now wore men's breeches. Form-fitting men's breeches. And a flowing shirt that plastered against her chest as she faced the wind.

Rafe cut his gaze to the wheel and Snake MacKenzie. The warning in the old salt's eyes made Rafe want to check his neck to make sure his head was still attached. Instead he slowly removed his hat and casually shielded the evidence of his reaction to Miss Mary Margaret St. John's provocative attire from angry eyes.

The woman would be the death of him yet.

On the first day of the second week of the voyage, Maggie emerged from the cabin and lifted her face to the warm sunshine. She stretched like a cat as the tropical heat sank into her bones, and she realized she'd not felt a twinge of joint pain in a week. She'd been right to come along on this trip. Right in more ways than one.

She looked to the starboard bow where Rafe stood at the ship's rail gazing out to sea. He wore the clothing she had presented him to mark the occasion of his first sail with pirates, and at the sight of him Maggie's mouth went dry. The white silk shirt and black breeches were a uniform of sorts for her pirate papas. But her papas had never filled out the clothes in quite the same manner as Rafe Malone. Her gaze trailed over the breadth of his shoulders and down his torso to where the breeches hugged his muscled buttocks, thighs, and calves. He was barefoot, and Maggie found the sight terribly alluring.

She hadn't spent as much time with him on this voyage as she would have liked. She had hoped for the opportunity to get to know him better. But between the sailing lessons Gus forced on Rafe and the fact Snake had assigned him to the watch opposite hers, she'd spent relatively little time with the man who so often occupied her thoughts. And fueled her fantasies.

Maggie's conversation with Luella Best had confirmed some things she'd come to suspect about Rafe Malone, and while she was not entirely certain she should trust him with their treasure—his talk about the value of his word was as yet still unproven—she did think she could trust him to assist her in another aspect of her life. Assist her without hurting her, that is.

Unless she totally misread the signs, Rafe Malone offered the opportunity for something she'd wanted for quite some time. Maggie was a woman now, with a woman's wishes and desires. She wanted to flirt and spark and spoon a little. She wanted to fall into infatuation. She wanted a beau.

She wanted that beau to be Rafe Malone.

Maggie liked the man who'd showed such kindness to Papa Gus and smiled so tenderly at a pair of baby girls. She enjoyed his terrible jokes and the outlandish stories he told about his highwayman days. She wasn't put off by his past as a thief. After all, the men she loved most in the world had once been thieves themselves. Heaven knows, she found Rafe Malone attractive. And that was putting it mildly.

She'd known men who were more classically handsome than Rafe, but none as intensely, powerfully masculine. The sheer force of his aura drew her like shavings to a magnet. She admitted that lowering her defenses around the man might be courting danger, but Maggie had been raised on danger. In many ways, she thrived on it.

Besides, she wasn't looking for anything serious. She didn't want a suitor. She wasn't looking for love, just a little romance.

At the girls' school she'd attended, Maggie had been taught all she cared to learn about love. She'd been eighteen and in love with a classmate's brother when her papas came to visit. Before they left a week later, she had learned firsthand the importance some people placed on family background and bloodlines. She had seen how shallow both love and a man's character could be.

The lessons had been painful, but she'd been better for the learning. She knew now that only a strong, intelligent, and independent man could appreciate a family like hers. She'd all but given up ever meeting him.

Maybe you've already met him.

Her mouth went dry at the thought. No. She couldn't, wouldn't think that way. It was one thing to flirt with an adventurer like her grandfathers, but another thing entirely to marry such a man. She'd spent the better part of her life being dragged around the world by men who didn't slow down until forced into it by age. While she enjoyed a little adventure herself, she didn't want a steady diet of it. What she wanted was a permanent home at Lake Bliss, a home filled with love and laughter. The home she'd lost when her parents died.

Maggie didn't remember her mother or her father. All she knew of them were the stories her papas had told in answer to her questions throughout the years, and a vague memory of a house that smelled of lemons. According to her grandfathers, Maggie's father had been a West Indies sugar planter. William St. John and his wife Catherine had rejoiced upon the birth of their daughter, but tragically, four short years later, yellow jack had struck down first Catherine and then her grieving widower. From his deathbed, fearing for his daughter's future, St. John had sent for his old and trusted friends, Captain Ben Scovall and his crew. With Maggie's parents gone, the papas took the young girl into their hearts and into their home—a world filled with action and adventure and very little boredom.

Now boredom was exactly what Maggie craved. She

wanted peace. She wanted tedium. And she couldn't quite picture Rafe Malone embracing that kind of life.

He'd joined this journey for adventure's sake, nothing else. He'd abandoned the responsibilities of his ranch and partnership with Luke Prescott without blinking an eye. That wasn't exactly a trait she intended to look for in a husband.

No, Maggie wasn't looking for a suitor. A beau, though, was another matter entirely. Rafe Malone would make a wickedly exciting beau.

Anticipation skidded up her spine as she approached him. Dressed in his breeches and silk shirt, Rafe Malone made a mouth-watering pirate. But something was wrong with the image he presented, and it made her smile. Maggie folded her arms and tsked. "You can take the man off the ranch, but you can't take the cowboy out of the corsair."

Rafe turned his head and looked at her, a wary light in his eyes. "What was that?"

"You wear your weapon like a gunslinger, Malone." She eyed the Colt Texas Paterson five-shot revolver strapped low on his hip. "A cutlass is more in keeping with your costume."

Shrugging, Rafe glanced down at himself, one side of his mouth tilting in a wry smile. "'Costume' is the right word for it. Almost as comfortable as my buckskins, but still a costume. Out here like this, though, it's not hard to imagine. Turn your ear just right and you'd swear to hear the cannon's thunder." His voice roughened as he added, "Turn your head just right and you can see treasure ripe for plunder."

A slow grin spread across his face and Maggie's heartbeat quickened. It was as piratical a gesture as she had ever seen. She eased away from him a half step. "The imagination is an incredible instrument."

He arched a brow, the knowing glint in his eyes questioning the courage of her response, before turning back to the water. "The sea is different from what I imagined. I never expected it to change so from one day to the next. From one hour to the next. The ride today is so smooth that Snake MacKenzie's hammock is barely swinging, while yesterday when the wind was blowing and the waves running high, this old tub reminded me of Brown Baggage."

"A portmanteau?"

"My racehorse. The fastest quarter-miler in Texas, in fact."

A horse. She should have known. "How is the *Buccaneer's Bliss* like a horse?"

Malone used hand motions to demonstrate his meaning while he spoke. "Yesterday she'd ride to the top of a roll, then plunge forward like a sprinter at a starter's shot. She'd hit the trough of the wave then rise again, tossing the water from her bows in a cloud of foam and spray. A high-mettled horse does the same thing, champing and shaking the froth from the bit." He paused a moment, then added ruefully, "I admit to being wrong about this boat. I should have known. Great spirit goes a long way in overcoming physical limitations."

Maggie's entire body went still. *Great spirit can overcome physical limitations.* It was the motto she'd lived by following the very first attack of rheumatism. That Rafe Malone recognized the truth of the statement, too, and stated it to her here at this particular moment felt significant. "I agree," she said slowly. "And I'm intrigued by the image you paint. The force of nature is awe inspiring."

"So is the force of man."

She gazed up at him, silently questioning his meaning.

"I hear timber straining and the wind whistling through the rigging, and I realize that man has taken the most unstable of elements—sea and sky—and bent them to his will. Man's courage and skill has harnessed the horse, Miss Maggie. He used his brain to ease his way over the wild and lonely paths of this world we live in."

"Not to be insulting, but that's profound thinking for a thief, Mr. Malone."

"It's profound thinking for a lawyer, too, and I used to be one of those."

"A lawyer!" From the deck behind them where Snake MacKenzie pretended to polish brass while he eavesdropped, the buccaneer's voice rang with revulsion. "Maggie, get a rope. Treasure or no treasure, I'm stringing him up by the thumbs. Lawyers are the whole reason we're in this mess."

While the younger man pointed out that a good attorney might have saved them from their legal troubles, Maggie tried to make sense of Rafe Malone's revelations. During a pause in the men's debate, she wondered aloud. "When did you have time to be a lawyer?"

He looked at her and grinned. "I studied law back before the Texas revolution. I was young, but I was good. Luke is fond of saying that the step from lawyer to thief was a natural professional move for me."

Snake grumbled something mean beneath his breath, then stalked away in answer to a summons from Gus. Rafe chuckled softly before turning a curious gaze on Maggie. "So, Miss St. John, now that you know my deep, dark secrets, why don't you share some of your own."

"Like what?"

"I don't know. I'm curious about you, lady. I wonder what is going on inside of that beautiful head of yours. Why don't you tell me what you see when you look at the sea?"

He'd surprised her with that one. Maggie gazed at the gray waters of the Gulf of Mexico and spoke from her soul. "I've lived a good portion of my life aboard ship. When I look at the sea, I see a nice place to visit."

"But not to live?"

"Not to live. I find adventure wearing."

He propped a hip against the ship's rail and folded his arms. Cocking his head, he asked, "Have you ever tasted a habanera pepper, Miss Maggie?"

She eyed him quizzically at the change of subject. "Yes. They're very hot."

Rafe nodded. "A little bit of habanera in a plate of beans turns something plain and ordinary into a delicacy worth savoring. Too much pepper makes it too hot to handle."

"And your point is . . . oh, I see now. You are certainly in a metaphorical mood today, aren't you?"

"Adventure is the spice of life."

"Maybe so, Mr. Malone." Maggie turned her gaze toward the west where Papa Ben and Papa Lucky worked and waited at Hotel Bliss. "But home is certainly the sugar."

Caribbean blue. On the deck of the *Buccaneer's Bliss,* gazing through the spyglass, Rafe finally had a name for the color of Maggie St. John's eyes. Caribbean blue, luring and alluring. A man could happily drown in such glittering depths.

The Yucatán coast lay before them like a jewel cache. Turquoise waters lapped against pearlescent beaches that disappeared into an emerald jungle. Excitement gushed like a drug through Rafe's veins as he lowered the glass and returned it to Gus. "So, master plunderer, when does this treasure hunt fork the saddle?"

"Come again?"

"Begin. When do we get started? When do we dig for the gold?"

"Well, for one thing, you're not digging nothing. The treasure isn't buried, it's hidden, and we've a few details to check before attempting to retrieve it. But if all goes well, I anticipate we will have accomplished our business here and be headed for home by day after tomorrow."

Rafe frowned, his gaze once again seeking the shore. He didn't like the idea of such a brief stay on land. After all, how much adventure could a man have in two short days? "That soon?"

"If all goes well. We will need to do some reconnoitering first. Don't forget there's a war going on down here. Snake and I will visit with some of our old acquaintances and find out what's been happening since Lucky and I were down here last. Gotta make sure no one has set up a camp or something along our route. As much fun as fighting can be, I'd just as soon avoid a war of our own with a local who thinks to steal our treasure as we tote it back to the boat from the cenote."

Rafe repeated the unfamiliar word. "Sin-oh-tay?"

"It's like a pool inside a cave that serves as a natural well," Gus explained. "The rivers in this country are all underground, and cenotes are the cracks in the surface that allow access to the fresh water. They are also good hiding places for treasure."

Rafe grinned. "A freshwater bath sounds right fine about now. So, when do we meet with your old friends? I have to tell you, as much as I've enjoyed the sail, I'm ready to get off this boat."

"If you feel that way after less than two full weeks, you'd better stick to raising horses, Malone," Gus said, shaking his head. "You'd make a pitiful sailor. You'll get your wish, though, because we'll reach the island by noon." He slid Rafe a sidelong look and added, "Just so you're forewarned, this afternoon may well be the most dangerous hours you'll face during the entire trip."

"Why? Are these old friends of yours that nasty?"

Gus shrugged. "They are murderers, cutthroats, and thieves."

"Sounds a lot like my old friends. I should fit in just fine."

"You're not going to have the opportunity to fit in, Malone, and that's what makes this afternoon so dangerous for you."

Rafe arched a brow. "Explain it to me, Gus."

"No, don't think I will. You are an intelligent man, Malone. You'll figure it out."

Rafe figured it out all right. He both figured it out and couldn't believe it was happening at the same time.

Shortly after noon, Snake and Gus left Rafe all alone on a sun-drenched tropical island with their most-prized treasure, his for the plundering. As the *Buccaneer's Bliss* sailed away and was lost to the horizon, Rafe turned to Maggie and choked back a groan.

She stood barefoot on the white sand beach, her glistening, waist-length hair flying unbound in the breeze. She wrapped her mouth around a banana and took a bite. Her eyes closed and pleasure filled her expression. When she ever-so-slowly ringed her lips with her tongue, savoring the sensuous pleasure of the fruit, Rafe threw his head back, glared at the sky, and swore softly.

It was going to be a long, hot, hard afternoon.

Pleasure hummed in Maggie's veins as she licked the last bit of banana from her fingers. *Mmm, I've missed this.*

She'd missed the fruit and this little slice of heaven. This tiny little island off the coast of Yucatán had always been one of her favorite places to visit. No one lived here, and all signs suggested few people other than she and her papas ever visited.

The land was lush and lovely. A wide variety of tropical fruits ladened the trees and sweetened the air. Birds filled the afternoon with a symphony of song. The surf lapped against the beach, the soothing sound melting over her like warm honey. Maggie called the island Eden, and glancing toward the man who shared the island with her, she felt like Eve studying the apple. Rafe Malone was pure temptation.

Maggie sucked in a breath. This beautiful island, the privacy afforded by her grandfathers' departure. The sea, the sand, the sun. The man. Life simply couldn't get more romantic than this.

"I still can't believe they did this," Rafe said, rubbing his jaw with the palm of his hand.

He hadn't shaved that morning. The dark stubble on his face and glare in his eyes as he gazed toward the horizon where the *Buccaneer's Bliss* had disappeared made him look dangerous. Maggie grinned. She'd always liked that in a man. "You can't believe they did what?"

"Left us here like this. Alone. After all that chin music they spouted about my staying away from you, and then they up and leave the fox in with the hen. It makes no sense."

"Maybe they think they've frightened you into good behavior with their threats."

He drawled, "Maggie, please. I'm serious."

She'd like to please him. Seriously. "Papa Gus explained it all before they left. They had no choice but to leave us both here. Do you not believe them?"

"I believe them. It makes sense that they needed to scout for information and that the village is too dangerous a place for a man to visit alone or to take a woman. I can even understand that having a stranger like me along might cause their old friends to clam up."

"So what else could they have done?"

Rafe didn't have an answer for that because one didn't exist.

"Quit your fretting and follow me, Malone. Do I have a treat for you! Have you ever tasted mango? I know of a tree not far off the beach."

He sighed heavily and glanced back toward the sea. She heard him grumbling something about buccaneers and sea sirens, and a shiver of delight raced up her spine. Was that how he thought of her? A sea siren?

"No, I've never tasted a mango."

"Then you're in for a culinary adventure, Malone. Be happy about it, all right?"

He looked at Maggie, then back at the sea. After a moment, he shrugged. "You're right. I came here looking for adventure, so I reckon I'd be a fool not to give it a try. Lead the way, Lorelei."

Malone appeared to relax after that. He asked dozens of questions about the island and its vegetation. He climbed up a mahogany tree and shimmied down a long palm. He tasted each fruit she offered him and spent twenty minutes trying to figure his way into a coconut. Maggie shook her head in amusement when he finally whipped out his Texas Paterson and plugged it.

After that bit of excitement, Maggie led him to her favorite spot on the island, a calm green-water lagoon rimmed by a sugar sand beach. "This is where I swim. Actually, I do more standing and watching than swimming. There are thousands of fish in this lagoon. You won't believe all the colors, Rafe. Come see." She reached up to open the buttons on her bodice.

He caught her by the arm. "What in blazes are you doing?"

"I'm going swimming," she said, looking at him in surprise. "Aren't you coming with me?"

He winced as though in pain. "Do you wear the same thing when you swim as what you wear to take a mud bath?"

She wore one of the bathing sarongs she'd acquired during their last South Sea voyage. *What did he . . . oh.* Maggie remembered what she'd worn when she inadvertently shared a mud bath with Rafe Malone. Nothing. He thought she intended to strip down to the bare skin right here in front of him.

She found the idea intriguing but a little too advanced for the current stage of their relationship.

Rafe's hand tightened around her arm. "Maggie St. John, are you inviting me to get naked with you?"

"No, Malone. I'm inviting you to swim with me. That's all. I'm wearing a bathing costume beneath my clothes." She tugged off the dress to reveal a bright orange and green sarong. As she removed the necklace from around her neck, she added, "I wanted to swim and watch the fish, and I thought you'd enjoy the entertainment, too. This lagoon is filled with the prettiest, most brilliant colors I've seen in my life."

Rafe studied her with a strange look in his eyes. "Prettier than a rainbow over Lake Bliss?"

Surprised by the question. Maggie paused and thought about it a moment. The colors of life in this Caribbean lagoon were flashy and fast. A rainbow painting the sky at home was bigger, grander. "Nothing is as beautiful as home."

"You are, Mary Margaret St. John."

The sound of her full name on his lips sent a quiver skidding across her skin. Her head jerked up, and she met his gaze. The heat in his eyes all but knocked her to her knees. Good heavens, what had she started? Maggie trembled as he slowly walked toward her. She was filled with fear and excitement and . . . need.

He stopped in front of her and raised his hand, brushing his knuckles along her cheek. "This is a dangerous game you are playing, lady. You've been inviting me to do more than swim since we left Galveston, and I'm about ready to take you up on the offer."

Was it true? Had her actions suggested more than she, in her inexperience, had realized? And if so, how did she feel about it? Did she want to take this beyond flirtation? Was she ready for seduction?

But before Maggie could make up her mind, Rafe turned and disappeared into the trees. She watched him go and muttered, "Promises, promises."

Rafe struck out blindly, not caring where he went as long as it was away from Maggie. Another minute with her—one more glimpse of that scrap of fabric she wore for swimming—and he'd have been on her as fast as small-town gossip.

As it was, the only thing stopping him was suspicion. What did she want? What was she after? What sort of scheme or scam did she and her pirate papas have in the works?

Rafe wondered if the treasure actually existed. It could be that this entire trip was an elaborate attempt to trap him into doing something he wouldn't want to do. What could that be? Shoot, he was game for just about anything as long as it wouldn't break his promise to Luke.

His promise to Luke.

Memories of that awful time during the war slithered over Rafe like a snake, and he picked up his step trying to outrun them. Failing. As he sped through the jungle, thoughts of his half brother Nick Callahan coiled around him. They constricted his chest and hissed in his ear. *Broken promises. False accusations. Bloody deaths. Senseless deaths.*

Rafe let out a yell when he broke through the trees onto the beach. He headed straight for the water, stripping down to his skin along the way. He dove into the cool surf and swam with powerful strokes, hoping the salt water and physical exertion would wash away the ugliness of the past and clear his mind to better deal with problems of the present.

He swam for almost an hour and felt tired but refreshed when he finally dragged himself from the sea. He plopped down on the sand and soaked in the welcome warmth of the Caribbean sun.

Until the sound of Maggie's scream chilled him all over again.

Rafe leapt to his feet, pausing only long enough to pull on his pants and boots and pick up his gun. As he raced for the lagoon, a second shriek ripped through the air.

"Stop it . . . stop it . . . oh!"

Fear rushed like poison through his veins. *Please, God, let me get to her in time.* Who was attacking her? Cutthroats, soldiers? It didn't really matter. Whoever it was had bought more trouble than he could imagine when he made Maggie scream.

At the tree line Rafe paused, his frantic gaze sweeping the area for Maggie. There, a spot of orange. Rafe's gaze locked on the battle raging before his eyes and shock stopped him cold. She didn't look hurt; she looked angry. Wet, bedraggled, and, most of all, furious.

And she was battling a monster for her dress.

Not a man but a monster. A real monster. Green and scaly, seven feet long and probably thirty pounds or so. It was the ugliest creature Rafe had ever seen. Like an overgrown horned toad, only different. A mouthful of vicious-looking teeth had hold of one end of Maggie's dress and she had hold of the other. She was growling; the animal remained silent.

Rafe didn't know whether to laugh or shoot the lizard. He called out to Maggie, "Is he dangerous?"

She spared him a glare. "No, but I am. He won't let go. Pretend he's a coconut, Malone, and shoot him. We'll have iguana stew for supper."

"No." Rafe approached the struggling pair, watching Maggie with a mixture of amusement and lust— wearing that wet bathing sarong, she might as well have been naked. He eyed the animal with distaste. He'd heard of iguanas, but this was the first he'd seen. *And I thought we grew things big in Texas.* "I don't kill what I don't eat, and I gave up eating reptiles years ago. Let go, Maggie."

"I want my dress back."

"Why? It's not worth wearing. Not anymore."

She spat out a stream of sea-creature names and Rafe decided to try out one of the pirate family oaths on his tongue. "Oyster!" he cursed. Then, grinning, he nodded. "You put the right emphasis on it and it works real good."

"Put a sponge in it, Malone." Maggie's jaw clenched. She planted her feet, inhaled a deep breath, and gave the fabric one furious tug. The ripping seemed to go on forever.

Maggie fell back onto her behind, her hands clutching her half of a dress split down the middle. The iguana swaggered off into the trees with the other portion.

"You know," Rafe drawled, watching the big lizard's tail swing back and forth. "That fellow's technique could use some work. I've ripped a bodice or two in my day, but only at my lady's request."

Maggie gawked up at him, speechless. Rafe plopped down on the sand beside her, leaned back on his elbows, and waited for her to speak. When she continued to stare at him, he added, "Just for my information—so I can keep my amorous skills up, you understand—what turned you against him to begin with? Was it his looks? Do you prefer a different shade of green, perhaps? You find shorter toes more attractive? Perhaps you prefer beards to dewlaps below your lover's lips?"

Maggie made a strangled noise, and Rafe pressed onward. "Or maybe his actions are at fault. Could it be you don't care to be spat at? Or maybe you didn't care for that darting business." Rafe demonstrated by whipping his tongue in and out of his mouth.

That did it. A twinkle kindled in her eyes and laughter bubbled up from inside her. Rafe's smug grin dissolved into chuckles as he dropped back upon the sand. "That had to be the funniest thing I've seen in years."

"I must have looked like a fool."

He pictured her then—the damp sarong plastered to her curves, the length of her bare legs, the fire in her eyes. "You looked ravishing."

In the time it took to say those three words, the laughter between them died, replaced by tension thick and hot and sweet. Rafe slowly lifted his back off the sand until they sat eye to eye, lips to lips. The moment seemed to stretch for hours as she beckoned him closer with those Caribbean blue eyes.

"They'll kill me," Rafe said, his voice rough and low, referring to the pirates. He lifted a hand, brushing a thumb across her cheek.

She shivered at his touch. "They may try."

His mouth slanted in a crooked smile. "What do you want from me, Maggie?"

"Romance," she said on a sigh. "I've never been romanced. My papas hover over me so. I think you are my chance, Rafe. I'd like you to give me just a little romance."

He considered it a moment. He didn't know how he felt about being Maggie's "chance," but he did like the idea of romance. He always had. "I'm good at that."

"I thought you might be."

He leaned forward, and as her lashes fluttered to her cheeks, he touched her mouth with his. She tasted of salt water, mango, and innocence. Soft and shyly, she returned his kiss, her response both uncertain and encouraging, fueling the slow burn that had been building inside Rafe since their mud bath rendezvous.

He slid his hand into her silky, molten-gold hair and pulled her closer. Her hands crept around his torso, and she held him tight. At the press of her breasts against his bare chest, a wave of wanting washed over him, and even though he knew better, even though he knew it was a mistake, Rafe took it beyond a kiss.

He lowered her to the ground and lay beside her. Heat pooled in his groin as he rolled her toward him. Even as she melted against him, he slipped his tongue past the velvet softness of her lips, exploring her intimately, thoroughly. A whimper of need escaped her throat and he captured it, savored the taste of it. Swallowed it to feed the driving ache inside him.

He craved her bare skin beneath his fingers, beneath his mouth. He yearned to suckle at her breasts. He hungered to bury himself in the sweet honey between her thighs. Breaking their kiss, he stared down into her eyes, past the flecks of blue and green and into her very soul. God, how he wanted her. Mary Margaret St. John. "Mary," he breathed.

A smile hovered at her lips and in her expression, he saw softness and wonder and . . . innocence. That damned innocence. *A little romance.* Fool woman didn't know what she was asking for.

It was enough. Just barely, but enough. With a groan, he pushed away from her and rolled onto his back. Throwing a hand across his brow, he lay gulping air back into his lungs as silence stretched between them.

"No one's ever done that before."

"Kissed you?" Of course, calling that a kiss was like calling Texas a little bit of land, but Rafe didn't know how else to put it.

"Called me Mary. I've always been Maggie or Magpie or Mary Margaret. When I was little, Papa Gus called me Snookums. The way you said 'Mary,' it sounded so . . . well . . . pretty."

After what just transpired between them, that's all she had to say? A comment about her name? Rafe cocked open one eye and stared out from beneath his arm.

She lay on her back, a pleased smile on her face, and Rafe didn't have a clue what to make of her. She was an innocent, yet she wasn't, both brazen and shy all at the same time. A pirate's virgin granddaughter.

She fascinated him. She drew him like lemonade on a hot summer day, and after one taste he knew he wanted more than a single sip.

And he'd called her a fool.

He rolled to his feet. Scowling, he paused to yank off first one boot, then the other. He hated to get sand in his shoes. "Listen, Maggie, about this romancing you want."

"Yes?"

"I don't think it's such a good idea."

Her smile faded and a blush stole across her face. Rafe realized she was embarrassed. Before he could say anything more, she was on her feet, dusting herself off, her spine stiff as a whalebone corset. "Please, just forget about it. I shouldn't have said . . . shouldn't have done . . . you didn't want—"

"To stop," he said flatly. "I didn't want to stop, Sugar. Believe me."

Her gaze flicked toward him, then away. Hesitantly, she said, "So why did you?"

"Because I'm afraid of your grandfathers."

"Uh-huh," she said dryly. "At least try to make it believable, Malone."

He grinned. This woman was too strong to stay disconcerted for long. Carrying his boots, he walked toward the lagoon, stopping to retrieve the scrap of Maggie's dress lying in the sand. At the water's edge, he dipped one bare foot into the water, swished it clean, then stood on the cloth as he washed his other foot. He used the sleeve of her dress as a towel, then pulled his boots onto his clean feet. "It's like this, Miss Maggie. Romance is a lot like sand."

She sputtered a laugh. "Excuse me?"

"I've had more than a nodding acquaintance with romance in the past, and I've learned a valuable lesson or twelve. Think about it. Sand can be soft and pillowy or hard and clingy. It can tickle your toes or cut your feet. It can rub you raw if you're not careful, and burn you even if you are. Heat it hot enough and you can make a weapon. Glass shards can kill as well as a knife."

Maggie folded her arms, unknowingly emphasizing the fullness of her breasts beneath her damp costume. Her expression darkened with frustration. "Where are you going with this, Malone?"

He swept her with his gaze, knowing a little frustration of his own, as he continued, "Sometimes, though, a grain of sand finds its way into an oyster, and then do you know what you get? Something so beautiful—something so perfect—it's coveted all over the world. But it takes a little time to grow a pearl. A person has to be patient. Otherwise that grain of sand has been wasted, and you'd have been better off making glass with it."

Maggie shook her head. "I don't understand a word you are saying."

"You know, I'm not certain I do, either. But I have a point to make, and it's in there somewhere." Rafe walked over to Maggie and took hold of her hands. "I lived a good share of my youth with Luke's family, and his mother had a hand in my raising. She put powerful store in manners and in treating ladies with respect. I wasn't called Gentleman Rafe Malone for nothing, Maggie. I don't want to hurt you. As much as I'd enjoy doing otherwise, I think it best we take this romancing more slowly."

He watched her closely as she considered his words, and when she offered a wistful smile, he felt as if a heavy weight had lifted from his shoulders.

"Do you think there's a chance we'll find a pearl, Malone?"

"Stranger things have happened," he replied, giving her hands a squeeze. Rafe leaned toward her, intending only to kiss her cheek, when the unmistakable scrape of a sword being drawn stopped him cold.

"I'll give ye one sentence to explain this." Snake MacKenzie stood at the edge of the trees, a hunk of Maggie's dress clenched in one hand, his cutlass held high in the other.

Rafe winced. "Of course, there's always the chance we'll choke on the oyster."

One hour after the *Buccaneer's Bliss* dropped anchor off the coast of Yucatán the following morning, Maggie trudged single file behind Gus and Rafe and in front of Snake along a questionable path through the jungle, biting her tongue to keep from asking her grandfathers, "Are we there yet?"

If the little island where they'd spent yesterday was Eden, this place was its opposite. The strong breeze that cooled along the shoreline didn't penetrate the dense inland foliage. The hot, humid atmosphere of the jungle was thick enough to taste; its scent a peculiar mixture of new life and decay.

Living in Texas, Maggie wasn't new to hot weather, but this wet heat managed to sap the strength right from her bones. Sweat sluiced down her back, plastering her linen shirt against heated skin. Periodically she stopped and lifted a wineskin to her lips, but the tepid water did little to quench her thirst.

Thunder rolled across the land, adding its noise to the clamor of the jungle. Mosquitoes whose size made their Texas cousins look like gnats hummed in Maggie's ears. From the treetops came the high-pitched howl of monkeys and the drone of cicadas pounding their membrane drums. Maggie wanted to put her hands over her ears and yell at them all to be quiet. She was miserable, but she refused to complain.

She hadn't spoken to any of the men since yesterday.

They'd acted like children, each one of them. Papa Snake, for charging ahead with that sword raised high, refusing to believe her explanation. Papa Gus, for throwing the punches Rafe didn't defend against. And Malone himself, curse his hide, for starting the battle by admitting he'd kissed her.

Why couldn't the man have used a little discretion? *I don't lie,* he'd told her flatly. Well what kind of moral outlook was that for a thief, for goodness sakes? And for a lawyer, at that? No wonder he'd changed professions.

But the worst part came after the scuffle when the men sat around sharing a smoke and swapping stories of the trouble caused by women in their pasts. The sympathy and understanding each expressed for the others made Maggie want to slap them all. Her mood didn't improve when the men tried to talk her into waiting aboard the boat while they fetched the treasure.

On their trip into the village, her grandfathers had learned that the fighting in the area between the locals and the government troops had moved south and away from their route to the treasure. With that being the case, Maggie had seen no reason why she should be left behind. They'd argued, three against one, and by the time Papa Snake had served up a delicious turtle stew, she would have dumped it over their heads had it not been so delicious. She'd bedded down for the night nursing a full-blown case of hurt feelings.

Now, faced with the discomforts of the jungle, she wondered if she hadn't made a mistake.

"Be careful here," Gus called over his shoulder, stepping cautiously over a fallen seybo tree that blocked the entire path. "Don't graze the trunk, whatever you do. The sap will eat a man's skin like acid."

Rafe took an exaggerated step over the log, then turned back and held out a helping hand first to Maggie and then to Snake. When the pirate hesitated, Rafe casually eyed the rough, scaly bark of the seybo and said, "We grow some nasty things at home, but I've never heard of a skin-eating tree. Scares me spitless."

"If you're frightened of a tree, best keep an eye out for snakes," Snake said, accepting Rafe's assistance over the obstruction. "They grow some down here that make rattlers look like garden snakes."

Malone knew just what tack to take to ease her papas' fearsome pride, Maggie realized. She couldn't deny his kindness where her grandfathers were concerned, and that meant more to Maggie than almost anything. Gentleman Rafe Malone. The name fit him.

They continued their trek along the jungle path and Maggie's snit began to melt. As if he sensed her feelings, Rafe glanced back at her and winked.

Gentleman *Rake* Malone suited him better, she decided. A small grin lifted her lips at the thought. Along with her smile came a cheering of her heart, and within minutes Maggie's outlook on the day had changed.

The jungle felt less oppressive and even her steps seemed lighter. She marched for a full quarter hour without once thinking a complaint. Instead of her earlier lethargy, Maggie knew a sense of excitement. Soon they would reach the treasure trove. They were only an hour or two away from securing the means to save Hotel Bliss and solve all their problems.

And on a more immediate scale, it wouldn't be long now until she took a refreshing swim in the cool, clean water of a cenote.

Although her papas and Malone didn't know it yet, she intended to join the thief on his cenote swim. Swimming alone was always a dangerous proposition; swimming alone in an underground river was simply stupid. Too much was at stake to take unnecessary risks, and besides, Maggie had heard stories about the underwater world for much of her life. She wasn't about to squander her opportunity to see its wonder for herself.

"The sopadilla tree is straight ahead," Snake called up to Gus. "Do you see it?"

"Yep." The pirate glanced over his shoulder to Rafe. "Time to pull out the machete, son. From here on out we blaze our own trail. It'll be tough going for a time."

"Why isn't there a path? I thought y'all were just down here."

"We were. But the jungle reclaims its territory fast. That's one reason this is such a good hiding place for our booty. Almost as soon as we cut our way through, the vines and bushes grow to close our path, concealing it from the casual eye."

Drawing his own broad-blade machete, Gus studied the sopadilla tree, chose a spot, then whacked his way into the foliage. The going proved hard but not unreasonably slow, and less than fifteen minutes later they reached a towering rock monolith that marked their goal.

"What the hell is that?" Rafe asked, staring up at the leering, fearsome faces carved into the stone.

"The Maya left calling cards like that all across this

land," Snake answered. "That's how we found our hiding place. Ben has a real interest in the old ruins, and each time we came here he'd drag us off on an expedition of sorts. We linked up with a guide who over time became a friend. He showed us the entrances to find the cave. The back way in—the one you'll be taking—is marked by carvings like that."

Rafe gave the images a mock salute. "Glad you warned me. I'd hate to run across one of those unexpectedly. Scare the bejabbers out of a man."

"There he goes being scared again," Snake said to Gus, disgust lacing his tone. "I'm beginning to get worried."

"Don't be silly, Papa Snake," Maggie said. "Rafe will do just fine."

The man in question quirked a brow as if amused or surprised by her show of support. Gus said, "Everyone quiet now. I want you all to listen good and make certain we're alone." Lowering his voice, he added, "We're almost there."

Finally, Maggie thought.

Once the pirates were assured of their solitude, they led Rafe and Maggie toward a slight rise in the landscape, their machetes hacking away at the incessant web of low scrub. "Careful now," Gus called. They stood at the top of a rise. The ground sloped steeply downward before leveling out again some thirty feet below them. "It's tricky to see, and if you don't watch where you're going you could stumble into the sinkhole."

"Sinkhole?" Rafe questioned. "Like the ones we have in the Texas hill country?"

"Yes, in a way. The land has crumbled in, forming a cave around a pool that is fed by the underground river. Follow me and you'll see. The path is gravelly, though, so footing is precarious. Watch that your feet don't slide out from under you."

They climbed down the small hill, assisting one another as needed. Excitement thrummed in Maggie's veins as the ground leveled out and she gasped with pleasure at first sight of the cenote.

The cave cut into the hill some twenty feet at its widest. Rock formed an arch over a pool of crystal-clear water that disappeared into deep shadows at the back of the cavern. Tropical flowers framed the edges of the arch, an explosion of oranges and reds, purples and yellows. Fruit bats sounded a baleful greeting from their ceiling perch.

Maggie hurriedly descended the rest of the path, halting at the very edge of the cenote, smiling at the majestic beauty of the scene.

"It's magical," Rafe said, his eyes alight as he joined her.

"The Maya thought so," Gus told him, coming up behind. "Similar basins dot the entire Yucatán peninsula. We're told it's not unheard of today for an occasional sacrifice to be offered up to the gods from places like this."

Rafe thumbed his hat back on his head. "Tell me y'all haven't taken up their religion."

Snake dropped his pack on the ground. "Not yet, but we damn sure might if you keep sniffing around our Maggie."

"Papa!" she protested. She didn't want any strife to mar this moment. She knew the peace would end soon enough as it was. It would end the minute she expressed her intention to accompany Rafe on his swim.

"C'mon, folks," Gus said. "Daylight's wasting. I want to go over the map one more time with Malone before we head out for the fissure."

"I know it by heart," Rafe said seriously.

"It never hurts to check things out one last time."

Rafe pulled a dagger from its sheath at his waist. Hunkering down, he began to trace in the dirt. Maggie felt certain he could draw it in his sleep if required. Her grandfathers had gone over the route at least five times a day since they'd left Galveston. Maggie knew it by heart, and she hadn't been the one the papas constantly had grilled with the facts.

Once Rafe managed to reach the inner chamber, retrieving the treasure would be a relatively simple process. The men carried a coil of rope and a dozen bank bags. The plan was for them to lower an empty bag tied onto the rope through the fissure in the rock above the treasure cave. Rafe would fill the bag and the papas would pull it up to the surface where they'd load the plunder into backpacks for the hike out of the jungle.

On the previous trip, they had debated the idea of widening the fissure enough for a man to fit through and retrieve the treasure that way. Two things had stopped them. First, it would forever destroy a great hiding place, and a man never knew when he might need one of those. Second, Lucky had recalled the promise Ben had made to his guide years earlier not to disturb the land. To do so risked a curse from the Mayan gods. They considered this plan far superior because it risked only Rafe Malone's life.

When Snake and Gus finally agreed that Rafe knew where he needed to go, they wished him luck and prepared to leave the cenote. Now that the moment was upon her, Maggie decided that action served better than words at this particular time. Briskly she shucked down to her bathing sarong. Rafe saw what she was doing before her grandfathers noticed, but this once, anyway, she proved quicker than he. As he reached out to stop her, she dove into the cenote.

The cold water shocked her, squeezing her lungs like an overly tight corset. She hadn't expected it to be this chilly, and she hoped the drop in temperature wouldn't trigger a bout of rheumatism as it had in the past. Her papas would really be angry then. But it was too late now to worry the question. She was committed to her course.

She surfaced just long enough to take a breath. Her

grandfathers' angry shouts rang in her ears as she dove beneath the water once again and swam for the tunnel that led off the right side of the cenote. A splash behind her told her Rafe had followed on her heels, and she pulled harder, kicked harder, swimming as fast as she could along the narrow opening. Around that first turn she'd find a hole in the rock approximately three feet below the surface. Once she made it through there, she'd be safe. Rafe couldn't force her back through the hole if she resisted, not without drowning her, anyway.

Coming up for air, she spied the leering face painted on the wall and knew she'd found the first marker. The tunnel hole would be directly beneath it. She took a breath and prepared to dive when a hand grasped her ankle. *Kelp you, Rafe Malone!*

Like a fish on a line, she went still for a moment. Then, just as he attempted to reel her in, she twisted and bucked and slithered from his grasp. She'd gotten away!

She kicked hard and pulled with her arms. In a flash, she made it through a hole and into the next chamber. She surfaced and treaded water while she investigated her surroundings. Sunlight beamed through cracks in the top of the cave some ten feet above Maggie's head and created the purest, gentlest blue she had ever seen. She could easily have hovered there, drinking in the beauty, had she not needed to find a place to stage the battle she fully expected to wage with Rafe.

He didn't disappoint her. No sooner had she grasped a rocky ledge along the tunnel wall than his head and shoulders burst from the water in the middle of the luminescent pool. He gave his head a shake, slinging water like bullets while his eyes fired flaming arrows straight at her. Pasting on a false grin, she said, "And I thought Loch Ness had a monster."

His shout echoed off the walls. "What the hell do you think you're doing?"

Maggie was nervous, but determined not to show it. She licked her lips. "I think that should be obvious, Malone. I'm going with you."

"The hell you are."

"The hell I am, too." Because she couldn't quite make herself hold his gaze, she glanced down into the crystal water. *Oh, my.* Rafe Malone swam naked.

His arms pumped the water and his biceps bunched. Shock lit his eyes. "You said a real swear word."

"I beg your pardon."

"You certainly should." He lifted one hand from the water and crooked a finger. "Come on, Maggie. You're going back."

Her long wet hair swirled around her shoulders as she shook her head. "No, I'm not, and if you try to make me I'll fight you. Even someone with your strength can't force me through that hole if I don't cooperate."

"You are some piece of work, lady."

"Thank you."

Rafe swam toward her, stopping only an arm's length away. "Why are you doing this?" he asked, the frustration in his voice echoing off the walls. "Is it trust? You don't trust me? You think I'll load up the treasure and swim it out of here? Swim it all the way back to Texas, perhaps?"

Maggie touched his shoulder. "I don't think you'll steal our treasure, Rafe. Not anymore, anyway. I simply don't think it's smart for you to make this swim by yourself. My grandfathers haven't used the back entrance to the cave for years and years, and even then their guide swam the route, not them. What if you run into trouble?"

He grabbed hold of the rock shelf and dryly drawled, "I didn't know you cared."

His choice of words caught Maggie off guard. The sense that something profound might come from her answer lapped at her consciousness. *I didn't know you cared.*

When she didn't reply, Rafe's gaze grew more intent. Maggie stared into his eyes and did her best to read the emotions in their jungle green depths. Anticipation? Apprehension? What did he want to hear?

What did she want to say?

Rafe was a rake, a rogue. He was the kind of man a woman could love but never get to keep.

Well, she didn't want to keep him, did she? She simply wanted to enjoy him for a while. Right?

I didn't know you cared.

Well, there was caring and there was *caring*. Maggie was prepared to admit to only the first. She cleared her throat. "I do care, Rafe. I probably shouldn't, but I do."

The moment hung between them, ripe and seductive. Rafe brushed a thumb across her cheek and then her lower lip. "Ah, Mary Margaret. What am I going to do with you?"

Leaning toward him, she answered with her eyes. *Kiss me.*

Aw, hell, he wanted to kiss her.

Sunlight lit the cavern from a dozen small cracks in the roof above them as Rafe stared at Maggie's lips, drawn like a thirsty man to water. He wanted to taste her, touch her, hold her.

But he also wanted to wring her neck.

He couldn't believe she'd jumped into the water out of the blue like that. She must have known neither he nor the pirates would allow her to swim into the treasure cave, so she up and took the decision from their hands. Willful little witch. How had those pirates managed her all these years? Obviously, they hadn't managed her at all.

Maggie watched him expectantly, and for Rafe, time seemed to slow to a crawl. *I do care,* she'd said with conviction and a hint of despair in her voice. Her confession warmed a corner of his heart even as it raised his defenses.

He gave his legs a little kick, backing away from her. He needed the distance, both physically and emotionally. Hard experience had taught him to be cautious where women and caring were concerned.

Rafe was a man who truly liked women; he enjoyed having a special one in his life. For years he'd viewed each romantic relationship as just one more adventure to savor, and certainly the women he'd known hadn't seemed to mind. But Rafe's perspective had changed a few years back when he had tangled with Elizabeth Perkins. He'd fallen harder than usual for the woman, and when she'd chosen to marry another man—a man with an impeccable reputation—he'd taken it like a bullet. Since then he'd been much more careful about allowing ladies into his heart.

Then he'd met Maggie, whose spirit and fire and loyalty and tenderness threatened all his good intentions. He had the sneaking suspicion that without even trying, Maggie St. John could make the fickle Elizabeth Perkins look like an also-ran in the heartbreak race.

After all, he was already halfway in love with the woman.

He croaked out his next words. "I hear your grandfathers shouting. Don't you think you should go talk to them about this?"

Her mouth pursed in a pout. "I don't doubt they're out there poised to grab me the minute I poke so much as a finger through that opening. But you'd better go explain that I'm going with you. Otherwise they're liable to try to swim in after me."

Rafe blew out a harsh breath. "Maggie, you are not coming with me."

"Yes, I am."

He restrained himself, barely, from dunking her head beneath the water. "Then why am I even here? If you are big and strong enough to make this swim, then why did those four old marauders come calling at my ranch?"

"Because we need you. I need you. I'm too afraid to try this swim alone even if my grandfathers would have let me, which they wouldn't. If you hadn't agreed to help, we'd all still be in Texas. So please, Rafe, go tell them you'll watch out for me. Let me watch out for you. I have a feeling we'll make a good team."

So did he. That was the problem. Without another word, he turned and dove beneath the water, swimming back to the outside pool.

Maggie had called it correctly. Gus waited on the other side of the wall, his lips set in an angry line. Snake stood ready with a rope. "Malone! Where is she? Tell me you didn't leave her in there."

Rafe eyed the rope skeptically. "Tell me you weren't going to tie her up."

"We weren't going to tie her up," they replied in unison, their flippant tone contradicting their words.

No wonder Maggie acted so crazy. With men like these seeing to her raising, he found it amazing she'd turned out as normal as she had. Willful but normal. And so damned delicious she made his teeth hurt. "She thinks I might need her help. As you have probably figured out, she wants to come with me."

"Well she can keep wanting," Gus grumbled, the silver hoop in his ear swinging like a pendulum as he propped a hip against a moss-covered rock. "I won't have her down there. It's too dangerous."

Snake rubbed his hand across his brow and moaned. "I knew we should have left her in Texas."

"It's a little late for that now," Rafe replied. "She's here, she's in that tunnel, and she claims she's not coming out until you have the treasure in your hands. Now, I could bring her out by force, but I'd just as soon not fight that battle. She'd have us all paying for it for weeks."

Gus started shaking his head back and forth, and Rafe could tell he was winding up to deliver an ear-blister. Hurriedly he added, "How about I let her tag along until we reach the chamber right before the deep dive? According to what you've told me, the going shouldn't be difficult or dangerous up to that point."

The pirates shared a look of resignation. Snake

drew his knife and grabbed Rafe's trousers from the ground. With a pair of dramatic slashes, he sliced off the legs.

Rafe scowled. "What the——"

"You'll cover yourself if you're swimming with my Maggie." He tossed the shortened pants toward Rafe, who caught them with one hand. Rafe yanked them on, sharing a glare with Snake even as he silently acknowledged the wisdom of the idea. The water was cold, but not so cold that his body didn't respond naturally to the sight of Maggie St. John all wet and luscious.

A glowering Gus traced the scar across his cheek and warned, "Protect her with your life, Malone. That's what it will cost you if any harm comes to her."

"Shoot, I've already figured out she'll be the death of me one way or the other. Let's get this over with, shall we, gentlemen? When can I expect to meet you at the treasure cave?"

"Your route underground is more direct than ours. We have a two-mile hike ahead of us. Taking the jungle into account, you'll probably wait on us for an hour at least."

Having struggled into his britches, Rafe gave the pirates a two-fingered salute. "Until later, then, gentlemen." Giving a wave, he dove below the surface.

Maggie met him as he emerged inside the second chamber. "I imagine they are not very happy with me," she said with a wince of regret.

"You have a gift for understatement," he replied dryly. "If you have been this much trouble all your life, I'm surprised they didn't sell you to that band of Gypsies that roamed the Texas gulf coast a few years back."

Maggie smiled and said simply, "They love me."

A smile quirked Rafe's lips. "You use it as a weapon against them."

"No more than they use my love for them to manipulate me. Where do you think I learned all my bad habits? Now, are you ready to proceed, or do you prefer to spend all morning discussing the vagaries of my character? I have already located the entrance to the next tunnel, so we can be on our way immediately."

She could be a mermaid, he thought. Her cheeks so rosy. Her eyes so bright. Alluring . . . luring.

What she had said finally filtered through the lust clouding his thoughts, and Rafe gave her a sharp look. "According to the map, the next entrance requires a dive of twelve feet. You searched for it alone?"

"My swimming skills are excellent. I grew up on the sea, remember? Follow me, Malone." With that she filled her lungs with air and dove. Rafe muttered a curse and followed her. Long strokes and hard kicks carried him down toward the faint beam of blue visible along the cavern's wall and the opening through which Maggie disappeared. Upon reaching the gap, Rafe clutched the slippery stone on each side of the hole and pushed himself through.

The water inside the second cavern glowed a brilliant azure blue. He fastened his gaze on the graceful kick of Maggie's long and luscious legs and propelled himself upward. As he broke the surface his gaze was drawn above him where sunlight beamed through an opening the size of a sea turtle's shell in the top of the cave. Turning his face toward the light, he basked in the warmth of the sunshine, grinning with pleasure.

"Look, Rafe," Maggie said, her voice filled with excited wonder. She gestured to an area directly below the hole in the ground where a perfect pyramid of glittering sand rose from the bottom of the cenote. "It must be the soil that falls through the roof. I'll bet it's been growing like that for years."

"Centuries, I imagine."

"I wonder how many other people have been here to see this? Not many, surely, or someone would have destroyed it. People are like that."

Rafe glanced at Maggie, then back to the pyramid.

A hint of yearning filled his voice. "But don't you want to know what it feels like? Isn't your hand itching to knock the top off that pyramid?"

Her laugh echoed off the cavern walls. "I should have known. That's just how little boys act, Malone."

"Honey," he drawled, caressing her with his eyes. "If you knew what is going through my mind right now, you'd know I'm all man."

The pale blue light couldn't hide her blush. Rafe chuckled softly. She'd called it correctly. Except for the thrum of desire that never left him when Maggie was around, he did feel like a boy. Childish excitement gripped him as he gazed around the chamber. Damn, but this cenote was a beautiful world. This swim was a fine adventure.

He was glad he shared it with Maggie St. John.

Maggie found the stash of J shaped hollow canes tucked behind a rock exactly where Papa Gus had told Rafe to look. Removing two, she swam back to Rafe who continued to hover over the sparkling pyramid, staring down at it with tempted fascination. "Don't you dare," she warned, poking his shoulder with one of the canes. "Come along, Malone. We've a treasure to rescue."

"But Maggie . . ."

The glint in his eye told her he was teasing. She rolled her eyes and struck out for the entrance to the next step of their journey, the narrow black tunnel leading off the north wall of the chamber. She took only two strokes before Malone caught up to her, stopping her by grasping her wrist.

"I'd like to practice a minute or two with this before we go," he said, holding up the cane. "You may be an expert with these breathing pipes, but my experience is limited to your grandfathers' coaching on the way down here. I'm liable to drown myself without a little rehearsal."

"I'm sorry. I didn't think." Papa Ben's Mayan

friend had taught Maggie how to use the breathing cane years before, and now she called upon those long-ago lessons to remind Rafe of the papas' instructions. He caught on fast and soon was swimming the circumference of the chamber without lifting his head. "Just remember not to panic when water comes down the pipe," she instructed when he removed the pipe from his mouth. "Blow it out of there. You won't have any trouble, Malone. There's not a doubt in my mind you can blow just as hard as any man."

"Watch it there, Miss Maggie. I've been known to kill folks for talking smart like that to me."

"You're lying."

"You're too quick for me." Flashing her a grin, he added, "Bet I can beat you to the tunnel, though." He dove toward the opening, splashing Maggie in the face.

On purpose, she thought.

She entered the tunnel behind him, mentally going over the route in her mind. This stage of the journey required an approximately fifteen-minute swim through a narrow water-filled tunnel with only a two-inch space of air at the top; hence the required breathing tubes.

The tunnel took a turn and total blackness engulfed them. Maggie concentrated on swimming, trying not to notice how the space surrounding her seemed to close in. She'd never seen such blackness as this. Anxiety crawled like a crab along her spine and she put extra effort into her strokes to stay close to Rafe. She concentrated on controlling her breathing, and the next five minutes passed a bit easier.

Then something slid along her foot, something long and alive. She shuddered. Maybe she should have stayed with her grandfathers after all.

In an effort to keep her mind off any real or imaginary monsters lurking in the water beneath her, she mentally reviewed her plans for the hotel's grand reopening party once they'd bought off Barlow Hill. She'd plan the affair for midautumn when the trees turned the thicket a riot of reds, yellows, and oranges. They'd have a croquet match and picnic and serve Papa Snake's renowned pumpkin cake with its sinful cinnamon icing. Maybe between now and then Papa Ben could build a couple more rowboats and they'd have races across the lake. In the evening they'd have a dance—a harvest ball—on the lawn outside. She'd hire an orchestra from Nacogdoches and wear the gown Papa Gus had bought her for her birthday. It was emerald green and she'd yet to have an opportunity to wear it.

Without meaning to, she imagined herself wearing that beautiful dress and dancing in the arms of a tall, broad-shouldered man with burning eyes. He stared at her lips, leaned closer . . . closer . . .

Maggie lifted her head for his imaginary kiss, and the breathing pipe bumped the top of the tunnel and slipped from her mouth. *Oh no!*

She grasped for it, certain she'd find it directly in front of her face. Nothing. *Dear Lord.* Pulling up, she frantically searched the water. The cane floated, so it had to be here. But could she find it while she was blinded by the total lack of light? Find it before she ran out of air?

You won't drown, Maggie, she told herself, trying to ignore the anxiety building in her chest. She could always lie on her back and get her nose above the water. It would be difficult to swim that way, but she could manage. She'd be all right.

Her fingers touched water and nothing else.

Oh, Lord.

The pressure on her lungs grew tight. She needed to breath. Something brushed her arm, and she lost a little of her valuable air to an underwater scream as she thrashed away from the sensation, sinking deeper into the water. Even as she swam away, she realized it had to have been Rafe. He must have noticed she'd not kept up and come back to help her. Relieved, Maggie pulled toward the surface.

At least, she thought it was the surface. She should have been there by then. Had she gone the wrong way? She couldn't tell. Everything was black. She was so turned around. She didn't know up from down. She couldn't hold her breath any longer.

I'll die. I'm dying. A roaring sound filled her ears as the blackness of the cenote invaded her mind.

Then something grazed her. Fingers. A hand around her ankle yanked her in the opposite direction. Too late. He was too late.

Rafe's hand gripped her chin, tilted her head as he dragged her through the water. Maggie fought to hold on to that last bit of breath.

If she lived through this, he was going to kill her.

Rafe held his breath as he shoved his breathing tube into Maggie's mouth and forced her lips closed around it. Inhale, damnit. All she needed was one good breath to make it around the upcoming horse-shoe bend in the tunnel and out into the next cave with its plentiful precious air.

Rafe had a lump in his throat the size of west Texas as he held her, his legs kicking to keep them afloat while propelling them toward the tunnel exit. He kept one arm wrapped around her chest, the other holding the pipe as he willed her to breathe.

He hadn't realized Maggie had fallen behind until he'd reached the end of the tunnel without her. Because the shaft was narrow and she'd remained near the surface, finding her hadn't been difficult. Until she'd panicked and swum away from him, that is. That had scared him half to death. It was pure dumb luck he found her again in this pitch black hellhole.

He felt her lungs expand, heard her cough. *Thank*

God. Hang on, Maggie, we're almost there. Good thing, too, because he was running out of air himself.

As he swam them around the horseshoe bend, light filtered from the cavern ahead to reveal a broadening in the tunnel that allowed room for him to lift his face from the water and draw a sweet breath. Turning his head toward Maggie, he was relieved to see her eyes open and clear.

He removed the cane from her mouth, tasted the coppery flavor of fear in his own. "It's all right now," he said, reassuring them both. "We're there. You can relax. There's plenty of air to be had here. Sunlight, too." Glancing around the cavern, he spied a rock shelf large enough for them both to sit upon. Without releasing his hold on her, he swam to the shelf. He hauled himself up onto the rock, then lifted her from the water and held her tenderly while coughs racked her body.

"Swallowed a little water, huh?" He brushed the hair back off her face and frowned at the paleness of her complexion.

She nodded but she wouldn't look at him, and Rafe found he wanted—no, he needed—to see her eyes. "Maggie? Look at me. Are you all right?"

Her voice emerged thin and quavery. "I got confused as to which way was up and which was down. I went the wrong way, didn't I? I almost . . ."

She started to shake like a hen in a dust bath. "Oh, Maggie." Rafe pulled her onto his lap and cradled her close. He murmured into her ear. "Hush now, honey. It's all over now. Everything's fine. I saved you."

She stiffened in his arms. "That just makes it worse."

She tried to sit up, but Rafe wouldn't let her. He stroked his hand repeatedly up and down her arm's cold, wet skin. "You'd rather I let you drown?"

"No," she replied, her voice weak. "It's just that I'd rather I got myself out of my own mess."

He pressed a kiss against her temple and tasted the sweet and deadly water of the underground river on his tongue. "Independence is a fine thing, Miss Maggie, as long as it doesn't get you killed. Shoot, that was one of the first lessons I learned when I took to thieving."

Finally she looked at him, and Rafe could see the lingering fear in her Caribbean eyes. More than anything else, he wanted to banish that cloud. And while he was at it, he could do a little forgetting himself. It made him cold inside to think how close he'd come to losing her.

"Did a member of your gang save your life?"

Ah, curiosity. Good. She needed something to think about other than her scare. "I worked alone, actually," he said, finger-combing her wet strands of hair. "I made it look like I rode with other men when I played robber along the trace, but in truth, I hunted those east Texas forests all by my lonesome. And if not for Luke, I'd likely have died out there all alone."

He tilted her chin up and gazed down into her eyes. "Because of independence, you see, Miss Maggie. My pride. I'd been back stabbed by someone I'd trusted, so I wasn't going to trust anyone ever again. Luke showed me different. It took awhile, but he finally showed me the error of my ways."

"How did he do that?"

Remembering, Rafe's lips slid into a slow grin. "He arrested me. Had to work hard to do it, too." He launched into the tale of the second time Luke had tracked him into the east Texas canebrakes and how Rafe had lost him by hiding beneath the rotting carcass of a gator at the edge of a swamp. As he talked, Maggie's eyes closed and she snuggled deeper into the arms that cradled her. Rafe almost sighed from the sheer pleasure of holding this woman.

"You're doing it again," she interrupted when he began to describe the alligator's stink.

"Doing what?"

"Talking. You've gone off on one of your tangents again." A smile hovered at the corners of her lips as she added, "You make a point in the most roundabout way I've ever seen. I've never known a man to do that before."

The question slipped out before he could stop it. "And just how many men have you known?"

Silence stretched long and black like the tunnel behind them. When she finally opened her eyes, the fear was completely gone. Instead, to his chagrin, Rafe saw sorrow and embarrassment, and it cut him to the quick.

"None," she said flatly. "It's one reason why I've been flirting with you, why I thought I wanted a little romance. Most women my age are married with children, but not me. I have overprotective pirates for guardians, and in one way or another they've scared off every man who ever came near me."

Rafe knew he should keep his mouth shut. He knew he should move her out of his lap and put some distance between them. Instead, the recklessness that was so much a part of his character had him dipping his head and whispering, "No, Mary, not every man."

And then he kissed her.

And she kissed him back. Her lips moved against his hotly, passionately. Desperately. The slightest of whimpers emerged from the back of her throat, and the sound of it made him hard as steel.

He wanted her. God, he wanted her. She had fire and spirit and courage. She was stubborn and reckless and intelligent and caring. And beautiful. So damned beautiful she made his heart stutter.

Rafe broke off the kiss and looked at her. Lush red lips, swollen and wet. The slightest of trembles to her flawless skin. A shimmering look in her eyes—sweet and needful and asking for something obvious—and also something more.

And Rafe knew as sure as the cenote water was clear that in this place, at this moment, Mary Margaret St. John was his for the taking.

An avalanche of need buried the last of Rafe's good sense, and he laid her back against the limestone ledge. Somewhere inside him he knew this was more than just sex. A part of him sensed that going forward would change his world, but he didn't care. Life was an adventure. She was an adventure he didn't want to miss.

Rising above her on his knees, he reached out and loosened the knot at the shoulder of her swimming sarong and bared her to the waist. Her body was a fantasy. Breasts full and perfect and crowned in pink like the coral of the island lagoon. He cupped their weight with his hands, then flicked his thumbs across her pebbled nipples. She gasped and their gazes met and held. Once again, Rafe recognized her innocence. He sucked in a breath through his teeth.

"We've gone beyond romance, Maggie," he said, his voice rough with desire. Hell, they'd gone so far he wouldn't be surprised if the water clinging to their bodies turned to steam. He tugged the sarong up over her breasts, hiding the temptation because he wanted to make a point, and he didn't need the distraction.

Well, he did need it. That was the problem. He needed his mouth on her badly. But he had a point to make, and he would never get the first word spoken if her breasts continued to beckon to him. He cleared his throat and repeated, "We've gone beyond romance and now it's your call. I sure as hell didn't expect for this to happen here and now, and I doubt you did, either. You probably are reacting to a near brush with death. Now, we could take this all the way, and I admit it would make me the happiest man this side of heaven at the moment. Or we can stop it now, and I'll survive, and I won't hold it against you. Much more, though, and neither one of us will find the stopping fun."

He leaned over and pressed a kiss to her forehead, then looked deeply into her eyes and spoke from his heart. "I want you to be sure, Maggie. You only have one first time. Are you positive you want it to be with me?"

Her slow, wistful smile would have brought him to his knees were he not already there. Maggie St. John was the true treasure hidden in this cenote, and Rafe held his breath, praying for permission to plunder.

She licked her lips and murmured, "You saved my life."

Well, hell. "I don't want a gratitude tumble," he snapped.

"You're the most handsome man I've ever known."

"Now that I like a lot better."

Maggie lifted her hand to his jaw and stroked him, seducing him with her touch and the husky flow of her voice. "You are kind to my grandfathers. You're warm and generous and you make me laugh."

He closed his eyes. "So do puppies, I imagine."

"Puppies don't make my skin tingle when they touch me. They don't make my blood run hot or my knees feel like butter. And Rafe, the way you say my name, the way you call me Mary, it makes me tremble inside. A warm, delicious shudder. You make me feel alive, Rafe. You're an adventurer. A thief."

"Former thief," he rasped as her fingers grazed his nipples. She was killing him. Then she quit touching him and that was even worse.

As the moment stretched, Rafe's heart fell. He heard her sit up. *Guess that was his answer. Well, hell. But it was better this way,* he tried to tell himself. Truly. He didn't want a woman who would suffer regrets when the loving was done, even if it did mean he'd walk stooped over for the rest of his natural born life. She was a virgin, damnit. Her first time should be in a plump feather bed with an entire night stretched out in front of her, not on a hard rock with four crusty pirates waiting with cutlass at the ready, prepared to run her lover through for even thinking about touching her, much less actually doing it.

But, damn, he'd wanted her.

Stoically he opened his eyes, and once again the lady surprised him. She sat beside him, her loosened sarong clutched to her chest, while a hesitant smile fluttered at the corners of her lips. Rather than refusal in her eyes, he saw a plea to listen. Maybe she wasn't telling him no after all.

She had him as confused as a fly in a butter churn.

Maggie's voice rang with sincerity. "I think that you—more than any man I've ever met—have the ability to understand me. Today you may be a respected Texas rancher, but you have a past. You know what it's like to be wicked. You know what I am, having been raised how I was."

Anger flared and melded with the lust pounding through his blood. "You are not wicked! If that's not the dumbest thing I've ever heard you say. You may act stupid sometimes, forcing your way along on this swim, for instance. And how did you manage to lose your breathing tube? You want to tell me that?"

"I was daydreaming. You were kissing me, and I went to kiss you back."

"Damn, Maggie," he groaned. "You are wicked after all."

She laughed softly. "No, Rafe, I'm not wicked, but I am different. I'm not like the girls at my school in Boston. I'm not like the society women who frequented Hotel Bliss, either. As much as my grandfathers tried to guide me and protect me and give me all the opportunities I could want, I still grew up aboard a pirate ship. I spent time in some of the roughest ports in the world among men who'd just as soon kill you as look at you."

"You shouldn't have been there."

"I loved my papas. I wouldn't have been anywhere else."

The simply stated truth created a warm-honey

feeling inside Rafe that had nothing to do with sexual heat. Love, pure and simple and freely given despite all the odds against it. It was something for which Rafe had searched but never found. Not yet, anyway.

Maggie continued, "I may be inexperienced, but I'm far from innocent. For my grandfathers' sake, I tried to be good, tried to be a lady, and for the most part, I've succeeded. But part of me wants . . ." She took his hand and squeezed it. "A part of me *wants.*"

"Maggie . . ."

She lay down upon her back, allowing the sarong to slip once again to her waist. Her eyes glistened like blue diamonds. She reached for him, pulling him down to her. Rafe groaned as their bodies met, ache to ache. Hard to soft. "You say you came along on this trip for adventure. Well, I have that same craving, too. Just because I'm a woman doesn't make me different in that regard."

Her expression turned devilish. "In fact, I'm thrilled that I'm here, caught literally between a rock and a hard place." She punctuated her point with a roll of her hips.

"That's bad, woman," Rafe said with a groan.

"I know and I love it. I want adventure, you see. We're here alone in this paradise and I want to take advantage of it. I want *you* to be my adventure, Rafe. It feels right. You feel right. Make love to me, please?"

Rafe was two layers of cloth and at most two thrusts away from exploding. This beautiful, exciting, warm, willing woman lay beneath him, asking for something he wanted to give more than he wanted to take his next breath.

He said the only thing he could say under the circumstances. "No."

No?" Maggie's heart seemed to stop.

"No," Rafe repeated and rolled off her.

Humiliation drizzled over her, quenching the fire that had burned so brightly just moments before. Quickly, she sat up, clutching her sarong against her chest, her fingers working furiously to knot the cloth at her shoulder. She wanted to die, to disappear in a puff of blush-colored smoke. She wished he'd never found her in the tunnel.

"It's not right, Maggie. Not for you. Not right now. A person doesn't make life decisions like that right after she damn near drowns. You are vulnerable."

"I'm not vulnerable."

"Yeah, you are."

"No, I'm not. I told you how I feel."

"Yeah, you did. And it was what you said that convinced me to stop. This has happened to me before, you know."

No, Maggie thought, *I don't want to die.* She wanted to kill him. Maybe drown him in the blue-water pool.

"Not exactly the same thing, of course. I mean, I never turned down sex in a cenote before."

Where was her gun? Her knife? She'd like to cut out his tongue. She could at least dunk him. She could reach over and give him a nice big shove into the water. Maybe get some leverage on him and hold him under.

But then the egotistical scalawag beat her to the punch by slipping into the pool himself. "I need to cool off, but this would work better if it were a bit colder." He hooked his elbows on the edge of the ledge and hung waist deep in the cenote, sucking in a sharp breath. "As much as I'd like attending to the part of me that's shouting for attention, experience has taught me I'm better off listening to my gut. I figured it out. It was the second time Luke arrested me. I'd just pulled off one of my more creative heists—I'd robbed an east Texas sugar plantation of their cash and jewels during the San Jacinto Day ball. Luke, curse his hide, said he knew it was me because the hair on the back of his neck stood up when he looked at the open safe."

Rafe smiled at the memory. "Prescott is funny like that, always sensing stuff. Anyhow, I thought I'd gotten away clean so I wasn't paying close attention. He caught up with me at Sally's Whor—uh—place and cuffed me slick as slime."

Frustration was a living, breathing monster inside her. "I don't really care—"

"It was as he attempted to haul me back to the Nacogdoches jail that he started talking," Rafe continued, showing no sign of having heard her attempt to interrupt him. "Gave me all sorts of chin music about why it was wrong for me to keep stealing. Now, everything he said made sense. I couldn't argue with one of his reasons. But the more he talked, the more convinced I became that I needed to stay my course. Luke has the hair on his neck, but I have my gut. I listen to it, Maggie."

She gave a snide sniff. "Maybe you should change your diet, Malone."

He frowned at her. "The point I'm trying to make here—"

"No!" She clasped a hand to her breast. "You actually have a point?"

"Yeah, I do." His glare would have scared a lesser woman. *"The point* is that despite a very strong argument originating below my belt, so to speak, my gut told me we need to go about this differently. Something is happening here between us, Mary Margaret. Something beyond romance or adventure. Because of that something, I won't take your virginity on a rock while your grandfathers are checking their watches."

"You weren't going to *take* my virginity, anyway. I was going to give it to you." Maggie's emotions were in turmoil. She didn't know what to think or feel or say, so she retreated into pride. "But that was a onetime offer, Malone. We're not going to go about this differently. You missed your chance."

He lifted one brow. "Oh, did I?" Amusement and something else—anticipation, maybe?—glittered in his eyes. He grabbed her ankle and tugged her into the water. His arms wrapped around her waist and he said, "You and your chances. Take a deep breath, Mary-mine."

She did, and it was a good thing, because his kiss stole it right back from her lungs. They floated, totally immersed in blue water, white magic, and golden fantasy. Bonelessly, Maggie gave herself up to Rafe. He brought her to the surface, told her to breathe, then took her down again. Finally, but still too soon, he led her back to the ledge. He cupped her chin in his palm, gazed into her eyes, and said, "You, me, Texas, and a bed. No grandfathers."

"No grandfathers," she repeated on a sigh.

"And plenty of time. I promise. But right now, I'd better go rescue a treasure. This is the last chamber. The one with the extra-deep dive that will take me to the chest. You wait here for me, and I'll be back quick as a minnow."

You, me, Texas, and a bed. Maggie cleared her throat. "I'm coming with you."

"No. Your grandfathers and I agreed. You'll wait here."

She felt dazed, her thought processes numb. "All right," she said vacantly. "You'll hurry back?"

He nodded. "Up on the ledge. I'll feel better if you're out of the water before I leave here."

Maggie exited the water without argument. She watched from the ledge while he lined up beneath the marker on the opposite wall, filled then emptied his lungs of air three times, and dove. And dove. And dove. The clarity of the water made him appear closer than she knew he was. She watched till he disappeared from sight. Then ever so softly, she murmured, "He promised."

She trembled, but not from fear of the physical effort facing her as she stood on her tiptoes, filled her lungs, and followed Rafe Malone. Under other circumstances she might have been afraid to face this dangerous dive so soon on the heels of a near drowning, but her mind was too busy recalling the moments just passed. *You, me, Texas, and a bed.*

He promised.

Down, down she went. Pressure gripped her chest, squeezing it like a vise as she found the opening she sought in the wall. Wiggling through, she tried to ignore the bursts of light shining before her eyes. *Pull, Maggie, pull.* Her arms pumped. Her legs scissored.

Her head broke the surface.

Gasping, she spent a moment treading water and replenishing her body with air. A fiercely bellowed curse attracted her attention to a rocky shelf some ten feet wide and thirty feet in length on the far side of the cavern. Rafe stood on the shelf beside a large wooden chest. Maggie was surprised the heat in the glare he aimed her way didn't start the cenote to boiling. "You hardheaded, stubborn fool. You'd think someone who grew up with four fathers would have had the ornery spanked out of her by now. Don't you have a lick of sense, woman?"

Short strokes sliced the water and took Maggie to the ledge where she pulled herself up and out of the water. She sat for a moment, catching her breath, then said, "Open the treasure chest, Malone."

"I can't. Gus has the key, and he hasn't lowered it down to me yet."

A muffled voice descended from above. "What are you yammering about, Malone? We can barely hear you."

Rafe's flinty gaze held Maggie's as he yelled back, "Just send the key."

A minute later, a rope threaded through a plate-sized hole in the roof of the cavern, a small burlap bag dangling at its end. "If I could figure out a way to fit you through that hole I'd send you up to them this very second," he groused. Stepping over to the rope, Rafe removed the bag and opened it. He fished out an ornate golden key.

Seeing it, Maggie's hand automatically went to her neck seeking the necklace that usually hung around her neck. It wasn't there today, of course; she always removed it before going swimming. But she knew at first glance that the key that hung from the chain was a miniature of the one Rafe Malone held in his hands. She burst into tears.

"What the—" Rafe stared at her in horror. "Maggie, what's wrong?"

"It's just like mine. My papas gave it to me on my ninth birthday. For the true treasure in their lives, they said. Isn't that sweet of them?" She gazed upward. "I wish I could hug them all right now."

Rafe shook his head. "Maggie, you set me back on my heels. Most women I know would be thinking only of what's inside this box at a moment like this."

She sniffed through her tears. "Haven't you figured out yet that I'm not like most women, Malone?"

He chuckled as he fitted the key into the lock. "Honey, I figured that out the moment you joined me in my mud bath. Now, come on over. Since you're here you might as well be in on the moment we crossed the Gulf of Mexico to experience. Personally, I feel like a boy at a mercantile candy counter." The metallic click of the releasing lock echoed in the cave. "Come take a look, Maggie. It's your grandfathers' past and your future."

Excitement thrummed through Maggie. She liked jewels as much as the next woman, and she couldn't wait to see some of the items her grandfathers had described over the years. A million butterfly wings fluttered in her stomach as she moved to stand beside Rafe. Hinges squeaked as he lifted the lid.

Maggie's heart thundered. A smile waited to explode across her face. The lid slowly rose.

And Rafe spat a vile curse while Maggie gazed down upon the contents of the chest in shock.

The coffer was empty. No gold, no jewels, no riches of any kind. The only item inside was a folded sheet of paper.

Maggie swayed on her feet as Rafe reached down and lifted the note from the bottom of the box. She clutched his arm to steady herself as he read aloud. "You stole my treasure. Now I've returned the favor."

Rafe shot a look at Maggie. "Who the hell is Andrew Montgomery?"

The name hit her like a fist and she reeled backward from the blow. "No," she said softly. "Dear God, no. It can't be. Not Andrew Montgomery." She glanced wildly around the cavern. "He can't have done this. The treasure must be here. Not him."

A bellow sounded from above, and Maggie gazed upward to see Papa Gus's face hovering over the opening in the roof.

"Maggie St. John! I should have known you'd follow him. Of all the stupid . . ."

Gus's face was shoved aside by Snake's. "I can't believe you followed him. That's it, lass. When we get back to Lake Bliss, you'll be punished. Confined to your room. I don't care how old you are. It scares me spitless—"

"It's gone, Papa," Maggie interrupted, her voice hollow. "The treasure isn't here."

A shocked silence preceeded Gus's word. "What?"

The placement of the chest inside the cavern made it invisible to eyes spying from above. Frustrated and angry and filled with fear, Maggie grabbed hold of one end of the trunk and tugged it into her grandfather's line of sight. Words exploded from her mouth. "It's empty, Papa! He's robbed us. He's stolen Hotel Bliss."

At that the fire drained out of her, leaving her weak. Rafe wrapped a supportive arm around her waist as her knees buckled. "We found a note," he said. "I put it in the bag."

The dangling rope slithered upward like a snake, and Maggie waited for the imminent eruption. To her surprise, she heard only quiet—a long, ugly silence.

Rafe stood with his legs spread, his hands braced upon his hips as he stared up at the hole in the roof, obviously awaiting the grandfathers' reaction. As the seconds ticked by, he turned his head and looked at her, arching a brow in silent inquiry.

Maggie couldn't have spoken past the lump in her throat even if she'd known what to say.

When finally a face reappeared above them, it was a solemn and subdued Snake who said, "If we hurry we can set sail for Texas this evening."

Rafe appeared baffled. "Just like that? Your treasure is stolen and that's all you've got to say? I'm due an explanation, don't you think? You had promised me a cut of the take, after all."

"We will make it up to you somehow, Malone,"

Snake replied in a voice devoid of emotion. "First priority needs to be getting our lass back to safety."

Rafe looked as if he wanted to argue, but changed his mind. "You're right. We need to get Maggie out of this place, but we have a bit of a problem in that regard. We're down to one breathing tube and sharing it would be an unneccesary danger. Since y'all no longer need to keep this chamber hidden, why don't you enlarge the hole and let us climb out."

Snake and Gus discussed the matter briefly and agreed that under the circumstances, they wouldn't worry themselves about any potential Mayan curses. Rafe and the grandfathers then spent the next few minutes debating the best way to go about chipping away at the hole. Maggie lost herself in thought.

No treasure meant no way to buy the hotel. No way to buy the hotel meant she might have to deal with Barlow Hill's other offer. The marriage offer.

Maggie sank to the ground and buried her head in her hands. They stood to lose the hotel. They were on the verge of being denied access to Lake Bliss water. What would happen to her grandfathers then? Ben's breathing trouble and Lucky's pain from his old shoulder wound. Gus's aching joints. Her own rheumatism. And what would Ben do without his garden to occupy his time? She hated to imagine it.

She loathed the idea of marrying Barlow Hill.

Rafe's voice interrupted her thoughts. "No, Snake, I don't think black powder is necessary. You can lash a rock to a tree limb for a sledgehammer. Once you've cracked the rock a bit, you can use a tree trunk as a lever and break it from the bottom up. It shouldn't be impossible. The ground isn't solid rock or there wouldn't be a hole to begin with."

"I guess we'll try it your way, Malone," Gus declared. "We can always go after the powder later if we find we need it. I don't fancy tangling with the locals today, anyway. The way our luck has been running, we'd end up with even more trouble on our hands."

"If I didn't know better, I'd think Lucky stowed away on the boat," Snake grumbled. "We might as well get to it, though. This may take us awhile. Do you need anything before we go?"

"How about some food? I worked up a powerful hunger this morning, and I'm pretty sure your granddaughter did, too."

Maggie shot him a suspicious look that he returned with an innocent smile. A couple of minutes later the papas lowered a bag filled with fruit and some of Papa Snake's special mesquite-smoked beef strips. They told Maggie good-bye, warned Malone to keep his hands to himself at the risk of losing them, and headed out to collect their tools.

Rafe grabbed a banana for himself and tossed one to Maggie. Slamming the lid of the treasure chest shut, he propped a hip on it, peeled his fruit, and said, "Now, tell me about this Mr. Andrew Montgomery."

"I'd prefer not to speak of him."

"Too bad, Sugar. I hired on to this adventure for a cut of the spoils. Since there's not going to be any of those, I reckon the least you owe me is a few answers. Who is he? The name halfway rings a bell with me."

Maggie shrugged as she broke the end off her banana. Why not tell him? She didn't see how it would hurt anything. Besides, Malone was crafty enough. Maybe he'd see a way out of this mess. "Andrew Montgomery is my grandfathers' worst enemy. They go way back. I remember meeting him once years ago in Barbados when I was little more than a child. My grandfathers bodily threw him out of our house. Over time they have cussed and discussed Montgomery at such length that I feel like I know him well."

"He is a pirate, too?"

"Yes. From what I remember, Montgomery is a younger son of an English earl who was on his way to the Indies when pirates attacked his ship. The Englishman chose to join the ranks of the marauders and eventually ended up a crew member on the *Mystique.*"

"Another pirate ship?"

"My Papa Ben was her captain."

"I see." Rafe thumped his hand against the treasure chest. "So he helped to capture the spoils we expected to find?"

"I guess he must have. I've never asked." Maggie took a bite of her fruit, then made a face. Food never did taste good when she was nervous. "I know that his shipmates—Lucky, Gus, and Snake—liked him and welcomed him into their group. I remember Snake calling him a bold adventurer."

"He's said the same thing about me."

"No wonder he keeps threatening to kill you."

Rafe tossed away his banana peel and reached for a hunk of dried beef. "So, this Montgomery made a good pirate?"

"My grandfathers taught him everything they knew. I want to say he was fifteen years or so younger than they, and I do remember the trip to India was his first sea voyage. He must have had a lot of learning to do."

"I'd imagine one would need to learn fast, too."

Maggie nodded. "I think he did. Papa Gus said he'd embraced the pirate's life and shown all the signs of becoming a leader."

"So, did he? What happened? Did he challenge Ben for his ship or something?"

Maggie stared into the cenote. "Perhaps. They wouldn't tell me. All I know is that something happened to drive a wedge between him and my grandfathers. They became the bitterest of enemies, and over the years, Montgomery has intruded into our lives from time to time."

"How is that?"

"Well, he settled in Texas after we did, for one thing."

Rafe perked up at that. "Galveston? I think Republic Shipping has a Montgomery at the helm."

"No." Maggie shook her head. "Not Galveston. East Texas. He's a cotton planter."

"Triumph Plantation. Southeast of Nacogdoches." Rafe snapped his fingers. "Of course. I knew I'd heard the name. I once robbed guests on the way to a party at his place, if I remember correctly. I even think he may have been a guest of the Prescotts a time or two. Luke has become somewhat prominent socially in the past couple of years. Honor is trying to talk him into running for Congress."

Rafe folded his arms. "The owner of Triumph Plantation a retired pirate. Don't that just beat all."

"Not so retired," Maggie replied with a grimace. She gestured toward the chest. "Obviously, he hasn't given up stealing."

Following that sad observation, conversation lagged. Rafe polished off another banana and a pair of mangoes. Maggie set her snack aside. She could feel him looking at her, but she wasn't in the mood to deal with bicker or banter or anything else. Barlow Hill kept coming to mind. She might never eat again.

Finally her grandfathers returned and went to work on the rock above. It took almost two hours of labor with the makeshift sledgehammer and a tree-trunk lever to enlarge the hole enough to accommodate Rafe's shoulders. Once Papa Snake declared the opening wide enough, Papa Gus tied a rope around a nearby tree and called for Maggie to climb up.

"Have them pull you out," Rafe scoffed. "You can't climb that rope. That's a good fifteen feet, woman."

Maggie didn't bother to argue, just wrapped her hands and feet around the hemp and began to shimmy upward. When she'd made it halfway up, he observed, "Well, I reckon a girl learns a few useful skills while living on a pirate ship."

At the top the papas lifted her out, and Maggie squeezed her eyes shut against the sudden glare of sunlight. Rafe made it out of the cave without incident, and they fell in line behind Gus for the hike back to the *Buccaneer's Bliss.*

"First time I ever went home from a robbery empty-handed," Rafe observed.

Maggie could almost feel his gaze on her backside as he added, "But then again, maybe not."

→ 9 ←

Lake Bliss, Republic of Texas

On the first night back at the hotel, Rafe turned away from the kitchen window and studied the grim faces of those seated around the table, ostensibly playing cards. Rafe had never seen such a hangdog group of men in all his born days. Not that he didn't understand. If someone had swiped his secret cache of stolen plunder, he'd have been down in the mouth, too.

Rafe had a stash of goods—weapons mostly—collected during his robber days that his amnesty agreement with the Texas Rangers had allowed him to keep when he went legal. He called the collection his old-age fund and accessed it only upon rare occasions. Coincidentally, Rafe's hiding place for his treasure was also a cave—a good strong Texas cave, that is—and ever since they'd boarded the *Buccaneer's Bliss* for the return trip home, Rafe had been itching to go check on his stash. It would be just his luck that Andrew Montgomery had branched out and robbed caverns all over the world.

This evening, however, his cache wasn't on his

mind nearly as much as the pirates' treasure. And the particular treasure he was thinking of wasn't the missing gold and jewels. Rafe had Maggie on his mind.

Not that such a state was anything new. She'd been a bother in that regard even before he met her, but ever since they'd boarded the *Buccaneer's Bliss* for the sail home he couldn't get her out of his head. He was worried about her. He'd caught her in a smile only once, and that was when she'd spotted Ben and Lucky on Hotel Bliss's front porch. She hardly spoke, certainly never laughed, and had spent the majority of the trip lying in her bunk trying to hold down her food. According to Gus, it was her first-ever case of seasickness. Rafe wondered if heartsick wasn't closer to the mark.

All that was enough to cause him concern, but what had happened half an hour ago made him downright frantic. Maggie had accepted an invitation to walk out with Barlow Hill after supper. "The bastard," he grumbled.

"Bastard is too good a name for Andrew Montgomery," Lucky observed. He banged his fist on the table and rattled the glasses. "We should have killed him years ago."

"I wasn't referring to Montgomery." Rafe pushed aside a gingham window curtain to gaze once again at the empty garden path. Why was this walk taking so long? "I was talking about Barlow Hill."

"The maggot."

"The louse."

"The chigger."

"The tick."

Rafe glanced back over his shoulder and shot them a glare. "Why would she agree to walk out with him, anyway? She detests the man. And if we are all agreed about his character, why did we allow her to go off with him?"

Gus took a long draw on his ale, then wiped his mouth with the back of his hand. He tipped his chair back on its two hind legs. "Did you say 'allow,' Malone? In relation to our Maggie? The Caribbean sun must have baked your brain."

"This business with Montgomery has tangled up all our thinking," Lucky said, scratching at the scar around his neck. "I for one never guessed he'd up and steal our treasure. Not since we gave him his cut when we kicked him off our ship. Drew has mixed business with personal. We always told him not to do that."

Gus laughed sourly. "Isn't that what started our problems to begin with, him doing something we told him not to do?"

Ben's voice joined the discussion for the first time since Snake reported the theft upon their arrival at Lake Bliss. "We have choices to make, Malone, and it's best that Mary Margaret not be included in the discussion. That is why I made no attempt to dissuade her from accompanying that idiot this evening. Rest assured that Mary Margaret is safe. We taught her well. She can handle the likes of him."

Rafe wasn't so certain. She'd had a look about her when she left. He wouldn't go so far as to call it scared—if he'd thought that he would never have let her go—but something about Hill didn't sit well with Maggie. That much was as obvious as the wrinkles in the buccaneers' brows.

"What choices are you talking about, Cap'n?" Lucky asked.

"I see three possibilities." Ben shuffled the deck of cards, then lay the top one, the four of spades, on the table. "One, we accept defeat and leave Lake Bliss."

"That ain't never gonna happen," Gus said with a scowl. "Maggie needs the water. I won't have her in pain, boys." Lucky and Snake nodded their heads fiercely in agreement.

"Two," Ben continued, placing a second card, the

jack of clubs, beside the first. "We could tell Mary Margaret the truth."

"Now what the hell good would that do?" Lucky shoved to his feet. "It'd hurt her heart and in many ways that's as bad as her joints paining her."

"It's what Montgomery wants," Ben said flatly, thumbing the edges of the card deck. "I know the man, and the note he left made it obvious. Telling her the truth is definitely one way to ensure Mary Margaret's future access to Lake Bliss water."

Gus sipped noisily at his ale. "She pestered me for answers all the way home. Even sick like she was." He set his glass down hard. "I'm not against telling her. You all know I've thought for years that we should let her make her own decisions."

Snake drummed his fingers on the table. "Well, I don't like it. Not one little bit. The lass doesn't need to make her own decisions because she has us. She's always had us. *We* have been there for her."

"Wait a minute," Lucky warned. "Let's not forget we are not alone here. We shouldn't be talking about this in front of Malone."

Ben sighed. "Sit down, Lucky, and give me your attention. I want you all to pay attention. We must speak of it in front of Malone." He drew a third card from the deck and lay it beside the others.

The ace of diamonds drew Rafe's gaze like a bloodstain.

Ben made eye contact with each of the pirates in turn. He didn't look at Rafe. "I believe I mentioned three choices? Well, Malone here is that third option."

That piece of news got Rafe's undivided attention. He cleared his throat loudly. "Excuse me, gentlemen, but I don't remember dropping my name into any hat."

Ben still didn't spare him a glance. "Andrew left the note to taunt us. He has kept the gold and jewels; we can be certain of it. Malone here could help us get it back."

Rafe started shaking his head even before Ben had finished his sentence. "I told you from the git-go that I wouldn't steal anything from anybody inside Texas's borders. Shoot, I won't hardly borrow."

Finally, Ben's clear blue eyes met Rafe's. "We won't require you to commit the actual theft. That is our duty and our pleasure. What we will need from you is a little reconnaissance. I'll leave the details to you, although I might suggest you use your position as owner of the Lone Star Ranch to gain entry to the plantation."

Frustration propelled Rafe across the room. He placed his hands on the table and leaned forward. "Watch what my mouth is getting ready to say, you old sea dogs. *I. Won't. Do. It.* Any participation on my part could be termed conspiracy, and that's enough to get me hanged."

He shuddered as a memory flashed in his mind. The stench of rotting corpses from the San Jacinto battlefield. The rough scrape of rope around his neck. The blow of the horse beneath him. The hate burning in his brother's eyes as he barked out the order. The confidence glowing in Luke's.

"I gave my word. I'm sorry you lost your treasure, but I can't do anything about it. Besides, it's time for me to head home and check up on things there. You need to find another way to keep Hotel Bliss. Find someone else to help you."

His voice seemed to echo in the sudden silence. Then, from behind him came Maggie's voice. "We will. Don't doubt it. We don't need you."

The woman's tone could freeze beef still on the hoof. Grimacing, Rafe turned to see Maggie standing in the doorway, her head held high, her eyes flashing. All that time he'd been on the lookout for her, and of course she showed up the minute his back was turned. Contrary female. She returned angry enough to spit, too, by the look of it. He wondered how much of it was Hill and how much of it was what she'd overheard him say. "Look, Maggie——"

"I don't care to look. Neither do I care to listen. My family and I have private matters to discuss, so if you'll excuse us, please?"

Now she was making him mad. "Snooty doesn't become you."

"Neither does cowardice look good on you, Malone."

Rafe narrowed his eyes and took an inadvertent step toward her as Ben cautioned, "Mary Margaret . . ."

She folded her arms and tipped her chin even higher.

"If you were a man I'd take that as a challenge," Rafe snapped.

"My sex has little——"

"Don't be using that word in mixed company, young lady." Snake jumped to his feet. "Malone, get on out of here. Our lass is right. If you're not with us, you're agin us. So leave us be; we have plans to make."

Rafe wanted to protest. He wasn't against them at all. But he couldn't break his agreement with the rangers; he wouldn't break his word to Luke.

Fine. Let 'em think what they wanted. He didn't care. If Maggie thought so little of him after what the two of them went through in that tunnel from hell, then she wasn't worth his time or trouble.

But why did that idea make his chest hurt?

"Sure," he said, ignoring the ache. "I thought I'd give my muscles a soak in the bathhouse, anyway. The mud down there doesn't sling around like it does up here." He swaggered toward the doorway where Maggie continued to stand. Upon reaching her, he stopped. Although she held her ground, her eyes grew wary.

Rafe smiled blandly and reached for his hat hanging on a peg behind her. His arm brushed her breast.

He heard her quick, indrawn breath and imagined the grinding of her teeth. Placing his hat on his head, he tipped it. "Evening, Miss St. John."

She gave her head a toss and her braid went flying. "Good-bye, Malone."

He walked outside and the door slammed behind him. He did not proceed to the bathhouse, however. As he strolled past Maggie, he'd seen something that changed his mind, something that left him seething and made him want to eavesdrop on the pirates' plans.

Maggie St. John—curse her fickle soul—had returned from her walk with a love bite on her neck.

With her hand resting against the door she'd just slammed, Maggie tried to ignore the pressure pushing at the back of her eyes. Exhaustion, she told herself. That's why she was on the verge of crying. The trip back home had sapped all her energy. To top it off, circumstances had forced her to cap her return with arm-to-arm combat with a buffoon who thought to blackmail her into marriage. That's what was wrong with her.

Her mood had nothing at all to do with Rafe Malone.

She crossed the room to the table and sank into a chair beside Papa Lucky. He reached over and clasped her hand. At his comforting touch, Maggie's temper deflated. She silently admitted something she'd long known. The saddest lies were those a person told herself.

"I thought he cared," she said softly.

Gus dragged his gaze from the direction of the window. "I think he does, Maggins. We all have a private demon or two, and I have the notion we just ran into Rafe Malone's."

As Maggie considered that idea, her hurt solidified into a slow, low-burning anger. "Why do you think that, Papa Gus? What did he tell you?"

"It's just a feeling I have."

Maggie sniffed. She wasn't certain she believed Gus. He wasn't above twisting facts around if he thought it best. Rafe may well have confided in him, and Maggie found she didn't care for that idea at all. He'd certainly never confided in her. But then, no one ever confided in her.

I'm tired of that. She was an adult. She deserved to be treated as such. Considering what she'd just gone through with sucker-fish-lips Barlow Hill, she believed she'd earned it.

Taking care to keep her neck hidden—no sense sending her grandfathers off on a tangent—she drew herself up, glared at her grandfathers, and said, "So, Papas, is Andrew Montgomery your private demon? Considering I'm fixing to lose my home due to this feud between you, I think it's high time I learned what started it. Who wants to tell the tale?"

Gus studied the froth on his ale and didn't speak. Snake stared up at the ceiling, Lucky at the floor. Ben Scovall contemplated his granddaughter. Abruptly he tossed the entire deck of cards onto the table. "You heard her, boys. What do you think? Choice number two?"

"How about number four?" Snake piped up. "It's one you forgot to mention. I say we kill Montgomery."

"Yeah." Lucky flexed his fist. "My hand is itching to swing my blade at that scoundrel's gullet."

Ben slapped the table with both palms. "And would that solve our problem or create a bigger one? The reason why we didn't kill him years ago still exists."

All four men looked at Maggie. Her stomach took a dive. "What? Why are you staring at me like that? What is this about numbers two and four? What aren't you telling me?"

"It's time," Ben said, squaring his shoulders. "She's a woman full-grown, boys. She should be part of this decision. We've raised her to be strong and sensible and secure in our love. She can handle this. She's our Mary Margaret."

Their Mary Margaret didn't care for the sound of that at all. She watched in wary anticipation as the papas hemmed and hawed, but finally all agreed with a nod. No one appeared too happy.

Now that the moment was upon her, Maggie was half-tempted to run from the kitchen and hide in her bedroom. Obviously, she wasn't going to like whatever news her grandfathers had for her. Maybe she didn't want to be an adult after all—not if it meant scenes like this one and the debacle with Barlow Hill.

A pregnant silence filled the kitchen, broken only by the nervous tap of Papa Snake's boot and the faint but doleful croak of a bullfrog from down by the lake. Maggie glanced toward the window. The frog sounded the way she felt. Maybe they should sing a duet.

"Mary Margaret," Ben said, his tone solemn but gentle. "How much of your early life do you remember?"

Maggie's head jerked around. The question surprised her. She'd expected unpleasant news about the hotel, perhaps a connection between Hill and Montgomery. "Do you mean before I came to live with you?"

"Yes."

She shrugged. "Very little at all. I have vague recollections of a lemon-scented house, but my first clear memory is of when I first met you all on the beach. I remember being so afraid."

Snake chuckled. "We were pretty scared ourselves."

Maggie folded her arms, bracing herself for Papa Ben to continue. Instead, Gus spoke up. "Let me tell it, Ben. I was there at the beginning with him."

"Go ahead."

Gus took hold of Maggie's hand and lifted it to his lips for a kiss, then said, "We sailed the waters of the

West Indies at the time. Montgomery and I were headed for a grog shop in Charlotte Amalie when we first met up with Lady Abigail Summers. Andrew took one look at the woman and was lost. A right beautiful woman she was, fresh off the boat from England and on the island to visit friends for the winter."

Lucky slowly shook his head. "Had the prettiest singing voice, too. Remember?"

"What I remember," Ben replied, "is that she was no more immune to Montgomery than he was to her. They seduced one another by week's end. We saw little of Andrew that entire summer. He didn't sail with us once."

Gus squeezed Maggie's hand. "He fell in love with her, Maggie. Fell hard. I think he'd have done anything for her—even return to his family in England."

"Fool boy," Snake said, shaking his head sadly. "He'd a warrant for piracy on his head by then, but he'd have done it anyway. If she'd so much as wriggled her little finger he'd have gone back and tried to finagle his way out of the charges against him. Andrew always was good at finagling."

The other papas nodded their heads in agreement as Gus continued the tale. "But as it turned out, Lady Abigail wasn't prepared to trade her manor life to be a pirate's woman, and when time came for her to return to England, she broke it off with Andrew and sailed away without looking back. The boy went a little wild then."

"He went a lot wild," Lucky interjected.

"He grew mean and bitter—especially toward women—and took up with some unsavory characters. And that's saying a lot coming from men such as ourselves." Gus paused in his story and sipped his drink in contemplative silence.

Maggie's hands curled into fists. She sensed he'd

been leading up to something, and she would bet he'd now reached that "something" part of the story. She wanted to grab him by the collar and shake him, telling him to spit it out. She wanted to run from the kitchen before he could speak, but she waited too long.

"Five years later Abigail returned to Charlotte Amalie. She demanded to speak with Andrew, but he refused to have anything to do with her. She tracked him down on Saint John Island. We were there with him that afternoon. I'll never forget it. A battle royal as violent as any I'd witnessed at sea. He refused to have anything to do with her. Or with . . ." Gus dragged a hand across his mouth, contorting the scar on his cheek, and tried again. "Or with . . ."

When Gus didn't continue, Ben cleared his throat and did the dirty work. "Or with the four-year-old girl she claimed was Andrew's daughter."

Maggie gasped as her grandfather pressed on. "It seems that Lady Abigail delayed her return home. She extended her holiday long enough to give birth to a pirate's child. She hired a caretaker for the infant, then returned to England and soon married. Years later, upon receiving notice that the nanny had died and desperate to keep her daughter's existence secret from her husband, Abigail decided it was Andrew's turn to support the child."

"You told me my parents were dead." Cold invaded Maggie's bones as betrayal hit her. "You lied!"

"It wasn't a total lie. We learned Abigail died within a year of leaving you with us."

"With him," Maggie protested, her thoughts a boiling mixture of confusion, anger, and grief. "She left me with him because she didn't want me. Only, he didn't want me, either."

"Not you, darlin'," Lucky said earnestly. "Abigail. He had closed himself off from her entirely. When she came to him that day it was as if she no longer existed.

And because he didn't see her, he didn't see her leave. And he refused to see that she left you."

"They abandoned me, both of them." Maggie found it difficult to breathe as her mind opened to that long-ago day on one of the world's most beautiful beaches. Old emotions hit her like new—pain, loss, and anguish—as the memory long suppressed overtook her. "She wore a dress the same blue as the sky," she finally said in a little voice. "He shouted at her. He shouted at you. You fought. I remember that. He knocked Papa Gus to the sand."

A chill shivered down her spine as her voice cracked. "They both walked away. They both left me!"

Snake surged to his feet. He braced his hands on his hips and leaned toward her. "Don't cry, lass. Don't you dare cry over them. Yes, they left you. But we didn't, by God. We took you and we fed you and we loved you. We didn't leave you then and we never will."

Lucky's hands balled into fists. "Andrew gave up his rights that day on the beach on Saint John Island," he declared. "He can't have you now, by God. I'll kill him first. I'll kill him and that idiot who stole our hotel if I have to. You're not going to go live with Montgomery. You're not!"

Maggie reared back as Papa Lucky's statement registered. "Is that what this is all about? He wants me to live with him? Why would he want me now when he hasn't wanted me all my life?"

Snake sat down, Gus snapped his jaw shut, and Lucky closed his eyes in a pain-filled grimace. Ben's eyes shied away from hers, and she knew then it must be bad. Silence descended on the room like a bitter cold storm as she waited for someone to answer.

Finally Ben drew a deep breath and exhaled it in a sigh. "That's not exactly true, Mary Margaret. Andrew tried to change his mind, but we wouldn't let him. We wanted to keep you."

"Keep me?" she squeaked. Her emotions were in a tumble. "What do you mean 'keep me'? What was I to you, a puppy?"

"No," he snapped back in an unusual display of temper. "You were our daughter."

Maggie slumped in her seat and shut her eyes. But she couldn't shut out her thoughts. They darted to and fro, trying to make sense of the details of what she had been told. "You said he tried to change his mind. Does that mean he decided he wanted to be my father after all?"

"Yes."

Her chest felt heavy. It took concentrated effort to fill her lungs with air. "When?"

"It's been a while," Gus said.

"How long is a while?"

The pirates shared a frown. Lucky cleared his throat and said, "Oh, twelve or fourteen."

"Months?"

"Years."

Years. She shuddered. Maggie gazed at each of her grandfathers in turn. Ben appeared stoic as always; Snake looked angry. Lucky nervously flicked his sapphire earring with a finger. And Gus, her dear sweet Gus, watched her with suspiciously damp eyes. "But I was still a girl then. I needed a father."

"Why?" Snake banged his mug on the table, his voice trembling with emotion. "You had us."

"Yes," she cried. "But I could have had all of you."

"No, you couldn't." Ben's gaze narrowed, his expression hardened. Cold fury sharpened his voice as he added, "He wouldn't have allowed it, Maggie. Those were his terms."

"What do you mean?"

"Ah, Maggie." Gus raked his hand through thinning white hair. "He intended to take you away from us permanently. He wasn't going to let us see you at all, and of course, we wouldn't stand for that."

"So you told me they were dead? That I was an orphan?" Betrayal cut through her like a knife. "You lied to me all my life?"

Silence fell hard and complete. It was as if the world had ground to a halt. Maybe it had.

Maggie knocked over her chair as she shoved to her feet, a storm of emotion ripping through her. Battering. Bruising. Somewhere deep inside she understood their motives. Somewhere in her heart she felt their love.

But right now she needed escape, and for the first time in forever, she had nowhere to turn, no one to turn to. When Gus reached for her she backed away. It hurt him, she could tell, but at this moment, Maggie had no room for anyone's wounds but her own.

Never in her life had she ever felt such ache as what now squeezed her heart. This hurt was different from the pain of rheumatism or the broken toe or any other physical ailments she'd dealt with during her life. This was like nothing she'd ever known before, and it overwhelmed her.

Her parents had abandoned her. Her papas whom she had trusted all her life had lied to her all her life.

And Rafe Malone was going home.

Tears overflowed as she turned and ran out into the night.

Standing outside in the shadows beside the kitchen's open window, Rafe stood motionless as he watched Gus Thomas trudge toward him. Despite the forgiving moonlight, the buccaneer had never looked so old.

"I saw you through the window," Gus said tiredly. "You heard?"

"Yeah."

"Go to her, Malone. It's time. She's all grown up now. She needs someone other than her papas to help her through this. I think you are the man she needs.

She may not know it yet, but you mean something to her. I can tell. You take care of Maggie. Take care of our little girl." He walked away then, off into the forest, shoulders stooped and feet shuffling.

Rafe tugged his gaze away from the departing pirate and glanced toward the hotel. Indecision seldom bothered him, but when he saw the light flickering in Maggie's bedroom window he didn't know whether to rope or ride. Was Gus right? Did she need him, or would his showing up at her door only make her feel worse? The last thing he wanted was to hurt her more when she was hurting this much already.

He'd eavesdropped, of course. Rafe never liked dangling questions, so he'd never considered walking away without divining the particulars about Ben Scovall's curious second choice. Now he almost wished he had. How could Scovall ever think access to the god-awful tasting Lake Bliss water could ever be worth that look on Maggie's face or the anguish in her voice?

Although he didn't make a conscious decision, Rafe's feet carried him toward the hotel and the light shining like a beacon in the night.

With the pirates all elsewhere, the hotel remained unusually quiet. The creak of a stair step beneath his feet sounded loud as a gunshot to Rafe, and the tinny notes of a music box waltz coming from Barlow Hill's suite blared like a brass quartet. In truth, he was surprised he could hear them at all over the pounding of his pulse. Rafe was as nervous as a tongue-tied attorney.

Briefly, he considered a detour by Hill's room to work off some of the tension. That damned love bite. It would feel good to smash his fist into Hill's fleshy jaw. First, though, he needed to check on Maggie.

At her bedroom door he paused, sensing he was about to wade into emotional depths deep enough to drown him. *Think of it as just one more adventure,* he told himself. Lifting a hand, he rapped his knuckles against the door.

She didn't answer.

"Maggie? It's Rafe. Open the door, Sugar." When she still didn't reply, he turned the knob and pushed the door open. "Maggie?" he repeated, taking a step inside.

The room was empty. She'd left her lamp burning, but Maggie was nowhere in sight.

The lighted lamp provided a clear signal of her state of mind. During his stay at Hotel Bliss, he'd noticed Maggie's frugality with the hotel's resources. She would never leave a lamp burning in an unoccupied room under ordinary circumstances. But then, these circumstances were far from ordinary.

Bet she went to the bathhouse. Hesitating only long enough to extinguish the lamp, Rafe exited Maggie's bedroom and headed for the baths.

The moon shone brightly in the starlit sky, clearly illuminating the path down to the lake. The bathhouses rose along the shore, shadowed retreats for weary bodies and heavy hearts. Eyeing the buildings, Rafe rolled his shoulders. Maggie had a good idea. For all his doubts about the curative powers of Lake Bliss water, he couldn't deny the mud baths' soothing qualities. After a day spent mostly on horseback, he wouldn't mind a wet dirt dip himself.

The hinges on the door of the ladies' house creaked loudly as Rafe stepped inside. He peered into the shadows. "Maggie?"

Again, no answer. The bathhouse was deserted. *Well, shoot.* Where could she be? He hadn't been that much behind her. She couldn't have gone too far. Exiting the building, Rafe retraced his steps toward the hotel, stopping at the halfway point along the path.

Something didn't feel right. Something about the night seemed strange, off-kilter.

He concentrated with all his senses. Listening, he heard the whisper of wind through the trees and the far-off howl of a coyote. He sniffed the air for lingering traces of her scent, but found only the sulfur smell of the lake. He looked inside himself, using his knowledge of her in an attempt to figure out where else she might have gone.

If she was in Hill's suite he'd wring her neck.

He dashed for the hotel and hurried up the stairs to Hill's room. Rafe didn't bother to knock. Throwing open the door, he marched inside. Empty. He glanced toward the second doorway. The bedroom. His mouth flattened into a grim smile as he stepped in that direction.

The sight that met him both disgusted and relieved. Hill lay spread-eagle atop his sheets, snoring. Naked as the day he was born. Ugly as a fresh-whelped hound dog. But alone, thank God.

Rafe left the suite a lot more quietly than he had arrived. And a lot more frightened. Maggie was in trouble. He knew it. He needed to check the stable, the carriage shed, and the smokehouse, but first he needed to get his gun.

He climbed a second flight of stairs to the third floor and made his way toward the last room at the far end of the hall. Fishing his key from his pocket, he inserted it into the lock and stepped inside. Without bothering with a light, he walked toward the bed where he knew he'd find his gun belt looped over a post.

As he reached for the leather, he realized he wasn't alone. He knew. He didn't know how, but he knew. "Maggie."

A chimney lamp rattled. A match flared. "Where have you been, Malone?"

The wick caught fire, and a golden glow drifted over the room like warm honey. Maggie St. John sat propped against his pillows, his sheet caught against her chest, her shoulders bare and taunting him. "Good Lord, woman. What in the name of Texas do you think you are doing?"

Her eyes glittered up at him, sad and sorrowful. She held her head cocked to one side, her chin at a proud, defiant angle. Had Rafe been less aware of her, he'd have missed the wobble in her voice as she said, "I'm here to hold you to your word, Malone. You, me, Texas, and a bed."

Maggie was running on instinct rather than thought. A wildness pulsed through her blood tonight, hot and fast and reckless. She furiously ignored the whisper of caution sounding in her brain.

She held her breath as Rafe absorbed the significance of her statement. He couldn't turn her away, not now. She couldn't bear it.

Maggie was lost. Adrift. Like never before, she needed a sense of belonging. Intuition told her Rafe Malone could give her that, if only for tonight, and feminine inspiration had driven her to his bed. Now, watching him, witnessing the protest taking form on his features, that instinct instructed her to act and forestall his objection.

Boldly she released the sheet.

"Ah, hell, Maggie." Rafe dropped his head back, closed his eyes, and groaned. "You could tempt a saint to sin."

"But you're no saint, are you, Malone?"

He looked at her then, a heated, hungry glance that spoke volumes. Nervousness clutched at her stomach, but she doggedly ignored it. Scooting over in the bed, she made room for him.

Rafe eyed the expanse of sheet, then dragged a hand across his face. "No, I'm not a saint, but I'm not a bastard, either. You're wrong, Maggie. You don't need to hold me to my word. You just need to be held."

"But I want to make love," she pleaded.

"I understand the feeling, believe me," he said with half a groan. "But that's not why you came here, whether you know it or not. You need a hug, Maggie St. John. A good hug."

Her name on his lips distracted her. "There never was a William and Catherine St. John. They made it up. They chose St. John because it all happened on a Saint John beach."

"Maybe." He flipped open the trunk at the foot of the bed and rummaged through its contents. The scent of sandalwood rose on the air, and Maggie unconsciously leaned toward it.

"What does it matter?" Rafe continued. "You are who you are no matter what your name. That's something I always liked about this country of ours, you know. Many a man came to Texas for health reasons—that throat disease threat. If a fellow needed a change of climate due to that particular affliction, he stood a good chance of recovering as soon as he crossed the Sabine. The trip usually cost his name, but all he had to do was pick a new one and go on. And look at what these men built, Maggie. An independent republic. Those men can be proud of who they are no matter what name they wore before they ran afoul of throat disease."

She knew he was trying to distract her, but she was curious despite herself. "Throat disease? Which one? Aren't there a number of such maladies?"

"With this particular infirmity the patient dies of a broken spine at the end of a few minutes and a rope." Rafe's pirate's smile slipped and a shadow entered his eyes as he added, "I confess I've been close to picking up that bug myself."

Wanting—no, needing—to chase his shadows away as much as her own, Maggie gave the response she sensed he desired. She chuckled and to her surprise, it felt good. She'd been doubtful whether she'd ever laugh again.

"You dare to laugh at the notion of my being

hanged?" Rafe teased. His expression softened, and a pleased light entered his eyes. He pulled a shirt from the trunk and tossed it to her. "Put this on, Maggie. A man can only take so much temptation, and if I'm going to spend the night with you without acting like a bastard, I need you to keep your bosom covered." Matter-of-factly, he placed his heel in a bootjack and tugged first one leg and then the other free.

Her heart seemed to stop. He had said he would spend the night. He wasn't throwing her out. A heavy weight lifted off Maggie's soul as she donned the soft blue chambray shirt.

Rafe whistled beneath his breath as he pulled off his socks. Then his hands went to the top button on the fly of his pants and froze. "Now that would be a plumb stupid move." He blew out a long breath, tugged his shirttail free, and climbed into the bed beside her.

He shifted her onto his lap and his arms wrapped around her, strong and steady and safe. Maggie rested her head against his chest and sighed with pleasure at the intimacy they shared.

He clicked his tongue. "I listened at the window earlier, Maggie. You've had an awful time of it, haven't you?"

She wasn't surprised that he eavesdropped. "I can't believe they lied to me."

His fingers gently stroked her arm. "Don't be so hard on those old corsairs, sweetheart. They did what they thought was best."

"I know. And I love them for it. I love them. I'm just . . . I don't know."

"Confused." He pressed a kiss against her hair. "You had a lot thrown at you this evening."

"You don't know the half of it," Maggie said with a grimace. She noted the slight increase in the tension of his chest muscles beneath her cheek.

A dry drawl rumbled from out of his chest. "Yeah, but I bet I can guess." He tilted her chin, exposing her neck and his thumb traced Barlow Hill's mark. "You want to tell me about this?"

"Not necessarily."

"Nonetheless, I want to hear. Why did you let him near you?"

Maggie tucked her head against him. "Can't we just forget about it?"

"You're in my bed, in my arms, wearing his pucker scar. I don't think we can forget it."

"I don't think that gives you the right to—"

He leaned his head down and kissed her. Hard. And Maggie welcomed him. Her lips parted and his tongue probed, roughly stroking hers. She tasted both his hunger and his frustration, and though the kiss flirted with violence, she also tasted his restraint.

Maggie's entire body went limp. This man was pure magic. He wove a passionate spell with his mouth, awakening hollow aches and sizzling nerves inside her. Instinctively, she tried to shift in his arms, to press herself against him. But Rafe wouldn't allow it. He held her captive in his lap, taking it no further than a kiss despite the hardened proof of his own excitement she felt beneath her thighs.

"God, Maggie," he whispered roughly, breaking the kiss. "You do know how to slip past a man's defenses. In the future I want you to remind me that kissing you is not a good way to prove my point. Now, tell me about Hill."

The name served to jerk Maggie from the sensual daze. She groaned and started to wrench herself from his arms, but abruptly changed her mind. She liked being wrapped in his hug. If he was going to force her to tell this story, at least she should get a little something out of it. She vented her frustration by giving the hair on Rafe's arms a tug as she said, "He wants me to marry him."

"What!" he yelped.

"Barlow Hill has made me a proposal. He wants a

lady-wife for the mansion he's building here at Lake Bliss, and he thinks I'm perfect for the position. If I marry him, he will allow my grandfathers to stay at the hotel."

Rafe's complexion turned Brazos River red and his eyes shot daggers. He squeezed his fist so hard the veins in his hands bulged and looked ready to pop. "The maggot. That's blackmail!"

Maggie had sensed he wouldn't like the idea any more than she, but she never expected such an extreme reaction. "You sound like my grandfathers."

"They know about this?" he asked incredulously.

"No, of course not. They'd kill him if they did, and we can't have that."

"Why not?"

"Hill was wary of my grandfathers from the first. He claims he has taken steps to ruin my family should he suffer an untimely death, and I believe him. The man has proved himself to be intelligent, after all. He owns Hotel Bliss."

"Well he doesn't own you. He needs to keep his mouth to himself. When did he propose this bit of extortion anyway? Tonight?"

Maggie shook her head. "He talked to me about this right before we left for the Caribbean. I told him I was going to New Orleans and that I'd see about a wedding gown there."

"You accepted him!"

"I never came right out and said it. He, however, seems to believe my acceptance is a given." She paused, shuddering at the memory of her struggle to free herself from his arms. When she spoke again, she couldn't stop her voice from catching. "I expected to come home with the treasure. I had no idea my father had stolen it. I had no idea I had a father."

"Aw, Maggie," he drawled, his voice a tender sigh. His fist relaxed and he gently stroked her hair, his touch both a comfort and a temptation. As a pair of tears overflowed her eyes to roll down her face he laid her back against the mattress and gently kissed them away.

It felt so right to lift her lips to his.

His mouth was warm and wet and sweet with the faint taste of cider. Maggie wanted this pleasure to ease her pain. She wanted Rafe Malone. In that chamber of her mind where her most honest thoughts took substance, she admitted she cared for him more than she'd ever cared for any man. Was it love?

Maggie shied away from the idea. She'd have to be a fool to love a man like Rafe Malone. A rambler, a rogue. He appealed to her for many reasons, not the least of which was because he was so much like the papas. But that same fact told her to guard her heart. Too many women had come and gone through her grandfathers' lives for her not to understand the folly of loving an adventurous man.

This wasn't about love. It was about comfort and caring, and for tonight that was enough. Tilting back her head, she lifted her face toward him and said, "Hold me."

"I am holding you."

She stroked a finger down his bare chest. "Make the hurt go away."

He fought it. He looked away, the cords in his neck bulging from the clench of his jaw. Tension hovered like a living thing between them.

Maggie stared into his eyes and whispered, "Please?"

The word seemed to shudder through him. She waited. She watched. Losing herself in the brilliant depths of his eyes, Maggie knew the moment he decided. Pleasure washed through her, sweet and clean.

"Aw, shoot, Maggie. I tried."

⇒ 10 ⇐

Rafe eased her back onto the bed and rose above her, his knees on either side of her hips. "You don't fight fair."

"I didn't realize it was a fight."

"Oh, it's a fight, all right. Let me show you."

His hands moved over her, spreading heat with every stroke. Nimble fingers worked the buttons of the shirt she wore, and she caught her breath at the warm brush of his fingers against the underside of her breasts. "Oh, Mary."

At the husky rumble of her name a sinuous shiver ran all the way to her toes. His heavy-lidded gaze took a leisurely trip down her body, leaving her aching for his touch. He whispered words of desire and wanting, erotic images that circled in her mind like satin ribbons. She would have responded with needy words of her own had the ability to speak not deserted her.

Rafe yanked off his shirt. His eyes were fierce with concentration, and the air surrounding him all but crackled with raw sexuality. Slowly, too slowly, his hand lifted toward her swelling breasts. When finally he touched her, his bronzed hand a vivid contrast against her white flesh, an exquisite sensation speared through her, and Maggie couldn't hold back a gasp.

"You are so beautiful, Mary. Seeing you starts a fire inside me. Touching you—" He flicked his thumb across a pebbled crest. "—Makes me ache. Tasting you . . ." He bent his head to her and traced his tongue slowly, wetly, arousingly around her nipple. "Tasting you makes me hungry for more."

He covered her with his mouth and began to feast.

Maggie threw back her head, arching her back, offering herself. His mouth was hot, his tongue so sweetly rough. Shivers rippled through her and she moaned, low and throaty. "Oh, Rafe."

He lifted his head then, showed her his pirate's grin, and his eyes glowed like polished jewels. "Oh, Mary," he growled in reply before devoting his attention to her other aching breast.

Darts of pleasure pierced her with every lave and nip and tug, sensations that tore straight to the hollow core of her, that achy, needy place inside her crying out to be filled. Maggie circled her hips seeking, instinctively demonstrating her need.

She knew a keen disappointment as his mouth freed her breast. He shifted, rolled back. His hands went to the buttons of his pants and paused. "Are you certain about this, sweetheart? A woman only has one first time. It's a wonderful gift—one I'll treasure forever—but I want you to be absolutely sure. No regrets."

"No regrets," Maggie whispered. "I want it to be you, Rafe."

He breathed a relieved sigh. "Thank God."

He stripped off his pants with swift, decisive movements, drawing Maggie's gaze inexorably downward. Her mouth went dry as he stood before her, naked and bold and . . . hungry.

Even as a responsive yearning quickened in her womb, a whisper of doubt fluttered through Maggie's mind. What if she didn't please him? What if in her inexperience she did something wrong? Even though she needed the comfort, needed the heat now melting the ice from her wounded heart, Maggie wasn't the type of woman to take without giving in return. Her pride wouldn't allow it.

Lifting her arms toward him, Maggie made a decision of her own. Virginity be damned. Heaven knew her upbringing hadn't kept her unaware. She was an intelligent woman. She could figure out what she didn't know. By the looks of things, she was doing all right up until then.

He came to her, took her hand, and lifted it to his mouth for a courtier's kiss. Hot eyes blazed down at her, and in them Maggie saw something that both soothed her fear and filled her with a woman's power.

This was more than lust. More than sex.

She went pliant with delight. Rafe Malone would remember the time she spent with him. Mary Margaret St. John would be more than just another of the women who had passed through his life and through his bed. She would be the one whose memory haunted him in the months and years to come.

Secure in her position, Maggie joined the battle.

She drew a deep breath and expelled it slowly. "I want to touch you. May I?"

"I think I might die if you don't."

The muscles in his long arms flexed as he lowered himself to the bed to lie beside her, and she chose to touch him there first. Her hand skimmed his bicep, felt the bulge of hard muscle beneath soft skin. She smiled, appreciating the feeling, enjoying the intimacy.

"You slay me, woman," he rasped as she pushed him over onto his back then brushed her fingers across his chest and his nipple.

Tanned skin quivered beneath her hand and she thrilled at her feminine power. Her palms spread out on his chest, her fingers tunneling into his chest hair. She stroked him as he had done her and gloried in his reaction as he sucked in a sharp breath. Maggie wanted to laugh. She felt so free, so delicious. So much a woman.

Her hands stroked lower and lower. When she skimmed below his navel his entire body grew taut, and he unleashed a growl. "Enough."

He grabbed her hands and pinned them to the bed, then fit his body atop hers. "You are a bold woman for a virgin, Mary-mine, and as much as I love it, you're about to end this when we've barely gotten started."

Maggie hardly heard him, so conscious was she of the heat of him poised against that achy core of her. The air surrounding them thickened and her body tensed in nervous anticipation. Unconsciously, she circled her lips with her tongue.

Rafe groaned and loosened his hold on her wrists as he lowered his head. He mimicked her action with his own tongue before fusing his lips to hers. He kissed her deeply, his tongue thrusting hard as she wrapped her arms around him. Maggie relished his hunger and knew it for her own.

His harsh breath sounded in her ear as he skimmed a finger up her thigh, and for the first time she felt a glimmer of apprehension. His hand found her, cupped her, kneaded her. Then he eased one finger inside her slick folds.

Maggie gasped. "Rafe?"

"Shh, honey. Relax."

Relax? She couldn't relax. His fingers were wicked, teasing her, teaching her of hungers she'd never dreamed existed. Her fear drowned beneath the tide of rising heat and need. Soon she moved against him, willingly, impatiently, beseechingly.

"That's it, Mary," he said raggedly. "Let me. Let me make it happen for you. Relax and let it happen."

Maggie writhed atop the sheets, trapped by his

fingers and the hot, boiling, glowing throb building in her core. Rafe drove her higher and higher. Faster. Faster. A pleasure-pain that made her want to scream. "Please!" She sobbed. "I can't!"

His tight voice whispered in her ear. "Yes, you can. We can. Ah, Mary, didn't I warn you this was a fight?"

Maggie lay with her head thrown back against the pillow, her eyes closed, so she didn't see him move. It didn't matter. Nothing could have prepared her for the shocking flick of his tongue against her softest skin.

"Rafe!" And Maggie shattered. Tides of molten pleasure crashed over her, sweeping her along in a spectacular journey of shudders and shivers and quakes.

"That's it, Mary-mine. Now share it with me, sweetheart." He eased inside her. "It'll only hurt—" He thrust his hips forward, breaching the barrier of her innocence, filling her with himself. "—A minute."

Maggie lay quietly, adjusting to the unaccustomed fullness, shaking with the aftershocks of her climax. "Liar," she whispered.

"Oh hell, sweetheart. I'm sorry. But it is—"

"It didn't hurt a minute, Rafe," she said, smiling, watching him through heavy-lidded eyes. "It didn't hurt at all." Now that she could think again, she remembered her desire to make this memorable for Rafe. She abandoned herself to her instincts and wriggled her hips.

He ground his teeth and didn't quite hold back a moan. "Mary Margaret, you are playing with fire."

"I know," she breathed, rotating her hips in the opposite direction, trying to determine whether the route made a difference.

"Siren," he muttered, as his hips began to move. "I intended to give you time to get used to me."

She didn't need time; she needed him, more of him.

She needed to satisfy the hunger burning in his eyes. She wanted to give back. Instinctively, Maggie arched up to meet his thrusts. "Look at me," she demanded. "Rafe, look at me. At who I am."

He did. He looked at her and never looked away. And when he poured himself into her, her name was on his lips. "Mary."

A long time later, when pulses had calmed and heartbeats had slowed, Maggie lay snuggled up against Rafe. Filled with tender joy, she drew lazy circles in the whorls of his chest hair and asked in the softest of whispers, "Rafe? Why Mary?"

He wore only a lazy smile and a sheet as he turned his head and pressed a kiss to her temple. "That's simple, sweetheart. Snake has his lass and Ben his Mary Margaret. Lucky has his Magpie and Gus his Maggins."

His eyes glowed like a pirate's treasure in the lamplight as he added, "Mary is mine."

Maggie dreamed she was down in the cenote. Her arm lay trapped beneath the treasure chest that was filled with rocks. She yanked and she tugged, but it wouldn't come loose. Then a noise sounded. A loud rumbling . . . snore.

Maggie's eyes flew open. For a second her mind remained a blank. Then, like a dam bursting, memories came flooding back to her. She realized her arm wasn't trapped by a treasure chest filled with rocks, but instead by the man whose bed she shared.

Oh, my. She wrenched her arm free. The body beside her mumbled sleepily then settled back into a snore. Oh, my heavens.

She'd actually done it.

Maggie rolled off the bed and onto her feet in a swift, smooth movement. Moonlight beamed through the unshuttered window, illuminating the broad washboard torso against which she'd lain mere seconds before. A dozen different images from the previous night flashed through her mind, and Maggie swallowed hard.

She bent and grabbed her dress up off the floor where it had fallen, then winced in the darkness at the unaccustomed soreness between her legs. She wasn't a virgin any longer.

No regrets, she'd told him. Well, she had kept that promise. At this particular moment, she was feeling all kinds of different emotions, but regret wasn't one of them.

Rafe Malone, I'm glad it was you.

In that moment, it was the one thing—the only thing—she could say for certain. Her mind was mired in confusion as she quietly donned her clothing. Whereas the need for comfort had brought her to this room hours before, now the need to escape sent her tiptoeing across the wooden floor toward the door. Cautiously, she turned the knob. The click of the latch sounded loud as cracking thunder to her ears. *Please don't wake up,* she thought, glancing back over her shoulder at Rafe. She couldn't face him now.

She wasn't certain she could face herself.

Soundlessly, she pulled the door open. She slipped out into the darkened hallway and pushed it shut behind her. Standing frozen, she listened for signs of stirring elsewhere in the hotel. All quiet, thank heavens.

Maggie returned to her own room, but at the doorway she paused. Her thoughts were all jumbled, her emotions a wreck. As much as she wished to escape to the forgetfulness of sleep, she knew the effort would be useless. She might as well take a walk and think her troubles through. Or at least make the attempt.

As she stepped from the hotel, nighttime wrapped around her like a moonlit sea. The light dew moistened her feet. She breathed deeply of the magnolia-scented air and exhaled in a trembling sigh. "Well, St. John?" she asked herself softly. "Which subject do you want to tackle first? Rafe Malone or Andrew Montgomery?"

A rueful smile twisted her lips. Considering she'd already tackled Rafe, so to speak, perhaps she should begin with him.

Maggie walked toward Papa Ben's rose garden, trading the perfume of the magnolia for that of the tea rose. She sat on the wooden bench and propped her feet atop a rock. She wiggled her toes and recalled how at one point during the second time he'd loved her, Rafe had kissed them one by one.

Maggie felt her cheeks warm at the thought. She'd acted the brazen hussy tonight in seeking out his bed. Her classmates at Mount Glazier School for Young Ladies would be completely scandalized. Maggie was scandalized, and she'd had a more progressive up-bringing than most.

She couldn't believe she'd actually gone through with it. She'd acted on instinct, not thought. What was it about Rafe that caused her to do that? Despite what had happened—or almost happened—in the Caribbean cave, she never would have guessed she'd go to him the first night back at Bliss.

Of course, she never would have guessed she would need comforting so much, either.

Maggie lifted her head and gazed toward the moon. She exhaled a heartfelt sigh. How was she supposed to feel? Somehow, she didn't expect most brazen hussies felt embarrassed. Maggie did, and her embarrassment dismayed her.

She was the granddaughter of pirates, not some simpering Southern miss. She'd chosen Rafe Malone to be her lover. She'd pursued him, seduced him. Sought comfort in his arms. So why did the memory of it make heat flush her cheeks?

Was she ashamed of what she'd done? Should she

be ashamed? At school they had preached the religion of commitment. She didn't want that, did she?

Well if she did, she'd made a mistake in choosing Gentleman Rafe Malone, adventurer extraordinaire.

But it hadn't been a mistake. Making love with Rafe had been the most glorious experience of her life. He'd made her feel beautiful. He'd made her feel like a woman. He'd made her feel wanted, and she'd needed to feel that tonight, needed it like never before.

Because her parents hadn't wanted her. Her father and her mother had given her away.

Maggie pushed off the bench and resumed walking. And what of Rafe? Had he truly wanted her, or had he simply slaked his lust? Did it matter?

It mattered. It shouldn't, but it did.

Maggie's pace sped up. She left the rose garden and headed down toward the lake, ignoring the ache in her knee and the occasional sting of stone and stick beneath her bare feet. She was so confused. What did she want from Rafe? Comfort, diversion from her problems, life experience? He'd given her all that. Why should it matter *why* he had done it?

Because to her peculiar, self-defined sense of morality, motives made all the difference. She'd used him, true, for comfort and escape, and for that perhaps she probably should feel shame. But in her defense, she'd brought more to his bed than her needs. She'd brought caring and respect and true, honest desire. And what of love?

No. She couldn't think of that. She wouldn't think of that. Nothing had changed. She still wanted peace and tedium. She wouldn't love an adventuring man.

But deep in her heart a little voice whispered, *Maybe it's too late, Maggie. Maybe you already do.*

Anger flared inside her. He wasn't a man she could love. She stopped her march abruptly and glared back toward the hotel, toward the dark window of Rafe Malone's bedroom. He wasn't an adventurer. He was a coward. This very night he had refused her grandfathers' request for help. How could she forget that? How could she ignore his betrayal?

Because despite what he said, if Rafe Malone cared for her at all—if she mattered to him at all—he'd have granted her papas' request. Instead he was leaving Lake Bliss.

And to her despair, she had the sneaking suspicion he'd be taking a little piece of her heart with him.

Rafe woke up alone.

He sat up in bed, gazed at the indentation of the pillow beside him, and two thoughts occurred almost simultaneously. First, he didn't like waking up by himself when he'd fallen asleep entwined with Maggie, and second, he should probably count himself lucky to wake up at all.

Gus may have given him tacit instructions to have his way with his granddaughter, but Rafe didn't want to think about the other buccaneers' reactions. Especially Snake's.

Rafe swung his legs over the side of the bed and rubbed his palm across his whiskered neck. He hoped his own razor would do the shaving today and not a pirate's cutlass.

As a precautionary measure, he armed himself with his Texas Paterson revolver before making his way from his room. He halfway expected to find a lynch mob of four gray-haired raiders waiting for him. Instead, the hotel was quiet but for the faint scratch of pen against paper coming from Barlow Hill's suite of rooms. Rafe stepped toward the sound, then stopped in the doorway. His fingers itched to draw his gun.

Hill looked up from the paper before him and slowly set down his pen. "Ah, Mr. Malone. Isn't this handy. I intended to seek you out this morning." He gestured toward a chair opposite the desk. "Please, come have a seat."

All in all, Rafe would rather have eaten dirt than

have visited with Hill, but he'd been a bounder himself long enough to know the importance of sizing up one's enemy. This blackguard thought to black-mail Maggie into marriage. *Well, he has another thing coming.* Rafe crossed the room, took a seat, and waited for the other man to speak.

Hill flourished a faith-peddler smile. "I understand your business is horses."

"Yep."

"You're a mustanger?"

"Nope. We breed horses to sell to the rangers. That and a racer or two. I own Brown Baggage." Rafe waited for the spark of envy and admiration he normally saw in other men's expressions when he mentioned the quarter-miler's name, but Hill's remained politely disinterested.

"I see," he replied, obviously not seeing at all.

Hill's failure to recognize the name of the fastest racehorse in Texas added to Rafe's disgust. Every self-respecting Texian knew his horses. Along with being a scoundrel, Hill was an embarrassment. Maggie deserved much better.

Rafe knew that already, of course, and somewhere between midnight and morning, when she lay sleeping so sweetly beside him, he'd decided to help her get what she deserved.

Without robbing her father, that is. Rafe would dance a waltz in a rattlesnake pit before he'd break his word to Luke. Thank goodness he had another way to help her and those crusty corsairs.

He stretched out in his chair and crossed his boots at the ankles, his mouth twisting in a lopsided grin. Part of the fun of solving Maggie's problem would be getting rid of the trouble named Barlow Hill. "So, are you in the market for horses? Is that why you wanted to speak with me?"

"Not precisely. Allow me to be blunt, Mr. Malone." Hill cleared his throat. "I was told you are visiting Hotel Bliss to do some horse trading with Scovall and his friends. How that ties in with your decision to tag along on Miss St. John's trip to New Orleans, I fail to see. That aside, you must be aware that I, not Scovall, own the hotel. I'm certain you'll appreciate that I can no longer offer you unlimited hospitality."

Rafe leaned forward and flipped open the wooden humidor on Hill's desk. He extracted a cigar, stuck it into his mouth, and chewed thoughtfully on the end for a full minute. "Are you kicking me out?"

"I would not put it in quite so crass a manner, but yes, I guess I am."

"You're in luck, then," Rafe said around the end of his cigar. Pushing slowly to his feet, he added, "I was planning on leaving today, anyway, so I won't have to tell you no." Hill's eyes rounded in surprise.

Rafe removed the cigar from his mouth and placed both hands on the desktop. He leaned forward, pinning the scoundrel with his best I'm-a-dangerous-criminal gaze, and drawled, "Let me give you a little piece of advice. Before I took up ranching, I was both a lawyer and a thief. Those particular professions provided me the skills to get what I want and protect what I have—legally or otherwise. Now, you might have wrangled a deed on this bit of land, but you don't own the people on it. So listen to me when I tell you to step with care around Miss St. John."

"Are you threatening me, Mr. Malone?"

"No. I'm telling you you'll live a much longer and healthier life if you keep those lips of yours to yourself."

Hill wisely and fearfully shrank back in his chair. Rafe turned his back and moved to leave the room. At the doorway, the bravely whining sound of the other man's voice made him pause.

"The *lady* and I have an understanding! I shall touch her however I wish, and you won't be here to stop me."

Rafe glanced back over his shoulder. "Have you

ever taken a real close look at Snake MacKenzie's cutlass? You could use the shadow of the blade to shave with." With that farewell, he quit the room and left the hotel.

Spring had slipped into summer during his trip to the Caribbean, and despite the early morning hour, the day was already hot and muggy. Rafe broke into a sweat the minute he stepped outside. The weather didn't improve his mood at all, and he was still stewing about Hill when he finally caught up with Maggie a good fifteen minutes later.

She and her pirate crew once again battled their way around their version of a golf course. Rafe watched her line up over her ball. When she waggled her hips he froze midstep, gripped by a fierce surge of desire.

"One look at her and I'm hard as a horseshoe," he muttered beneath his breath. He'd have thought last night would have taken the edge off, but no. Today he wanted her more than ever before.

Having previously learned his lesson, Rafe waited for Maggie to finish her shot before advancing toward the group. He approached the grandfathers with a fair amount of trepidation, keeping his hands positioned to make a defensive draw should it become necessary. But other than a razor look from Gus, the marauders betrayed no sign of knowing where and how their beloved granddaughter had spent her night. And Maggie, well, she wouldn't look at him.

Rafe didn't like that any better than waking up alone.

He sidled up beside her. "Good morning."

She didn't reply, leaving that up to Lucky, who turned a fierce glower toward him and snapped, "There is nothing good about this morning, so shut yer trap."

Must have hit one into the lake, Rafe thought.

Without giving him so much as a glance, Maggie

marched away from Rafe, headed for her ball. He watched her, irritated and annoyed, until he realized what likely put the starch in her step.

Maggie was embarrassed. That had to be it. And such an emotion wouldn't sit well on the shoulders of a strong woman like her.

Rafe could have kicked himself. He should have waited until they were alone to approach her. Maggie would have dealt better with the normal morning-after awkwardness without an audience of overprotective grandfathers.

He looped his thumbs around his belt loops and sighed, wondering if heading back to the hotel now would improve matters or only make them worse. While he pondered the problem, Gus meandered up beside him and lowered his voice to a near whisper. "Maggie seems happy enough this morning."

Rafe almost tripped over his own feet at that. He looked around to make certain they weren't being overheard, then gestured toward the woman currently chastising the bushy-tailed squirrel who had dared to dart across her path. "This is happy?"

"This is normal. Yesterday's revelations were hard for her to swallow, and temper helps to get them down. She's not heartbroken, though. In fact, she may just be stronger than ever. I reckon we have you to thank for that."

Rafe didn't quite know how to answer him. This was the closest he'd ever come to having a father thank him for taking his daughter's virginity. "Uh, my pleasure."

Gus wrenched his eyes closed. "I don't want the details, Malone. This isn't easy for me, you know."

Rafe hadn't been sure. This entire situation was as strange as a sidesaddle on a sow. "What about the others? Do they . . .?"

Gus's mouth lifted in a sneer. "You weren't gelded right after breakfast, were you?"

They didn't know. Rafe breathed a little easier as

the band of tension surrounding his lungs released. Not that he was afraid of the pirates or anything like that. He simply wished to avoid any unpleasantness. Maggie didn't need it, and come to think of it, neither did he.

Up ahead, Snake drew his knife and with one fast slash hacked off the limb of a dogwood blocking his shot. Rafe sucked in a breath. Maybe the pirates worried him just a little, after all. He cleared his throat. "Has she said anything today about what she learned last night? About Montgomery, I mean?"

Gus slowly shook his head. "Not a word. We've talked about it among us, though. Ben is convinced she'll go to Andrew at Triumph. Maybe not immediately, but soon. We have less than two months until Hill's deadline to buy the hotel. She'll want to save Lake Bliss for our sakes. We just want to be sure it's available for her. Hill is a squirrelly son of a flounder, and we don't trust him not to deny Maggie's access to Bliss water just for the halibut."

Rafe was momentarily distracted by the combination of animal and fish in the old salt's speech. Just for the halibut? A light dawned. *Just for the hell of it. Oh.* "Do you think Montgomery will provide the funds needed to meet Hill's price?"

"Yeah," Gus said, his lips twisting in a bittersweet grin. "Drew visited us not long after we settled at Lake Bliss. Tried to take her away from us. That's when we told him about her illness. Judging by his reaction, I feel certain he'll protect her now. He'll give her enough of the treasure to buy back Hotel Bliss and secure her access to the water."

"What did he do?"

"This, among other things," Gus said, pointing to the scar on his face. "He decided to quit the fight to make her leave Bliss so that she could have the treatment she needed. But before he left, he swore he'd make us pay. He promised us that someday he'd cause us to lose what we valued most of all. When we told Maggie the truth, well, I reckon Drew got his wish. We hurt her bad."

"It's true you hurt Maggie, but you didn't lose her. She has forgiven you. She wouldn't play golf with you otherwise."

The pirate's tired expression crinkled into a smile. "Yeah, you're right about that, Malone. She's some kind of woman, isn't she?"

Damn right she was. And Gus only knew the half of it. Rafe rubbed the back of his neck. "Do you really believe that if Montgomery steps in and saves the day he'll try to keep y'all separated?"

Gus's smile faded. He cleared his throat and nodded. "One thing about Andrew: when he gives his word, he keeps it. The two of you are alike that way."

Not caring for the comparison, Rafe scowled and asked a question that had occurred to him last night while Maggie was sleeping. "About Montgomery. Could he and Hill be partners in this scheme to take Hotel Bliss away from you?"

"I never even thought of that." Gus's gray eyes went hard as steel as he considered the question. "I don't know, Malone. Drew has a mean streak in him, for certain, but a plan like this would have taken years to set up. You should have seen what Maggie went through trying to fight our case in the courts. Poor thing wore herself down and had the worst spell she's had in years. To think Andrew would cause his own flesh and blood so much hurt, well, it's hard for a man to fathom."

Rafe scowled. "He didn't care about hurting her when he left her on a beach, now did he?"

"That was different. He couldn't think straight. Abigail hurt him so badly, and the two—Maggie and she—were all tied up together in his mind."

"Are you defending what he did? I can't believe you, Gus. I thought you hated Montgomery."

"I do. I did. Well, clam it." He yanked a bandanna from his pocket and dragged it across his perspiring face. "I don't know what I think except that matters aren't always black and white. Sometimes a man has to massage the gray with his brain a bit before he can figure out what's right and what's not."

With the idea of a connection between Montgomery and Hill rumbling around Rafe's mind, Rafe asked, "Is Montgomery the type of man who would want his daughter to marry water barrel scum like Barlow Hill?"

Gus drew up short and speared him with a look. "What kind of nonsense is that?"

"Never mind." Rafe had a hunch that telling the pirates about Hill's nefarious plan might put a plow to a field best left untilled. Knowing Maggie, if she'd kept the information to herself this long, she had good reason. Rafe wanted to know about that and a whole lot more. Awkwardness or no, the time had come for him to share a little conversation with the lady.

He got his chance one shot later when she sliced her ball off into the woods. Casually he joined her in the search, and when they were both beyond the pirates' sight, he cornered her against a cottonwood. He hadn't intended to kiss her first off, but now that her lips were so handy, he couldn't help himself. "Good morning, Mary-mine," he said, his thumb stroking her face before his mouth claimed hers.

She tasted sweet as honeysuckle nectar, and for a moment Rafe forgot the questions he wanted to ask. When he finally broke the kiss, a sensual haze clouded her normally crystalline eyes. Rafe grinned and she blinked. As her eyes cleared her complexion pinkened like a dogwood in spring.

"I'm not yours," she said snippily.

"You were last night."

Maggie's blush deepened. He kissed her again, and when she melted against him, Rafe briefly considered laying her down on the forest floor and taking the matter further. But recalling the proximity of her guardian pirates, he decided on a more prudent course of action. Firmly, he set her away from him. "I have some questions. We need to talk."

She pressed her fingers against her lips and closed her eyes. "Why do I let you do this to me?"

"I think we do it to each other," he replied. Catching hold of her hand, he lifted her knuckles to his mouth for a kiss. "It's the same for me, honey. I ask myself the same blasted question."

"Questions. I don't want to answer questions. I don't want to talk. I need to find my ball." She kicked at a heap of leaves.

"Maggie, I know you're probably feeling shy about last night, but—"

"I'm not feeling shy about last night," she interrupted.

"Awkward, then."

"Not awkward, either. I'm fine. Last night was fine."

Fine? The best sex of his entire life was just fine *for her?* Rafe folded his arms and stared at her, his mouth hanging open. *Well, hell!* "Are you sure?" he asked, giving her another chance.

"Positive!"

That just got all over him. "Fine, then. Fine yourself." Rafe gave a nearby clump of brush a good kick. Searching for the golf ball, of course.

Maggie, too, turned back to the task at hand, and the next few moments passed in tense silence as they searched the forest floor.

But Rafe couldn't leave it at "fine." Once he'd calmed down a bit, he spoke up. "All right, Maggie. If you're not feeling bashful, how come you have a burr under your blanket?"

"I don't have a burr under my blanket."

"Yes, you do." He halted and braced his hands on his hips. "I can tell. What's the problem, Maggie? Go ahead and run it by me. Maybe I can help."

It was the wrong choice of words for him to use.

"Help?" Her gaze filled with scorn. Bitterness

dripped like venom in her words. "Gentleman Rafe Malone help us? Ha!" Twigs cracked beneath the violence of her steps as she rushed away from him.

Rafe muttered a curse and hurried after her. Reaching out, he caught hold of her arm and drew her up short. "Now wait just a minute. What did I do to deserve that?"

"Nothing." She gazed at him through angry, tearful eyes. "That's exactly it, Malone. It's what you said you'd do. Nothing. It would be so easy for you to get our treasure for us. You have all the right skills. I don't believe for a moment that you'd be careless enough to get caught at it. You're too good. But you refuse to help us, so now I must figure out another way." She jerked from his hold, lifted her chin, and abandoned her search for the ball, hurrying back to the meadow and her grandfathers.

Rafe grabbed at a small cottonwood branch, stripping it of its leaves, scowling as he watched her flee. Wasn't that just like a woman? She sharpened her tongue on his hide, then went running back to her daddies before he could so much as spit.

Her attitude pricked his pride. She all but ignored what had happened between them last night, and it stuck in his craw. He damn well knew he'd pleased her—a number of times, in fact. She'd given him her virginity, then left his bed with nary a howdy-do. Women weren't supposed to act that way. They were supposed to cling and moon on about love.

Instead, Maggie St. John dismissed him entirely and took to worrying about the Barlow Hill/Hotel Bliss/Andrew Montgomery trouble. When he finally chased her down, all she did was blush a little and chew him out for refusing to put his neck in a noose by stealing for her.

Damn, that woman was something else. She hadn't even given him a chance to tell her about his old-age fund. He'd had an idea how to help, but did she give him the chance to tell her? No. She yammered at him like a fishwife. "Well, you can just stew in your own juices a tad bit longer, Mad Maggie. Serves you right."

Rafe gave a pinecone at his feet a good strong kick, then turned on his heel with the intention of returning to the hotel. Maggie's scream stopped him in his tracks.

"Papa!"

→ 11 ←

The air echoed with Maggie's cry as she watched Papa Snake clutch at his chest and collapse. The grimace of pain plowing deep furrows in her grandfather's pasty complexion filled her heart with terror. Her own hands mimicked his actions when his meaty fingers curled into fists.

Fear fueled her movements as she rushed to his side and was joined by her other papas, each of them reaching for the flask tucked away in vest or trouser pockets. Down on her knees, she lifted his head into her lap.

Ben squatted beside her, lifting the small bottle filled with Bliss water to Snake's pale lips. "Get a good sip," he said, his voice controlled as he tipped the container.

Snake drank, then coughed, then took a second drink.

Maggie pulled a handkerchief from her pocket, and with shaking hands dabbed at the sweat on his brow. His skin was clammy, his breathing shallow. It made her so very afraid.

"What's wrong, Snake?" Lucky fanned the downed

man's face with his hat. "Did you get hold of a bad slice of bacon or something?"

"Gotta horse sitting on my chest," he panted out in reply.

It must be his heart, Maggie realized. *Oh, dear Lord, no.* She spied the foreign look of fear in her Papa Snake's eyes, and her own heart began to ache. Trembling with nerves and at a loss on how else to help him, she said, "Take some more water, Papa." Then she started to pray.

"We better move back and give him some air," Gus said.

Snake breathed a weak curse. "Hurts. Hurts bad."

Tears stung at Maggie's eyes, and she blinked hard, trying desperately to prevent them from falling. Snake hated it when she cried.

"What's wrong?" Rafe's voice cut across the pasture and Maggie lifted her head, gazing at him as though he were a lifeline. He ran toward them, his long arms and legs eating up the distance with gratifying speed.

Maggie remained silent while Gus repeated what had happened. Ben and Lucky appeared hesitant and uncertain. They glanced from Rafe to their fallen comrade, then back to Rafe once again.

"What do we do?" Ben asked, his voice tight.

Emotion squeezed Maggie's insides. This had never happened before. In emergencies, Papa Ben was captain of the family ship. Her papas always had the answers; they always led the way. This reversal of roles frightened Maggie even more.

Rafe knelt beside Snake, and with a gentleness in his expression new to Maggie, he laid his fingertips against her papa's neck and felt for a pulse. "Well, you'll be glad to know you're not dead yet, Snake MacKenzie. Your heart's still ticking."

"But somebody put my chest in a vise."

Rafe smiled gently. "Have you had spells like this before?"

"Yeah . . . couple of . . . times."

Maggie rolled back in shock. This was the first she'd heard of it.

"What did you do to get to feeling better?"

"Bliss water. Rest."

Ben cleared his throat. "We've dosed him good with water, Malone. I don't know what else . . ."

"Let's take him home." Rafe slipped one arm beneath Snake MacKenzie's shoulders, the other beneath his thighs, and hoisted the old man into his arms. Standing, he said, "Hang on there, Snake. I'll try to make this as smooth and as quick a trip as possible."

Dizzy with fear, Maggie lurched to her feet and followed after them, almost running to catch up with Rafe's long ground-eating strides. The other papas trailed behind, moving as fast as their aged legs would carry them. *Please, God*, she prayed. *Take care of Snake. Don't let him die. Please, God.*

She stayed behind Rafe but close enough to hear the low, gasping words her papa muttered. "Hate being old. Not much of a man anymore. I hurt."

"Hold on there, Snake. I'll have you to your bed in two wags of a hungry dog's tail."

A couple of minutes later, Snake spoke again. "Tired of fightin'. Hill. Now Montgomery. Makes me so damned tired. Sometimes I wonder if I should . . ." He gasped in pain and rasped, "Quit."

"No," Maggie moaned softly. He couldn't quit. Snake never quit at anything. He couldn't start now! She saw Rafe's arms squeeze her papa tighter.

Rafe glanced at her, his eyes saying something. A question? A warning? He smiled reassuringly, winked, then said, "Hell, no, you can't quit. Maggie needs you. You have work yet ahead of you, and you're the only one mean enough to do it. She needs your protection."

"From . . . what?" Snake opened tired eyes dull with pain.

"Not from what. From who. Your Maggie needs protection from me, Snake MacKenzie. Remember what you've warned me against these past weeks? Remember your promises? Well, you gotta be around to keep them. I touched her, Snake."

"Rafe!" Maggie yanked on his shirt. "What are you doing? Are you trying to kill him?"

He ignored her, continuing in a savoring tone, "I made about as free with my hands as a man possibly can."

"You mean . . . ?" Snake rasped, attempting to lift a feeble hand.

"Yep."

Seconds passed like minutes, then life sparked in the old pirate's eyes. "I'm gonna kill you."

Maggie heard the renewed strength in Papa Snake's voice, and her mouth dropped open in surprise. Now she understood Rafe's wink.

Rafe met Snake's gaze and nodded. "I reckon you need to try. But first you'll have to get well, old man. I don't fight invalid old quitters. If you want to make me pay for taking your granddaughter's innocence, you have to live through this first."

Snake blew a harsh breath filled with pain. "Reckon I'll do it then, Malone. I'm gonna. cut your nuts off and serve them to you for supper."

A wide smile broke across Maggie's face. Now she knew for certain Papa Snake would be all right.

Rafe sat sprawled on the horsehair sofa in the hotel's parlor, his legs outstretched and his arms crossed over his chest. Although he presented a picture of total relaxation, inside he was strung tighter than a two-dollar fiddle. The doctor was in with Snake MacKenzie.

Maggie and her grandfathers proved less successful than he in hiding their anxiety. Maggie about wore a path in the floorboard varnish. Gus and Lucky played a vicious, almost violent game of chess, while Ben stood staring out the window toward the lake, his fingers drumming against the glass over and over and over. Rafe thought Barlow Hill had shown admirable perception when, after one look at the pirates' tense expressions, he had declared his intention to spend the rest of the afternoon with the carpenters and laborers camped at the building site on the other side of the lake.

Maggie heaved a sigh, catching Rafe's attention. The poor thing looked so darned pitiful that his arms ached to hold her. The rest of his body just plain ached. He'd made the normally four-hour trip into the nearest town and back to fetch the doctor in a little under three. The hard ride had him yearning for a mud bath, but he wasn't going anywhere until he heard what the physician had to say about his patient.

Finally, the squeak of a hinge from above and the heavy thud of footsteps on the stairs announced that the doctor had finished his examination. Rafe stood as Gus and Lucky turned away from their game. Ben allowed his hand to drop to his side. Maggie steepled her hands over her mouth, wobbling on her feet until Rafe took her elbow and offered his support.

Dr. Terence Moore trudged into the parlor, his head tilted to one side as he massaged his neck. "The patient is resting well, you'll be pleased to know. Based on his description of his symptoms, I believe it was a seizure of his heart. I take it as a good sign he made it this long following his spell. If he survives the night, I expect he'll live."

Maggie swayed against Rafe. Ben turned away from the window, faced the doctor, and asked, "What do we do to help him?"

"Pray," replied the doctor. "That and continue the doses of that water of yours. I am uncertain how it benefits the body, but it obviously doesn't seem to hurt. I'll be the first to admit the science of medicine has plenty left to learn."

"And tomorrow?" Maggie asked, her voice thready.

"When he wakes up tomorrow, how should we minister to him?"

Dr. Moore offered her a kind smile. "You must make him stay in bed for at least two weeks. After that, he can resume his activities on a limited basis. He should not be subjected to any strains, anxieties, or tensions—the least little upset could kill him, I'm afraid."

Lucky folded his arms. "That means the dog Barlow Hill can't even walk upstairs."

"The cur."

"The mongrel."

"The mutt," Rafe added, unconsciously filling in for Snake. He was worried. Had he done the wrong thing by telling the pirate about him and Maggie? Had he caused even greater damage to the man's health?

The doctor continued, "Your friend did illustrate a keen will to live, however, and that is the best possible medicine for him."

Rafe blew a long breath, grateful to have that concern dismissed. He realized his grip on Maggie's elbow was tighter than necessary and he forced his hand to relax. Not that she noticed. He wasn't sure she even knew where she was. Shoot, she hadn't been this upset when she damn near died in that cenote. He hoped Snake MacKenzie realized how lucky he was to be loved by this woman.

"Can we see him?" she asked.

The doctor nodded. "One at a time. Someone should be with him all night."

Maggie gave Ben a pleading look. He smiled gently at her and nodded. She flew from the parlor and up the stairs as Ben announced, "We will take three-hour watches. Malone, since you rode for Dr. Moore here, you are excused from duty."

Rafe had no intention of skipping his turn, but he wouldn't argue about it now. He listened without speaking as the pirates bombarded the doctor with questions about Snake's condition, and upon exhausting that topic moved on to their own aches and ailments. When the doctor declared his intention to conduct examinations on them all, Rafe excused himself and headed for the bathhouse, detouring by the kitchen to grab a bottle of cider and swipe one of Snake's Havanas.

Inside the three-walled structure, he lit the cigar, stripped off his clothes, and eased into the warm mud with a heartfelt sigh. Soothing heat seeped into his muscles, relaxing the knots created by tension and toil. Finding a seat on the submerged ledge, he rested his head against the log wall behind him and closed his eyes. Memories of the day's events stole through his mind in a riot of color and emotion.

He felt pretty good about Snake MacKenzie's chances. Twice in his life he'd seen a man die of heart seizures, and both of them died within an hour of the attack. Snake was simply too tough an old coot to kick up his heels without making Rafe pay for his trifling with Maggie.

Clearing his mind of all thought, Rafe drifted into a comfortably hazy half-sleep as his body recharged. He smoked the cigar and took occasional pulls on the bottle, the tangy-sweet cider a sensual compliment to the tobacco.

The voice sneaked up on him like a dream. "How do you feel, Rafe?" Maggie asked.

He cocked open one eye. She stood framed by shadow just inside the door, appearing weary and worried and still in need of that hug. Rafe's lips curled in a rueful grin. Somehow he didn't think she'd appreciate his obliging her at this particular moment. He removed the Havana from his mouth. "How do I feel?" he repeated, closing his eyes. "I reckon that happy as a pig in slop is the most appropriate description, under the circumstances."

His hearing keen, he heard her move closer.

"I came here to thank you for your assistance today," Maggie said. "Carrying Papa Snake home. Riding for the doctor. I don't know what we'd have done without you."

Rafe thought he'd earned a moment of self-righteousness. "So Gentleman Rafe Malone helped you after all. Guess you jumped the gun by haranguing me this morning." She winced and he immediately wished he'd kept his mouth shut. "Forget I said that. Let me start over. You're welcome, Maggie. I was happy to be of help."

She moved to the edge of the mud bath and sat, then began to unlace her shoes. Rafe tried to ignore the erotic pictures that flashed in his mind at the innocent exposure of a bit of ankle. He swallowed hard. "You must be tired."

"I have had an eventful twenty-four hours."

She rolled down her stockings and plopped her bare feet into the mud bath, teasingly close to his thighs. Rafe eyed the expanse of bare leg in front of him and couldn't help but ask, "You want to join me, sweetheart? I'll scoot over and make room. Or better yet, you can sit in my lap."

"You are wicked, Malone."

"That's why you like me so much."

She smiled then, the first one he'd seen on her face all day. It made Rafe feel surprisingly good. "You know what, Miss Maggie? I think you lied to me. I think you were feeling a bit bashful this morning."

She looked out toward the lake and shrugged. "Maybe."

"You don't feel that way now, though."

In the process of lifting her feet from the mud and wiggling her toes, she froze. A myriad of emotions played across her face before she plopped her feet back into the bath. "Today's events make that all seem silly."

"Not silly, Maggie. Just normal." Rafe ground out

his cigar on the planks beside the bath. "I was sorry you weren't with me when I woke up this morning."

She turned her face away, but he could still see the blush staining her cheeks.

Smiling, he spoke in a low, sincere tone. "It was a fine night we passed together, Mary. The finest in my memory."

"Can we change the subject, please?"

"All right. What is it you want to talk about?"

"Not what. Who. I want to talk about Andrew Montgomery. I want to ask you one more time. I need your help, Rafe. We all need your help. Please, tell me what it would take to convince you to bring us my grandfathers' treasure?"

Rafe cracked a laugh that was anything but amused. "Let's see, to convince me to steal for you in Texas, I reckon you'd have to lasso the moon and hogtie it to the sun."

"But, Rafe—"

"I gave my word, Maggie," he said flatly. "It's the one thing nobody can take away from me; I'd have to give it away. I'm not about to do that. I'm not going back on my word."

"But that makes no sense!" She threw out her hands, palms up. "You're a thief, you steal from people. Why would breaking your word bother you so much?"

"Why?" Rage at the question flared like a match to dry grass. Rafe shoved to his feet and climbed from the bath, heedless of his nakedness. "You know what happens when people break their word? Women die on battlefields, that's what. Bloody, ugly, needless deaths. And smart men become fools who hide from the truth. Fools ready to hang an innocent man rather than face their own failings."

"What are you talking about?"

"I'm talking about honor. I'm talking about who a man is in here." He struck his chest with his fist. "About the consequences possible when a man betrays himself. I've been on both sides of it, Maggie. I've felt a noose around my neck because another man broke his word. And I . . ."

He couldn't say it. He couldn't force the words through his throat.

"You what, Rafe? You broke your word to someone? You did it for them, but you won't do it for me? I'm good enough to bed, but not good enough to cause you to bend your precious honor?"

"Damn you, Maggie St. John! It's not like that at all." He raked his fingers through his hair. "You want to know? You want to hear the gory details? Fine. I'll tell you."

Rafe braced his hands on his hips and loomed over her. "Yeah, I broke my word. To the very same man you want me to betray now. Luke Prescott. And the last time I went back on my word to Luke, people died. Because of me and my broken promise, a very lovely, very special woman and her two innocent children now lie in their graves. It was my fault, Maggie." He thumped his chest with his finger. "My fault."

"Oh, Rafe."

He whirled around, unwilling to see what must be in her expression. Disgust, revulsion, loathing, perhaps. Heaven knows, he'd seen them all and more. For years he'd seen them in his own eyes every time he looked into the mirror, never leaving until Luke Prescott had tracked him into the east Texas canebreaks and offered him the opportunity for redemption.

"I can't help you, Maggie. I'm sorry, but I cannot steal that treasure for you. But, there is something I can do to help. I have some wealth of my own put away, and you are welcome to use it to save Hotel Bliss. I had intended to tell you about it earlier, but I never had the chance. It's not all in cash, so it may take me a little time to convert it. I expect I can bring you somewhere around seventy thousand dollars. That should be enough to pay off Hill. I wouldn't think this property is worth much more than fifty."

"Wait a minute, Rafe. This is happening too fast. What do you mean—"

"I mean that I'm leaving first thing in the morning," he interrupted, impatient with the thought of doing any more explaining. He needed to get away from her, right now. He couldn't bear any more questions. He walked to the edge of the lake where the setting sun cast a glittering ray of diamonds upon the surface. "I'd be obliged if you'd go on back to the hotel now and leave me to finish my bath in peace."

He waded knee-deep into the water before stretching out into a dive. Right before his head submerged, he heard her say, "You offer to pay me? You would do that?"

The warm water surrounded him, washing away the residue of his mud bath. If only the memories Maggie St. John had stirred inside him could be washed away so easily. He'd rather do just about anything than think of that horrible time.

Captain Nicholas P. Callahan. Nick Callahan. Liar, murderer, fool. Half brother. Rafe would never forget the look on his face when he slipped the noose over Rafe's head in the shadow of the San Jacinto battlefield.

Rafe came up for air. He shook his head, flinging droplets of water from his eyes, slinging off the black thoughts. He wouldn't think of Nick, or of his wife Rosa, or of Luke's first wife, Rachel. The women he and his brother had failed. He'd think of Maggie and of his own efforts not to fail her now.

What was she thinking? Did she hate him now? Did she understand his reasoning at all?

His arms plowed the water as he considered the best way to turn his cache into cash. He reckoned that no matter how he went about it, the process would give him a few willies. A lot of his past was tied up in that stash. He'd learned some hard lessons early on in life, and for the longest time the valuables hidden away in that central Texas cave had symbolized his security.

But now he had the Lone Star and the partnership with Luke. He didn't need his old-age fund, not nearly as much as Maggie needed it.

Maggie. His own sweet Mary. What was the woman thinking?

He's making me a whore.

Maggie slumped onto the bench beside the mud bath, staring sightlessly at her mud-caked feet, emotions rolling through her like too much rum. She bedded down with him one day, and the next he offered her money. Just call her Maggie St. John, two-bit whore. All right, not two bits. A seventy-thousand-dollar whore. Tears overflowed her eyes and spilled down her cheeks.

You're not being fair, Maggie.

"I don't have to be fair. I've had a very difficult day. Two very difficult days. A difficult year, in fact." She swiped at the moisture on her cheeks and sighed. "Oh, Rafe."

He hadn't meant it the way it sounded to her; she knew that. He truly was trying to help. He might well have offered the money anyway had last night never happened. That's the kind of man Rafe Malone was. Generous and kind as well as adventurous.

Rafe didn't know his generosity fell way short of the outrageous purchase price Hill had set for the Lake Bliss property. Hill wanted 125,000 American dollars—more than many of the richest plantations in the republic were worth. More than Maggie and her family had a chance of raising without their treasure, even with Rafe's financial help.

And Rafe wasn't offering his professional skills.

That's what she needed but now realized she'd never get. Rafe Malone had his own monsters with which to deal.

Her throat tightened as she recalled the grief that had been etched across his face. How selfish she had been. She'd never even stopped to wonder what forces in his past had combined to make Rafe the man he was today. That wasn't well done of her. As the granddaughter of four very dear criminals, she should have known better. Most men didn't turn to a life of crime without a reason. Rafe's tirade of a moment ago had hinted at his.

Women die on battlefields, he'd said. What women? The woman with the children? Who were they to him? His own family? Maggie shuddered at the thought.

And smart men become fools who hide from the truth. Fools ready to hang an innocent man rather than face their own failings. Who was the fool who put such anguish in Rafe's eyes? Who had been hanged? Who had done the hanging? Was that the event that created Gentleman Rafe Malone? Was it a combination of events? Maggie realized she needed to know the answers. But Rafe was leaving. *Oh, God.*

Self-pity was a yellow-fanged monster peering over her shoulder.

Maggie fought the sentiment. She knew better than to let it win. Years of battling rheumatism had taught her the importance of standing tall against such pathetic behavior. Straightening her spine, she inhaled a deep breath and blinked away her tears. She'd learned the trick to winning was to always think forward. By planning for the future, one dwelled less in the pain of the present.

So, which of the problems currently on her plate did she wish to consider first. The loss of her home? Papa Snake's health? Barlow Hill's proposal? Andrew Montgomery's very existence? Why, she could go on this way for days.

A logical course would be to take each difficulty in order. That would mean first she'd need to deal with . . . Rafe's leaving.

Maybe another approach would be preferable after all.

Maggie rose from the bench and began to pace the floor. After a moment's thought, she decided to address the problem that had brought her down to the bathhouse tonight. Time was running out and she had to get her hands on that treasure.

So how could she go about it?

The solution wasn't difficult to find once she opened her mind to the possibility. In fact, now that she'd thought of it, she couldn't believe she hadn't considered it from the first. The sheer volume of troubles she faced must be at fault. She'd simply had too much to worry about and she hadn't been thinking straight. She'd let her grandfathers do her thinking for her, and she had believed what they had told her without question. Well, the papas' confession last night had taught her the fallacy in that course of action.

She knew she was a strong woman, an intelligent woman. It wasn't like her to look to men to solve her problems. "I'm through with that mistake," she muttered, kicking a small stone toward the lake. She didn't need a man to recover the treasure for her. She didn't need Rafe, or the papas, or any other man.

She would do it herself.

A little smile lifted the corners of her mouth. Who better than a prodigal daughter to infiltrate the enemy's castle? Who better than a simpering, helpless female to put Andrew Montgomery off his guard?

Staring blindly out at the lake, Maggie envisioned the scene. She'd fawn and flatter and flutter. Her dear daddy wouldn't know what hit him. She'd steal the treasure right out from underneath him slick as . . . Gentleman Rafe Malone.

At that thought, awareness of her surroundings drifted back to her. She heard the crickets chirping from the willows along the bank. She smelled the magnolia blossoms perfuming the evening breeze and smiled at the beauty of the sunset painting the western sky in a pallet of blues, purples, and mauves. It wasn't a fiery eventide tonight, but a gentle going. A peaceful good-bye.

Which brought her gaze to Rafe as he swam across Lake Bliss, his arms cutting the water with brisk, powerful strokes.

Maggie felt as if she'd been out there swimming with him. Putting her mind back to work after letting it wallow in emotion invigorated her, made her feel stronger. She could deal with the cards life had dealt her.

Tomorrow, Rafe Malone was leaving. Tonight, she would tell him good-bye.

Rafe swam until his muscles screamed for rest. He swam until his mind found at least a semblance of peace. By the time he turned and headed for shore, he'd managed to lock the majority of the memories plaguing him back into his mental strongbox. As he set his feet into the muddy bottom of Lake Bliss and waded toward the bathhouse and his clothes, he figured he had at least a fifty-fifty chance of sleeping without nightmares tonight.

Sometimes when he thought about the war, the bloodier recollections had a nasty habit of slipping the lock and playing havoc with his dreams.

The deepening shadows of twilight cast the bathhouse in a filmy half-light. Rafe grabbed one of the clean towels stored on wooden shelves along the north wall and swiped it across his wet chest.

"Rafe?"

The sound of her voice shivered across his skin, and he froze, every cell of his body leaping to full alert. He had assumed she would leave as he had asked. More the fool he for ever making any assumptions about Miss Mary Margaret St. John.

He wrapped the towel around his waist and turned to face her. His voice sounded rough. "I thought you'd gone back up to the hotel."

"No."

She moved from out of the shadows, and Rafe caught his breath at the picture she made. Her dress was the same one she'd worn all day, a serviceable midnight blue cotton with a scoop neck that skimmed the tops of her breasts and warmed her tawny skin. Her hair tumbled in enchanting disarray, and her Caribbean eyes were luminous with the remnants of tears.

Rafe cursed beneath his breath. He had made her cry, and he hated it. Maggie had enough troubles to deal with. She didn't deserve to have him add to them. Emotion churned deep in his belly. Sorrow and frustration. The craving to pull her into his arms and hold her. The need to comfort her in her pain. The black tide of hunger to drag her down to the floor and take her again and again until neither one of them had the energy to worry about anything anymore. "You'd better go now."

She clasped her hands in front of her. "I need to tell you something."

"Be quick about it. I'd just as soon not get caught down here like this by your grandfathers."

"They won't be down here. Lucky is sitting with Papa Snake for the evening shift, and Gus has already gone to bed so he can pull the middle-of-the-night stint. Ben got roped into a chess game with Barlow Hill. I've seen that man take an hour to make one move before. Why, one time—"

"Talk to me, woman."

"I am."

"Not about the skunk's chess game," he said,

rubbing the bridge of his nose between thumb and forefinger. "Tell me what you waited here to tell me."

"Oh, all right." Her gaze flickered toward him, then away again. "I was wrong to try and force you to do something that would cause you so much pain, and I wanted to apologize. Also, I wanted to thank you for all you've done for us—for me and my grandfathers. You are a good man, Rafe Malone. The very best. And your magnanimous offer to provide the cash we need to buy Hotel Bliss is, well, I can't put into words how much it means to me. You'll have my undying gratitude."

Rafe harrumphed. He didn't want her gratitude. He wanted her to leave here, now, before he wanted her to stay so much he wouldn't let her go. "Fine. You've thanked me. You can skedaddle out of here."

Maggie took a step toward him. Rafe stifled the strange urge to take a step back. His nostrils flared as he caught her scent, soft and sweet and damned alluring. Beneath the towel he went hard as a hammer.

"I can't," she replied, her feet carrying her in front of him. "I can't leave until I've given you a proper good-bye."

Maggie reached up and pulled his head down to hers. She kissed him with a tender passion that coiled around his heart like a song. Finally she stepped away, and Rafe knew a deep sense of loss.

A wistful smile accompanied her words. "It was a right fine adventure, one I'll always remember. Good-bye, Gentleman Rafe Malone."

The words of farewell lashed him like a whip, and Rafe realized he wasn't prepared to hear them. Hell. The adventure wasn't over. Nothing was ended. In fact, he felt plumb full of adventure just waiting to explode.

It happened when she turned her back to him and took a step toward the door. He gripped her shoulder, whirled her around, and allowed his frustration to sound in his voice. "Don't you know what you do to me? Dammit, woman, you started this. And now, by God, I want to finish it."

He jerked her against him. His mouth swooped down on hers, hungry and desperate. With the last trace of his control he wished she would push him away. It was the only way he could force himself to stop.

But Maggie didn't push. Instead, her arms lifted, her fingers inching across his bare back. With a groan, he deepened the kiss. She met each thrust of his tongue, dug her nails into his back. The sweet sting literally brought him to his knees, and Rafe dragged her down with him.

He couldn't be the tender patient lover of the night before. The thrill of the adventure, thrill of Maggie St. John, thrummed in his veins and destroyed his composure. Rafe went wild, his hands stripping and ripping on the edge of violence until she lay as naked as he against him.

His restless fingers found her wet and hot and ready for him. But Rafe wanted her as mad as he, and so he battered her senses with his touch, his teeth, and the taste of his dark passion.

She writhed beneath the onslaught of his mouth against her breast. She bucked as he nipped the sensitive skin at the nape of her neck. She cried out as he laved his way down her belly and drank from the font of her sweetest honey.

Rafe couldn't think, could only feel as her hands dragged through his hair, her heels dug into his back. He heard the sob of his name on her lips as the first set of tremors racked her, adding fuel to the fire of his lust.

Rafe never let up. He asked for more, demanded more. He took her higher and faster and farther until the power of a second climax had her shaking like leaves in a gale.

Now. He had to have her now. He knelt between her thighs, gripped the sweat-slick skin of her buttocks, and lifted her. He drove himself deep into her welcoming heat and a groan slipped from his throat. "Mary."

He rode her hard, lost in the electric, sensual storm that raged inside his mind. But he wasn't in there alone. She was right there with him. He watched her eyes darken to deep-water blue as she plummeted over that hard-earned peak. As her muscles contracted around him, Rafe gave a wordless cry and emptied himself into her.

A proper good-bye.

The next morning, it was Maggie who woke up alone.

Rafe made the trip back to the Lone Star Ranch in a hard four days on horseback. He rode with the devil on his heels and his conscience perched on his shoulder, screaming in his ear with the passage of every mile. But despite all the mental haranguing, he couldn't bring himself to regret the nights spent with Mary Margaret St. John. In fact, he could hardly wait to get back to her.

Midafternoon of the fourth day, Rafe rode into Bastrop, stopping by the newspaper office just long enough to place an advertisement for the auction he intended to hold in nine days. He figured that would give him plenty of time to retrieve his cache of goods from their hiding place and categorize them in some semblance of order for the sale. That way he could make it back to Hotel Bliss in right around two weeks—not bad, if he said so himself.

He dropped by the Winning Ticket Ranch and ended up staying for supper. He entertained the Prescotts with stories about the trip and handed out the gifts he'd brought back for the children, an assortment of seashells, rocks, and other jungle prizes. To Luella, who so often suffered from rheumatism, Rafe presented a large bottle of Lake Bliss water. He soon had everyone laughing over his description of the dress-attacking iguana. Jason, especially, was mesmerized by the existence of such a creature.

"Sort of a cross between a horny-toad and a lizard, isn't he?" the boy observed as he gazed at the pen and ink drawing Rafe had attempted.

"Yeah," Rafe replied. Taking the opportunity to gig Jason about a recent prank, he added, "Except he's a bit too big to be putting down anybody's dress during the sermon in church."

Jason's complexion flushed as pink as the peach he was eating for dessert.

Rafe waited until the children were in bed to address his plan to liquidate his old-age stash. The announcement was met with a varied reaction. In the process of taking a draw on her pipe, Luella choked and coughed at Rafe's news. Luke crunched a lemon drop, his brows lowered with concern. Honor sipped her tea as her lips lifted in a smug, secretive smile.

Seeing it, Rafe grimaced. "Don't read more into this than what exists. All I'm doing is helping out some friends."

"That's a mighty big piece of help, Rafe," Luke observed. "You sure you know what you're doing?"

Rafe shrugged. "The stuff is just sitting there. To be truthful, I'll be glad to rid myself of the chore of keeping all those guns oiled."

"So you'll be a partner in the hotel with that handsome Ben Scovall?" Luella asked once she caught her breath.

"Well . . ." Rafe drawled. "Not exactly."

"He's giving them the money outright, Luella," Honor said, her knowing gaze never leaving Rafe's face.

Luke's stare cut from his wife to Rafe. "Is that true? You're giving the cash as a gift?"

Rafe nodded and Luke cursed, tapping the ashes off

the end of his cigar with more force than was necessary. "You bedded her, didn't you? Honor called it. We bet honors on naming the first filly out of Orange Blossom. Now I'll get stuck with another horse named after a flower. Son of a gun, Malone, couldn't you have kept your britches buttoned this once? I'll bet those pirate papas of hers had a fit."

Rafe didn't like having his private life made the source of bets, but he knew it was useless to protest. Hoping to lead their speculations in another direction, he said, "Actually, my actions helped to save Snake MacKenzie's life."

Luella gasped. "Snake? What happened to dear Snake?"

Rafe told them about the brigand's collapse and the doctor's diagnosis of a heart ailment.

Luella shook her pipe stem at Rafe. "I should go to Hotel Bliss. That sweet little Maggie will need help. Honor, you and the children can manage by yourselves for a time, can you not? Rafe, you will take me with you when you go back there? You are returning soon?"

"Here's your hat, what's the hurry," he replied dryly.

Luke appeared puzzled. "Why would you think you should go to Lake Bliss, Luella? You hardly know these people."

"That's the point, dear." Honor tucked her arm through her husband's. "Luella and Miss St. John's guardians are all of an age."

"Oh," Luke said, the light obviously dawning. When it came to flirting, Luella Best could teach most of the women in Texas how the cow ate the cabbage.

Rafe grinned. "If you can be ready to leave ten days from today, I'll be happy to escort you, Luella. I'm sure Maggie will enjoy having another woman around the place, and you will certainly find the mud baths to your liking."

"I don't know if I want her to go," Honor said with exaggerated concern. "She might not want to come back."

"Oh, of course I'll come back," the older woman said, clucking her tongue. "Gentlemen friends add spice to an old girl's life, it's true. But I can't leave my grandbabies for long, you know. I'd purely pine away from loneliness."

Rafe took his leave a short time later and arrived home shortly after dark. After a brief discussion with his foreman, he headed for bed. It felt good to be back at the Lone Star; his back all but giggled when it settled down into his own mattress to sleep. But as one day passed and then two, he was discomfited to discover how life around the Lone Star Ranch had changed. Where before he had enjoyed working mostly in solitude, now Rafe was lonely. To realize he missed a quartet of crusty corsairs made Rafe shake his head in wonder. However, the depths to which he yearned for Maggie came as no real surprise at all.

Shortly after noon on the fourth day following his return to the Lone Star, Rafe completed his inventory of guns and other assets in his cache. He heated leftover stew for his noon meal and had just poured the steaming mixture into a bowl when he heard the thundering thuds of a horse approaching fast.

"Honor must have sent one of the boys over to help," he said to himself. Lifting the bowl, he carried it toward the door, pausing to spoon a bite or two into his mouth along the way. Treasure sorting made a man hungry.

He walked out onto the porch just as the rider halted his mount beside the hitching post. To Rafe's surprise, it wasn't Micah or Jason Best come to help, but another person entirely. "Ben Scovall!"

The pirate's first words were enough to turn Rafe's appetite to dust. "It's Mary Margaret," Ben said. "I fear she has gone off and done something stupid."

Rafe went cold. Had she gone and married that son

of a bitch Hill after all? "What happened? Is it . . . Hill?"

"The worm? No, he's still hanging on at the hotel, lording his power over us all. Excluding Mary Margaret, that is. She's run off."

Before Rafe could ask another question, the old man swung wearily from the saddle. When his heels hit the ground, he nearly doubled over coughing. Rafe helped him inside, then quickly poured a cup of water. "Here. Drink this. I'll care for your horse while you catch your breath. Then you can tell me all about it."

"She wrote you a letter. It's in my saddlebags."

Rafe led Ben's horse to the barn and with quick, efficient movements, saw to its needs. He grabbed the bags and headed for the cabin, but halfway there his curiosity got the better of him. He untied the lace and tossed back the flap. A folded sheet of paper lay on top.

Bad news. His gut told him so. Rafe's heart beat double time, and his mouth went dry as a west Texas July. Slowly, he removed the sheet, then slung the saddlebags over his shoulder. Paper crinkled as he unfolded it. His eyes scanned the page and rage kindled inside him. Damn fool woman.

He stomped toward the house, waving the letter like a flag. "What the hell is this, Ben? Thanks but no thanks? Keep your money. You aren't rich enough to help? No need to come back to Hotel Bliss?" He threw the bags on the floor beside the chair where the old pirate captain sat. "I'm willing to hand over my life's savings, and she doesn't want it?"

"I read the letter. That's not what she said."

"Not in those exact words, maybe, but that's the gist of it." Rafe yanked a chair back from the kitchen table, flipped it around, and straddled it. Tossing the paper down onto the table, he asked, "What's this all about? What has she up and done?"

Sighing wearily, Ben raked his fingers through his

snow white hair. "She told us about your offer. Before I go any further, allow me to express my appreciation for your generosity. It was more than kind."

"But it wasn't enough?"

"Hill's selling price is one hundred twenty-five thousand American dollars."

Rafe's mouth dropped open in shock. "That's crazy! That property isn't worth half that much. What is he thinking?"

"He never intended to sell us back the land. Knowing what our treasure was worth, we manipulated him into making the offer. Anything less and he would have balked."

"But a hundred twenty-five thousand?" Rafe pushed to his feet and began to pace. "That's robbery! And I should know!"

Ben Scovall shrugged. "The money meant little to us. Mary Margaret is all that matters, and now she's in trouble. We're not a hundred percent sure, but we think she's gone to Triumph."

"Montgomery's plantation. Isn't that what you'd predicted she would do?"

"I thought she'd reconcile with him. It never occurred to me that she'd try and steal back our treasure."

Rafe froze midstep. "Excuse me? What did you say?"

"She intends to do the stealing herself. She left the same day you did. We didn't discover her note until the next morning. She asked me to bring this letter to you, and she asked Gus to watch closely over Snake."

"And Lucky?"

"She said she knew we'd go after her, but someone had to stay with Snake. She figured Gus needed the rest following the Caribbean trip, so that left Lucky for the task. He and I rode together as far as Huntsville. We missed her by less than a day. She caught the coach north to Nacogdoches. Lucky headed after her while I came here."

"And Triumph Plantation lies a day's ride from Nacogdoches." Rafe thought it over a few minutes, then said, "Maybe she's just going to visit with him. Maybe this has nothing to do with the treasure."

"That's not what she said in her note."

"Damn." Rafe resumed his pacing. "But it's not a sure thing Montgomery will catch her. Your granddaughter is smart; she might just outwit him."

"But what if she doesn't?"

"Tell me what he'd likely do if he caught her red-handed."

"Mary Margaret has his eyes. When he looks at her, he will see her mother. Everywhere but the eyes, that is."

"Will that help or hurt?"

Ben Scovall sighed. "He loved Abigail. Heart and soul. Then he hated her just as much. As far as I know, he has not laid eyes on Maggie since before she went away to school. She has matured during those years, and she now looks exactly like the woman who sliced out Andrew's heart. I have no guess as to how he'll react once he sees her. Except, if he were to catch her in the act, I fear it would bring back ugly memories." Ben paused and cleared his throat. "Malone, I need to ask a favor of you."

Rafe rubbed his jaw with the palm of his hand. "You want me to go after her."

"Yes. Gus felt certain you would."

"Gus is an intelligent man. Tell me everything you know about Montgomery."

They spent the next twenty minutes cussing and discussing Maggie's father and developing a plan to save her from herself. "I'll leave this afternoon," Rafe said. "I'll write a letter and you can take it over to Luke's for me. He'll help you do what's needed to handle the auction. I don't see a need for you to rush back to Lake Bliss once that's taken care of. Stay a few days either here or with the Prescotts and rest up a bit. Luella will be tickled to have the company."

Ben drew himself up tall. "I do not require rest. I could travel with you today if need be."

"I know, but you'll be more help to me here in Bastrop dealing with the auction. Besides, I'm liable to catch up with Lucky somewhere along the way."

"Try Gallagher's Tavern and Travelers Inn," Ben suggested, giving in gracefully in the face of Rafe's argument. "It's a coach stop a day this side of Nacogdoches. They'll be able to tell you if either Mary Margaret or Lucky has been through that way."

"Gallagher's? I know the place well. I once hid behind the bar when the posse chasing me decided to drown their frustration in some of John Gallagher's Irish."

"He didn't turn you in?"

"John Gallagher? Heavens, no. He liked me. He said my gift for blarney was the finest he'd seen this side of the Emerald Isle itself. I've passed some mighty fine hours at that tavern. Mighty fine."

"I'll tell you what, Malone." Ben reached into his pocket and pulled out a Spanish gold coin. "Find my Mary Margaret and bring her home safe and sound, and a bottle of Gallagher's best is on me."

"Now that's an offer I can't refuse. I'll do my best, Ben." Rafe tucked the coin into his shirt pocket. "You have my word on it."

→ 12 ←

Dawn painted a blush across the east Texas sky as Maggie sat beside the window watching the day come alive. The soreness in her joints had kept her awake a good portion of the night, and now she grimaced with pain as she lifted her arm and pushed a frilly yellow curtain farther back. The faintest of smiles touched her lips as she watched a big yellow dog chase a frog across the yard in front of Gallagher's Tavern and Travelers Inn.

The inn's door opened and a pair of young boys spilled out onto the porch. With shouts of laughter they launched themselves after the animals, and for the next few minutes devoted themselves to running off some of the high spirits a good night's sleep and hearty breakfast could create in two little boys.

Maggie wanted desperately to run and play with them. Instead she bided her time here in the small bedroom built onto the inn's summer kitchen which, like at Lake Bliss, was a separate structure from the inn's main building. Her room was not one the inn's current proprietor, Mrs. Craig, ordinarily rented. But upon witnessing the difficulty Maggie experienced while climbing the stairs to the guest rooms, Mrs. Craig had clucked her tongue with concern and shown Maggie down the hill to this cozy little place.

The spell had come on slowly. In hindsight, Maggie acknowledged she'd ignored signs of it before leaving Lake Bliss. The stiffness in her joints. The heat in her knees, ankles, and even her toes. Still, it hadn't been until she climbed down from the stagecoach at Gallagher's after three days of constant travel that she realized just what she was facing. A full-fledged rheumatic attack. The challenge had returned with a vengeance.

And she had only one bottle of Bliss water packed away in her baggage.

Knowing what to expect, Maggie had done what she could to prepare for the onslaught. Mrs. Craig had been a godsend, checking on her periodically throughout the days. Although younger and certainly more sprightly, she reminded Maggie of Luella Best in a number of ways. Maggie liked that. For some reason, it made her feel closer to Rafe.

Maggie blinked back the tears that flooded her eyes at the thought. Funny how she could lie in bed tormented by waves of racking pain, and she never cried a drop. But all she had to do was think Rafe's name and the waterworks commenced. "You're pitiful, Maggie St. John. Purely pitiful."

She was also getting tired.

Turning away from the window, she eyed the bed. It seemed so very far away.

A knock sounded on the door. "Magpie? Are you awake?" Lucky's muffled voice called.

He had arrived yesterday, and Maggie had to admit she'd been happy to see him. She'd known from the start that at least one of the papas would come after her, but she had fully expected to have tricked the treasure away from Andrew Montgomery by the time her grandfathers arrived. She hadn't planned on getting sick. "Come in, Papa."

Door hinges squeaked and Lucky stepped inside. He took one look at her and scrunched his face into the scowl that had struck fear into men across the seven seas. "What are you doing out of bed! You'll cause yourself harm walking around when you're in the shape you are in. Come now, girl, haven't you a lick of sense?"

Maggie smiled and asked softly, "Help me back to bed, Papa?"

A thread of fear entered Lucky's narrowing eyes, and Maggie silently cursed herself. One of her methods for fighting the illness was never to ask for help unless she truly needed it. She'd learned long ago that maintaining her independence in little ways made a big difference in how she felt about herself. Her grandfathers understood that, so when she'd requested Papa Lucky's assistance, she'd inadvertently caused him added worry. That only made her feel worse.

Lucky put his arm around her waist. "Lean on me, child."

"I'm not a child," she protested, because he would expect it.

"Then quit acting like one." He lowered his voice to a mutter as he escorted her back to bed. "Only brings one bottle of Bliss water with her. Won't stay in bed when she needs to. Frets herself into sickness."

"Now, Papa," Maggie said.

"It's the truth, Magpie. I know in my heart that worry brought on this spell. Ben was wrong. We never should have told you about Drew." He emptied the last of Maggie's bottle of Bliss water into a glass and held it out for her to take. "It's been too much for you. Losing the hotel, losing the treasure, almost losing Snake, then taking off on this fool's mission—it's little wonder you've stirred up the Old Devil."

Old Devil was the pirates' nickname for her rheumatism. Maggie couldn't argue with him. For one thing, she agreed that anxiety played a negative role in a person's health. Things simply didn't flow right when a person was tied up in knots. Second, Maggie didn't have the energy to argue. Her excursion to the window seemed to have sapped the energy right out of her bones even as it fed the flames in her joints. "I think I'll sleep some more, Papa."

"That's a good idea, but I want you to drink your water first." Lucky supported her back while she took the tonic. When she emptied the glass, he lay her gently upon the mattress and tucked the covers up around her chin. She gritted her teeth against the groans that moving wrenched out of her.

Hovering, Lucky sighed. "I need to tell you something, sweetheart. I've spoken with Mrs. Craig. She's agreed to let you stay here as long as we need. She's promised to keep an eye on you for me while I'm gone."

The feverish feeling that accompanied particularly bad attacks swept over her, and Maggie had to force her eyes open. "Gone?"

Lucky nodded. "You just drank the last of your bottle of Bliss water. If I leave today, I should be able to get back with a new supply before you empty the bottles I brought along."

"But you shouldn't leave so soon," Maggie protested weakly. "You rode too hard and fast getting here. You should rest."

"You're a fine one to talk, missy." Lucky leaned down and kissed her brow. "I'll be fine. I'll rest better when I know you're on the mend. But I need you to promise me you'll quit fretting yourself to death. Otherwise, I'm liable to worry myself into a sickbed, too."

Maggie nodded. It wasn't a difficult promise to make. She hardly had the gumption to even think, much less worry. With each minute that passed her strength slowly ebbed, sapped by the influenza-type ache settling into her bones.

"Rest now, Magpie. I'll be back quick as a rumor,

and once we get you watered up, we'll kick the Old Devil's butt all the way to hell."

Maggie hummed a sigh in response, then sank into the dark, swirling vortex of pain-haunted sleep.

Rafe spent the first day of the ride cussing Maggie's foolishness. He passed the second day blaming the pirates for not teaching her better. The rest of the trip he chewed out himself for being stupid enough to spend days in the saddle to rescue a woman who would likely do her best to kill him once he saved her.

But beneath all the chiding lay a bedrock of concern. Maggie intended to steal a fortune in gold and jewels from a man whose motives for doing the things he'd done remained suspect. She could end up getting herself hurt.

The summer afternoon was hot, still, and stifling as Rafe arrived at the shamrock-shaped wind chimes that marked the turnoff to Gallagher's Tavern and Travelers Inn. He eyed the dark cloud billowing in the western sky, noted the tinge of green that often meant hail, and was grateful he'd managed to reach his destination before the storm descended. Riding past the summer kitchen on his way up to the main building, he caught a whiff of cinnamon in the air and hoped he'd find a slab of peach cobbler on his dessert plate that evening. He knew from previous visits that Gallagher's cobbler was a treat not to be missed.

Rafe reined his horse to a halt at a hitching post in front of the inn. As he swung from the saddle, the front door opened and a cloud of dust billowed out onto the porch, followed by a woman wielding a broom. Rafe's lips tilted in a grin. The widow Craig was an old acquaintance of his. He'd lived in her Nacogdoches boardinghouse for a time a few years back. He tipped his hat to the robust woman and said, "Afternoon, Martha."

Her head snapped up. Slowly her eyes widened and a smile wreathed her face. "Gentleman Rafe Malone, you scoundrel! What brings you back to this neck of the woods? Are you running from the law again? Will you hide in my flour barrel like the last time?"

"It was an inspired hideout, you must admit. Fooled Luke Prescott but good."

"He walked right past you," she replied, chuckling. "So can I expect to see that handsome young man later today, too? Seems like the two of you always ran in a pair."

"Not this time. I'm here by myself. In fact, this time I'm the one doing the hunting instead of the other way around."

The widow Craig shook her head. "Not for the law, surely!"

"Nope, this is personal."

"Well, I want to hear all about it. You'd best go stable your horse first, though. It's fixing to come a toad-strangler. I'll have a drink waiting for you in the tavern. Do you still prefer cider to spirits?"

"Most of the time. But today I think I've earned a whiskey. Pour me one of Gallagher's Irish, would you?"

Ten minutes later, Rafe shut the barn door and hurried up toward the inn. A blast of wind whipped across the yard. Rafe made a grab for his hat as it threatened to blow off his head, while above him an upper-story shutter tore loose of its latch and banged against the wall.

He made it inside just as the first raindrops fell. Martha waited for him in the large room that opened off the entry hall. Rafe hung his hat on a wall hook, then took a seat on a stool beside a long, polished oak bar. They discussed changes at the inn since the last time he'd visited. She informed him of John Gallagher's recent death and passed along news of Gallagher's young son and married daughter. "Rowdy Payne and I are taking care of matters here at the inn until Katie comes home," she told him. "I've enjoyed the job. All the hustle and bustle keeps me young."

"Have you been busy?"

"Very. In fact, our rooms are booked up for tonight. You'll have to take one of the cots up in the attic."

Rafe sipped his whiskey. It burned a trail of fire down his throat. "Speaking of guests, I mentioned earlier that I'm looking for someone."

Martha set her own drink down on the bar and leaned forward. "What did he do? Rob someone? Kill someone? Did somebody dare to cross Gentleman Rafe Malone?"

"I reckon you could look at it that way if you wanted." Rafe swirled the amber liquid in his glass. "Actually, the person I'm looking for is a woman. A lady by the name of Maggie St. John. I doubt she'd be using an alias. She's tall for a woman, five foot six or seven. She has the prettiest blue-green eyes I've ever seen." He paused, trying to decide how best to represent her indescribable beauty.

"What do you want her for?"

"Her family sent me. She's on the verge of doing something really stupid and I need to—" He broke off abruptly when he looked up and saw the peculiar expression on the widow Craig's face. "Martha? Do you know something about her? Have you seen her?"

"Oh, I've seen her, all right. And I'm afraid you're wrong. That poor little sweetheart isn't on the verge of doing anything."

Rafe's heart all but stopped. *Dear God. I'm too late. Montgomery must have hurt her.* He forced words past the lump in his throat. "What do you know about Maggie?"

"She's here."

"Here? Now? At Gallagher's?" Rafe shoved to his feet. "Which room? What's the matter with her? Why did you say she's poor?"

Martha shook her head and snorted. "Maybe because she has you on her trail. Settle down, Rafe. I won't have you barging in on her. Not the way she's feeling now."

"She's hurt?"

"She's ill. Rheumatism. In a girl that age, don't that beat all?"

Rafe's heart pounded. She was sick? "That's all that's wrong? He didn't wound her or anything?"

"That's all!" Martha scoffed. "Well, I should think it's enough. And you will, too, once you see her. The poor thing is suffering."

"But she's not shot or anything." He needed to be clear on that.

"Of course not. Why would you say that? Who would hurt that sweet child. Certainly not her grandfather. Never in my borned days have I seen such a hard-looking man treat a woman with such gentle care. That scar around his neck is downright frightening."

Lucky had found her. Suddenly Rafe needed to sit down. His knees had gone weak and wobbly. He took a fortifying sip of his drink, then asked, "Is her grandfather with her now?"

"Oh, no. He left a few days ago. He's gone after her medicine, some special tonic water they've run out of. He said that's the only thing that'll make her better." Her brow crinkled in a worried frown as she added, "But to be honest, he seemed worried about whether the medicine would do the trick. He said when it gets this bad she really needs the mud baths, but that she couldn't tolerate the trip home in the shape she's in."

"The shape she's in?" Rafe repeated, his throat tight.

"She's in such awful pain, Rafe. But she won't let me give her any laudanum, just a little of the Irish now and again. I'm worried about her. Her grandfather asked me to watch over her until his return. I do hope he hurries, though."

"How long has she been here?"

"Going on eight or nine days, now."

"And she's been sick all that time?"

"Not as sick as she is now. It got much worse once we ran out of her medicinal water."

Bliss water. He remembered the bottle one of the pirates had stuck in his saddlebags before he left the hotel. Thank God he had never removed it.

Rafe needed to see her. Right then. "Which room is she in?"

"She's not in a room. I gave her Katie's room down at the kitchen. She couldn't climb the stairs in the shape she's in, and besides, it's much easier to heat water for her baths down there. Hot baths seem to help. In fact, I intended to fix one up for her just before you arrived. Rowdy has already hauled the water and put it to heating for me."

Before she finished speaking Rafe was moving toward the door. He would stop and grab the water on the way. "I'll take care of it, Martha. Thank you."

"Wait one minute, Rafe Malone. I'll do it. You cannot give that dear a bath. You're a man!"

"I'm glad you noticed. Don't worry, Martha. Maggie and I are close friends. I'll be a perfect gentleman, I promise. That's who I am, don't forget. Gentleman Rafe Malone." He lifted his hat from the hook and shoved it onto his head.

The widow hurried after him. "I don't know about this, Rafe. The thought of you bathing that poor sick girl just doesn't seem right."

Rafe paused at the top of the porch steps and glanced back over her shoulder. Martha Craig was all but wringing her hands in worry. "Don't fret, ma'am. Maggie won't mind."

"Well, if you're certain. Oh, and Rafe, check the Dutch oven. I mixed up an embrocation, hoping that might give her ease. I used my best brandy and butter in it, and my homemade rose-scented soap to offset the smell of the onions. She may want to apply it after her bath."

"Liniment," Rafe said, nodding. "That's good. I

have a recipe for horse liniment I sometimes use for my own aches."

Martha stared out across the yard toward the kitchen, then back at him. "I don't feel right about this, Rafe. How do you know she won't mind? Who is she to you?"

Rafe met her gaze and said simply, "She's my Mary."

Then he dashed out into the pouring rain.

Maggie lay in a haze of pain, uncertain what day it was and not entirely positive where she was. She drifted in and out of sleep, one state just as bad as the other. Awake, she had to deal with the fire burning her joints; asleep, the nightmares.

It was as if the rheumatism had a life and a mind of its own. An evil but intelligent creature, it refused her the rest her body required to battle its effects by filling her sleep with monsters both real and imagined. In her sleep, Maggie clashed with a fire-breathing Barlow Hill. She dueled an Andrew Montgomery whose sinister grin revealed teeth made of shards of ruby-colored glass. In her dreams, Maggie swam surrounded by slithering eels. She ran from rabid javelinas and wrestled hungry coyotes. She warred with the monsters all by herself.

She missed her papas. She needed them. She felt so alone. So very alone.

In that, Maggie knew, lay the danger. Fighting by herself, for only herself, gave strength to the enemy— the temptation to surrender. She wearied of waging the battle alone. She needed reinforcements. She was tired, so very tired.

The most dangerous monster of all, self-pity, sat poised and ready to pounce.

Maggie twisted her head back and forth on the pillow as her dreams receded. She needed help, but who could she turn to? Not the papas, not this time. Things were different now from when she'd fought the rheumatism as a girl. Years had passed and somewhere along the way she'd switched roles with her grandfathers. The men had become like her children and she their parent.

Ben and Snake, Gus and Lucky. For nearly all her life, they had been there for her whenever she'd needed them. They'd been her strength and her support. Her problem solvers. Now it was Maggie's turn to be that for them. They weren't strong anymore. They needed *her* to help *them* fight. They needed her strength.

Lying on the bed in the kitchen cabin at Gallagher's Tavern and Travelers Inn, Maggie looked deep inside herself for a little more grit. No matter how easy it would be to give up and allow self-pity to take control of her will, she knew she couldn't let it happen. She had to fight this cursed condition for her grandfathers' sakes. She had to beat this illness, defeat it and her own weakness of will, so she could stand strong against Andrew Montgomery and Barlow Hill and Papa Snake's heart trouble and Papa Ben's breathing problem, and all the rest.

But, oh, how she wished she had someone to lean on. Just for a little while. *This damsel in distress sure could use a hero to hold off the dragons just until she got her strength back.* Finally facing the challenge of full consciousness, Maggie muttered, "Where is a knight in shining armor when you need him?"

"Here I am," a cocky voice rumbled. "However, I wear my armor on the tarnished side. That shiny stuff attracts way too much attention when a man is trying to hide from his pursuers."

She must be worse off than she had thought. She imagined she'd heard Rafe's voice. With effort, she turned her head. A shape took form. A figure. She blinked once. Twice. *Oh, no. Now I'm hallucinating.*

Rafe Malone peered down at her, the concern in his deep green eyes at odds with his easy grin. "Well, Sleeping Beauty awakes. It's about time. I've reheated your bathwater twice, and that's a lot of work, you know."

"Rafe? Is that really you?"

"Yep. And I come bearing Bliss water." He slipped his arm beneath her shoulders and propped her up. "Open your mouth, Maggie. Take a big ol' sip."

He put a cup to her lips, and the familiar bitter taste filled her mouth. He made her drink until she could hold no more. Then Maggie closed her eyes once again and tried desperately to make sense of her thoughts. She was so confused. "How did you get here?"

"On my horse, of course." He winked.

She groaned as much from his wit as from the pain resulting from her effort to roll from her back onto her side.

"Stop that, love. I hate to hear that sound. Now, what do you want? What can I do to help you? Do you need to sit up? Are you hungry? Or do you want to take your bath first?"

"Why are you here?" *And why wasn't he wearing a shirt?*

He shrugged, and even in her condition, Maggie noted the ripple of muscles across his chest.

"I have to be somewhere," he said. "Considering it's pouring a gully-washer outside, I reckon beneath a roof is a good choice."

Maggie closed her eyes and tried to concentrate. "You left Lake Bliss."

"So did you."

"But I'm in east Texas. Your ranch is in the hill country."

"Yeah, and you owe me a new saddle for the one I've worn out chasing you down. But we'll settle all that once you're feeling up to snuff. C'mon, let's get you into the tub before I have to heat the water yet again. Martha says the hot baths help you."

Cool air kissed her skin as he whipped the covers off her. Maggie kept her eyes closed as she felt his fingers at the buttons of her cotton nightgown's scoop neckline. She thought she should probably protest his familiarity, but she didn't have the energy. Besides, his touch was gentle and tender and just how she imagined a knight errant's would feel.

"The mercantile must have run a sale on buttons when you sewed this gown," he grumbled. "You have enough of them, don't you think? Lift your hips, love, and I'll slip it out from under you."

"No," Maggie said. "I can't." Today her hips hurt worse than anything.

"No need to be shy." His fingers continued to work the buttons that ran the length of the gown. "Maybe that's not it, though. Is that where it hurts, Maggie? In your hips?"

She didn't want to snivel, but the sweet concern in his voice made it easier to confess the truth. "It hurts all over."

His hands froze and after a moment's pause, he said, "Well, maybe I should kiss it better, then. Everywhere it hurts. Medicinal purposes, you know."

Maggie opened her eyes. "Malone," she replied, the tiniest bit of starch in her voice. "How could you even think—" She broke off abruptly when she saw the teasing twinkle light his eyes.

"There. That sounds much better. I don't like whiny women."

He'd done it on purpose just to rile her. A smile flirted with the corners of her mouth as she settled back onto her pillow. Mentally bracing herself for the pitchforks in her joints, she lifted her hands and pushed his away. "I can do it."

"I know you can, Maggie." He reached out a finger and gently traced it across her forehead as if he were smoothing away the wrinkles. "You can do anything you put your mind to. I know that without a doubt. But let me help you here, all right? It's not like I'll be seeing anything I haven't seen before, and if it makes you feel better, I won't even look."

"Your word on it?"

"Aw, Maggie!"

"Aw, Rafe." She allowed her hands to fall back to her sides as weariness overcame her. She'd exhausted the little spate of energy Rafe's appearance had given her and didn't even have the gumption to be embarrassed by her nakedness. "Don't let me drown."

"You have my word on that." Rafe stripped the gown off her body, then carefully slipped one arm beneath her shoulders and the other beneath her thighs. "I don't want to hurt you. You tell me if I do."

She clamped her teeth against crying out as he lifted her from the bed. She'd already whined once, and she figured that should be her limit. Besides, being in his arms was almost like a healing balm itself. "If I could bottle this up, we could sell it at Hotel Bliss along with our water."

"What's that, love? Am I holding you wrong?"

"No. It's just right." *You're just right.* She lay her head against his shoulder and closed her eyes.

Rain drummed against the rooftop, punctuated by an occasional crack of lightning and boom of thunder. As he carried her from the bedroom into the kitchen, the scent of burning cedar drifted like ribbons on the air. Cedar and Rafe Malone. Maggie breathed deeply of the combined fragrances and sighed with more pleasure than pain.

"Fair warning, fair lady. It's time for the big dip. Yell if it's too hot, and I'll yank you out."

For all his talk of dipping and yanking, Rafe lowered her into the oval tin tub like the most fragile of fine crystal. She leaned her head back against the tub's hard rim. Seconds later Rafe tucked a folded towel between her and the metal lip, and Maggie smiled her thanks for that and more. The heat from the water seemed to soak into her swollen joints, soothing them and bringing her relief. Questions nagged at her mind, but the fatigue washing over her convinced her they could wait. Sleep beckoned and she surrendered to it, saying in a soft, drowsy voice, "Thank you, Malone. You're good medicine."

As Rafe lifted a poker to stir the smoldering logs in the fireplace, he realized his hand was shaking. Taking a quick inventory, he discovered the rest of him pretty much had the shivering fits, too.

Maggie hurt and it killed him to see her this way.

He'd about shed a shoe when he first got a good look at her. Pale as new milk and weak as a sick kitten. When she'd looked at him with those beautiful eyes grown dull and glassy with pain, Rafe had felt a stab of hurt in the general vicinity of his heart. She was such a strong woman, and to see her brought down like this just tore him apart. If he could have freed her from her suffering by taking it on himself he'd have done it fast as double-geared lightning.

He glanced back at the tub where she lay sleeping and wondered if too long a soak could adversely affect her condition. She'd been napping now for a good twenty minutes. He'd added hot water twice. Maybe he should try and wake her up. It would be just his luck to cause her harm when he was trying to help.

Lord knew she needed some help. He wished one of the pirates were here to answer some of the questions buzzing around his brain. He wanted to know how long spells like this one usually lasted. More than a week seemed like a hell of a long time. Also, was it normal for her to lose weight like she had? The poor thing was skin and bones. Why did she refuse the laudanum? Was there a medical reason, or was it Maggie's own stubbornness—something she had in abundance?

A little groan from the bathtub sent him hurrying to her side. Was she awake? No. Her eyes were still closed and she lay without moving. Rafe started to turn away when he spotted something that froze him in his tracks. A tear. A single tear had slipped from under her long lashes and was running down her cheek.

Maggie was crying in her sleep.

Rafe took it like cannonball to the gut. This strong, stubborn, doesn't-know-the-meaning-of-the-word-surrender female hurt so fiercely that she was crying in her sleep.

Rafe closed his eyes and gritted his teeth, his hands clenched at his sides. He felt helpless as a field mouse in a hawk's shadow. If he'd been a few days earlier, then he could have ridden to Lake Bliss for more water, instead of Lucky. He'd have made better time. He could have gotten the water back to her sooner. Damn it all, she needed relief.

And he needed to give it to her.

The significance of that thought washed over him. Never one to lie to himself, Rafe admitted that what he was feeling wasn't solely about Maggie's needs. He couldn't stand to see her hurting. He couldn't bear to see her cry. He needed to help her.

He loved her.

His eyes going wide, Rafe took a step backward. Good Lord. It was true. He'd gone and fallen in love with Mary Margaret St. John. Maggie with her hard head and harder-headed grandpas. Maggie with her crystal laugh and Caribbean eyes. Maggie with a curse on her body that sapped all the strength and joy and spirit from her being.

He loved her. The knowledge flowed like whiskey through his blood, warm and intoxicating. How had he gone so long without realizing it? Rafe wasn't a stranger to love. He'd been in love before, a number of times. He liked being in love.

But you've never been in love like this.

Rafe backed up until his knees hit a chair, and he sat down abruptly. He rubbed his palm across his jaw and considered the thought. Was it true? How could it be true? Take Elizabeth Perkins, for instance. He'd been in love with her. He'd courted her for months, even proposed marriage. Hadn't it hurt like a son of a bitch when she turned him down to marry another man? Hadn't he still been wallowing in misery almost a year later when she gave that other man a son?

Yes, but it was your pride that was hurting, not your heart.

Maggie had the power to rip his heart plumb in two.

Well, hell. It was true. What he felt for Maggie was bigger than anything he'd ever felt for any other woman. What he felt for her was greater than his feelings for all the other women who'd passed through his life combined.

In the bathtub Maggie stirred, and Rafe stood and crossed to the tub. As her eyes fluttered open, he smiled at her. "Hey, sweetheart. It's about time you woke up. I was beginning to fear Martha would come in and try to make prune pudding out of you for dessert."

Maggie gave a tired smile. "No, peach cobbler is on tonight's menu."

Rafe lifted her from the water, helped her dry herself with a towel, then gently laid her on a soft pallet he'd prepared before the fire.

"I want my clothes," she weakly demanded.

"I have some liniment I want to rub on you first. I think it might help."

"Not horse liniment," she said. "I've used that before. It doesn't do any good, and the stink doesn't wear off for days."

"This isn't horse liniment. It's something Martha fixed up for you. You'll like it. She used her rose-scented soap to make it." He brought the bowl over and knelt beside her.

"Onions," Maggie said weakly.

"Just a little bit. What I smell most is the brandy." He dipped his fingers in the thick, slick mixture and said, "Lie still and let me work this into your skin. Let me know if I rub too hard."

At first her muscles remained tense. "This embarrasses me," she admitted.

"Don't waste any energy on something as silly as that, honey. You need all your focus on getting well."

As he gently worked the ointment into her skin, Rafe distracted her with a story about Honor and Luke's girls. Slowly she relaxed, and soon he realized she'd drifted back into sleep.

But Rafe didn't stop his tender touches. His hands massaged her swollen joints, silently speaking of his sympathy, his admiration for her strength, his need to exorcise her pain.

His desire to act out his love for her in a million large and small ways each day.

"Aw, hell, darlin'." He cupped her swollen knee joint, absorbing its heat between his palms and fingers. He wished he were a good enough thief to steal this pain away from her. He'd give damn near anything to make her better. That's how a person felt when he was in love.

And God knows, he did love her. Passionately. Profoundly. Blissfully.

Bliss. Lake Bliss. Lake Bliss water. Good God, he was in trouble.

His hands fell away from her. Absently he used the towel to wipe them clean of greasy liniment. Then, with the gentlest of touches, he reached out and brushed away the teardrop that clung tenaciously to her cheek. Bliss water. The pirates had searched the world to find it for her. Bliss water helped save her from this misery.

How could he love her and not do everything within his power to spare her this pain? How could he love her and allow Lake Bliss to slip through her hands?

He couldn't. He wouldn't. So where did that leave him? He damn sure wouldn't let her marry Barlow Hill. While he could set up a scheme to obtain water for Maggie and her crew even if they didn't live at

Lake Bliss, he didn't see how he could duplicate the mud baths anywhere else. If she needed the mud baths when she got this sick, then she should have them. She would have them.

Rafe didn't have enough money to meet Hill's price for the hotel. He could try and secure a loan, but in cash-poor Texas he knew of no one who had the kind of funds he required readily available. Luke certainly didn't. His money was all tied up in the Winning Ticket Ranch.

Rafe inhaled a deep breath, then blew it out with a heavy sigh. His choices were limited. Real limited. A man couldn't beg upward of fifty thousand dollars in the short time they had left before Hill threw the pirates out of Hotel Bliss. Neither could he borrow it. That left only one option.

He had to steal it.

⇥ 13 ⇤

Rafe took a quick glance at Maggie, assuring himself she was in no danger of drowning in her sleep during this second bath of the evening, and crossed the room to the door. Pulling it open, he stared out into the rain.

Could he do it? After all that had happened in the past, could he break his word and steal the money Maggie needed? The question had haunted him for the past two hours. A man's word. A man's honor. What was it worth?

A lot, that was for sure. Damn near every horrible thing that had ever happened to him could be traced back to a man's lack of honor, either his own or someone else's.

A scene from the past flashed across his eyes. His father standing in the front parlor of their home, confessing his sins only when the truth—the two wives, the two young sons—stood face-to-face.

Rafe's thoughts leapt forward. Brothers reunited. Captain Nick Callahan of the Army of the Republic of Texas. Too selfish to keep his word and too cowardly to admit it. Blaming others for his own mistakes.

Where was the honor when he and his lies put the noose around his brother's neck? That memory led back to one Rafe had buried the deepest—the instance of his own broken word.

Luke, leaving home headed for the Alamo, hugged his children and kissed Rachel good-bye. Then, he held out his hand for Rafe to shake. "Watch over them for me, will you?" he asked.

"Sure, I will," Rafe replied. "You can count on it."

But two weeks later Nick Callahan had arrived and convinced Rafe to join up with the Texian army. Shortly afterward, rumors of the advancing Mexican army convinced Luke's adored wife to take her children and flee in the panic that became known as the Runaway Scrape. The three of them had died while trying to ford the Colorado River.

Because Rafe had broken his word and wasn't there to protect them.

Though he and Luke had never discussed it, Rafe knew it was the truth. Luke's family had died because Rafe had broken his word to Luke. A shudder raked Rafe's body. Here he was contemplating the dishonorable act all over again. Could he go through with it?

He turned his back to the rain and reentered the small cabin. His gaze sought and lingered on the woman asleep in the tub. A man's word was worth a lot, true. But Maggie St. John was worth a hell of a lot more. For her, he could do it. Anything was worth sparing her more pain. For Maggie, he would willingly sacrifice his honor.

"I'll do it."

Rafe smiled. Maggie's eyes fluttered open. Her gaze focused on his face. He was pleased to see that the strain in her eyes had eased a bit. "Feeling better? Has that Bliss water had time to go to work yet?"

She nodded. "I do feel better. The baths are a help. What will you do?"

"Wake you up," he lied. "I've been afraid you would get waterlogged if you stayed in the bath much longer. It's a good thing you woke on your own. Now I don't have to give the cold water splash a go."

She crossed her arms over her chest. "You were going to pour cold water on me?" she asked, her voice strong with affront.

Rafe made a show of scratching his cheek. "Well, no, probably not. You're a vindictive woman, Maggie. You'd have paid me back in a way I wouldn't have liked."

"Bet on it."

He flashed her his pirate's grin and said, "Now, let me warm up a towel and then I'll help you out of there."

"I'll do it myself." She sat up straight, her movements easier than Rafe had seen since his arrival.

"Let me help—"

"No." She shook her head. "Rafe, please. I'm feeling much better. I can do this myself."

"Are you sure? I don't want you swooning on me or anything."

She gave him a reproachful look. "You told me once before you didn't take me for the swooning kind. Have you changed your mind?"

"I don't guess so," he replied truthfully. Trusting her to know her own limits, he turned around and walked back to the fireplace. He lifted the poker and jabbed and prodded logs as he listened closely to the sounds of Maggie rising from her bath. He heard the splash of water and a slight footfall on the puncheon floor, and held his breath as he waited to detect the near-silent swish of the towel against her skin. At first groan, all bets were off.

But Maggie didn't groan. Instead, he heard her walk slowly into the bedroom. A minute later the bed ropes yawned, and he sneaked a look. Maggie had donned a demure white cotton gown. She sat on the bed with her hair draped over one shoulder, a silver-backed brush in her right hand.

Rafe caught her wince as she twisted her shoulders,

and he decided that was close enough to a groan to warrant his interruption. He stepped into the bedroom and approached the bed. Slipping in behind her on the mattress, he swiped the hairbrush from her hand before she could manage a protest.

"You have beautiful hair, Mary Margaret." The silky golden-red strands washed across his fingers, reminding him of gentle waters of the Caribbean island lagoon at sunset. He glided the brush through her hair, his strokes long and repetitive and tender. Emotion swelled in his chest, and Rafe felt compelled to voice the words that rumbled up from deep inside him. "It hurts me to see you hurting."

Her spine stiffened. "Don't, Rafe."

"Don't what? Don't feel for you? Or don't tell you how I feel?"

"Either one."

"Why not?"

"You'll distract me and I can't afford to be distracted. Standing up to you requires a lot of energy, and I simply don't have it right now. You'll run right over me."

"I won't run over you," he chided. "I'm not running anywhere, Maggie. I'm staying right here."

"That's what I'm afraid of."

Rafe's hands stilled on her hair. "Don't be afraid of me, Maggie. You don't ever need to fear me."

"Papa Ben must have told you where to look for me. Why are you here, Rafe?"

He didn't know how to answer her. He didn't want to cause her any more upset; it couldn't be good for her condition. But he didn't want to lie, either. He set the brush down on the night table beside the bed and divided her hair into three sections. After braiding it loosely, he fished in his pants pocket for a string, which he tied at the bottom of the braid. He stood, propped the pillows against the headboard, and eased her back against them.

Maggie watched him expectantly as he pulled a

chair close to the bed and took a seat. He took her hand, holding it gently, and studied her face. "You're awful peaked-looking, Maggie. Why don't we wait and discuss this when you're feeling better?"

"Tell me why you followed me."

Rafe shook his head slowly. The woman was laid out like a corpse, but still stubborn as a mule. He might as well put it all on the line or she'd get herself riled and to hurting again. "Ben believes you were headed to Triumph Plantation, but he doesn't think you intended to stage a reunion with your long-lost father. The pirates think you were out to steal the treasure. Were you?"

She didn't reply, just stared at him with her mouth firmed.

Rafe let go of her hand. He propped his feet on the end of the bed, leaned back in his chair, and folded his arms. "Of course, it's possible you only intended to have a chat with your father, to try and convince him to work out a deal with the buccaneers."

Maggie's eyes narrowed. "I wouldn't speak to that man if he were the last person on earth. I know Ben felt he had to offer me the choice to acknowledge the man whose seed gave me life—I won't call him a father, and I wish you wouldn't either—but Ben should have known me better. I won't kowtow to Montgomery. Him and his cryptic notes and contemptible demands. My papas need me, and they need Lake Bliss. You were there, Rafe. You saw Papa Snake. He might have died without a dose of Bliss water."

Ah, Maggie. I see how it is with you. That's all it takes. "So, you're admitting that when you left Lake Bliss you intended to steal the treasure from your, uh, from Montgomery?"

"It's not stealing, it's just taking back. Did you leave your ranch thinking you were going to stop me?"

He allowed the barest hint of his frustration to filter

into his voice as he said, "From the looks of things, Maggie, you've already been stopped, and I had nothing to do with it."

"I've been delayed, that's all."

"Uh-huh."

"I'll be back on my feet in no time. And I'll get the treasure, you just wait and see."

Rafe set his feet on the floor with a thud. "Since you seem to be feeling well enough to argue, why don't we talk about that? How did you plan to do it? Waltz right into your father's house and ask him where he stashed the treasure? And what were you going to do once you had it in your hot little fingers? Slip it into your handbag and carry it off? How much would a hundred twenty-five thousand dollars in gold weigh, anyway?"

"You are so-o-o funny, Malone," she drawled, folding her arms across her bosom.

Rafe noted the movement and was distracted enough to flash a little smile. It was the first time he'd seen her move naturally since he'd arrived at Gallagher's. Rafe stood and leaned over her. He lowered his head and kissed her cheek. "Quit your fretting, Maggie-mine. It's bad for you."

Straightening, he added in a casual tone, "I bet you're hungry. Martha left a soup on, or if you'd rather, we could dig into that fresh peach cobbler."

As he turned and headed for the outer room, her breathless voice brought him to a halt. "Rafe, I won't let you stop me."

He shot her a look over his shoulder. Despite her renewed vigor, the effects of her illness showed in the lingering brackets of pain visible around her mouth and eyes. His annoyance drained away. The words to tell her of his decision to steal the treasure hovered on the tip of his tongue. But for some strange reason, he couldn't force them out, not even in the face of the suffering etched across her face. Well, hell. He had to tell her something to ease her mind, but what?

He sucked a deep breath into his lungs, then slowly expelled it. "I know how important saving Hotel Bliss is to you, Maggie. I understand it now better than ever. Listen to what I tell you. I won't allow you to lose it, all right? One way or another, we will beat Barlow Hill at his own game."

"You won't try to stop me from going to Triumph?"

"I give you my promise that you won't need to steal the treasure from Montgomery."

Maggie's eyes slowly blinked. "You promise? You're giving me your word?"

"Yeah." He turned away.

Her words surrounded him like a soft mist. "Then I can believe it. I don't need to worry anymore. I know you value your word more than anything."

He exited the room without speaking. It would have been kinder for her just to shoot him, he thought as he ladled hot soup into a bowl for her. Wasn't that just like a woman to find a man's most vulnerable spot and poke at it?

Of course, she hadn't done it on purpose. She didn't know she was as wrong as she could be. He had found something worth a helluva lot more than his word.

Rafe had found Maggie.

When Maggie awoke the following morning, it took her a moment or two to figure out what was different. Her joints still protested any movement; little change there. The sky was bright, but that wasn't it, either. The rain had ended and the clouds cleared off shortly before sunset last night. She pulled the pillow lying next to her on the bed over her face to shield her eyes from the rays of sunshine beaming through the window. That's when she realized what it was.

The scent. His scent. He'd slept in the bed with her last night. For some reason that seemed even more intimate than the occasions when they had made love.

Before Maggie could decide how she felt about that, Rafe's voice filtered into the room through the partially opened window. "Look what the coyote dragged in," he drawled nastily.

His tone of voice was enough to cause Maggie to drag herself from the bed. She'd never heard Rafe speak with such loathing. Who could he be talking to? Gritting her teeth, she shuffled her way toward the rocker that sat beside the window. Sinking into it, she gazed outside.

A stranger sat atop a bay mare, both hands resting casually on the saddle pommel. A straw panama hat shadowed his face and a blue chambray shirt molded shoulders every bit as broad as Rafe's. Maggie's gaze drifted over him, stopping at the badge pinned to his chest. A lawman.

No wonder Rafe didn't sound happy to see him.

The stranger said, "I was surprised when one of my lieutenants told me he'd witnessed your arrival here yesterday. I thought he had to be mistaken, but here you are in the flesh. What's the matter, Malone? Did your conscience finally get the better of you? Did you decide to allow me the pleasure I have anticipated all these years?"

"You'll never slip a noose around my neck again, Callahan. You had your chance and you let it get away."

"Only because you hid behind a hero. Is Luke Prescott here to save your ass again, Brother dear?"

Maggie's eyes went wide. Brother? She didn't know Rafe had a brother.

"What do you want, Callahan?"

"I want to know why you've returned to east Texas. Please, tell me you intend to take up your thieving ways again here in my jurisdiction. I want to start planning the party I intend to throw at your hanging."

Rafe gave a harsh laugh. "You'd like that, wouldn't you? It'd take a real load off your shoulders. After all, I'm the only person alive who knows what a liar you truly are. Rachel and Rosa are dead now, aren't they?"

Maggie gasped as the stranger, Callahan, whipped his gun from his holster and pointed it at Rafe's heart. "God damn you, Malone."

"Oh, I've been damned for decades, Brother, so your curses don't worry me a bit. The only part that bothers me is knowing you'll be standing right beside me in hell. Remember, Rachel Prescott and her children have been whispering in God's ears for nigh on a decade now. Even though it's my fault they died, you're not free of blame."

"That was war, Malone," Callahan said, his voice a scathing rasp. "I regret that Captain Prescott's family lost their lives, but I am not responsible."

"Oh, really?" Rafe drawled. "Is that what you try to tell yourself about Rosa, too?"

Callahan's roar of rage brought Maggie to her feet. She turned away from the window as he swung off his saddle. Moving as fast as her protesting joints would allow, she grabbed up her robe from the foot of her bed and slipped it on. Then she hurried toward the door.

The two men rolled in the mud, punches flying. Callahan had lost his hat, and with a start, Maggie realized that were it not for the fact he wore a blue shirt and Rafe a brown one, she couldn't have told the two men apart. Not at first glance, anyway.

Brothers with different last names but near-identical features. Brothers hitting one another. All her life Maggie had wished she had a sibling. "What a waste," she muttered. Reentering the cabin, she grabbed a bucket filled with water left over from yesterday's baths. Wincing from the effort, she carried the bucket out onto the porch and waited for them to roll within reach. Then she threw the cold water on the brawling brothers and yelled, "Stop it! Now!"

Both men paused and looked at her. Blood lust glimmered in identical green eyes. Maggie had seen enough fistfights in her life to recognize when one had ended. This one was far from over. Making a quick decision, she allowed the pain she was feeling to sound in her voice as she said, "Rafe, I need help." She released her knees and collapsed to the porch, grimacing at the jarring of her body against the floor.

She watched from half-closed eyes as Rafe shoved away from Callahan. In an instant he was on his feet rushing toward her. Callahan followed on his heels. "What's wrong with her?"

Gently, Rafe scooped Maggie into his arms and carried her into the cabin. "Sweetheart, what do you need? What can I do?"

Her eyes fluttered open. "I could use a hot bath."

"Let me get you to bed, and I'll put the water on."

Maggie's gaze met Callahan's, and she recognized the knowing curiosity in his look. Even as she flushed with embarrassment, she realized she'd accomplished her purpose. Neither man's eyes continued to glisten with danger.

Rafe carried her into the small bedroom while Callahan stood awkwardly in the outer room. After laying her gently on the mattress, Rafe tucked her beneath the covers and returned to the kitchen, pulling the door shut behind him.

Maggie sighed heavily. What a bother. She couldn't hear a thing going on in the kitchen with the door closed, and she wasn't about to miss this. She tossed down the covers, climbed awkwardly out of bed, and made her way slowly toward the door. Cautiously, she cracked it open.

Rafe was speaking. ". . . Better things to do than play games with you. State your business and leave."

"Who is she?"

The metal tub scraped across the puncheon floor as Rafe dragged it in front of the fireplace. "Go away, Callahan. The Texas Rangers have no cause to concern themselves with me."

"Is she your wife? I hope to hell not. You're hard on wives, aren't you, Malone? Or is it only other men's wives you destroy?"

Rafe's voice grew as cold as a blue norther wind. "I'd love an excuse to kill you."

"The feeling is most definitely mutual. I'm here to give you fair warning, Malone. I and my men are the law in this part of Texas. You cross the line in my territory in the least little way, and I'll see that you pay. With your life. The conditions of your pardon are etched in my mind, and the rangers will be watching you while you're in east Texas. If we catch you doing anything the least bit illegal, it won't come to a trial. I'll string you up by the nearest tree and whistle a tune while I'm about it. This time Prescott won't be around to interfere."

Rafe showed him a mocking smile. "Consider me duly warned, then, dear Brother. Now, if you'll excuse us? I must check on the lady. And shut the door on the way out."

Seeing Rafe headed her way, Maggie tried to hurry back toward the bed. She didn't make it.

"Oh, Maggie," he said. "Your head is harder than red Texas granite. Was a little bit of snooping worth the pain?"

"Yes. He threatened you, Rafe."

He settled her onto the bed, then sat down beside her. "You're feeling better today, aren't you? Your eyes are clearer."

"I slept well last night. Rest helps. Moving is more of a nuisance today rather than a torment. Tell me about that man."

"Let me get your bath first."

"I've changed my mind. I don't want a bath. I want to know about your brother."

"Please don't call him that," Rafe replied, tension carving furrows on his brow.

"It's what you called him."

He raked his fingers through his hair and grimaced. She waited expectantly until a reluctant smile tilted his lips. "Stubborn, mule-headed woman. I don't know how those pirates put up with you."

"I told you before, Malone. They love me. Now tell me about your brother. His threats worry me, and it's not good for my condition for me to be upset. Papa Ben believes anxiety contributes to these attacks, you know."

"Manipulative and stubborn. You should be ashamed."

"I am." She took his hand and gave it a squeeze. She waited for him to look at her, then said, "But I'm also your friend. It sounds to me like I've brought you trouble without meaning to."

Rafe lifted her hand to his mouth and kissed it. "A friend. I like the sound of that. Not that it covers everything between us, but until we get a chance to hammer out the details, I reckon the term fits well enough. What happened just now has nothing to do with you, honey."

"Still, I want to know. I could use a good story to distract me from my aches and pains."

Rafe snorted. "Any story I'd have to tell about Nick Callahan is far from good."

Maggie eased over in the bed and made room for Rafe. "Kick your boots off, Malone, and tell me about it."

"You're a forward woman, Miss St. John, inviting me into your bed in the middle of the morning. What would your grandfathers say?"

"Before or after they gutted you?"

"Ouch." Rafe yanked off his footwear, then settled in beside her. "You're gonna pester me until I give in, aren't you?"

"Yes."

Smiling, Rafe leaned his head against the carved oak backboard and draped one arm around Maggie. He closed his eyes. "Nick Callahan is my half brother."

Maggie rested her head against his shoulder. "You had the same mother?"

"Oh, no. Nick and I were both unfortunate to be

sired by Wallace Malone. That's the name he used when he married my mother. He called himself Wallace Callahan when he married Nick's."

"He was a widower?"

"He was a bigamist."

"Oh."

"That's what my mother said when Nick and his mother showed up at our door one afternoon and she introduced herself as my father's wife."

"Oh, Rafe. What happened?"

"Her name was Ellen Callahan. Apparently my father had used that alias when he went north to set up some sort of business scheme to cheat this woman's family out of a substantial amount of money. I don't know if it was part of my father's plan or not, but Ellen ended up pregnant by him. When her father demanded marriage, my dear daddy went along with it, conveniently ignoring the fact he had another pregnant wife back at home. Anyway, he deserted Ellen before Nick was born and returned home to my mother as if nothing had happened."

"Your father sounds like a real charmer," Maggie observed.

"'Charmer' isn't the word I'd use," Rafe dryly replied. "Anyway, as fate would have it, a decade later Ellen Callahan spotted him on a train. She followed him home and went a little crazy. Went a lot crazy, actually."

"You were there?"

Rafe took a long time to reply, and when he finally spoke Maggie heard a wealth of feeling in his emotionless tone. "Yeah, I was there. I had a front-row seat. Ellen Callahan waved a pistol around as the sordid story spilled from her lips. Her father had disowned her. My father had ruined her life. She pointed the gun at ol' Wallace and pulled the trigger just as my mother stepped in front of him. One bullet got them both. I couldn't get the bleeding stopped."

"Oh, Rafe, how horrible."

"She lost all control at that point. Screaming and shouting at both me and her boy. Nick tried to help me, but the blood . . ." His eyes drifted shut. "They died within minutes of each other."

Observing the expression on his face, Maggie's heart broke. What an event for a child to witness! "Did Nick's mother go to jail?"

"No. She killed herself. Before the sun set that night, he and I were both orphans."

"How awful for you both," Maggie said softly, shaking her head. "I can't imagine how you must have felt. Is that what caused this animosity between you two? Surely you realized neither one of you were at fault for your parents' actions."

"'Animosity'?" He let out a mirthless chuckle. "That's a little weak for what we feel, isn't it? 'Hatred' is a better word, Maggie. I hate him and he hates me, but it's not because of what happened with our parents. Actually, for a time he and I were friends. Now, though, either one of us will kill the other if we get half the chance."

"So what happened?"

Words vibrated from deep inside Rafe's chest. "After the killings, we went our separate ways. Nick ended up with family on his mother's side, and I hooked up with a peddler. We traveled all around the South. While he was busy selling, I was busy thieving. Eventually, it was the stealing that led me to the Prescotts. Luke's pa caught me in the act. I stayed to work off my debt and didn't leave."

"And where does Nick fit in? You must have seen him again sometime."

"We met up again back in Thirty-five. Ran into each other in Nacogdoches. I was in town doing some lawyering, and Nick had plantation business to attend to. He'd taken up cotton farming and had himself a nice little spread. We entered the mercantile at the same time and only realized who the other was because we looked so damned alike."

"You could be twins."

"Yeah. I'm better looking, though. I'm older than him. Older by a week. Good ol' Wallace had a busy February that year."

He paused pensively and Maggie prodded, "So it wasn't hatred at first sight there in the mercantile?"

"Not at all. Actually, we liked each other. We were bound by blood—literally and figuratively. He lost as much as I did that day his mother came calling."

Rafe brushed his fingers slowly up and down Maggie's arm. "We saw each other periodically over the next year. Nick was a personal friend of Sam Houston, and when they called up an army to fight the Mexicans, he was first in line to join. That's the tragedy of the political ideals, Maggie. Nick had 'em. Luke had 'em. For a little while, I pretended to have them. And look at the trouble they brought."

She had difficulty following his line of thinking. "You didn't support the revolution?"

"I supported it. Shoot, war became inevitable the minute Mexico decided to flex its fist and bring Texas under national authority. They had invited Anglos to settle Texas to provide a buffer between them and the Indians, then they got scared when the colony began to grow and prosper. Especially when it became too closely allied to the great enemy, America. The Mexican government thought to solve the problem by bringing Texas to heel, implementing taxes and laws the Anglos couldn't abide. Legally, the Mexicans had every right to attempt to govern the province under their terms. Morally, the colonists couldn't let them do it."

Rafe shrugged. "I looked at the war a bit differently from Luke and Nick and the majority of Texans. For me, the Texas revolution wasn't as much about taxes and self-government as it was a clash of two very different cultures that were simply too disparate to coexist peacefully. Luke and Nick fought it because it was the right and honorable thing to do. I fought because I knew the war would happen sometime, and I figured better to get it over with now while my side still stood a chance at winning. Not very heroic of me, was it?"

"I don't know that I'd say that," Maggie said, lifting her head from his shoulders to look up at him. "Another way to look at it is that you fought the war so that those who came after you wouldn't be forced to. It seems to me that fighting a war for your children's sake is the very best of reasons."

His eyes warmed. "That's something I like about you, Maggie. You think for yourself. I haven't always done that myself, and it has caused me a world of grief in the past."

"Oh, really? That surprises me. Was your brother somehow involved?"

"How did you guess?"

"It wasn't all that difficult. You've been circling around the subject for some time now."

Rafe studied the quilt on the bed, tracing the outline of a star made of calico and gingham. "Callahan tracked me down in Bastrop in early March of Eighteen thirty-six. He was recruiting men for Sam Houston's army. I didn't want to fight for Sam Houston. The man was, and still is, a drunk. He reminds me too damned much of my father. Luke had already left for the Alamo by then, and since I had no plans to go anywhere at the time, he had asked me to watch over his wife and children while he was gone." He turned his face away. "I said I would."

Maggie tried to recall their discussions on the trip to the Caribbean. Hadn't Rafe told her Luke lost his first wife during the war?

He cleared his throat before adding softly, "I gave him my word that I would protect them, Maggie."

The pain in his voice made her want to groan. He obviously felt responsible for Luke's dreadful losses.

"I let my brother's talk of liberty and justice get the better of me. I left with him. I left Rachel and Daniel and Sarah Prescott to drown in the Colorado River as they fled the rumors of the advancing Mexican army. That's my sin, and it's one I'll have to live with forever."

"Wait a minute," Maggie protested. "You're not being fair to yourself. It's awful what happened to Luke's first family, but you can't take the blame for their deaths."

"I know that. And I don't take all the blame. My dear brother Nick gets to share the culpability. Before I left with him, he gave both Rachel and me his promise to send two of his men back to the Prescotts to escort Rachel and her children to safety."

"He didn't do it?"

"He didn't do it."

"Oh, Rafe." Maggie wrapped her arms around him and gave him a hug. Now she better understood his emotional response when she asked him to steal the treasure. Stealing wasn't what he balked at; breaking his word to Luke again was the problem he couldn't overcome. And now that she understood, she couldn't say she blamed him.

One question in particular continued to plague her, and she tried to put it gently. "You said something to him about slipping a noose around your neck again. Did that have something to do with Luke's wife?"

"No, that had to do with Nick's wife. His bad judgment got her killed, but he tried to lay the blame on me." Rafe's mouth clamped closed. He rose from the bed and walked swiftly toward the door. "I promised Martha I'd chop her some wood. I'd best get to it or she won't be serving me any of her cobbler for desert."

Maggie sat up. "Rafe, wait. Tell me what happened. Please?"

He paused, head bowed. Then he walked out of the bedroom, out of the kitchen without another word. Blast the man. Didn't he know her well enough by now to know she wouldn't put up with being ignored?

She walked gingerly toward the wardrobe and pulled her favorite cotton print from the hanger. Had she not been so upset on Rafe's behalf, she'd have welcomed more enthusiastically the marked improvement in her condition.

It took her a good fifteen minutes to make herself presentable. She wasted another five minutes hunting for her shoes, then finally gave up the search. Barefoot, she walked out of the kitchen and into the sunshine, pausing to lift her face to the sky. The sun's heat kissed her cheeks and soaked into her skin. Then, the rhythmic thud of an ax to wood drew her gaze to the woodpile, and a different type of heat flushed through her.

Rafe stood facing away from her, his discarded shirt lying beside him upon the ground. Sweat ran in rivulets down his broad corded back, his muscles bulging then releasing with every swing of the ax. His movements were smooth and skilled and angry. Maggie thought he must have chopped a week's worth of wood already.

She breathed deeply, inhaling the tangy fragrance of pine and the pleasing scent of newly cut wood. She stepped closer, stopping some ten feet away from him, and waited. He knew she was there, Maggie could tell. One little flinch gave him away. But he continued to chop and she continued to stand, determined to wait him out. She didn't speak, simply waited. Finally, as she had known he would, Rafe gave in.

He chucked the ax across the clearing and it flew a good fifty feet before falling to the earth with a thud. Bending, he scooped his shirt off the ground and used it as a towel to wipe the sweat from his torso as he slowly turned around. In a controlled voice, he asked, "What are you doing out of bed?"

"You ignored me."

"Maggie St. John, you are stubborn as a rusty lock and impossible to ignore."

"Tell me."

He scowled and raked his fingers through his dark and damp hair. "You're not going to let this go, are you?"

"No, I'm not."

"If I tell you will you go back to bed where you belong?"

"Actually I'd like to go up to the inn and visit with Martha for a bit."

"You're feeling better?"

"I am."

"Good. Lucky thing I had a bottle of Bliss water in my saddlebags. It may be days yet before your papa gets back with more."

"Lucky thing indeed. What did your brother do to you, Rafe?"

A mockingbird's chatter filled the silence as he stared at her a long moment. When he finally spoke, his tone was hard and bitter. "I learned what had happened to Rachel Prescott and her children shortly before the battle of San Jacinto commenced. I started drinking, and I got angry—riled up, spur raking, pawing the dirt mean. I waged war on the Mexicans with a vengeance. The Texians won the battle in eighteen minutes, but the slaughter went on for more than an hour. It was a carnage, Maggie, and I was right there in the midst of it. I'm not proud of what I did, but I'm not making excuses. It was war and war is an ugly thing. But I wasn't the only crazy fool out on that battlefield, and some men committed acts much more vile than mine."

Rafe bent over and scooped his hat off the ground. He set it atop his head and pulled the brim low on his brow. "I admit the circumstances looked damning, and I know Nick wasn't himself at the moment. But I told him I didn't do it. I looked him in the eye and swore on the graves of our parents. He should have believed me. He should have accepted my word. And he damn sure shouldn't have done what he did the following day."

"What was that? What happened, Rafe? What did Nick do?"

Rafe shut his eyes. "Nick's wife Rosa was following the army. He kept saying he'd send her home, but he never did. Ol' Nick enjoyed the comforts of having his wife nearby too damned much. She was there at San Jacinto during the battle. And afterward, when it became a slaughter. She died."

"And he blamed you?"

Rafe opened his eyes and pinned her with a stare. "He went to the other officers. He spoke to General Houston himself. My brother, that bastard, stood on the San Jacinto battlefield and swore before the whole goddamned Texian army that I raped and murdered his wife."

➤ 14 ◄

She'd used up all her energy.

Rafe scrutinized Maggie's appearance as she visited with Martha Craig in the summer kitchen while the widow prepared supper for the inn's guests. While he savored the aroma of roasting ham, he frowned at the dark circles under Maggie's eyes. He took careful note of the strength of her voice and intensity of her smile, and decided he'd give her five more minutes. Then, he'd make her go back to bed even if he had to carry her.

He should never have told her about Nick. She'd gotten so angry on his behalf that he feared she'd surely set back her recovery. It was a good thing the widow Craig had come scurrying down the hill when she had, or Rafe might have finished the story about his rendezvous with a tree limb and a noose. That would have stoked up her temper even worse.

Rafe swallowed a sigh. Too bad she wasn't asleep when his brother rode up. She would never have learned about Callahan and the trouble he'd caused Rafe in the past. As much as he appreciated Maggie's stirring defense on his behalf, and as little as he liked secrets between people who cared for one another, he found he didn't like her knowing the more humiliating details of his past. It stung his masculine pride.

He'd never been one to worry about what people thought of him. He couldn't remember ever caring quite this much before. But then he'd never loved anyone quite this much before, either. "Maggie, that's enough," he said when she volunteered to peel some potatoes. "I want to get you in bed."

"Why, Rafe Malone!" Martha Craig said in a scandalized tone.

"I didn't mean it like that, Martha, and you know it. Look at her. She's still sickly. I'm just trying to take care of her."

"Malone!" Maggie protested, narrowing her eyes and sitting up straighter in her chair.

Considering how tired she looked, Rafe was surprised she had that much vinegar left in her. He flashed her an encouraging grin. "I figure we have three more doses of Bliss water left in the bottle. Do you think you should take one of them now or save it till later?"

She muttered something about dumping it on his head, and Martha clicked her tongue. "I swear you two act like old married folk."

Maggie's gaze flew up to meet his. Now she looked worried as well as tired, and Rafe shot her a teasing wink to distract her. As he did so, the idea of marriage settled through him like fine whiskey. Marriage. To Maggie. The notion had hovered on the edges of his mind for a while, but he'd never actually looked at it straight on. Maybe he should think about it. Think about it seriously.

Something told him he'd find more adventure in marriage to Maggie St. John than he would if he set out to explore the entire West.

"Come on, love," he said gently, taking her hand and tugging her to her feet. "I want you to rest up real good so you can harangue me properly later when I tell you what I have planned for tomorrow."

"I'd rather hear the rest of the story you were telling me out by the wood pile."

"Oh, I think I covered all the high points already. I'd just as soon leave the low ones out of it. Now, you never answered my question. Do you want a snort of Bliss now, or do we save it for later?"

He saw the argument in her eyes, but when she took a step and grimaced, she apparently changed her mind. "Later. I think I will lie down for a bit. But don't think I intend to allow this matter to drop. I want to hear the rest of the story, Rafe."

She leaned on him as he helped her into the bedroom. As she climbed into bed, he fluffed her pillow. When she lay down, he murmured, "That's my girl."

"I'm not your girl, Malone," Maggie said tiredly.

"Not yet, sweetheart." He leaned over and kissed her cheek. "But soon. Real soon."

The hearse arrived at sunset.

Having already tucked Maggie into bed following a light supper, Rafe had moseyed up to the inn. He was seated on the veranda sharing a smoke and conversation with a pair of buffalo hunters who were indulging in a rare night on a real mattress at Gallagher's when the funeral wagon rolled into the yard.

"Why, lookie there," said the burly hunter around his pipe stem. "I haven't seen a coffin carriage that showy since the last time I passed through New Orleans. Looks like a fancy fish tank on wheels, don't it?"

Stripes of vermilion and gold outlined the large rectangular windows that spanned all four sides of the shiny black lacquer carriage. Brass lanterns swung from the two front corners, while ornately carved wood vase holders occupied the back. Black crepe curtains trimmed with black tasseled fringe concealed the interior.

Every person on the porch watched with interest as it lumbered past the inn and toward the summer kitchen. "Hot damn, would you look at that!" exclaimed the scrawnier of the hunters when one of the drivers tipped his hat. "Wonder where that fellow got his scar? What do you think? Comanche? Apache?"

"Maybe he tangled with a corpse who wasn't ready to give up the ghost," suggested his partner.

Rafe skidded his gaze off the vases and toward the driver's box. He recognized the hat first. "Gus?" He blinked hard and looked again. It *was* Gus. And Lucky rode beside him.

Lucky, the same son of a bitch who was supposed to be on his way to Lake Bliss to replenish Maggie's supply of water.

Anger lashed Rafe like a whip. What the hell were those old men doing? Lucky couldn't have made the trip to Lake Bliss and back in three days, and where in the world had he met up with Gus? And what about Snake? Had Ben returned to Lake Bliss from Rafe's ranch already? Or had Gus left Snake home alone despite his heart ailment? Rafe didn't even want to think about why they were driving a hearse.

Grumbling beneath his breath, Rafe descended the porch steps and strode toward the summer kitchen where the wagon had rolled to a stop. When Lucky and Gus climbed down from the driver's box, walked around to the back of the hearse, and swung the door down, Rafe's steps slowed. He spied the end of a polished rosewood casket. Oh, no. Snake. It had to be Snake. Rafe broke into a run. This would kill Maggie.

The two old pirates reached into the wagon and slowly slid the casket from its shadowed interior. They angled it toward the ground, and for the first time Rafe saw that the coffin had no lid.

It did, however, have a corpse.

Well, hell, Rafe thought as he identified the body. Sorrow rolled through him. Snake. That poor bastard. For all the threats and fire in his words, he'd been a man who sat tall in the saddle.

Rafe reached toward his head to remove his hat when something happened that pulled him up short and damn near had him tripping over his own feet. Gus had extended a hand toward the burying box . . .

And the corpse lifted a hand to take it.

For a moment, Rafe's mouth went dry as a west Texas desert. Then with a grumble and a groan, Snake MacKenzie climbed out of the box. He appeared amazingly pink-cheeked for a dead man.

When Rafe was certain he wasn't about to expire from a heart attack himself, he thanked God that the aging buccaneer was alive. Laughing without humor, he slowly shook his head and pinned the three pirates with his gaze. "What are you sea mules up to now?"

Gus looked at Lucky. "Sea mules? I don't believe I've ever heard of them, have you?"

"Never. I've heard of sea urchins, but not sea mules."

"Doesn't matter," said Snake, glaring at Rafe. He held out his hand. "Gus, give me a weapon. I have me a polecat to kill."

Gus shot a stream of tobacco juice toward the ground. "You can't kill him, Snake."

"I sure as shrimp can." Snake squared his shoulders, shaking only a little at the effort. "I told you what he told me. I told you what he did to our Maggie."

"Don't get so worked up," Lucky said. "You'll keel over, and we'll have to use this coffin for real. The fact of the matter is that despite your promises, you can't kill Malone unless Maggie gives you the go-ahead. Besides, Malone doesn't matter. It's Maggie we're here to help, so let's get about it."

Rafe recovered from his surprise and rounded on Lucky. "You say you want to help Maggie? Then why aren't you on the road? She needs that Lake Bliss water you went to fetch."

"We have Bliss water." Gus moved the coffin out of the way then motioned toward Rafe. "Once we realized Maggie left without a good supply, Snake and I decided to bring her some. We have a full dozen small kegs inside the hearse. Make your muscles useful and unload it for us."

Rafe stepped closer to the hearse, then stooped over and peered inside. Sure enough, he counted twelve small water caskets lining the insides of the wagon. Relief rolled off him in waves. He broke into a smile, then glanced at the pirates. "You don't know how glad I am to see those barrels. She's been powerful sick."

The pirates demanded an update on their granddaughter's condition, and Rafe filled them in on the particulars. When he concluded by informing them that their granddaughter was currently sleeping, Snake, expressing the desire to stretch his legs, joined Lucky in the short walk up to the hotel to secure rooms for the evening. Gus and Rafe watched the two men go. "You people are crazy," Rafe said, observing the ailing pirate's careful steps. "Snake was supposed to stay in bed for weeks."

"Don't you worry none, Malone," Snake said over his shoulder. "I'm not about to croak until I make you pay for your villainy."

Rafe showed his lack of concern with a snort. He turned his attention to the water kegs, sliding the nearest cask from the bed of the hearse and hoisting it onto his shoulder. "I'll come back for the rest in a bit. I want to have some of this ready for Maggie as soon as she wakes up. Her anxiety level is gonna shoot through the shingles when she learns that Snake climbed out of his bed and into a coffin to make the trip up from Lake Bliss."

"Now hold on, boy," Gus replied, scowling. He grabbed Rafe's sleeve, stopping him. "I'll have you know that this buggy was a perfect solution to the problem of how to get here. Snake couldn't abide the ride without lying down, and the springs on our wagon were shot. It jostled him too much. When we spotted the hearse along the El Camino Real with its empty burying box, it seemed like a sign from heaven."

The unmistakable odor of Lake Bliss water oozed from the keg, surrounding Rafe as he gave the old pirate a sidelong look. "Those kind of signs tend to make most folks nervous."

"Don't you know Snake MacKenzie better than to think he'd be scared of a coffin?" Gus replied with a chortle. "Why, by the time we added the extra padding to the box he swore it was the most comfortable bit of traveling he'd ever done." He paused a moment, then asked, "How is she doing, Malone?"

Rafe set the keg on the ground. "Not good. The worst of it seems to come and go. She'll feel better for a time, then all of a sudden it hits her like a buffalo charge. It's hard to watch, Gus. Real hard."

The old pirate nodded sagely. "I'd weep like a baby after my turn to sit with her. Now you see why we searched the world over for a cure. You have to understand why it's so important we save Hotel Bliss."

Rafe nodded. His gaze drifted toward the window of the small room off the kitchen where Maggie lay sleeping. With her uppermost in his mind, he voiced his decision for the first time. "I've decided to help, Gus."

"The treasure?" Excitement lit the buccaneer's eyes. "You'll go after the treasure?"

"Yeah."

"How come? What changed your mind?"

Rafe considered all the possible replies, distortions, and deceits he could tell them, but for some reason he spat out the truth. "How can I not help? I love her."

For a moment, Gus froze as stiff as a new rawhide rope. Then satisfaction shimmered across his face and settled into smugness. "We have nine days before our option to buy the hotel expires. Can you leave tomorrow?"

"Wait a minute. Nine days? I thought you still had months before you had to leave Bliss."

"The judge's deadline for us to leave the hotel was six months. Hill, the buzzard, wouldn't give us that much time as far as the sales contract goes. We only have nine days left."

"Then I'll head out at dawn."

"Good. I'll go with you, of course. I reckon my fanny can stand a day in the saddle and surely the innkeeper has a horse I can rent."

Rafe folded his arms. "I don't work with partners, Gus."

"You will this time." The old man squinted against the setting sun as he gazed at Rafe. "One man can't possibly haul the entire treasure, and if you're going to bother with grabbing some of it, what's the logic in not snatching it all?"

Rafe opened his mouth to protest, but then reconsidered. While he much preferred the idea of working alone, what Gus said made sense. He risked the same punishment no matter how much, or how little, he stole. Might as well get Maggie the whole tamale while he was about it. He jerked his head toward the kitchen. "Lucky will take good care of her, won't he?"

"Yeah. Her and Snake. Before we leave maybe we should see about getting a bed for Snake set up down here so Lucky won't need to be tramping back and forth all the time."

"What in the world possessed you to bring him here, Gus?" He gestured toward the hearse. "Weren't you afraid that casket might come in a little too handy?"

Gus removed his hat from his head and slapped it against his thigh. Red dust rose in a cloud at the motion. "Let me give you a clue about old folks, at least about the four of us. We may be wrinkled-up winter on the outside, but inside we are hanging on hard to spring. We are free men, Malone. Men with dignity. Nobody is gonna tell any of us what we can and can't do."

"But Snake could—"

"No 'buts' about it. Snake wanted to make this trip, and while the rest of us had the right to argue with him, not a man jack among us had the right to stop him. Maggie understands that. You'd best come to understand it, too. We come as a package, after all. When you marry her, you marry us, too."

"Marry!" Rafe's head snapped around to glare at Gus. "Who said anything about marriage?"

Gus's brows lowered in a scowl, and in its cold fury Rafe saw signs of the young pirate who had cast fear into the hearts of men across at least five of the seven seas. The buccaneer barked, "You said you love her."

"I do."

"You love her. You bedded her. You'll marry her."

Rafe's chin came up. He didn't like being put on the defensive. "Not necessarily."

The old man braced his hands on his hips and leaned forward. "Careful, Malone," he said in a low mean voice. "I'm the only person standing between you and Snake MacKenzie's cutlass."

Rafe didn't want to point out the foolishness of thinking that Snake, in his current condition, could possibly cause serious injury to Gentleman Rafe Malone. Instead, he attempted to diffuse the situation by speaking candidly. "You're rushing me, Gus. You're rushing us. I just figured out how I feel about her, and Maggie has been awfully tight lipped as to how she feels about me. I may not be as old as you, but life has taught me a few lessons of my own. I have less than a handful of rules that I live by now, and those are sacred."

He ticked them off on his fingers. "I don't get drunk anymore. I stay the hell away from politics. And I refuse to even consider marrying a woman unless we are both slop-silly in love."

Gus pursed his lips and rubbed his chin thoughtfully. "Slop-silly in love, huh?"

Rafe nodded. "Wearing one another's brand burned into our hearts."

Gus moved his hand to scratch the nape of his neck. Wincing, he said, "Now that you mention it, I don't know that Maggie is that attached to you."

No matter how correct the observation might be, hearing it from Gus got Rafe's back up. "She's attached to me," he snapped. "Why, she probably does love me but is keeping the news to herself. That's a difficult thing for a person to admit the first time they fall in love, you know."

Gus shook his head. "Nah, that's not it. Maggie's been in love before."

Rafe's heart fell to his knees. "She has!"

"Yep. Some fella back at school plumb near broke her heart."

Rafe made a conscious effort to relax his hands now fisted at his side. In all the talk and secrets they'd shared, she'd never once mentioned any schooltime beau. Wasn't that a fine howdy-do? Still, Maggie couldn't have loved the scoundrel too awfully much. She'd come to Rafe's bed a virgin.

"Look," he said to Gus. "We can save this entire discussion for later. Right now I think we should wake your granddaughter long enough to get her dosed up with Bliss water and on the road to recovery."

Gus nodded. "That's right. Maggie's health comes before anything else. But promise me something, Malone. As soon as she's better, I want you to get this question settled. You find out whether she's slop-silly in love, and if she's not, you do what needs doing to get her that way." He paused for a moment before asking, "Have you told her you're going after the treasure? That's bound to help."

"It's not why I've decided to help, and no, I haven't told her what I'm doing. I don't want to bribe her into loving me, Gus. That cheapens it for both of us. And I don't want any of you to try and influence her, either. When we leave in the morning, I want Snake and Lucky to keep their mouths shut about where we've gone and why."

"The kelp you say," Gus replied with a scowl. "Maggie needs to know what we're doing. The poor gal has fretted herself half to death over the thought of losing the hotel. I don't doubt for a second that contributed to the attack she's suffering through this very moment. Why would you even consider allowing her to continue to worry?"

Rafe didn't know how to explain his feelings to the old marauder. He wasn't certain he understood them himself. On the one hand, he'd be proud as a peacock in full spread to present her with the means to save her home. On the other hand, the knowledge that Maggie would know he had broken his word to Luke left Rafe shuddering with a deep and stinging shame. "Lie to her, then," he gruffly replied. "Whatever it takes short of clueing her in on the truth. I won't have her knowing, Gus. I want your promise. I want your word."

The old pirate shrugged. "Let's go check on Sleeping Beauty, shall we? I need to see how she's doing for myself."

Rafe didn't realize until four hours into the ride the following morning that Gus had never given him his word.

Maggie woke up slowly. As she shook off the heaviness of sleep, she slowly came to realize a difference in the signals her body was giving her. Moving wasn't as difficult this morning. She rolled over in bed without gritting her teeth and flexed her knees without biting back a groan. A smile hovered at the corners of her mouth as she slowly opened her eyes.

Sunshine lit the room. The scent of frying bacon drifted from the kitchen. Snake MacKenzie's opinionated voice debated the pros and cons of adding ale to the batter for fried okra with the widow Craig. It was music to Maggie's ears. Her smile burst into full blossom and she flung off the covers and slid off the bed and onto her feet. "What a glorious morning."

Last night she'd gone to bed with a sense this might happen. The papas' arrival alone had made her feel better. Once she'd finished scolding Snake for leaving his bed at Lake Bliss, she'd rejoiced in the improvements she spied in his appearance. While he continued to look tired and weaker than normal, she took the color in his cheeks and the grin on his face as a good sign. As they dosed her to the gills with Bliss water, the papas had talked about their trip, and she'd laughed at their stories until her sides hurt. Too soon, her grandfathers' voices had joined Rafe in shoeing her back to bed, all of them demanding her promise to put her energy into getting well.

Now, to her joy, it looked as if their combined efforts had done the trick.

She found fresh water in the pitcher on the dresser and quickly washed and dressed. Happiness filled her, and she hummed a high-spirited song. It was always a pleasure to overcome her illness, and this time was no exception. She delighted in the ease with which she lifted her hands to her hair to braid and pin it. Gazing into the looking glass, she pinched her already colorful cheeks and considered the next battle she had to fight.

The time to save Hotel Bliss was ticking away. She couldn't waste another day. Obviously, now that the papas and Rafe had arrived she'd need to readjust her plans. Maybe Rafe had an idea on how to help without compromising his promise. "We will need to have a strategy meeting," she said to her reflection. A distinct growl from her stomach caused her to grin and add, "Right after breakfast."

She found Lucky and Martha seated at the kitchen table. Snake stood over a pot on the stove. A quick glance around revealed neither Rafe nor Gus. Perhaps they'd already eaten.

"Good morning," she said brightly.

"Why look at the sprightly spring in her step," marveled Mrs. Craig.

"Magpie!" Lucky's expression lit like dry kindling. "You're back, aren't you? Whipped that old nasty devil all over again. Lord-a-mercy, girl, it's good to see you looking so perky."

"It's good to feel perky." Maggie stopped beside Lucky and bent to kiss his cheek before moving on to Snake. She wrapped her arm around his waist then peered into the skillet. "Bacon and fried ham. Are you making flapjacks, too?" When he nodded, she continued, "Good. I'm hungry enough to eat a horned frog backward."

"She even has her appetite back." Lucky smiled over his cup of coffee at the widow. "That corks it, then. Maggie's whipped the Challenge again."

It felt good to pitch in and help with breakfast. The inn had seven overnight guests, not including Maggie's bunch, and the widow Craig declared herself thrilled to have surrendered her cooking duties to Snake. "It's been a long time since I've been able to put my feet up this time of day," she said. "While I'd likely get tired of it over time, for this morning it's downright relaxing."

While she labored beside one beloved papa and listened to stories told by another, Maggie's heart felt light and happy. Even Snake's grumbling about her cooking skills made her want to sing. A couple of times it crossed her mind to mention Andrew Montgomery and the treasure, but she decided not to risk ruining the first meal she'd felt like eating in days with topics certain to sour the stomach.

It wasn't until after they toted the hot food the short distance to the inn and she, Lucky, Snake, and Mrs. Craig joined Gallagher's guests at the long dining-room table that she glanced around and asked, "Where are Gus and Rafe? Have they already eaten breakfast?"

Lucky got a look on his face that suggested he'd bit into a lemon, only he was eating a flapjack and Papa Snake never put anything the least bit sour in his recipe. One glance at Papa Snake confirmed her suspicion. The papas were hiding something. "Lucky? Where is Gus?"

The pirate cleared his throat. "Well, I don't rightly know. I haven't seen him for a bit."

"Snake?"

He squinched his eyes and frowned as if in pain. Laying down his fork, he lifted a hand to his chest. "Well, rip me sails, I do believe I'm feeling a peculiar catch in my lungs."

Maggie shot him a narrow-eyed glare. More likely he was feeling a pang of guilt. Snake never had been able to lie to her worth a clam. "I've heard that a dose of truth medicates that condition well."

When neither of her grandfathers deigned to answer, Maggie looked at the widow Craig. That woman offered a vague smile before turning her head to ask a buffalo hunter about his intended route west. Frustrated, but recognizing it wouldn't do to air the family laundry in front of strangers, Maggie bided her time until the guests had finished their meals and left the table. At that point, she gave each of her grandfathers in turn a pointed look. "Where are they?"

When once again the men ignored her, she decided desperate measures were called for. She reached across the table and swiped Papa Lucky's plate right out from beneath his fork.

"Hey, Magpie! I'm not through with that. This is the first time Snake has cooked since his spell. Those are the best flapjacks I've had in a coon's age."

"They'll be the best ones you've worn on your lap if you don't come clean."

"Clean!" he replied, slapping his chest in affront. "Why, Magpie, I took a bath just last night."

"Where are they, Papa?"

Lucky grimaced, then said, "Gone."

"Gone where?"

"I can't rightly say."

"You can't or you won't?"

Snake piped in. "Malone didn't want you to know."

Maggie folded her arms. "Excuse me? So you've switched your loyalty from your granddaughter to Gentleman Rafe Malone? *You,* of all people, Papa Snake?"

From the look on his face, he'd taken a bite of the same sour flapjack Lucky had gotten hold of earlier. "It's not like that, Maggie," he said, foundering.

"That's right, Magpie. It's not like that."

"Then explain to me why should I think otherwise. From where I'm standing it looks like the four of you have ganged up against me. For all I know, Papa Ben is in on this, too."

"Now wait a minute, gal. Ben doesn't know anything about this. How could he? When Malone headed here, Ben planned to return to Bliss. None of us have had the chance to tell him what's been happening. Ben is innocent."

Maggie jumped on that like a duck on a june bug. "But you two are guilty!"

The two men shared a look. "She's stubborn," Lucky said.

"I'm afraid we'd need ten yoke of ox to pull her off her position," Snake replied.

"We gave it a good try." Lucky nodded.

"Gave them a decent head start." Snake flicked his earrings with a finger.

"Are you ready to quit?"

"I've done sheathed my cutlass."

Lucky swiped his napkin across his mouth. Snake took a quick gulp of coffee. "Well?" Maggie asked.

"Triumph," Lucky said. "They've gone to Triumph Plantation."

Snake added, "It's what we've wanted all along, Maggie. Malone is going to steal back our treasure."

"No!" Maggie covered her mouth with her hand and slowly sank back against her chair. She recalled the agony in Rafe's voice as he explained his reasons for refusing to steal the treasure when she had begged for his help. She remembered the anguish visible on his face. Why? Why was he doing this? He'd hate it. He'd hate himself.

"He'll hate me."

→ 15 ←

Maggie used every sea creature she could think of to curse Rafe Malone as she hurried toward the summer kitchen. She was mad enough to eat bees. How could he have gone off to ruin his life without speaking to her about it first?

Stealing the treasure from Andrew Montgomery meant he'd break his word to Luke. Not that he'd get caught. Rafe was too talented a thief for that. But in taking the treasure, he'd be giving away his soul. She couldn't allow that to happen.

But then, neither could she abandon her papas by allowing them to lose Hotel Bliss. Time had all but run out. Her untimely bout with the rheumatism made her original plan to trick Montgomery out of the treasure impractical. Even if she could catch up with Rafe and convince him not to interfere with her plan, she couldn't be certain of securing the treasure in time to get it back to Hotel Bliss before the deadline.

Stopping in her tracks, she stared at a squirrel perched on the limb of a nearby loblolly pine and asked, "So what do I do? How can I even consider trying to stop Rafe? Yet, how can I not do everything in my power to stop him?"

She wanted to lie down and bawl.

Too bad she wasn't at home. If she were home, she'd make a beeline for the lake. A swim in the soothing waters of Lake Bliss would do her a world of good at the moment. Along with working any lingering stiffness from her joints, swimming always offered her the opportunity to do some of her best thinking. And it would take some really hard contemplation to work her way out of this conundrum.

She started moving again, though now she stepped more slowly. A shadow of a thought hovered at the back of her mind. Maggie knew it was there, sensed what it meant, and tried her best to ignore it. There had to be another way.

Maggie kicked a bright yellow dandelion. Maybe she should ride up to Andrew Montgomery's house and ask for his assistance flat out—no trickery or manipulation involved. But what if he said no? What if too much bad blood existed between him and the papas for Montgomery to ever agree to help? Dare she risk it?

No, not when another way out existed. Not when two little words would save not only Rafe but the papas, too.

Maggie could hold back acknowledgment of the solution no longer. Two little words said to Barlow Hill: I do.

"Oh, God." Maggie bent over double.

She couldn't do it. She simply couldn't face such a fate. She couldn't stand the thought of him touching her. Memory of his lips upon her neck made her nauseous. Marriage to Barlow Hill would be miserable. Horrible.

It could be short.

Maggie slowly straightened. She drew a deep

breath, then exhaled in a rush and resumed walking. A short marriage to Barlow Hill. Maybe she could handle that. She could think of it like a bout of rheumatism, something unpleasant but bearable, because it didn't last forever. A short marriage to Barlow Hill. "I could do that."

The question became, how would she see it ended?

Murder was out. Although she knew her papas wouldn't hesitate to accommodate her, she couldn't live with murder on her conscience. Divorce sounded nice. Annulment even better. The trick would be to arrange matters so that she ended up with the property when the bedsheets split, so to speak.

The longer she thought about it, the more she warmed to the idea. Women enjoyed more liberal property rights in the Republic of Texas than they did in the United States. It might take a little effort on her and an attorney's part to get the details the way she'd need them, but chances were good she could manage it.

An attorney. She'd need to find a good one right away. She wouldn't trust the man who'd represented them during the Lake Bliss lawsuit to draft a handbill, much less a legal document. Who did she know who was a lawyer?

Hadn't Rafe told her he'd once read law?

A laugh sputtered from her mouth. Somehow she couldn't picture going to him for legal advice, under the circumstances. She'd ask Martha to recommend a man. Someone from Nacogdoches. That way Maggie could detour by town and have papers drawn up before returning to Bliss.

She whirled around and retraced her steps to the inn where she found the widow Craig upstairs changing bedsheets. Maggie explained she needed an attorney and asked for the widow's recommendation.

Mrs. Craig frowned. "A number of lawyers do business in Nacogdoches, dear. I'm not entirely certain whom I should recommend. I must say that if you intend to make trouble for Gentleman Rafe, I'll refuse to help."

Maggie shook her head. "It's not like that, Mrs. Craig. You see, Rafe is putting himself in danger by trying to help me. I need to stop him before something terrible happens, and I need a lawyer's assistance to do it. Please help me, Mrs. Craig. I need an attorney with excellent skills, but someone whose ethics are a tad bit questionable. And I need him fast."

"Rafe is in danger, you say?"

"Dire straits."

Martha thumped her lips with an index finger as she thought. After a moment, she nodded. "Lester Bodine is the man you need. His office is on the square."

"Thank you, Mrs. Craig." Maggie took hold of her hands and kissed her weathered cheek. "Thank you for everything. I owe you so much. As soon as you're able, I want you to visit us at Hotel Bliss. I'll personally lead you through a mud-bath regime that will leave you feeling twenty years younger."

"You don't owe me anything, child. Just take care of our Rafe. That rogue holds a corner of my heart."

As Maggie hurried downstairs, she tried to block the troublesome idea that where her own heart was concerned, Rafe had claimed much more than a corner.

She made a brief detour to the inn's office where she penned and sealed a letter, then exited the building in search of her grandfathers. She found Snake and Lucky near the carriage house, each with a wrench in his hand as they tended to some minor repairs on the hearse, each fussing about the quality of the other's work.

Maggie's heart filled with love at the sound of their bickering. It was wonderful to see Snake back in fighting form, and she was determined to keep him that way. Owing to Snake's delicate health, she should present her plan in a sensitive manner. In other words, Maggie needed to lie.

Approaching her grandfathers, she pasted on a smile and asked, "Hi, Papas. What are you doing?"

Lucky looked at Snake. "She's got that tone in her voice."

"Aye." Snake folded his arms and glared at her. "What is it this time?"

Maggie gave her head a toss. She'd best be careful now. This had to be done with just the right touch. "Don't you give me that look, either one of you! I've come to apologize for running out on you at breakfast this morning."

The papas shared a glance and said, "Uh-huh." Snake added, "What do you have up your sleeve?"

Maggie offered him a brilliant smile and replied, "Actually it's in my pocket. It's a letter." She whipped out a sealed missive. "I've made a couple of decisions, and I need to ask for your help. Both of you."

Lucky lifted his hat off his head and scratched the back of his neck. "We were right again."

"I can already tell I'm not going to like this."

"Yes, you are, Papa Snake." Maggie stepped forward and took his hand. "The news that Rafe has gone after the treasure for us has lifted a huge burden from my shoulders. I was angry earlier because before I got sick, I wheedled some information about Triumph Plantation from one of the other guests. Rafe took off before I could tell him about the secret room off Montgomery's office."

"A secret room?" Snake asked.

"Yes," Maggie lied. "That might be where he keeps the treasure. Rafe needs to know about it before he wastes too much time looking in other spots."

"She's right," Lucky said.

"Of course I'm right." Maggie waved the letter. "That's why one of us needs to take him the information."

"It has to be me." Lucky grabbed the letter from her hand and turned it over. "Why did you seal it? Did you write something you don't want me to see? Do you and Malone have some secrets between you?"

"What's the need for secrets?" Snake stuffed his wrench in his shirt pocket and added, "Malone confessed to me himself. I have decided to put off killing him until after he steals the treasure, you'll be pleased to know."

"Thank you, Papa Snake," Maggie dryly replied. She would have preferred a different distraction from the fact she'd sealed the letter, but under the circumstances she'd take what she could get. "Papa Lucky? When do you think you'll be able to leave?"

"Here's my hat, what's my hurry, little girl?"

"Now, Papa." She flashed him a tender smile. "Don't get your feelings hurt. I'm trying to do what's best for all of us. The sooner you leave, the sooner you'll get to Rafe so he can steal the treasure, and then the sooner we'll be home with the deed to Lake Bliss back in our names."

"That sure sounds nice. Tell you what, soon as I can get a horse saddled up, I'll be off." Lucky tucked the letter into his pocket and turned to Snake. "You watch out for Magpie while I'm gone, you hear?"

"We'll watch out for each other, Papa," Maggie replied, slipping her arm through Snake's.

They'd watch out for each other all the way back to Lake Bliss. Once she was certain Lucky was on his way to Triumph, she intended to talk Snake into his seat inside the hearse and head for Nacogdoches. The timing of her plan would be imperative. She didn't want to marry Barlow Hill a day earlier than necessary, but she also couldn't wait so long that Rafe could possibly arrive at the hotel in time to stop her. If he even wanted to stop her, that is. Would it bother Rafe to know she planned to marry Barlow Hill?

Maggie suspected the answer would be yes. Because, for Rafe to willingly break his word to Luke, he must have powerful motivation, something as strong as the reason why she would voluntarily marry Barlow Hill. Maybe he loved her.

Just as she loved him.

Moonlit darkness surrounded the three-storied Greek Revival manor house on Triumph Plantation. Blending into the blackness of the pine forest, Rafe's gaze roamed across the six polished walnut columns supporting the front gallery, searching for signs of movement. The house remained dark and quiet, just as it had for the past three hours.

Rafe laid his hand on the shoulder of the man standing beside him and gave it a silent squeeze before slipping from the cover of the trees. Stealthily, he made his way across the clearing toward the house, confident that his partner would follow at his signal as prearranged. Gus had high hopes for the success of the night's efforts. He was convinced that Montgomery would keep the riches nearby, and that a thief of Rafe's skill would locate the stash quickly. Rafe hoped like hell he was correct. The deadline for closing the deal with Barlow Hill was approaching fast.

Except for a few hours of badly needed sleep, he and Gus had effectively used the time since their arrival at Triumph. The day before, they had searched the cotton gin, the blacksmith's shop, and the carriage house. Their luck had taken a turn for the good when Andrew Montgomery loaded a valise into a buggy and informed his housekeeper he'd be away from Triumph for two days. The planter's absence had given the thieves a perfect opportunity to search the main house.

Last night Rafe and Gus had slipped into the house and made a cursory search of the unoccupied rooms, including Montgomery's bedroom. Rafe had been surprised to find a drawing of Maggie framed and decorating a bedside table. Failing to locate any sign of the treasure, they had descended to the first floor with the intention of giving the study a thorough search. The housekeeper had thwarted their plans, however, when she chose to deal with an apparent attack of insomnia by curling up with a book in the plump leather chair occupying that room.

Tonight they hoped to enjoy better success.

Rafe made a circuit around the house, watching and listening for any sign of wakefulness from within. Except for the drone of a pair of crickets and an occasional hoot of an owl, all remained quiet. Rafe moved to the north side of the house and paused just outside the study's French doors.

He didn't expect to find the treasure in the study— that would be too easy—but he did hope to discover a clue that would lead them to the cache. Should their efforts prove unsuccessful, upon Montgomery's return to the plantation, Rafe intended to abandon the idea of stealth and go straight to threats.

The bastard deserved a good scare. Montgomery deserved a helluva lot more than that for his sins against Maggie. But as much as Rafe would like to beat the peewaddling out of Montgomery the first chance he got, if they found the treasure tonight, revenge would have to wait. Punishing Andrew Montgomery was his desire, not Maggie's. She needed him to get the treasure to Lake Bliss before Barlow Hill's deadline.

Rafe lifted his face toward one of the windows in Montgomery's suite of rooms. *Someday, you son of a bitch. Someday soon.*

Rafe pulled a white handkerchief from his pocket and signaled Gus to join him. Cautious servants had secured both the doors and the windows in their master's absence, but locks proved little deterrent to a man of Gentleman Rafe Malone's skills. Within minutes he'd gained entrance to the house by way of a second-story window. Swiftly and silently, he made his way downstairs and into Andrew Montgomery's study, shutting the door behind him. He used the heavy drapery to muffle the click when he flipped the lock on the French doors and allowed Gus Thomas to slip inside.

"Any trouble?" the pirate whispered.

Rafe shook his head. He loosened the drapery ties and covered the windows before lighting the lamp on Andrew Montgomery's desk. While the pirate searched the bookshelf, Rafe sat in the desk chair and tried the drawers. The bottom left refused to open. He removed a letter opener from the middle drawer and jimmied the lock. The drawer slid open, and Rafe turned his attention to the files inside.

The two men labored silently for almost ten minutes, then a soft exclamation attracted Rafe's attention. Gus had discovered the safe.

Rafe carried the lamp closer to the false wall behind a section of the bookshelves. He studied the lock intently, then **his** lips lifted in a slow smile. He was familiar with this brand. He knew its tricks. Handing the lamp to Gus, he reached into his pants pocket and removed a small pick he'd lifted earlier from the stable. He rested his ear against the steel door and went to work. Fifteen minutes later, the safe swung open.

Inside he found a small amount of cash and a number of legal documents. He pushed aside a gold pocket watch, then removed a ribbon-tied packet of letters. The salutation drew his eyes like a magnet: *To my beloved daughter, Mary Margaret.*

Rafe's brows arched. He'd always sensed the pirates hadn't told the entire story. He motioned for Gus to hand him one of the empty canvas bags he carried, then he dumped the cash, the documents, and the letters inside, leaving behind the watch.

"Is that all there is?" Gus asked worriedly.

Rafe reached into the safe and removed a small blue velvet pouch with gold braided drawstrings. "Except for this."

Gus's eyes lit with excitement as he swiped the bag from Rafe's hand. "This is it! Laffite awarded these jewels to Captain Ben for saving his life. If everything is still here, this should be enough. Look, Malone. Hold out your hand." He opened the drawstring and tipped the pouch. Glittering jewels—diamonds and sapphires and more—dribbled out onto Rafe's palm.

Just as light spilled into the room from the entry hall.

"Well, well, well. Look what we have here." Nick Callahan stood at the doorway of the study holding a Colt revolver in one hand and a hangman's noose in the other. He moved into the room followed by a pair of men carrying pistols and wearing stars on their vests. "It's the middle of the night. I see an open safe and a bag of loot. Gentlemen, it looks like we have a case of broken parole."

"Well, shoot," Rafe muttered. He briefly considered dosing the light and diving for the floor, but with five guns pointed his way, that option appeared suicidal. Eyeing the noose dangling from his brother's hand, Rafe decided waiting around didn't hold much appeal, either. If not for Gus, he'd have given the first idea a try. "Well, shoot," he repeated.

"Not unless you make me," Callahan replied with a snide smile. While one of the rangers set about lighting the rest of the room, Callahan slowly twirled the rope. "I'm gonna hang you, Malone. Finally. Nothing is going to stop me this time."

Rafe had the nagging suspicion he might just be right. "You set us up. How did you do it? I'd have sworn I wasn't followed from Gallagher's."

"I'm afraid you succeeded in giving us the slip. Mr. Thomas, however, wasn't that lucky. Now we've caught you dead to rights, and you are gonna hang."

"Wait a minute." Gus stepped in front of Rafe. "You haven't caught us dead to anything. You represent the law. You have to be legal about this. Malone wasn't stealing, so he hasn't broken his parole."

"Not stealing?" Callahan laughed and gestured toward the gems sparkling in the palm of Rafe's hand. "What do you call this?"

"Taking back," Gus replied. "Those jewels belong to Captain Ben Scovall. We're here to retrieve them on his behalf."

As Gus launched into a long and meandering explanation about the treasure and how it came to be in Montgomery's possession, Rafe's gaze fastened on one of the jewels in his hand, a two-carat aquamarine. It made him think of Maggie. She should wear this gem. It matched her eyes. Caribbean blue. Chances were he'd never see her again.

He felt a yawning sensation in his chest. Funny how things worked. All the times over years he'd faced his own death, he'd never regretted it quite as much as he did now. *Ah, hell, darlin'. I never told you I loved you.*

"Look," Callahan said, waving the rope impatiently. "Your story is all very interesting, but it's not accomplishing anything other than delaying a hanging."

"I don't mind," Rafe said.

"Well, I do," Callahan snapped.

Rafe caught movement at the doorway, out of the corner of his eye. Careful not to call the others' attention to the fact that a shadow-cloaked figure was sneaking into the room behind them, he tried to discern the newcomer's identity. Hope flared inside him, and then he realized just who tiptoed toward his half brother. Rafe couldn't stop the groan bubbling up from his throat when he spied the footstool in his rescuer's path.

Sure enough, just as he lifted an ancient gun to Nick Callahan's head, unlucky Lucky tripped over the stool and went sprawling, knocking down Callahan in the process. His gun exploded and the rangers dove for cover—needlessly, Rafe knew. Lucky never would be lucky enough to actually hit someone who needed hitting.

Callahan recovered quickly enough to draw a bead on Rafe before Rafe managed to do more than palm the dagger he kept in his boot. "Hold it right there," his half brother said as Gus rushed over to where Lucky lay moaning.

Gus ignored him and knelt on the floor beside his friend. "Did you break anything this time, Lucky?"

"I think I'm all right."

"I think he broke me," one ranger complained, protectively cradling his left arm as he climbed to his feet.

Gus's eyes widened in admiration. "What do you know about that. Maybe your luck is finally changing, Lucky."

The loud click of revolvers being cocked suggested otherwise. Rafe glanced up to see Callahan and the second ranger with guns at the ready, their jaws set and their eyes granite hard. Texas Rangers never did like being taken for fools, and Lucky had come darned close to doing just that.

Lucky struggled to sit up. "We've got trouble, Gus."

Gus took a glance around the room and said dryly. "Nah."

"It's Magpie." Lucky sought Rafe's gaze as he added, "She's gone and done something stupid."

Tension shuddered up Rafe's spine, and he got a cold, hollow feeling in the bottom of his stomach. "What?"

"I should have looked at the letter right away. She fooled me completely. Said she had a good idea where the treasure was stashed. Something she'd wheedled from one of Gallagher's guests about a secret room off Andrew's office."

Fear shuddered through Rafe. "What has she done, Lucky? Is she here?"

The rangers whirled around, guns at the ready. Callahan swore with disgust and kept his gun on Rafe.

Lucky reached into his vest pocket.

"Careful, old man," Callahan warned. "One wrong move and I'll shoot you."

"It's a letter. A letter from Magpie to Malone. I don't know what she's thinking." He slowly removed a folded sheet of paper and held it out for Callahan to see. "She's gone crazy. I think the sickness must have affected her mind this time. Have you ever heard of that? Is it possible to get rheumatism of the brain?"

"What the hell has she done?" Rafe demanded, ignoring the gun pointed at his heart as he set the jewels on the desk and snatched the letter from Lucky's hand. His gaze skimmed the page. "Oh, no. I'll kill her. Just wait til I get my hands on her, I'm gonna kill her."

"Goddamn it, Malone," Callahan shouted. "You're not going to do anything! You're going to be dead!"

If Callahan had been any other man, any less of a gunman, Rafe would have launched for his throat. As it was, he was forced to control his temper and use his brain, because he needed to come out of this alive.

He needed to stop that hardheaded, softhearted Maggie St. John from marrying Barlow Hill.

He sucked in a deep breath, then blew it out slowly. "Look, Nick. You and I need to talk. You're fixing to make another big mistake, and another innocent woman is going to suffer because of it. Can your conscience stand it? If Maggie gets hurt that'll be three women on your soul, Callahan. Rachel, Rosa, and now Maggie. Could you live with yourself?"

Callahan's face drained, then flushed with color. Rafe read the intent in his eyes and braced himself. With a roar of rage, his brother launched himself at Rafe.

They fell to the floor. Callahan landed a hard punch to Rafe's jaw. "It's you. You killed her. You got drunk and you raped her and you killed her." He dropped his Colt to wrap his fingers around Rafe's neck.

It was just the opportunity Rafe had been looking for. With a wide swipe of his hands he shoved the gun toward Gus. At the same time, while his brother's hands squeezed his throat, he jabbed upward with the dagger, pricking Callahan's skin just above his jugular. For barely a second, Nick's hands relaxed. But it was enough. Rafe gasped in a breath and shoved with his feet, rolling them both over until he sat on his brother's chest, knife at the throat.

He felt the gun at the back of his head almost immediately. One of the rangers said, "Drop it, Malone."

Gus's voice followed right away. "You drop it, Ranger."

"Everybody drop everything," the second ranger said. "I've got everyone covered."

Rafe's gaze never left his brother's. "This is between you and me, Nick. Let's settle it once and for all. Call off your men. Tell them to wait outside. Otherwise, we'll have a blood bath on our hands."

"Captain?" one of the rangers asked hesitantly.

"Go. Wait outside."

Rafe added, "Gus, Lucky, that includes you, too. My brother and I need to talk."

"Brother?" Gus asked in a shocked tone of voice. "Callahan is your brother?"

"It's a hell of a deal, old man," Callahan answered.

Rafe waited until the room emptied, then he rolled

off Nick and onto his feet. He returned the knife to his boot, then asked, "You want a drink?"

Nick sat up, rubbing his hand across his neck. "Yeah."

Rafe pulled the stoppers off a pair of decanters and sniffed. "Rum or whiskey?"

"Whiskey."

Rafe splashed the liquor into a pair of crystal glasses, then handed one to Nick once he'd climbed to his feet. Rafe nursed his along while Nick tossed his back, then poured himself a second. "All right. You have the floor. What is it you want to say?"

"Maggie St. John is in serious trouble, and I need you to give me the chance to get her out of it. I give you my word I'll come back here or meet you wherever you want afterward. We can settle this problem between us once and for all. But right now, I need to go take care of Maggie."

Callahan's laugh was anything but amused. "Let me get this straight. Your light o' love is in trouble, and you've come to me for help. Me. Isn't that rich? You murder my woman, but you ask me to help you save yours."

Light o' love? Rafe wanted to deck him for that alone. "I didn't murder Rosa, Nick. Let me tell you—"

"No!" his brother shouted. "I don't want to hear it. I wouldn't believe it anyway. Most likely this story about your lady is all a lie, your sly way to try to escape the noose. You are a liar and a thief, Malone. I've caught you in the act. You broke your goddamned parole, and I have two men with me who saw you do it. I'm a Texas Ranger, sworn to uphold the law. Even if I wanted to let you go I couldn't and I wouldn't."

"You sure about that?"

Callahan paused for a moment, then shot Rafe a narrow-eyed glare. "Yes. Yes, I am. It's my duty."

"Well, shoot, Nick." Rafe reached up to scratch

behind his ear, then with the speed and menace of a striking rattlesnake, he threw his fist and coldcocked his half brother. As Nick Callahan slid to the floor unconscious, Rafe stood over him, rubbing his aching knuckles. "I always did consider 'duty' a four-letter word."

→ 16 ←

Barlow Hill scratched his name across the bottom of the paper, and Maggie swallowed a sigh of relief. He'd bought it. The conceited fool had bought it. Smiling, she watched him sign a second copy, then accepted the pen he offered and wrote her own signature on the specified lines. *God bless you, Lester Bodine, Attorney at Law.* Not even Gentleman Rafe Malone, thief extraordinare, could have done it any better. Part one of her campaign to legally wrestle Hotel Bliss away from Barlow Hill was a fait accompli. Now all she had to do was marry the toad.

Maggie's smile dissolved like a wet sugar cube.

Hill lifted the paper to blow a soft stream of air over fresh ink. "I didn't expect you to suggest a marriage contract, Maggie, although I will agree it is good business. You certainly learn from your mistakes, don't you?"

"My mistakes?" Maggie asked, more because she felt he expected a reply than out of curiosity.

"It was the lack of attention to legalities that brought us together to begin with, was it not? Your guardians should have researched the title they purchased instead of assuming its validity. Of course, it's all worked out in the end, hasn't it?"

You only think this is the end, you weasel. Maggie responded to his insipid smile with a fake grin of her own.

Hill handed her one copy of the contract, saying, "I agree it is a good idea to legalize our union before we spring the secret wedding entertainment on our guests at the reopening of Hotel Bliss. Matters are tidier that way. I'm happy you thought of the idea, my dear."

Staring at his signature, she said, "As I explained earlier, my grandfathers aren't particularly pleased with the idea of my marrying—you or anyone. It's best we have matters concluded before Lucky and Gus return and all four of them join forces against me."

"I will not allow them to cause you trouble, my dear. As of noon tomorrow you will be my wife. Your grandfathers will no longer have you under their control. I will."

With great difficulty, Maggie managed to keep her mouth shut, but her mind rumbled phrases about who would control whom. She folded the document and tucked it into her pocket.

Hill continued, "I don't want the surprise wedding compromised. I trust you will find a way to ensure your grandfathers won't speak out of turn and make our news public? That is very important to me, Maggie. I have grand plans for that party. I won't see them spoiled."

"You needn't worry about what my papas will say, Barlow," Maggie said with a smile. Better he concern himself with what they might do. Maggie knew she'd be hard-pressed to keep them from making her a widow before the sun set tomorrow.

"Very good. Now, I am needed across the lake

today. The workers are laying the Italian tile in the front parlor, and I intend to oversee their efforts. You should have seen the mess they made installing the marble hearth. It was dreadful!"

"Dreadful," she repeated, her mind not on any stupid marble hearth but on the event scheduled for the following day. "Well, I'd best let you get to it, then."

She exited the study, slipped outside, and allowed her smile to break free. She'd done it. Now she needed to store this most important of documents in a safe place. With that thought in mind, she headed for the bathhouse. Ever since a dishonest guest had rifled her bedroom and swiped her favorite string of pearls a little over a year ago, she'd kept a lockbox secreted away behind a storage bin in the bathhouse. It was the perfect place to keep this treasured possession.

The wooden door creaked as she pulled it open and the sulfuric smell of the mineral springs hit her like a fist. Hoping to catch the cross breeze off the lake, she left the door propped open while she fetched her box from its hiding place.

As always when she opened the box, Maggie spent a moment enjoying each of the treasures stored inside. Sitting on the packed dirt floor, she smoothed the creases from the skirt of a linsey-woolsey doll's dress. She lifted a shell from the pink sand beach of a South Sea island to her ear and listened to the ocean. Returning it to the box, she removed the breathing tube she'd brought back from the cenote, Rafe's tube, the one he'd used to save her life. The smooth, yet knobby cane glided beneath her fingertips. She brought it to her mouth and tasted the jungle and the salty tang of the sea. But she didn't taste Rafe. The taste of him, the scent of him had faded from the tube and from her life.

Where was he now? she wondered. Had Papa Lucky reached him in time? What had he thought when he read her note? Was he saddened by her news? Relieved?

Maggie replaced her prizes, added the marriage contract, and tucked the box back into its hiding place. Sighing, she rose and began to pace the three-sided bathhouse. Between the log-lined pits that formed the mud bath and the springs bath, she paused and gazed out toward the lake. Heat shimmered above the surface, and the water beckoned. Maggie eyed her bathing sarong hanging on the wall and thought, *Why not?*

She closed the bathhouse door, and her fingers quickly worked the buttons on her bodice. She hummed a tune as she slipped her arms from her sleeves. The dress slid past her hips and billowed to the floor.

When she bent to pick it up and hang it on a peg, a groan ghosted from the shadows. Maggie wasn't alone. She whirled around. "Rafe!"

He loved her so damned much.

He would have told her, too, if he weren't so godawful angry at her. Marrying Barlow Hill. Over his dead body.

Rafe felt dangerous. Reckless. It didn't help his temper any to realize that despite his fury, one good look at her made him hard enough to drive a railroad spike, even before she'd taken off her dress. He gritted his teeth against the need that pulsed through his veins. Even as his fingers lifted to rip at the buttons on his shirt, he told himself he wouldn't indulge. He had questions to ask her, one in particular that had vexed him every inch of the way from Triumph Plantation to Hotel Bliss. He ground his teeth and spat out the words, "Am I too late?"

"Too late? How did you get here so fast?"

"I forked the saddle and never quit, that's how." He stripped off his shirt and flung it onto the ground. "Damnit, woman, have you done it? Have you married that lowdown, cold-blooded fool-headed ferret yet, or am I in time to stop you?"

Maggie's mouth opened and closed like a fish out of water. "Rafe, I . . ."

In a flash of revelation, he realized it didn't matter. She was his. His and no other's. "How do you feel? Lucky said you were better. Are you better?"

Wide-eyed, she nodded.

Good. Great. She looked good. She looked wonderful. *Ah, shoot.* Rafe took a step toward her knowing that nothing—not his temper, not her foolishness, not even a sea slug scum of a husband—would keep him from loving this woman. Here and now. And always.

He took another step toward her, and she said, "Rafe, you must understand. I—"

He grabbed her by the shoulders. He wanted to know. He couldn't bear to know. "Are you married?"

She opened her mouth, but Rafe didn't really want to hear the answer. He jerked her against him, and his mouth crushed down on hers, angry and desperate. If she'd fought him he might have stopped, but instead she wrapped her arms around him and held him tight.

She tasted of molasses and moonlight and Maggie, and Rafe strained against the tethers of his control. He groaned against her lips. "Don't let me hurt you. Tell me if I do and I'll stop. I swear."

"I don't want you to stop. Oh, Rafe, I need you."

He dragged her down to the ground. The man who'd cared for her so gently, so tenderly at Gallagher's didn't exist on this hot, steamy summer afternoon. Full of fear and fury and exhaustion, Rafe hovered on the edge of violence. His teeth scraped down her neck, his hands ripped her chemise, baring her breasts to the heat of his gaze and to his mouth. He suckled greedily.

His need was like the cenote at night, dark and dangerous, an underground river of hellish lust that swept him powerlessly along its molten tide. He wanted her with him, to share this glorious, gleeful heat. His mouth devoured. His fingers delved.

And Maggie writhed right along with him, bucking and choking back a scream when her muscles gripped his fingers, contracting in the waves of her release.

But Rafe wasn't through with her. Not yet. He took her up again, groaning along with her as she shivered and shuddered and called out his name. Naked now, they rolled as the pressure built inside him to a fevered pitch. His legs extended out over the sunken bath and grazed the heated water of the springs. Purposely, he rolled again and they slipped into the bubbling water. Currents of heat gushed around them and inside him. *Now, it must be now.*

His feet found purchase and he stood, holding her at the waist, lifting her, backing her against the wooden wall. "Wrap your legs around me," he ordered.

She arched her neck, her back, and gasped a quaking breath. And he took her standing up.

He drove himself deep inside her. Pounding her. Again and again and again. Panting. He watched her face as she plunged over the peak once more.

Then, as the tide of his lust was swept up in a turbulent, tumultuous, tempestuous storm of love, he emptied himself into her, calling out her name.

"Mary."

Rafe was embarrassed. Maggie could tell. She also picked up on the fact that he was still a little bit angry. If she'd any bones left in her body, she might have worked up a good snit over that. But as matters stood, she felt entirely too good to feel bad.

She sat on the rock ledge in the springs bath staring dazedly at the opposite wall. *The* wall. The wooden wall that probably should be bronzed. A smile played across her lips.

Sitting next to her, Rafe noted it and scowled. "What are you laughing at?"

"You. Me. Us." She sighed contentedly and added, "If separations mean homecomings like that one, I think I'll send you away more often."

"You didn't send me away."

"I know. You left. On a fool's mission, I might add."

Rafe formed an oval with his hands, then eyed her neck as though he were measuring it.

Maggie shut her eyes, wishing she'd kept her mouth shut. They needed to talk about this, obviously, but she sure could use a little more peace before engaging in the battle certain to come.

Her wish proved futile when he dragged a hand across his face and said, "We need to talk, Maggie."

"Can't it wait?"

His eyes narrowed, glowing like a cat's in the shadows of the bathhouse. "It has waited too danged long already. Have you done it yet, Maggie?"

"We just did it."

He cleared his throat. "Not that."

"Then what?"

He pinched the bridge of his nose and spoke matter-of-factly. "Murdered Barlow Hill."

"Murder!" She sat up straight. "What makes you say that? I intend to marry him, not murder him."

He pinned her with a glare. "Same thing. If you've married him, then I have to murder him. I'd just as soon not have his death on my conscience. Not when it's a needless one."

Maggie folded her arms. "You obviously have been spending way too much time with my grandfathers. Why would you want to murder Barlow Hill?"

"I don't bed married women!"

"Well, you didn't bed me. You walled me." She glanced at the structure under discussion and smiled smugly. "Quite nicely, too."

"Maybe you are the one I should kill, after all. I'm really angry with you, Maggie."

The sentiment warmed her heart. Now that blood

was flowing to her brain again, Maggie had managed to put it all together. He wouldn't be so angry if he didn't care. He wouldn't have made such tumultuous love to her if he didn't care. Maybe there would be a future for them yet.

After her marriage to Barlow Hill ended, of course.

She pushed across the water and sat beside Rafe. Looping her arm through his, she said, "Let me explain, Rafe. Listen to me, please."

His hand stroked up and down her bare thigh. "Did you marry him, Maggie?"

"Not yet." She tangibly felt the tension leave his body. It returned in a flash when she added, "The wedding is scheduled for noon tomorrow."

"It's not going to happen."

Maggie shrugged. "Yes, it is. The sooner I marry him, the sooner I can save the hotel. I have a wonderful plan, Rafe. Let me tell you about it."

With crisp, concise language, Maggie told him about her meeting with Lester Bodine and the intricacies he'd explained about marriage laws in the Republic of Texas. "It's a widely known fact that women have community property rights in this country. We counted on Barlow being aware of it."

"Barlow?" Rafe's voice rose to a near roar. "You call him Barlow now?"

"Most women do call their fiancés by their first names." Beneath her hand, Rafe's thigh muscle tensed. She hurried on with her explanation. "What is not so well known, and what I counted on Hill being unaware of is the dispensation of gifts in a divorce case. This will be his first marriage. There is no reason why he would know that gifts are not listed as community property. I gave him a long, obscure reason why I wanted him to give me the hotel as a wedding gift, but all the time I was playing to his greed. I told him I was soon to come into a large amount of money. I told him about the treasure, Rafe."

"What!"

"I told him my grandfathers had a vast amount of gold and jewels, but owing to the warfare in Yucatán, they couldn't get to it in time to meet the deadline for buying the hotel. I also informed him that they've promised half of it to me as a gift on my wedding day. When I agreed to marry Barlow, I said that I wanted a show of good faith. Because the hotel meant more to me than any jewelry, I wanted him to give it to me as a wedding gift. In turn, I'd give him the treasure. He thinks the contract doesn't matter because it'll all be community property anyway. He signed the paper, Rafe. All I have to do now is say 'I do,' and the hotel will be ours!"

"And you'll be married to the grouper!"

"Well, yes, that's the down side. But I'll start divorce proceedings immediately."

"On what grounds?"

"I'm not worried about that. I'm certain I can find something."

Rafe dragged his fingers through his wet hair. "I can't believe you actually intended to do this. Your grandfathers obviously didn't spank you enough when you were young. Hell, Maggie, you knew I'd gone to Triumph. Why would you even consider doing something this drastic? Why would you whore yourself by marrying Barlow Hill!"

Maggie froze as a bitter chill seeped through her. How could he? How dare he? With her chin up and her spine straight, she rose regally from the bath. Naked and dripping, she stared down at Rafe. "Whore myself? Isn't that the same as what you thought to do? Tell me, Mr. Malone, why is my sleeping with Barlow Hill any more of a moral transgression than your breaking your word to Luke Prescott? Seems to me two whores are soaking their sins in mineral water this afternoon."

"Damn you, Maggie." If looks could kill, she would have been struck dead in that instant. He rose from the water like a sea monster, angry and wrathful and destructive. And as beautiful as a god.

Emotion churned inside her as she watched him stalk across to where his clothes lay. She scuttled to retrieve her dress and held it before her, shielding herself from the burning fury of his gaze. Rafe snagged his pants off the floor, but instead of donning them he reached into a pocket and withdrew a velvet pouch. "Count your blessings, Maggie. You've been saved from your moral decline. I acted faster than you."

He threw the pouch at her, and Maggie caught it instinctively. She stared down at the small bag, and awareness stole through her like a disease. *Oh, no.*

Tears filled her eyes as slowly, fearfully, she lifted her head and looked at him. She saw bitterness. Hostility. Anguish. Dear God, no.

He showed her a caustic grin. "You don't need to whore yourself now, Maggie. I beat you to it."

Maggie dropped the pouch on the ground as if it were a hot coal. Clutching her dress to her chest, she blinked back her tears and asked, "Why, Rafe? Didn't Lucky reach you in time? Didn't you know I'd already solved the problem?"

"Solved the problem!" Rafe barked a laugh as he shoved his legs into his pants and yanked them up. "You call sacrificing yourself on that shark's bed a solution? Well, I don't!"

"Better I sacrifice my body than you your honor."

"I have no honor!" he shouted. "I'm a thief, Maggie. A very good thief. And everyone knows there is no honor among thieves."

With that he stalked toward her and scooped the pouch up off the floor. "Put your dress on, Maggie," he said coldly. "Then let's go find Barlow Hill. Let's go pay your wedding ransom."

Before Rafe had the opportunity to settle up the sale of Hotel Bliss with Barlow Hill, he ran into Snake

MacKenzie. Literally. Snake's fist, to be precise. He lay sprawled on the ground rubbing his aching jaw as he squinted up into the sunlight at the gleeful buccaneer.

"Well, scrape my barnacles," Snake said. "That felt good."

Rafe ran his tongue over his teeth, checking for any damage. "What did you do that for?"

"If you have to ask, you are dumber than I gave you credit for, Malone. You should be glad you've still got your head, in fact. Having to wait until I got my strength back gave me time to calm down. Still, I'd flay your hide today if I didn't think it would break Maggie's heart."

Rafe glanced back toward the bathhouse where he'd left the woman when she refused to accompany him on his visit to Hill. Break her heart? Shoot, after the little scene they'd shared, she'd likely hand her grandfather the knife. "Maggie is not very happy with me at the moment."

"Do you know about her plans?"

"Her wedding plans, you mean?" The pirate nodded, and Rafe continued. "She wrote it in the note she sent with Lucky."

"Are you going to stop her?"

"Yeah, I am. But I have to ask, Snake, why the blazes haven't you put a halt to it already?"

Snake scratched his whiskered cheek. "Oh, don't think I didn't give Maggie a piece of my mind once I pried the details about her scheme out of her."

"I'm amazed you had any available to give," Rafe muttered beneath his breath.

"Ben is back from your place, and he and me, we argued our lungs out," Snake continued. "I even faked another heart spell. But she saw through me, and she wouldn't be dissuaded. So we put our heads together and decided we'd allow the wedding to proceed. Then we'll kill him, of course. We'll slit the bilge rat from stem to stern and solve her problems.

Being his widow, Maggie will automatically inherit his holdings, Hotel Bliss included. Remember, Malone, the only reason we haven't killed him already is that he told us he'd willed his estate to the Masons in the event of his untimely death. Once he marries, though, his widow will get it. We just have to make her one. I won't pretend I don't like that idea."

Rafe shook his head. How had Maggie managed not to strangle these pirates over the years? "You aren't going to murder Barlow Hill."

"The slug," Snake said automatically. "Why not? Do you want to do it?" He rubbed his jaw, pondering, then added, "I guess that would be all right. I was looking forward to it, though. I still have what it takes, you know."

"I'm sure you do," Rafe drawled dryly. "Where is he? Up at the hotel?"

"Nah. He's across the lake at the house he's having built, overseeing the overseer. Something about tile. I'll say this for the worm, when he puts his mind to something, he gets it done. That house has gone up fast. So, how you gonna kill him, Malone? Shooting? Stabbing? Dare I hope cat-o'-nine-tails?"

Rafe blew out a heavy sigh. "Sorry to disappoint you, Snake, but I don't intend to kill him."

"Well, somebody has to kill him. We can't let him stay married to Maggie."

"We're not going to let him marry Maggie in the first place. We don't have to. I found your treasure, Snake. Part of it, anyway. Enough to buy off Hill."

"The rattlesnake."

"The cottonmouth," came Ben Scovall's scathing voice.

Rafe twisted his head. He wasn't entirely surprised to see the woman on the suave buccaneer's arm. Not this woman, in particular. Luella Best wore a pair of man's breeches, carried a ruffled, white silk parasol, and flashed that familiar, flirtatious smile. "Hello, Luella."

"Well, if it isn't Rafe the Rogue." Her wise eyes twinkled at him, and she blew him a kiss. "I knew you'd arrive in time. I tried to tell Pepper here that you'd come to save the day, but he didn't have quite the confidence in you that I did."

Pepper? Rafe noted how the tips of Ben's ears turned pink, and he arched a questioning brow toward Snake. The pirate reached out a hand and helped Rafe to his feet before grumbling softly in his ear. "As in peppermint candy. I suggest you don't ask."

Rafe covered his laugh with a cough, then dusted the dirt from his behind.

"Now, tell us about the treasure," Snake demanded. "Does Montgomery know you got it? Did you have any trouble? Where is it? Where are Lucky and Gus? Did you get the whole thing?"

"I got enough, and that's all that's really important. Gus and Lucky will be along later. I needed to travel fast to get here by Hill's deadline."

"The cur."

"The knave." Ben stared out over the lake toward the home under construction. "I must say I am anxious to see the deed done. Shall we approach the lion in his den?"

Gazing past Rafe, Luella clucked her tongue. "Judging by the looks of things, that will have to wait. First you must get past the tigress on the rampage."

The men all turned as one. "Uh-oh, boys," Snake said. "She is loaded for bear. Who is gonna take her on?"

"I will," Rafe said, his lips settling into a grim smile as he watched Maggie approach.

Ben grimaced. "You sure, Malone? Have you ever done this before?"

"No. But how difficult can it be?"

The pirates, and even Luella, groaned collectively. The lady reached over to pat Rafe on the arm, but she spoke to Ben. "Pepper, I think we should all participate. I've come to know Rafe pretty well. Dealing with frustration is not one of his strong suits. I'd hate to see him hurt himself. Or hurt her, either."

"I'm not going to hurt her," Rafe replied, his gaze meeting and accepting the challenge clearly visible in Maggie's eyes as she drew near. "I'm going to beat her."

Maggie halted her march next to them, her bag at her side. "Who wants to join me in a game of golf?"

Maggie took aim at the flag fluttering in the afternoon breeze some thirty yards away and gave her ball a whack. The small brown sphere sailed up and over the stick marking the hole. Way over.

"Seashells, Maggie!" Snake exclaimed from his seat atop the folding camp stool Ben had assembled for his use. Though his health was much improved, he still tired easily. He talked of itching to get back to the game, but at the moment he seemed content to stroll along with the players as an observer. "Try to hit it hard next time, why don't you? What did you eat for lunch? I think I'd best get me some of that."

She tossed her papa Snake a mutinous glare as Ben moved to stand behind Luella Best. "Leave Mary Margaret alone, Snake," he grumbled.

Luella flashed Ben a brilliant grin and batted her eyelashes fast enough to stir up a wind. "Let's hit a good one this time, Pepper. I must say I've been caught by the spirit of this game. I would so much like to do well."

"We will give it our best, Luella." But Ben's hands-on effort to help the widow hit the golf ball resulted in an ugly slice. Ben muttered under his breath. Luella nudged him with her elbow in a teasing manner, then said something in his ear that brought a slow smile to his face.

Despite her ill humor, the sight lifted Maggie's heart. Returning to Hotel Bliss to the news of Papa Ben's budding romance with Luella had been the lone bright island in an ocean of darkness. The widow had returned with Ben from the Winning Ticket Ranch, supposedly to treat her rheumatism in the healing waters of Lake Bliss. After watching their interplay and seeing how spry the elderly woman appeared, if Maggie not had personal knowledge of the benefits of Bliss water, she'd have suspected the widow of faking her illness to spend time with Papa Ben.

The woman was a practiced flirt. Likable, certainly, but still a flirt. Maggie was determined to keep a close eye on her. She wouldn't have Papa Ben hurt.

"Oh dear. That shot was even worse than Maggie's," the elderly woman said.

Maggie stiffened and battled to hold back a snappish retort. Ben eyed her uneasily and said, "Uh, Luella. It's probably best if you don't comment on her game today."

Luella blazed on as if she hadn't heard him, and as if Maggie weren't well within hearing distance. "I do so admire your granddaughter, Pepper. She's a strong woman. Just like my dear daughter-in-law, Honor. I do think if they had the opportunity, the two of them would be great friends. Next time I come to take the waters here at Lake Bliss, maybe I'll bring Honor with me. That would be nice, don't you think so, Maggie dear?"

Maggie gave up pretending not to listen. "I liked Honor when I met her in Galveston."

"She's a gem. And you realize, Hotel Bliss is not all that far from the Winning Ticket. We could visit back and forth quite often. You girls have a lot in common, you know. Honor has me to put up with, and you have your grandfathers. Speaking of whom, I simply can't wait to meet Mr. Lucky and renew my acquaintance with Mr. Gus. I had hoped they'd return to Lake Bliss before my departure, but it doesn't look like that will happen now, does it? Luke will be along any day now to fetch me home."

"Luke is coming here?" Rafe's voice boomed from behind them.

Snake turned around. "Malone! You finally sank it, hmm? So what did you take on that hole, twenty strokes?"

"Twenty-seven."

A muscle twitched at the side of his jaw, and Maggie wanted to laugh. The hardheaded, slick-handed thief had actually thought he could beat her at her own game. Well, she'd shown him. She'd whipped him up one side of the makeshift golf course and down the other. It should have made her feel good, wonderful, stupendous.

Then why was it all she wanted to do was cry?

Rafe glared at Luella. "Luke is coming to Lake Bliss? Soon?"

"Yes. Sooner than I'd like, I'm afraid." She smiled shyly up at Ben. "If I had known how pleasing I'd find the . . . waters . . . here at Lake Bliss, I'd have instructed him to wait another week. As it is, I expect him tomorrow or the next day."

Rafe paused for just a moment, then abruptly threw down his club. He looked straight at Maggie for the first time since the first hole when he'd gone behind her in the game by seventeen strokes. "I'm tired of waiting. I'm going to go find Hill and take care of this situation once and for all. No more delays. Are you coming?"

"No."

"Fine."

"Fine, yourself." Maggie lifted her chin and turned her back on him, calmly setting up for her next shot. Inside, however, she was far from calm. As she heard him stalk away, she could no longer hide the trembling in her hands. The weight in her pocket grew heavier and heavier with each of Rafe's steps.

He would be furious. Absolutely, positively incensed.

What he shouldn't be was surprised. A girl didn't grow up among professional thieves without learning a trick or two herself. As clumsy as he'd been with his club, bumping into him on the first hole had been easy. His anger had worked in her favor, too. If he'd been paying attention, he might have noticed the lightening of his pocket.

Maggie reached into her own pocket and fingered the velvet bag. No, Rafe wouldn't be happy that his stolen goods had been stolen out from under him. But what else could she have done? Let him betray his honor and maybe even sacrifice his life when two little words out of her mouth would solve the problem instead? She hardly thought so.

That wasn't how a woman treated the man she loved.

➤ 17 ◄

Upon discovering the theft of the jewels, Rafe gave himself an hour to calm down. Then he gave himself another hour to consider his options for how to deal with Maggie's little larceny. It wouldn't have taken him nearly as long if he hadn't paused every few minutes to marvel over her audacity. So it was midafternoon by the time he tracked her down to her bedroom, picked the lock on her door, and slipped soundlessly into her room.

The shuttered windows cast the room in a dim light. Rafe's gaze was drawn to the bed where Maggie lay fully clothed atop her bed, frying in the stifling summer heat like a fish in a skillet. He felt certain she'd hidden the jewels in a place that would take him days to locate, so he didn't bother to search. Instead, he sat upon the bed and stroked his thumb across the silky skin of her cheek. When, finally, she looked at him, and he saw the anguish boiling in those Caribbean depths, every one of his prepared arguments slid right out of his thoughts.

He cleared the lump from his throat and said, "You are the most loyal, courageous, and loving woman I have ever met, Mary Margaret St. John. In the relatively short time I've known you, you have taught me more about the world and the people in it, and especially about myself, than I have learned in the last ten years all rolled in together. You are a good person. Too good. Here you are ready to marry a man you can barely stand to look at, all because you think you need to take care of your papas and even me."

She blinked once but didn't say anything. Rafe continued, "There is something you forget, though, honey. Your papas and I are men. I know that sometimes you must think that's an insurmountable problem, and maybe you are right. But one thing about being a man, you see, is that we have our pride, and pride ranks right up there in a man's brain with honor and principle. And virility, of course."

She met his gaze then, and Rafe bit back a grin. He knew the virility crack would get her.

"Maggie. Sweetheart. I appreciate what you are willing to do for me from the bottom of my heart. But I can't let you do it. Knowing that you married Barlow Hill, the skunk, would unman me. It would be like taking your Papa Snake's favorite cutlass to my own jewels, if you follow my meaning. I'm a man, darlin', and I must fight my own battles, not ask you to fight them for me."

Her voice was thin and tormented. "But it's *my* fight you are waging, not yours. I got you into this. I should be the one to get you out."

"No, Maggie, you didn't get me into anything I didn't want to be in. Neither did your grandfathers, no matter what they might think. I made the decision to go on this treasure hunt because I was bored and looking for adventure. I can't complain now that I have found it."

The sight of the single tear spilling from her eye tore through his heart, and he knew it was time to press his point. It was time to finish it. "You must give me back the jewels, Maggie-mine. I appreciate the effort, but you can't protect me. Not now. It's too late. The damage has already been done. I've already done what I swore I'd never do again, and to complicate matters, I got caught doing it."

Maggie gasped and sat up in bed. "You got caught? By who? Montgomery? Oh, God." Her eyes widened with fear. "Tell me it wasn't your brother!"

"All right, I won't tell you." Rafe gave a lopsided grin and lifted her hand to his lips for a kiss. "The rangers are hot on my backside, love. And according to Luella, Luke is arriving tomorrow. If the rangers get to Lake Bliss before I get away, I'm a dead man. If Luke gets here before I leave, I'll wish I were dead. So tell me what you did with the treasure, Treasure. Let me take care of you before I leave. I have to do that. I'd rather Luke Prescott hanged me himself than leave here knowing you intended to go through with this travesty of a wedding."

"Leave? You're leaving?" Another tear ran down her cheek.

Rafe had to look away then. The emotion in her eyes cut his heart out, and he felt like crying himself. He needed to finish this, then and there. It was ripping him in two to do **this**, and that damned manly pride he'd told her about wouldn't allow him to let her know. "I have no choice if I want to save my neck. I'll admit I've grown rather fond of it these past thirty-odd years."

Her voice cracked as she spoke. "Where will you go?"

"West. I hear a man can still find a lot of adventure in the West. Texas has grown too civilized these past few years. It's been difficult to find a good adventure. Should be easier in the West."

Maggie steepled her hands in front of her mouth. She rolled off her bed and began to pace the room. Rafe watched her, wary, a lump the size of the Gulf of

Mexico in his throat. Hell, hanging couldn't hurt a man worse than this. Leaving her would kill his soul just as dead as any rope.

He loved her, loved her like he'd never loved before. But he couldn't tell her that, not now. It would only make matters worse.

His gaze drifted down to her bare feet. For some reason, she looked uncharacteristically vulnerable without her shoes.

"I'll go with you."

His head snapped up. "What?"

"I'll go west with you. I like adventure, too, Rafe. You asked me once before if I cared to go adventuring with you. Well, I do care. Take me with you. I want to go."

"You can't go!"

She swayed on her feet, taking it like a blow.

Cursing, Rafe shoved to his feet. Two furious strides took him to her. "Not because I don't want you, damnit. Believe me, that's not it at all. What about Hotel Bliss? What about your grandfathers? What about the water you need?"

"They'll be all right. I'll be all right."

Maggie whirled around and opened the door to her wardrobe. Pulling down a box from the uppermost shelf, she rifled through what Rafe recognized to be the clean rags she undoubtedly used during her monthlies. When she pulled out the blue velvet pouch, Rafe knew it proved how well she knew him. He'd never have gone searching through those.

She handed him the pouch, saying, "Take it. Pay off Barlow. The papas will have the hotel, and we can leave tonight."

His hand clutched the bag tightly. "Sweetheart, you don't understand. I'm not coming back. I've broken my parole and the Texas Rangers know it. I can't come back."

"I do understand! My papas will be all right. They'll have Bliss water for their aches and pains."

"Well, what about their heartache? Losing you could kill a man. Believe me, I know!"

She whirled around. "Losing you will kill me! I love you, Rafe. God help me, I love you!"

She loved him? He stared into her eyes. *Read the truth. She loved him. God help them both.*

"Ah, shoot, Maggie. I—"

"No." She laid her hand against his mouth. "You don't have to say anything. Please, don't say anything. Just listen to me. I'll be good for you, Rafe. You said it before. I'm loyal and I'm courageous. Heaven knows, I've had plenty of experience with adventure. I won't tie you down. Let me come, please."

One of her tears fell upon his hand, scalding him. Rafe yanked her against him, tucked her head against his chest, and wrapped his arms around her. "Maggie . . ." He choked and cleared his throat, then tried again. "Maggie, you're not thinking straight. What about your papas? They are not young men. If you left, you probably would never see them again. I can't take you with me and do that to you, to them. They cared for you when you were young. You should be here for them now that they are older. And what about the rheumatism? You need the Bliss water, too, Maggie. That's why I did what I did. And that's why . . ."

I'm leaving you behind. Rafe couldn't say it. He sucked in a deep, strengthening breath. Firmly, determinedly, he set her away from him. He stared down into her watery Caribbean eyes and felt himself drowning. He knew then he had to be honest. Maggie deserved it; she deserved to know how he felt. And maybe he deserved to tell her, too. "I love you too much to let you come with me, Maggie. I've got to go, but you have to stay. It's that simple."

"Rafe, no."

He slipped the jewels into his shirt pocket. "Give me one last kiss, Mary. Kiss me good-bye."

From the doorway to Maggie's room came the

sneering sound of a familiar voice. "What perfect timing."

Not again! Rafe closed his eyes. *Well, shoot.* He had thought he'd have more time.

"Go ahead and kiss him good-bye, Miss St. John," Nick Callahan drawled, gesturing with his Colt Texas Paterson revolver for her to go ahead. "I reckon I can allow my brother such a boon before I hang him."

Maggie was in a panic.

Waves of heat rippled up off the dry grass leading down toward the lake, down toward the old oak with its spreading branches. The oak where the hangman's noose dangled like a sin from a thick branch.

Nick Callahan had brought a posse with him, a handful of scraggly deputies he'd collected along the way from Triumph Plantation. He'd announced his intention to use Rafe's own horse to do the deed. Maggie had wanted to slap both the brothers when Rafe expressed thanks for Callahan's consideration.

Now she watched in horror, her heart in her throat, as the lawman looped a rope around Rafe's wrists behind his back. "No, you can't," she protested yet again. Her knees went watery and she sagged against Papa Snake, who wrapped an arm around her. Luella Best stood white-faced and trembling beside Papa Ben, nervously twirling her parasol.

"Damnit, man! Get Maggie out of here," Rafe demanded, sending Snake a pleading look. "Take her across the lake to Hill's house. She doesn't need to see this."

"None of us needs to see this, Malone." Ben stepped forward and addressed Nick Callahan. "You are making a mistake, son. One you will regret the rest of your life."

"What I regret is taking this long to get the job done."

Maggie shook her head slowly. Her gaze shifted

between Rafe and his half brother. "This is so sad," she said, speaking to them both. She squared her shoulders and stepped away from Snake. "You are family. You are *brothers*. Do you know how lucky you are to have one another? All my life I've wished for a brother or a sister. You have that precious bond between you and here you are ready to throw it away."

Callahan tossed her a look. "I appreciate your sentiment, Miss St. John, but in this instance the argument is a poor one. Our family tie isn't one to be proud of, under the circumstances."

"Pride has nothing to do with it. It's blood, and it's a history, and it's a connection no one else on God's earth shares with you. It's priceless and here you are ready to throw it away because of what, some rigid sense of right and wrong that takes none of the extenuating circumstances into account?"

"Extenuating circumstances?" Callahan repeated, arching a brow.

"Love, Mr. Callahan. Your brother did what he did out of love for me. He tried other ways to solve my troubles first, but when all else failed he was willing to risk his life, to break his highly valued word to a dear, dear friend, because he loves me. And you know what? I love him just as much. I'd break a law or two if Rafe needed it. I'd break a law or two if my grandfathers needed it. We're not talking murder here, Mr. Callahan, or any other crime that caused injury to another person. We're talking theft of goods that were stolen goods in the first place. Is that truly worth a man's life? Is it truly worth your *brother's* life?"

"The law is the law, ma'am, and I'm here to uphold it."

"Bah," she said scornfully. "You're here to follow through on some personal vendetta. Your behavior that day at Gallagher's Inn proves it."

"He broke his parole!"

Maggie threw out her hands. "Well, I broke a toe one time. Nobody wanted to kill me."

Snake piped up. "That's right. And I've broken ribs more times than I can count." He glanced at Ben. "Didn't you break your arm years ago? On that voyage to Madagascar, wasn't it?"

"No, I don't believe so," Ben replied, picking up the change in conversation without hesitation. He held Luella's gaze for a meaningful moment and appropriated her parasol. Moving away from her, he started pacing, pausing beside Maggie to hand her Luella's parasol. Then he bowed his head and scratched behind his ears. "If I remember correctly, Snake, the arm was on the Tahiti trip. Madagascar was Lucky's leg."

"Lucky's leg!" Snake snapped his fingers and took to striding around in a wide circle himself. "How could I forget about Lucky's leg? He whined about it for a year afterward."

"That's true. Still, he wasn't near as bad as Gus was that time he got his nose broke."

Snake hit his forehead with the palm of his hand. "Now that was a mess. Never saw so much blood. And the hollering? Remember that, Ben? Remember how he wore out his throat with all the carrying on?"

"I remember," Maggie said, twirling the parasol as she stepped forward to join her grandfathers in their route. They were up to something. She'd watched them play this game a number of times in the past, and she knew to follow their lead. "He threw a fit because Magic Tongue Sally did it. Gus always has hated being bested by a woman."

She hazarded a glance at Rafe and Callahan. The ranger returned her look, his expression dumbfounded. Rafe arched his brows, silently mouthing the words "Magic Tongue Sally?"

Ben, assuming his customary leadership role, widened the circle they paced as he continued with Maggie's conversational thread. "That's why Gus won't play you in golf, Maggie. You get the drop on the three of us at the word 'go.'"

"Now wait a minute," Snake said, halting just in front of one of the lawmen. "Maggie doesn't beat me in golf."

"Yes I do, Papa Snake." Maggie stopped beside a second lawman, not meeting his eyes, but carefully observing his stance. If she'd interpreted Papa Ben's instructions properly, she figured to hear the word "go" at any moment. "I beat you just this morning. Rafe was there. He'll tell you."

Rafe studied Maggie closely, obviously trying to figure out how she wanted him to answer. Finally he said, "Uh, Maggie. Do you think now is the right time for this?"

She put her hands on her hips. "Well I don't know when else we might get around to it. Your brother, here, is ready to hang you any minute. For my sake, Rafe, tell us."

"Yes," Ben agreed, stopping within arm's length of a third ranger. He braced his hands on his hips. "Tell us, Malone." Ben waited until all eyes had shifted toward Rafe, then he said, "Tell us. Go on." And with that, he lunged toward the ranger and laid a knife against his throat. Snake moved simultaneously with Ben, the gun he'd slipped from the ranger's holster now pressed against the lawman's temple. Maggie, not as practiced as her papas with such maneuvers, threw herself at her ranger and knocked him to the ground. Before he recovered from the surprise sufficiently to knock her off, she'd stuck the pointed metal end of the parasol against the thin skin of his lower eyelid.

"Son of a bitch!" Callahan exploded. "Do you people want to get yourselves killed? What do you think you are doing?"

"It is what we like to call a Caribbean cutoff," Ben replied, twisting his knife so that sunlight glinted off the blade. He slipped the revolver from the lawman's holster, then gave a little warning whistle and tossed the gun to Maggie, who exchanged her questionable weapon for a sure one. "You can't get Malone without sacrificing at least one of your men," Ben continued as Maggie rose to her feet and backed away from the deputy with the gun aimed at his heart. "Not all three of us will lose in a fight."

"Oh, my," Luella said, rapidly patting her chest. She gazed helplessly at a fourth deputy and said, "Young man! Help! My heart!" She swayed on her feet and let out a little scream. The young lawman lowered the pistol he had aimed at Papa Snake and rushed over to help her.

And he was surprised with a little pistol in his side to show for it.

"I'm sorry, son," Luella said, smiling kindly. "I'm afraid I must stand with my friends on this."

Rafe started chuckling as Callahan let out a stream of curses. "I can't believe this. How could I let you people get the drop on me again? I should have hanged you immediately rather than let you stand around jawing. I'm a Texas Ranger, by God. I'm better than this!"

"Yes, you are," Rafe agreed. "You have a fine reputation, Nick. I've kept up with you over the years. I have to admit I'm surprised the buccaneers fooled you."

"Well, I'm not!" Maggie said. "It's perfectly obvious to me why you delay this stupid endeavor of yours. For all your talk, you don't truly wish to kill your brother. You understand what I meant earlier about family. You know what else, Mr. Callahan? In many ways you and your brother are very much alike. You both have a highly refined sense of honor."

Callahan cried, "Honor! The man is a thief!"

"But he's an honest thief. An honorable thief."

"He's Gentleman Rafe Malone," added Luella Best.

"That's right," Maggie agreed. "But he's something else, too. He's human, only human, just like you are, Mr. Callahan. And human beings make mistakes. Family members make mistakes. The operative word here is 'forgiveness.' We have to learn to forgive one another when we err. Rafe has told me of some of the history between you two. You don't need to hang Rafe; you need to forgive him. Just as Rafe needs to forgive you."

"Forgive him?"

The ranger's scornful laugh grated like sand against Maggie's ears. With every word he spoke, his tone grew harsher, louder, and meaner.

"It'll be a cold day in hell before that happens, lady. You say he told you some of our history. Did he mention how he'd raped and murdered my wife?"

For a long, unbearable minute, Nick Callahan's shout echoed across the land. Maggie saw the shock on her grandfathers' faces and watched with satisfaction as it faded into obvious dismissal of the ranger's charge. They believed in Rafe, as they should. As she did.

Then, heedless of the gun against his temple, Rafe whirled on Callahan. "Damn you, Brother! Listen to me. For once in your life, believe what I say, because I'm telling you the truth! Rosa was almost gone when I found her. I didn't rape her. I didn't cut her. I held her until she died."

The gun pointed at Rafe shook with the force of Callahan's fury. "You did it! You killed her! You were covered in blood!"

"It was a battlefield! People tend to get bloody on a battlefield. Some of the blood on me was Rosa's, but not most of it. I couldn't exactly tell you under the circumstances. I avenged her for you, Nick. I took a Mexican bayonet from a corpse and gutted the bastard who'd done it—Colonel Jack Randolph."

"No!"

Maggie's heart stuttered as he aimed the gun inches from Rafe's face.

"The colonel didn't do it," Callahan cried. "He was killed during the battle."

Rafe looked down at the gun, then up at his brother. He spoke in a quiet, controlled voice. "Listen to me. For once in your life, listen to what I'm saying. *I. Did. Not. Hurt. Her.* I was drunk, yes, because I'd just heard about Luke's family. But seeing Rosa sobered me up fast. Randolph still had his pecker hanging out, for God's sake. Randolph is the one responsible. Not me."

Rafe's tone rang with honesty and anguish as he added, "I wasn't responsible, Nick, and despite the blame I've tried to load on your shoulders ever since, neither were you."

Maggie held her breath, her gaze locked on Nick Callahan. The moment drew out silent and long as his inner struggle shone on his face.

"It wasn't your fault, Nick," Rafe said softly.

All the fight seemed to drain right out of Callahan. He lowered the gun and closed his eyes. A shudder racked him. "Yeah, it was," he said, his voice cracking. "I didn't send her home. I should have sent her home."

"You botched it, true," Rafe said, glancing upward toward the thick branch—the hanging branch—on the old oak tree. "Just like you bungled it by not sending a man back to protect Rachel Prescott when you told me you would. But as far as your killing either one, well, I was wrong. I shouldn't have blamed you. Randolph killed Rosa, not your poor judgment. It was my own guilt talking where Rachel is concerned. I broke my promise to Luke, and that's no one's sin but my own."

"Sins," Callahan muttered. "So many people and so many sins." He slowly turned his head and looked at Maggie. "Maybe you were right, Miss St. John.

Maybe forgiveness does need to be the motto of the day, but it's not that easy to do."

"I understand," Maggie said. "You've held hatred in your heart for a long while, and it takes time to let it go. But it's the right thing to do, Mr. Callahan."

Slowly, hesitantly, the ranger captain returned his gun to its holster. Relief flooded Maggie like a tide. It would be all right. Rafe would be safe. Her lips began to lift into a smile until Callahan's next words stopped her cold.

"The problem is, forgiveness and understanding don't negate the fact that a crime has been committed." He pinned his brother with his gaze. "Rafe, you stole something from the safe at Triumph Plantation, not to mention the fact y'all drew guns on lawmen. You broke your parole. It's my job as a ranger to deal with it."

Snake harrumphed. He jabbed the gun against his deputy's temple, drawing a squeal from the frightened young man, and grumbled, "Like we told you before, ranger, he didn't steal it. He repossessed it on our account."

"You stubborn old goats!" Nick Callahan exclaimed, rolling his eyes in frustration. "Can't you see this Caribbean cut-off of yours is likely to get at least one of you killed?"

Ben twisted his lips wryly. "It might come to that, true. I certainly hope it doesn't."

Coming from somewhere behind Maggie, a new voice entered the fray. "I don't see why it should."

Snake sucked in a sharp breath. Ben's posture grew rigid. Making sure to keep the lawman pinned down with the parasol, Maggie glanced over her shoulder and froze. Papa Lucky and Papa Gus had stepped out of the trees, pistols pointed and expressions fierce. But the man who demanded Maggie's complete and total attention was a stranger, someone whom she recognized at once.

The gun slipped from her hands and the deputy

rolled out of harm's way. Maggie stood frozen, her mouth as dry as a west Texas July.

Looking into the stranger's eyes was like looking into a mirror. Andrew Montgomery.

Her father.

When Maggie had thrown her arms wide and yelled about her broken toe, Rafe had gotten his first sneaking suspicion that he wouldn't die that afternoon. When the pirates swashbuckled their way into surprising Nick's motley crew of deputies, he'd upgraded his survival chances to pretty darn good. Then, when Gus and Lucky burst into view with Patersons at the ready, he'd silently declared himself home free.

That was before he got a good look at the fellow who tagged along with them. The minute he spied the masculine version of Caribbean eyes, he realized the dynamics of the situation had taken a drastic change.

Andrew Montgomery had come to call at Hotel Bliss.

Rafe's gaze immediately went to Maggie. Had she guessed the stranger's identity? The pasty appearance of her complexion told him yes, she had. Rafe ached to go to her; he wished one of her papas would wrap her in his arms. But the tableau of lawmen and defenders remained frozen, weapons pointed and ready, as Montgomery stepped into the circle. He walked toward Maggie and stopped directly in front of her.

Rafe whipped his head around and glared at his brother. "She needs me." Then, with his hands still tied behind his back, he strode past Montgomery and took position behind the woman he loved.

Montgomery asked, "Did you mean it?"

Rafe clenched his jaw when he spied a shudder rippling down her back. She cleared her throat before asking, "Mean what?"

"Forgiveness. We listened from the trees. You said

family members make mistakes and must learn to forgive one another. Can you do it?"

Rafe couldn't see her expression, but the stiffness in her spine gave him a clue as to what she was thinking. He moved closer, fitting his chest to her back, offering her his silent support. She leaned against him just slightly enough to let him know she needed him; then her shoulders rose with a deep breath. "Why should I?"

Montgomery dragged a hand across his mouth. Anxiousness shone in those eyes so similar to Maggie's as her father flicked his gaze upward to meet Rafe's. *Careful,* Rafe silently warned him. *Hurt her any more at your own peril.*

Montgomery gave a slight nod, then returned his gaze to his daughter. "Because, Mary Margaret, I love you. I regret how I failed you, and I'm begging your forgiveness."

"You love me?" Maggie said with a disbelieving laugh. "How can you love me? You don't even know me!"

Gus stepped forward. "I think now might be the time for you to offer up your good-faith gesture, Andrew. Right now before this nonsense goes any further."

Montgomery nodded and seemed to tear his gaze away from Maggie. Addressing Nick, he said, "Captain Callahan, you and I are a long way from home."

"Yeah," Nick replied.

When he didn't elaborate, Montgomery continued. "My friends tell me you are under the impression that Mr. Malone here is guilty of burglarizing my study."

"I caught him red-handed."

"How convenient you were present at Triumph at that particular time. How did it come about?"

"Triumph Plantation is in the center of my territory. It's natural that I visit it on my patrols."

"I see," Montgomery said, nodding. "Of course, I

also see that you didn't see what you think you saw, Captain Callahan."

"Come again?" Callahan cocked his head and folded his arms. "What sort of scam are you playing, sir?"

"No scam. I've been told you found Mr. Malone, a known thief, in my study late at night with the safe open. I can easily see how one might believe the man to be in the process of committing a crime."

"The bag of jewels in his hand was a good clue, too," Nick replied dryly. "So was the fact that the gems were there when he coldcocked me and missing when I woke up."

"Perhaps Mr. Malone should have handled that aspect of the situation a bit differently. However, I had given him a directive and time was very much of the essence. I needed that bag of gems here at Lake Bliss as soon as possible."

"How much are those pirates paying you for this, Montgomery?" Nick asked.

"I'm telling you the truth. Rafe Malone didn't steal from me. He was delivering a gift from me to my daughter. Captain Callahan, he didn't break his parole. You can't hang Rafe Malone."

Nick glanced at Rafe, then thumbed his hat back off his forehead. "You're lying. Rafe stole the jewels and the packet of letters. I know it as sure as I'm standing here."

"Uh, Captain?" one of the deputies asked. "Could I make a suggestion? If we're not gonna hang Malone anytime soon, don't you think we should bid these folks good day and let them put their guns away?"

"'Fraid this old man's palsy will accidentally trip a trigger, son?" Lucky asked, grinning wickedly as he exaggerated a tremble in his hand.

The deputy grinned sickly. Nick snorted. He sauntered over to where Rafe stood behind Maggie and reached for the knife sheathed at his hip. "Give me your wrists."

"It's over?" Rafe asked.

"I need to gnaw on it a little bit, put it all together in my head. Your lady's argument about family and forgiveness makes some kind of sense. And, since her father's lies have let us both off the hook, I think perhaps we'd be foolish not to explore the possibilities."

Rafe felt the knife sawing the rope, and then his hands swung free. He rubbed his wrists as he turned around and faced his brother. "I can live with that."

Nick extended his hand. "Better than hanging, anyway. Right?"

"You said it, Brother." Rafe gave his brother's hand a shake and they shared a crooked, hesitant smile.

Nick turned and spoke to the pirates and Luella. "If y'all would be so kind as to put your weapons away, I'd like to pay my men so they can return to their homes."

"Excellent," Luella piped up. "And, boys, I've some sweet tea up at the hotel if you'd care for some." She tucked her hand through Nick's arm and began to lead him away.

Now that the more immediate threat had been dealt with, Rafe directed his attention toward Maggie. *Poor thing. She looked positively whipped.* And no wonder. It had been an eventful few minutes.

With the lawmen gone, the pirates closed ranks, flanking Rafe and Maggie, folding their arms across their chest as they faced their old enemy. Ben spoke for them all. "All right, Andrew. Here's the chance you've wanted for years. Talk to our Maggie."

Maggie's heart pounded as Montgomery faced her, hat in hand. "May I speak with you alone?"

Snake let out a snort. "Maybe when the ocean changes from blue into pink and purple polka dots."

"Now, Snake," Gus said. "Give Andrew a chance here."

"That's right," Lucky added. "Drew has been awfully helpful so far. Why, if he hadn't been so quick to jump in after me when I fell off my horse while we were fording the river, we wouldn't have gotten here in time."

"It's up to Mary Margaret," Ben said, frowning at the bickering men. Turning to her, he said, "I think it might be a good idea, though. Otherwise, we may drag this out until morning."

Maggie slowly shook her head. "You should stay. All of you."

"Do you want me to kill him for you, Maggie?" Snake asked. "You say the word and it's done."

It lent a normalcy to the moment that brought a smile to her lips. "Thank you, Papa Snake, but I want to hear what he has to say."

"Well, if you change your mind, just say the word," he gruffly replied.

"I'm not leaving, either," Rafe declared. He threaded his fingers through hers and gently squeezed her hand.

"I don't want you to leave." Rising on her tiptoes, she pressed a quick kiss against his cheek. "I need you beside me, Rafe." He preened a little at that, and his action gave her strength. Finally, she was ready to face her father.

Andrew Montgomery looked every inch the successful planter. He was a handsome man, she realized as she studied him closely. He stood tall and distinguished-looking in his black frock coat. The wide-brimmed, low-crowned hat he wore didn't completely hide his salt-and-pepper hair. And his eyes, well, they were hers. Turquoise blue and uncertain. Hesitant. Anxious. So very much like her. Maggie swallowed hard and asked, "What is it you want to say?"

He cleared his throat and gave a little grin. "Now that the moment is here, I'm not quite certain."

Maggie took a step closer to Rafe. He wrapped a supportive arm around her shoulders as Montgomery continued. "I listened closely when you spoke to the ranger about family and forgiveness, and I am hoping you will extend that generosity of spirit to me."

Maggie gazed out at the green-tinted water of Lake Bliss, emotions blowing through her like the trade winds. Anger, hurt, hope—she didn't know how she felt. She didn't know how she should feel. Gripping Rafe's hand in a tight squeeze, she asked the question uppermost on her mind. "Why didn't you want me?"

Andrew Montgomery grimaced. "You don't start with the easy ones, do you."

"Are there any easy ones?"

He shook his head. "Not in this situation, no." Exhaling a long sigh, he stuck his hands in his pockets and followed the path of her gaze toward the lake. "Allow me, if you will, to start at the beginning. I believe if you understand my background, perhaps you'll find it easier to make sense of my mistakes. I am the second son of an English earl. My brother inherited the title upon my father's death, shortly before my eighteenth birthday. The new earl and I didn't see eye to eye on many things—we detested one another, to be truthful—so when he ordered me to America to research a potential investment, I willingly went along. When pirates attacked the ship and offered me a position on the crew, I jumped at the chance to join them."

"He had a swashbuckler look about him," Gus piped up. "We thought from the first that he'd make a good hand." Lucky and Snake nodded their agreement. Ben's expression remained impassive.

"I was young and cocky," Montgomery continued. "I know in my bones I'd have died that first year had Ben and the others not taken me under their wings. For a while, life was good. It was a grand adventure. And then I met your mother."

"Lady Abigail Summers," Maggie said.

Montgomery nodded. "Yes. Abigail."

"The she-cat."

"The vixen."

"The peahen."

"The nag."

"The bitch," concluded Montgomery.

Maggie realized then that the papas' routine was even older than she'd previously known.

Her father bent and scooped up a handful of pebbles. He tossed one, then another toward the lake, falling short each time. "I'd never seen a more beautiful woman. I won her, and somewhere along the way I fell in love."

"I've been tying rope all my life," Snake sagely observed, "and I've never yet run across a set of knots the likes of which she tied in Andrew."

Montgomery sent the remaining rocks sailing, and this time a pair of them made it to the water. "She was my dearest dream. My deepest desire. But it wasn't like that with her. For Abigail, love was nothing more than a game. She didn't love me. I was only a holiday diversion for her. Still, even knowing that, with her having said it to my face, when she left me I wanted to die."

The grandfathers nodded solemnly. "You almost did die once or twice," Gus said. "Remember that knife fight with Pegleg Purcell?"

That started a discussion of various bar battles and street fights. Maggie's frustration built like steam in a stew pot. "Papas, do you think you could hold off on the reminiscing for a bit? I'd like to hear the rest of this story."

"Sorry, Magpie." With shuffling feet and sheepish looks, the pirates finally settled down.

Montgomery sucked in a breath, and let it out with a whoosh. "It didn't take too long for the love I felt for Abigail to turn to hate."

"So you hated me, too," Maggie said, taking it like a lash to the heart.

Not meeting her gaze, Montgomery smiled and shook his head. "Not at all. I pray I can make you understand this. In my young and foolish mind, on that day when I first learned of your existence, I gazed not upon your sweet shining face, but on the deceitful, hurtful visage of your mother. Even as a child of four you had her look. You favor her even more now. In fact, you are the very image of Abigail."

"The beautiful wench."

"The lovely witch."

"The elegant wanton."

"The sumptuous whore."

"Hey!" Rafe rounded on the pirates. "Take care with the names you use, you old barnacles. He said Maggie was her image."

Ben's face turned the slightest bit pink. "Yes, you are right. We apologize, Mary Margaret."

Montgomery gave the pirates a quelling look, then returned his attention to Maggie. "Looking at you, I saw nothing of me. So, I saw nothing."

"And my mother? What did she see when she looked at me? Obviously not love."

"I don't know about that," Gus said, his eyes solemn and honest. "I think in her own way she loved you. I do know that day on the beach she didn't want to give you up." He glanced around at the other papas. "Don't you agree?"

They all nodded, and Maggie felt the tiniest spark of warmth invade an old, cold hurt.

Ben said, "Abigail was a weak woman, Maggie. She didn't have the strength to keep you, to own up to her responsibilities in the face of public censure. She didn't have your strength."

Montgomery cleared his throat, recalling Maggie's attention. "Neither did I. Seeing her again like that made me crazy. In my pain, I decided she lied. I told myself you weren't my child, that she'd taken a lover and tried to pass his get-off as mine. I was wrong, of course. Captain Ben and the others tried to make me see it at the time." He lifted a finger to a small faded scar on his temple. "They gave it an excellent effort."

Lucky grinned. "We beat you like a tied-up billy goat."

Montgomery ignored him. "I was a dangerous man those first years after she left me. Mean and brutal and ruthless. Then, after she brought you to the island, I only grew worse. If you believe nothing else I say here today, believe that you were better off with these men than with me during those first few years. To this day I am grateful they took you in."

"As well you should be," Ben grumbled.

Rafe muttered something under his breath that Maggie couldn't quite pick up. A belligerent light shined in his eyes and impatience bristled in his tone as he said, "Let's go to the whip, shall we? If you were so dad-blamed grateful they took her in, then why did you steal all the treasure from the cenote?"

Montgomery looked deeply into Maggie's eyes as he answered. "Because I wanted this opportunity to speak with my daughter. They wouldn't allow me to see her. They refused—"

"Now wait a minute," Snake interrupted.

"You watch your tongue," Gus warned.

"Hush!" Maggie demanded. "All of you. I want to hear what he has to say, but—" She turned toward her father. "—I won't listen to anything bad about my papas. If they wronged you, it was done out of their love for me. Tell me what you will, as long as you keep your slandering tongue off my papas."

Montgomery's grin was unexpected. "No wonder they are so proud of you. Gus and Lucky boasted about you all the way from Triumph to Lake Bliss. And I see now that what they said was true. Very well, Daughter, I'll do as you ask. Suffice to say that some time ago—years ago—I realized the errors of my ways. But because I was still too proud, too protective of myself, I made unreasonable demands upon your guardians. We ended up in a winner-take-all war for you as a result of it. That war ends here today."

"It does?" Ben asked.

Andrew Montgomery faced his old captain. "I want that more than anything. I don't want to take her away from you, Ben. I simply want you to share her with me. I want the chance to know my daughter. I want the chance to prove my love for her. And since I'm exposing my soul here, I might as well tell you the rest. I'd like to be your friend again—yours and Snake's and Gus's and Lucky's. I've missed you."

"You'd better hold right there, Andrew," Gus said. "You're bordering on sappy. Corsairs don't get sappy."

Montgomery turned to Maggie. "What do you say, Miss Maggie? Will you give me this chance? Will you allow me into your life? Will you forgive me?"

Maggie heard the echo of Nick Callahan's words. Forgiveness wasn't that easy. She looked up at Rafe, silently asking for guidance.

"It's your decision, love," he told her. "Look to your heart. It'll tell you what to do."

Forgiveness. Could she practice what she preached? Maggie closed her eyes and thought of all he had explained. She understood him better now, and she could empathize with what he'd done. But getting those feelings from her head to her heart where a little girl's hurt had burrowed in years ago wasn't that simple. "I need time."

Andrew Montgomery, her father, nodded. He blinked away the suspicious sheen glistening in his eyes and gave a poor imitation of a brave smile.

"Well, shoot," Rafe said, snapping his fingers. "I have an idea. Ben? Why don't you lead your buccaneers here back up to the house. Fetch that bag of jewels from my brother so we can make the deal with Barlow Hill."

"The cottonworm."

"The cankerworm."

"The lugworm."

"The bollworm."

"The woodworm."

"Good Lord," Rafe said with a grin. "Y'all do entertain a man. Maggie and I will be up to the hotel directly. Tell Luella I'd appreciate it if she saved me a glass of that sweet tea."

"What is it, Rafe?" she asked once they were alone.

"Two things. First of all, there's this." He tugged her into his arms and gave her a long, luscious, toe-tingling kiss.

"Hmm," Maggie said when he finally drew away. "I needed that. And what was the second thing?"

"What second thing?"

She laughed. "What's your idea, Rafe? Does it have something to do with my father?"

He gave his head a shake. "Dang, woman, you kiss the smart right out of my head."

"If only I could do the same with your mouth."

"Honey," he leered. "You're welcome to do anything your little heart desires with my mouth."

"I'll save the thought for later. Now, do you have something to tell me about Andrew?"

"No. Something to show you. Wait right there a minute." Rafe walked over to the tree where his horse was tethered. Unbuckling the strap on his saddlebag, he flipped back the cover and reached inside. Maggie's curiosity blossomed when she saw the big stack of ribbon-wrapped letters he pulled from within.

He carried them back to her and presented them with a sense of ceremony. "I don't know what these say. I found them in the safe with the bag of jewels. It's Montgomery's handwriting and they are addressed to you. Maybe if you read them, you'll find your answers."

Maggie stared down at the cream-colored parchment in her hands. "I'm scared, Rafe."

"Don't be scared. I'll be right here with you. I'm sort of hot, though. Why don't we go dip our toes in the lake while you're doing this. All right?"

Slowly, Maggie nodded. Soon they sat side by side,

bare feet dangling over the bank into Lake Bliss. Rafe put an arm around Maggie and leaned her against him, whistling a happy fiddle tune beneath his breath.

Maggie broke the seal on the topmost letter and began to read.

My darling daughter. Today is your tenth birthday. I would give everything I own to be with you today.

Rafe's heart felt as big as Texas as he watched Maggie welcome her father into her life a short time later. Her eyes were red and swollen with the remnants of the tears she'd cried while reading the stack of birthday, Christmas, and, later on, Texas Independence Day letters her father had written her but never posted. The words he'd penned had given her a glimpse of his past regrets and future hopes, and made it easier for her to allow the healing of forgiveness to begin.

When Maggie hugged her father for the first time ever, Andrew Montgomery's face lit with a smile as bright as the sky on a cloudless summer morning. The pirates, for the most part, took it in stride. Snake's scowl softened with grudging acceptance. Ben gave the proceeding a look of guarded approval. Lucky got so excited he swallowed the stub of his smoke, and Gus grinned with the smug satisfaction of a job well done.

Talk almost immediately turned to Barlow Hill.

"I say we head on over to that house of his," Lucky said. "Get this over with before supper. Snake put a ham on to cook this morning, and I'd just as soon not share my meal with that toad one more time."

"He's expecting to marry Maggie in the morning," Ben observed. "I halfway anticipate some trouble from him."

"Shoot," Rafe scoffed. "He can't give us any trouble. We come armed with a contract, a calendar, and a bag of precious gems. His hands are tied." Sliding Callahan a glance, he added, "And besides, we've got the law on our side."

"Will wonders never cease," Gus said.

"I never expected to see the day, that's for sure," Snake added.

After further discussion, the decision was made to wait until Snake pulled his pecan pie from the oven before heading over to Barlow Hill's lakeside mansion. The pirates all agreed it wasn't fair to make Snake miss out on the fun, and nobody wanted to risk burning the dessert. They congregated on the front porch while they waited, Nick, Luella, and Ben each lighting up their pipes while the others sipped tall glasses of sweet tea.

Lucky had just taken out his harmonica to play a tune for Maggie when the thud of approaching horse's hooves attracted their attention. Rafe identified the mount at once, and he uttered a soft curse. The familiar sorrel cantering up the drive was ridden by the one man in Texas Rafe didn't want to face. Not now, anyway. Not this soon. He'd counted on having until tomorrow to figure out how best to say the words that had to be said.

Luke Prescott reined his horse to a stop to calls of welcome from Luella and Ben. Maggie rose from her seat and stood beside Rafe, slipping her hand into his. Touched by her gesture of support, he smiled tenderly down at her, then braced himself and said, "Hello, Luke. We didn't expect you this soon."

The former Texas Ranger slid from his saddle, grimacing a bit as his legs hit the ground. "I left the

Winning Ticket early." He smiled at Ben Scovall. "After all the talk you gave us about Lake Bliss water, when my bum leg got to paining me, Honor decided I simply had to come give it a try. Personally, I think she just wanted to get rid of me for a bit."

"You two still arguing about baby names?" Luella asked.

"Yeah." Luke scowled and stretched the kinks from his muscles. "I don't know why she's so dead set against Thelma."

He fastened his reins to the hitching post, then accepted Luella's welcoming hug with a grin and a return squeeze. "Lawsy, Luke, take care with an old woman's bones," Luella laughed.

"Where's an old woman?" Luke asked, looking around.

Luella slapped his shoulder. "Brought that silver tongue of yours along with you, I see."

They spent the next few minutes discussing the conditions of Luke's trip from the Winning Ticket, then Maggie asked if he'd like a tour of the hotel. But before Luke could accept her offer, Rafe interrupted. "He mentioned his leg is hurting. Why don't I show him the bathhouse first. Let him try out the mud baths on that old wound of his."

"What about the maggot?" Gus asked, pointing across the lake toward Barlow Hill's mansion. "You want to be in on that, don't you, Malone?"

"Yeah. Definitely. But I need to talk with Luke—"

Maggie took hold of Rafe's arm and looked keenly into his eyes. "We'll wait. You have your talk with Luke, Rafe. Once you're finished, we'll go see to our landlord."

Rafe nodded. If he could still walk when Luke got through with him, that is.

His partner knew him well enough to sense more in the moment than a dunk in a vat of recuperative mud, and he arched a brow toward Rafe in question. For the first time in memory, Rafe couldn't meet his friend's gaze. "Grab your saddlebags and follow me," he said gruffly, striking out across the yard.

Luke did as he asked, and neither man spoke again until they'd entered the gentlemen's bathhouse. Rafe pointed out a hook on the wall for Luke to hang his clothes. "You want to tell me what's going on?" Luke asked, stripping out of his shirt.

"Not necessarily," Rafe replied as he yanked off his boots.

The pirates had equipped the gentlemen's bathhouse with plenty of masculine accoutrements, including a well-stocked bar and a humidor filled with Havanas. Naked, Rafe splashed three fingers of bourbon into a pair of glasses, appropriated a couple of smokes, and carried them over to the square-shaped mud bath where Luke stood eyeing the sludge suspiciously. "This is supposed to make me feel good?"

"Happy as a pig in slop," Rafe replied, handing his friend his drink.

Luke glanced at the glass in Rafe's hand. "Liquor, Malone?"

Rafe lifted the glass in salute. "False courage."

"Well, hell." Luke grabbed matches from the pocket of his pants and proceeded to light his smoke. After taking two deep contemplative draws, he demanded, "What's wrong, Rafe?"

With his drink in one hand, his unlit Havana clamped between his teeth, Rafe slipped into the mud. He gestured for Luke to join him.

Luke tested the temperature of the mud bath with a toe, then shrugged and stepped right on in. He took a seat on the rock bench opposite Rafe. "This stuff stinks."

"It's not so bad. They've rigged a cistern on the roof so a person can rinse off with rainwater if he finds the smell too offensive. It's better in the ladies' bathhouse, where you can rinse off in the spring where the water enters the lake. That water is hot as a pistol and hasn't soaked up the scent of the lake yet."

"You spend much time in the *ladies'* bathhouse?"

Rafe managed a grin. "As much time as she will allow me."

"I assume you mean the delightful Miss St. John?"

"Yeah." Rafe took a sip of his drink. The liquor burned a fire down his throat. "I love her, Luke."

"So what else is new? You fall in love with every woman you run across."

"Maggie is different."

Rafe took a puff on his cigar.

"Obviously she's a little different. I haven't seen you drink over a woman since Elizabeth Perkins threw you over for Jasper P. Worrell."

"I'm not drinking because of Maggie."

"You're not? Then maybe you better tell me the why of it."

"Yeah, maybe I should." Rafe blew out a long, smokey sigh. "I've a story to tell you, partner, and it's not very pretty."

"I'm listening."

Rafe twisted his lips, exhaled a deep breath, and said it flat out. "I betrayed you."

The former ranger straightened. "Betrayed me?"

"Yeah. I broke my word to you, Luke. I went back to my old ways."

"You're stealing again?"

Luke's incredulous look made Rafe want to bury his head in the mud. "When I left the Lone Star this last time, I ended up at Andrew Montgomery's cotton plantation. I stole a bag of jewels from his safe."

"Good God, Rafe. Your amnesty! Is that why Callahan is here? Did you get caught?" Luke shoved to his feet. "What are we doing sitting around in a damned mud bath? We need to be figuring a way out of this. They'll hang you, Rafe. I'll be damned if I let that happen." He shoved his fingers through his hair, heedless of the trail of sludge he left behind. "You'll have to leave Texas. Go west."

"What!" Rafe was amazed. He had anticipated a

number of reactions from Luke, but this wasn't one of them. Luke had always been a by-the-book type of man. His honor went bone deep, and he had little tolerance for those whose integrity didn't run so strong. In fact, Rafe had often wondered why Luke hadn't given him the boot years ago. "Didn't you hear what I said? I swore on my life I'd never steal again, and then I went and did it anyway. Aren't you going to ask me why?"

"I could ask, but the answer doesn't matter all that much."

Rafe was flabbergasted. "How can you say that?"

"I know you. I know the man you are today. If you acted the thief again, I know you had a very good reason to do so. Tell me how I can help you. I'll be damned if I'm gonna let you hang."

Suddenly, unaccountably, Rafe got angry. He tossed back the rest of his drink, then slammed his glass down upon the ground. "I don't know why the hell not. I deserve to hang, Luke. I deserved it years ago, and I've always been too much a coward to face it, to face you. I let you down in the worst way. You know it, and I know it."

"What are you talking about?"

"Come on, now, Luke. We both know what wasn't said the day you asked for my oath that I wouldn't steal again. It had something to do with your being a ranger, true. But it had more to do with your being Rachel's husband and Daniel and Sarah's father."

Luke grew marble-statue still. "What does my first wife and family have to do with any of this?"

"It's what I said I'd do! It's what I'd promise I'd do! I didn't watch out for them, Luke. I told you I would, and then I went off with Callahan. I broke my word to you and your family *died.*"

The word echoed through the bathhouse.

"You stupid son of a bitch." Disgust rolled off Luke in waves. "I can't believe we're not related by blood. You and I are so much alike it's scary."

"What—"

"Hell, Rafe. You aren't to blame for what happened to Rachel and the kids, any more than I am. Have you felt this way all along? Has this been eating at you ever since the war?"

"I told you I'd watch out for them. I left them, and they died."

Pain shimmered in Luke's laugh. "Did it ever occur to you that it was my fault? Rachel and the kids weren't your responsibility. They were mine. I'm the one who should have been there to help them cross the Colorado. I'm the one who should have been there to pull them from the water before they drowned."

"But *I* was the one who promised you I'd keep an eye on them," Rafe insisted. "You are my family, Luke. Your family is my family. I failed them and I failed you."

"Oh, really? Well, how about the times you've saved my family? Saved me? Aren't you the man who pulled me from a river not long ago? Aren't you the one who protected Honor from that sorry excuse of a father of hers in my absence? Hell, Rafe, use your brain. Did Rachel berate you when you left with Callahan to join Houston's army?"

"No."

"Do you think if she were standing here today she'd blame you for not being with her when it came time to make that river crossing?"

"No. She wasn't that kind of woman."

"And, by God, I'm not that kind of man either! I never once blamed you, Rafe. To be perfectly honest, it's not very flattering for you to think I would."

Rafe closed his eyes. "It's not that I thought you blamed me, so much as I blamed myself. I loved them, you know. As much as I love Honor and your new family now."

"I know. It killed me to lose them, and I carry that hurt with me every day. But hear what I say, Malone. You are in no way responsible for what happened to

Rachel and the babies. The oath I asked you to give had nothing to do with them. It had everything to do with you. You're like a brother to me, Rafe, and I didn't want to lose you, too. I've learned a lesson or two since Honor came into my life. It takes a strong man to forgive a man who wrongs him. It takes an even stronger man to forgive himself. Now, I don't think any forgiving needs to be done, but you apparently do. So quit being a weak sister and forgive yourself, all right? Then tell me why the hell you put yourself in danger of getting hanged all over again."

Rafe studied Luke's eyes and read the truth of his words. A wave of relief as big as the Gulf of Mexico washed over him, and a slow smile broke across his face. Everything was going to be all right.

He reached for Luke's matches and lit his cigar. Settling back into the mud bath, he said, "You see, it all started with a cutlass against my neck and a call to adventure."

Luke and Luella stayed behind at Hotel Bliss when Maggie, Montgomery, Rafe, and the pirates headed for Barlow Hill's lakefront mansion. Nick tagged along to lend the event an official air.

"Our timing is just right," Snake said, motioning toward the wagonload of departing day laborers. "If I end up having to kill him, it'll be better to do it without witnesses."

Nick's jaw dropped. Rafe made a dismissing wave with his hand, silently telling his brother not to be concerned.

They filed up the front steps and entered the house. Barlow Hill came hurrying toward them. "What is the meaning of this?" he demanded. "You're tracking dust into the house!"

Rafe glanced at the pirates and said, "I think Maggie should have the honors."

She nodded her thanks and stepped forward. "Mr.

Hill, we have had a change in plans. There won't be a wedding tomorrow."

Rafe frowned at Maggie's choice of words. *No wedding? Well, maybe he'd have to do something about that.*

Ben Scovall stood beside his granddaughter. He removed the contract for the sale of the Lake Bliss property from his jacket pocket and unfolded it with a flourish. "Recall our agreement, Hill? Well, we have met your terms."

Hill grabbed the contract from Ben's hand and glanced over it briefly. "I don't . . . I never thought . . ." His head snapped up. "You have somehow acquired one hundred twenty-five thousand dollars?"

Lucky grinned. "Show him, Gus."

Gus pulled the blue velvet pouch from his pants pocket. Working the bag open, he said to Hill, "Hold out your hand."

"What? Why?"

"Never mind." Gus knelt and emptied the bag. Gems in a splendor of colors spilled out onto the entry hall's hardwood floor.

Barlow Hill gasped. "Good Lord."

"It's the money you demanded for Hotel Bliss, and then some," Lucky said.

Snake added, "Consider it a bonus for a quick departure. Like, by tonight."

Moving at a snail's pace, Hill knelt beside the gems. Wonder filled his voice. "Look at the size of that ruby. This is worth a fortune!"

"And it's all yours with a signature at the end of this paper," Ben said. "Who has the pen?"

"I do," Lucky said. "Got the inkwell, too. I think there is still enough in it even though I spilled most of it in the grass."

Hill's eyes were as round as coins. "I don't understand. You're giving these jewels to me? Maggie informed you of the wedding tomorrow, and this is her dowry?"

Rafe put his boot down on top of the ruby that had caught Hill's notice. "Boy, are you stupid. You aren't marrying Maggie, Hill. You are leaving Hotel Bliss. For good. Before supper."

Hill's head came up slowly. "Leave Bliss? After everything I went through to get it? Leave my house? Leave my wife!"

"She's not gonna be your damned wife!" Rafe gave the ruby a kick and sent it banging off Hill's knee.

"Malone, watch your language around the lady," Lucky warned.

"No!" Hill shoved to his feet. "I won't give up my house. I made so many plans. Why, I've invited the crème de la crème of Texas society to attend the Hotel Bliss reopening. We are going to have a secret wedding like Lord Bellingham and Lady Millicent. It'll be the talk of Texas for decades!"

Gus rolled his eyes at Lucky. "What the sardine is he sputtering about?"

Snake drew his cutlass and took a step forward. "Listen up, you rice rat. I'd like nothing more than to have an excuse to take off your head. It doesn't even have to be a good excuse. But my sweet granddaughter doesn't want you killed, so I'm going to try to avoid it. I suggest you admit legal defeat here and now, gather up your loot, and go. Otherwise, I might be persuaded to listen to what my own heart is telling me to do." With a quick twist of his wrist, he used the tip of the cutlass to flick a sapphire toward the door. "Fetch, boy."

"Your greed has been rewarded, Hill," Lucky added. "So, sign our contract, take the jewels, and hightail it outta here. We have the law on our side this time."

Hill scrambled to gather up each and every gem, leaving them in a small pile on the floor. Reaching for the last one, he paused. "Wait a minute. You do not have the law on your side." He pointed toward the contract Ben continued to hold. "That calls for dollars, not diamonds. You haven't met the terms. You can't take away my Bliss."

"For crying out loud!" Nick Callahan exclaimed. "He's going to quibble over a petty point like that when you're giving him twice the value? Go ahead and stick him, Snake."

"Wait!" Panic swelled in Hill's eyes. "You're wearing a Texas Ranger's badge. You're a lawman. You can't tell him to kill me. That's a crime!"

"Well, so is being stupid!"

Lucky looked at Nick. "It is?"

"Well, if it's not," Maggie observed, "it should be. Barlow, didn't you tell me when you first proposed marriage that you'd like to relocate to New York if you had the funds?" She pointed toward the gems. "There they are."

"But Maggie, I like it here now," Hill protested. "I want you for my wife. I want you in my bed."

"Well, shuck an oyster," Rafe muttered. "I'm done messing around." He grabbed the pen from Lucky and shoved it into Hill's right hand. He held out his hand to Ben for the contract, then laid it carefully on the floor. Turning to Hill, he said, "You know, Barlow, there's jewels—" Rafe's hand darted out and grabbed him by the scrotum. "—And then there's jewels."

Hill squealed as Rafe yanked him to his knees. "If you value either kind, I suggest you scratch your John Hancock across that page right this second. Otherwise, you'll be regretting the loss of your . . . treasure . . . the rest of your life."

Barlow Hill took the hint. Seconds later, Rafe folded the contract and handed it to Maggie as Hill made a beeline for the door to a chorus of comments from the pirates.

"Have a speedy trip, bark beetle."

"Don't show your face around here again, boll weevil."

"Don't be spreading any tales about us, buffalo bug."

"Now might be a good time to relocate out of Texas, apple maggot."

"Good-bye and good riddance, jigger flea."

Rafe couldn't hold back his laughter at the look on his brother's face.

The pirates and their Maggie descended the front steps of the house, their conversation happy and filled with excitement. Noting his brother had lagged behind on the veranda, Nick paused and asked, "Rafe, you coming?"

Rafe pivoted and reentered the house. He took in the graceful arch of the staircase and the spaciousness of the rooms. He could almost hear the giggles of children sliding down the polished oak banister.

"Rafe?" Nick repeated, having followed him inside.

"In a minute," he told his brother. A slow grin spread across his face and he added, "In fact, why don't you wait here with me a minute. I have an idea for a job, and I could use an extra hand."

"A job?" Nick asked.

"Yeah. A job." Rafe laughed softly. "Gentleman Rafe Malone has to work tonight. I'm gonna make the most valuable heist of my illustrious career. You wanna help?"

Maggie had a difficult time falling to sleep that night. The events of the day replayed themselves over and over in her mind and kept her heart pumping. Supper that evening had been nothing short of a celebration. Snake had outdone himself with the food, Gus and Lucky had broken out their fiddle and guitar, and she and Luella had danced until her feet hurt. The older woman had been beside herself with joy at her relatively pain-free movement and refreshed herself between dances by alternating sips of Bliss water and Papa Ben's finest bourbon. The pirates, including her father, had reminisced at length about old victories and defeats, as had Rafe, his brother, and Luke Prescott.

Finally, when first Nick Callahan and then Luella and the papas declared themselves off to bed, Maggie had waited for an expected invitation to join Rafe for a celebration of a more private type.

But the invitation never came. He merely kissed her on the cheek—on the cheek—and sent her up to bed saying he'd see her in the morning.

She'd fumed about that a good hour. She and Rafe had matters to discuss, important matters such as where they went from here. She hoped somewhere. People didn't declare their love for one another, then simply walk away.

In an effort to distract her mind from her maddening lover, she'd taken out her father's letters and reread them. That took her thoughts in an entirely new direction. She and her father still had much to talk about, so many hurts to overcome. But they'd made a good start today. She could feel good about that.

She heard the clock in the entry hall chime midnight before she finally gave in to slumber. She was enjoying a deliciously sensual dream when the touch of something soft at her neck tugged her from sleep.

Maggie opened her eyes. Light from a bedside lamp illuminated the room in a soft yellow glow. A figure came into focus. *Good Lord.* Maggie blinked hard, then looked again.

There was a pirate in her bedroom holding a feather against her neck. Dressed in tight black breeches and a flowing white silk shirt, the young, handsome, irresistible pirate wore an earring clamped on one ear and a wicked gleam in his emerald eyes. Maggie stretched sensuously and said, "I do very much hope you are here to ravish me, sir."

"Aye, wench," he replied, his slow Texian drawl putting a unique twist to sailor's speech. He drew the feather slowly across her sensitive skin. "I fully intend to shiver your timbers and swab your deck. But first, me beauty, I've a question to ask."

"Hurry up about it, then. My timbers are anxious to shiver." Maggie's gaze locked on his mouth as he loomed above her. She tilted her head back to receive his kiss, but instead, his sweet seductive breath caressed her face.

"Tell me, Miss St. John, do you consider yourself an adventurous woman?" he asked.

"An adventurous woman? Oh, yes. Definitely yes."

"Would you be interested in a . . . holiday of adventure?"

"Holiday of adventure? And just what would this holiday of adventure entail, Captain Pirate, sir?"

"Could be some fighting."

"Fighting?"

"Maybe some fussing."

"Fussing!"

"Definitely some fu—"

"Captain!"

"—Un. Fun, Miss St. John."

"Fun. Well, yes, fun is good."

"I'm glad you think so. And then, of course, what pirate adventure would be complete without lashes?"

"Lashes?"

"Hundreds of them." He gave her neck a long, slow lick.

"Lashes," she repeated on a sigh.

"So, Miss St. John, what's your answer? Care to come adventuring with me?"

"When do we leave?"

"Immediately."

"Don't forget your feather, Captain."

"Never." Slipping his hands beneath her, he lifted her from the bed. But instead of lowering her to the floor, he slung her over his shoulder.

"Rafe!" Maggie protested in a whisper. "What are you doing? Put me down."

He gave her a quick slap on the behind. "See, I told you there would be fussing. Now hush, me beauty. Let me pirate you away to paradise without alerting the watch."

"Paradise? We're leaving Bliss? Aren't you going to let me get dressed."

"Ah, Maggie my love, there is Bliss, but then there is bliss. That's part of the adventure. And you wearing naught but your nightclothes is part of my bliss."

"You are good for my vanity, Rafe Malone. Bad for my stomach, slung over your shoulder like this, but good for my feminine pride."

"I'm glad. Now, quiet. This is the delicate part of the plan." He carried her through the hotel and out the front door. Once out on the lawn, he repositioned her so that he carried her in his arms. Maggie liked that much better. With her arms looped around his neck, she was able to nibble at his earlobe.

At first, she didn't pay attention to where he carried her. But once the walk had lasted a good fifteen minutes, she became curious, lifted her head, and looked around. "Hill's house? You are taking me to Hill's house?"

"This isn't that idiot's house. This is my pirate's lair."

"Oh," she said, gazing up at the dark facade of the half-completed mansion. "It's not much like the pirates' lairs I'm familiar with."

"I'm not like any pirate you've ever known before." With that, he swept her inside the mansion and set her bare feet down upon the cool tile floor.

"You are a cocky man, Rafe Malone."

He wiggled his eyebrows salaciously. "In more ways than one."

Maggie laughed and threw her arms around him. "Oh, Rafe, I love you."

And with those words, the atmosphere of gaming

and playfulness altered. The air grew thick and heavy with anticipation. He leaned forward to kiss her, barely brushing her lips before he abruptly pulled away. "No. Not here. I wouldn't be able to stop. Nick and I didn't go to all this trouble for me to jump the gun and never get you there."

"Nick? What does Nick have to do with it?"

Rafe grabbed her hand and pulled her toward the stairs. "He helped me with my plans."

"He did?" She wasn't certain how she liked that. Some things were meant to be kept private, after all.

He stopped to give her one short, fierce kiss, then led her to a room at the far end of the second-floor hallway. "Wait here. Let me light the lamps." He disappeared into the room, shutting the door behind him.

Maggie couldn't quit smiling as she hugged herself. Mrs. Rafe Malone. Maggie Malone. Mary Malone. "Yum," she said softly. Being Mary Malone sounded downright delicious.

The door cracked open. "Shut your eyes, love."

Smiling, she did as he requested and walked blindly into the room. She heard the door shut behind her, then the click of a lock being turned. "Now?" she asked.

"Yeah, now."

Maggie opened her eyes to an explosion of color. What must have been thirty bouquets of wildflowers lay scattered across the room. Fabric from at least a dozen bolts of cloth hung draped across the walls and floor. Candles burned in containers of a variety of shapes and kind. He'd even propped one in a sand-filled shoe. A quilt lay spread across the floor beside a basket piled high with fruit and cheeses and bread. She spied a bottle of wine and a pair of the hotel's best goblets. He'd obviously raided the hotel of every pillow he could find, because they lay spread across the floor all over the room. And the bed. *Oh, my, the bed.* Pink rose petals covered the entire surface of the mattress lying on the floor against one wall. Papa Ben would have a fit when he next caught sight of his garden. Maggie laughed delightedly. "Goodness, Rafe. This isn't a pirate's lair. It's a pasha's harem."

"Pirate, pasha, what's the difference." He swept her into his arms and lifted her off the floor, twirling her slowly around and around. "Tell me again."

"Tell you what?" she teased, knowing exactly what he wanted.

"Maggie," he warned. He let her slide down his body until her feet touched the floor.

"I love you, Rafe Malone."

He breathed a soft heartfelt sigh. Slowly, he drew back from her, gazed deep into her eyes, and gently traced a finger down her cheek. "As long as I can remember, I have been searching, and I've never been sure just what I was searching for. I thought it was love, so I looked for love. I thought it was family, so I looked for family. I looked for an occupation and a passion and a reason for existing. Nothing that I acquired or came into my life filled whatever was missing inside me. Then I met you. You are what's missing in my life. You are my heart, the very air I breathe. You are my soul."

He grasped her hands, lifted them to his mouth, and pressed a kiss against her knuckles. "You are my adventure, Maggie. I need no other. I desire no other. I love you. Will you stay with me? Will you be my wife?"

Emotion filled Maggie's heart. Tears glistened in her eyes. "I love you, too, Rafe Malone. Yes, I'll be your wife. Something tells me it will be the adventure of our lives."

He stood beside the bed and held out his hand toward her. "Come, Mary, lie with me. Make love with me."

She went to him with joy in her heart and peace in her soul. And amidst the petals strewn on the bed, they repeated their pledge to one another with words and body and the joining of their hearts. Tears filled Maggie's eyes with the beauty of their loving, and when exhaustion finally claimed them, she fell asleep with a smile on her face.

The chatter of a mockingbird outside the window woke her the next morning. For just a moment, she didn't remember where she was, but then the memories of the previous night came flooding back. She stretched like a cat and smiled, turning her head to offer Rafe a good-morning kiss.

But Rafe wasn't beside her. She sat up and looked around. He wasn't in the room at all. She sniffed huffily. Maggie didn't appreciate waking up alone following a night like the past one.

The perfume of roses surrounded her as she rose from the mattress, restoring her good humor. He probably wanted to get back before the papas started stirring and had decided not to wake her since she'd gotten so little sleep the night before. "I'll forgive him," she murmured, grinning at the idea. "This time." After all, she wouldn't want to have to tell their children they'd been married with the barrel of a shotgun—five shotguns—at their backs.

She pulled on her nightgown and looked around, hoping he'd thought to leave her a change of clothing when he decorated his decadent pirate lair/harem. That's when she noticed the note on the floor beside the door. Curious, she bent and picked it up. She recognized his bold handwriting right away.

My dearest Mary. Thank you for the most wondrous night of my life. You'll find some fruit and cheese in the basket atop the quilt. Make yourself at home. Someone will be by for you later. All my love, Rafe.

PS. The door is locked. You've been abducted. You'll be released once your ransom has been paid.

"Abducted!" she screeched. "Ransom!"

Tossing down the letter, she ran first to the door. Locked. "That eel. That moray eel." She ran to the window and leaned outside. It was a good fifteen to twenty-foot drop to the pile of debris—sharp-edged rock and brick—below. If it were grass she might have attempted the jump, but the brick made it too risky to attempt safely. She settled with leaning out and shouting, knowing she was too far away for anyone to hear. "Malone! Swash your buckle right back here. You are in trouble now!"

"You've done what!" Ben Scovall exclaimed.

Andrew Montgomery shouted, "I'll kill you, boy!"

Snake went running for his cutlass and Lucky took a swing at him and knocked a lamp off a table. Gus simply folded his arms and smirked. Luella Best glanced worriedly at Luke, who gave her a sly wink, then stared hard at the toes of his boots.

Rafe, once again wearing his pirate attire, stood in the parlor at Hotel Bliss, his legs spread wide and his arms crossed over his chest. "I've kidnaped Maggie."

"Well, what the sea turtle did you go and do that for?" Lucky demanded.

"Because I want the pirates' treasure."

The room fell silent, the buccaneers' eyes going round. One by one, the pirates looked to their leader, to Captain Ben Scovall, who scrutinized Rafe with eyes that burned like blue flames. "What game are you playing, Malone?"

"It's no game, Captain. It's my life."

"What are your demands?"

Rafe turned to Montgomery. "From what I understand, you took much more from the cenote than one pouch full of jewels. Correct?"

Montgomery nodded stiffly.

"Very good. Then my first demand is that you agree to split the spoils five ways. And I mean five equal ways. Now, as a show of appreciation I want you to subtract the value of the jewels we gave Hill from one of the shares."

"Well, that won't be nothing," Snake snapped. "Those gems were full of flaws."

Rafe arched a brow and stared at Montgomery, who shrugged and said, "I expected my former partners to come for the treasure at some point. I'll admit I forgot Snake's expertise in judging jewels."

"As soon as I got a good look at 'em, I knew it was a bag of culls. They did the trick, though. Hill, the buzzard, signed the property over to us fair and square."

Unable to help himself, Rafe started to laugh. From the sounds of it, Barlow Hill got his due after all. "Smart, gentlemen. Very smart."

"Get to the point, Malone," Ben said, a muscle twitching in his jaw. "What do we have to do to get Mary Margaret back immediately?"

Rafe nodded, returning his attention to the matter at hand. "Will you agree to my first demand, Mr. Montgomery?"

"I will."

"And just where can we find the loot?"

"It's here," he groused.

Ben, Gus, Snake, and Lucky shouted in unison. "What!"

"I buried it beneath that pecan tree out behind the hotel."

Snake sputtered. "Wh-wh-why in the kelp did you do that?"

Montgomery turned a glare on him. "I liked the idea of you looking all over the world for it and having it buried beneath your nose all the time."

Gus looked at Rafe and observed, "Drew always was an ornery one. Now you see where she gets it. Like they say, a pearl doesn't swim far from the oyster."

"I don't think I've ever heard that particular saying," Rafe replied, his voice strangling on a laugh.

Montgomery whirled on Rafe. "Get on with it, man. What else do you want?"

Rafe rubbed his hand across his jaw in a considering manner. "Well, I'm a man of pride, you know, and that means I must provide for my own." Crossing the room, he lifted Luke's saddlebags from the table where his partner had left them at his request. He untied the leather lace and flipped first one pouch, and then the other open. Reaching inside, he withdrew a stack of bills from one bag and a heavy leather pouch from the other. He gave the bag a shake. The familiar clink of coins sounded like gunshots in the room. "My second demand is that you sell me half of Lake Bliss."

Lucky's legs seemed to go right out from under him as he slumped into a chair. "Half the hotel?"

"Not the hotel. The lake. I want to buy the house that sand lizard was building and half the land you now own." He tossed the coins to Ben and the bills to Gus. "Luke brought me the proceeds from the auction of my old-age stash. I've decided to invest it in bliss."

"Wait a minute," Ben said, scowling. "Let me understand this. You've abducted Maggie, and before you'll give her back you want us to give you our treasure. But at the same time, you're using your own money to buy our land. It makes no sense!"

Shaking her head, Luella stepped into the middle of the circle of men. "Pepper, dear, you're too angry, and you're not thinking straight. Rafe doesn't—"

"Luella," Rafe warned. "I do. I will. You can count on it. And I want their agreement before we go any further."

"Now, Rafe."

"I mean it, Luella. This is very, very important to me."

She sniffed. "Well, all right. But only because the cause is one I champion myself."

"You champion his cause?" Ben Scovall exploded. "Why, Luella Best, I thought I knew you! I gather I have misplaced my trust!"

"You've misplaced your sense, old man," she fussed, bracing her hands on her hips. "I won't have a beau talk to me in that tone of voice. You may address me again with an apology, Captain, and not another word prior to it." She turned to Luke. "I've preparations to make. Come with me, son. I'll need some help carrying things." Luella marched from the room, her head held high. At the doorway, she paused and gave a haughty sniff.

Smiling, Luke spoke to Rafe. "I reckon you'd better get this thing done before somebody gets hurt and your brother is forced to act in an official capacity. Where is Callahan, by the way?"

"I expect him anytime now. He rode into town on a personal errand on my behalf."

"Ah, I see."

Rafe thought he probably did. Luke was sharp as Gus's cutlass and most likely right when he said Rafe should see to the conclusion of matters. Reaching into his jacket pocket, Rafe withdrew a stack of papers. "I don't know if you are aware of this, but in my previous life I read law. Calling upon those old skills, I have drawn up contracts for you to sign agreeing to what we've discussed here today."

He spread the sheets out on the nearby desk, lifted the pen from its tray, and dipped it into the inkwell. Holding it out first to Montgomery, he said, "Sir, if you'd please go first?"

Montgomery stomped over to the table and scratched his name across the documents where Rafe indicated. When he was done, Lucky, Snake, Gus, and Ben followed in turn, the latter being the only man taking time to read the contracts. "Wait a minute, Malone. You have Montgomery splitting the treasure with the four of us. I thought you wanted it."

Gus snapped his fingers. "Of course. I don't know why it took me this long to see it. Luella was right. We let our anger interfere with our thinking. Malone does want our treasure, men. Our most valuable treasure."

Rafe snatched the signed contracts from Ben's

hands, folded them, and tucked them into his pocket as slowly, one by one, the light came on in the pirates' eyes. Montgomery swallowed hard.

"He wants our treasure," Snake breathed, laying a hand over his heart.

"Our greatest prize." Lucky buried his head in his hands.

"Our most precious gem." Gus nodded, a bitter-sweet smile upon his face.

A tear dripped from Ben Scovall's eyes. "He wants our Mary Margaret."

"That I do, gentlemen. No need to get your barnacles in a bend, however. I want Maggie for my own, but I'm willing to share. After all, my children will need their great-grandpapas around to teach them about the sea, now won't they?"

"Great-grandpapas?" the pirates spoke in unison.

"You've given me everything I've asked for as payoff for her, but I'm afraid it isn't enough. It could never be enough. You see, Maggie has stolen something from me, and there is no ransoming it back. The little thief has stolen my heart. I love her, gentlemen."

Ben cleared his throat. "And what of her feelings? Does she return your love?"

"She does. She told me so. Hotel Bliss will host a wedding today, after all. Our wedding. I'll allow nothing to interfere with it. But you are her papas, and honoring you as such, I'm asking for your blessing, gentlemen."

Gus was first to shake his hand. "You've got a halibut way of going about it. You take care of her, Malone."

"You treat her right," Lucky said.

Montgomery dipped his chin in a bow. "I like you, Mr. Malone. You've got nerve. I'm sure that'll come in handy dealing with my daughter, considering how she was reared by these reprobates."

Ben shook his head as he shook Rafe's hand. "You scrambled my thinking, Malone. Now I shall be forced to make it up to Mrs. Best. I think I will find a way to make you pay for that."

"But not today," Rafe said.

"No, not today."

Rafe turned to Snake, who sat scowling out toward the lake.

"Seems like just yesterday she was a little thing scrambling around on the ship's rigging or ringing the watch bell. Now she's a woman grown. It's difficult. It gets an old man right here." He hit his chest over his heart with his fist.

"I love her, Snake. I'll protect her with my life, just like you've done all these years. And I'll need you there to watch my back. Will you do it?"

He raked his fingers through snow white hair. "On one condition. Give us a baby, a great-granddaughter. I'll be a better teacher this time around. I'll teach her not to get hooked up with a man the likes of you, Malone." He held out his hand.

Accepting it, Rafe said, "That's a deal, Snake. That's a deal."

Rafe crossed to a nearby table and the tray he'd placed there earlier. Tugging a cork from a bottle, he poured three fingers of Bliss water into six different glasses. He passed out drinks to each of the pirates, keeping one for himself, and lifted it in toast. "To Maggie."

The papas' voices echoed, "To Maggie."

Maggie yelled out the window. "Rafe Malone, when I get my hands on you I'm gonna snatch you baldheaded!"

She yelled so hard and so long, she almost didn't hear the knock on the door. "Maggie, honey?" Luella called. "Maggie, don't throw anything. It's just me coming in."

"Luella! Thank God! Do you know what he's done? Do you know what that son of an oyster has dared to do?"

"Yes. He got Andrew Montgomery to split the treasure equally with your papas. He also used his old-age fund to buy this house and half the Lake Bliss land from them. Then, as his final bit of magic, he managed to convince your papas to bless your upcoming nuptials. They are waiting downstairs to escort you to your groom."

Shocked, Maggie stumbled back against the wall. "My what?"

"Your groom. Rafe is waiting at the hotel with Luke and Mr. Nick and some preacher the ranger fetched from town. And then there's been the nicest surprise. Apparently my Honor up and decided she needed to witness the Lake Bliss treatment on Luke's leg, so she loaded up the children and headed after him. They arrived not half an hour ago. We just think it's wonderful that all the Prescotts will be here to share this special day with you and Rafe."

"Special day," Maggie repeated.

"Yes, special day. Everything is all set for you to marry. All you have to do is change into this pretty yellow dress I brought over with me. Honor found it in your wardrobe, and she says to tell you it's a good-luck color for a wedding dress. Probably you'll want to brush your hair, too. It's looking a little mussed, Maggie dear." Luella held the dress up to Maggie and sighed. "You'll be a beautiful bride. Simply beautiful."

"I'm going to kill him. I can't believe he did this."

"Isn't he romantic! Why, I swear, if I could find a man who would go to the lengths Rafe has gone to in order to make this such a special day for you, why, I'd marry the man in a heartbeat. He met your grandfathers on their own terms, Maggie. Gentleman thief to pirate. I was so proud of him. Even if he hadn't done it before, he earned their respect then. That will make it so much nicer for you, you realize. Of course, not that we won't miss him over at the Winning Ticket.

But he says he's keeping the Lone Star, and it's not so terribly far from Lake Bliss." She batted her eyelashes and added, "Besides, I wouldn't be surprised if Pepper discovered a desire to invest some of his new wealth in the horse-breeding business. We'll see plenty of you, I'm certain of it."

Though Luella had been the one talking, Maggie was the one having trouble catching her breath. *A wedding. Today. Mrs. Rafe Malone. Mary Malone.* "What are we waiting for, Luella? Let's get moving!"

An hour later Honor Prescott's eldest son played a march on the parlor piano as Maggie, a vision in yellow calico, entered the hotel escorted by her papas. All five of them.

Rafe barely even noticed the pirates, so intent was he upon his bride; this was the first sight he'd had of her since leaving her naked and asleep in his fantasy lair early that morning.

She was so beautiful. His heart swelled with love and threatened to overflow. Their eyes met and held. He smiled at her, his rogue's smile. His pirate's smile. Damned if he hadn't won the prize of prizes.

She reached his side and stopped. Looking up at him, she said in a soft voice only the two of them could hear, "I love you, Rafe Malone. I love you with every bit of my heart. But if you ever dare to lock me up again, I'll take Papa Snake's cutlass to you. Do you understand?"

"Yes, ma'am," he said as his body responded to the saucy sparkle in her eyes.

"Then marry me, Malone. And be quick about it. I made a few changes in your pasha's abode. I think you'll find them, ah, captivating."

Rafe winked at her, then nodded to the preacher, saying, "Give us the short version, will you, Reverend?"

When the time came to make her vows, Maggie had

to raise her voice to be heard over the sniffles and coughs of her overly emotional papas. Then the preacher turned to Rafe.

"I, Rafe Malone, take you, Mary Margaret St. John, to be my lawfully wedded wife. I promise to love you, honor you, and cherish you all the days of my life." He lifted her hands to his mouth and pressed a kiss, his pledge, against her fingers.

"You have my word on it."

**POCKET STAR BOOKS
PROUDLY PRESENTS**

THE BAD LUCK WEDDING CAKE

GERALYN DAWSON

**Coming Soon
in Paperback
from Pocket Star Books**

The following is a preview of
The Bad Luck Wedding Cake . . .

Tye McBride's nose twitched, then wrinkled. His eyes cracked open and immediately started to water. "Good Lord," he muttered into his pillow. "What died?"

The smell was enough to knock a buzzard off his dinner.

The stink interfered with his thought processes, too. His mind was flowing as slow as molasses. Where was he? Scenes from the previous evening flashed through his mind. Hell's Half Acre. Rachel Warden's whorehouse. Ah, hell. Afraid to look, Tye rolled onto his back and cautiously felt the mattress beside him. Nobody there. Good.

Slowly, he opened his eyes fully. The familiar gaslight fixture hanging from the wall told him he was home. This was his bedroom in the apartment above his sister-in-law's seamstress shop, Fortune's Design. So, if he was at home, alone, then what the hell was the stench?

He twisted his neck toward his armpit and sniffed.

Wasn't him. He lifted his head and squinted against the light filtering through the windowpane, trying to judge the time. Early morning. Very early morning, by the looks of it. When had he come to bed? Had he slept at all? It didn't feel like it.

Groggily, he sat up. He grabbed his pillow and held it against his face, cloaking the odor permeating the room. He forced himself to concentrate, and finally, one by one, memories of the previous evening trickled through the muddle in his mind. Tinny saloon music. The scent of stale perfume and hard liquor. Gunshots. Just another night in Hell's Half Acre.

Located in the heart of Fort Worth, Texas, the Acre was a relatively small piece of real estate that served up more violence and vice per square foot than any other place in America. Liquor, gambling, and women were the core industry of the Acre; murder and mayhem oftentimes the product.

Tye was a man who enjoyed his vices, so during the months since he'd made Fort Worth his home, he'd spent a good deal of time in that part of town. His favorite haunt, The Green Parrot Saloon, offered dining, drinking, dancing, gambling, and whoring all under the same roof—a type of one-stop entertainment emporium. Tye enjoyed the ambiance and convenience the Parrot presented. He'd made a friend of the owner, who had laid in a supply of Tye's favorite soda water in deference to the fact that he'd sworn off liquor.

"But I didn't go to The Parrot last night," Tye muttered, remembering. "I went to Rachel Warden's. Why?"

He groaned as the reason came to him in a flash. His nieces. His brother Trace's daughters. The girls known in Fort Worth as the McBride Menaces.

And the puppy.

The dog was the reason for his mush-mindedness. He'd paid for a puppy, not a poke, at the whorehouse last night. After putting his nieces to bed, he'd headed to the Acre and bought the six-week-old mutt from one of Rachel's girls.

The puppy was a cute little boy dog with small dappled paws, a terrier snout, and a beagle body. Tye knew the girls would love him, and heaven knows they needed another pet to distract them from the fortune-telling goldfish that had them so enthralled these days. He reminded himself of that fact off and on all night when the pup's constant crying kept him awake. It wasn't until he'd let the damn thing sleep in bed with him, curled up against his belly, that the pup finally went to sleep.

But the dog wasn't in his bed now. He glanced around his bedroom. The animal wasn't anywhere to be seen. Then, Tye spied the half-opened door. "Aw, hell."

He swung his legs from the bed, and a fresh whiff of the putrid odor hit him like a fist and served to clear the rest of the cobwebs from his mind.

The puppy. The smell.

Even as his gaze searched the floor, he knew the stink was different from what he could expect to find from an untrained puppy. This was more of a burnt-fur smell.

His eyes widened and his chin slowly dropped. The puppy. The smell.

Tye's troublemaking nieces.

In his mind he heard the echo of little Katrina's voice as she begged him for a pet. *I'll take good care of it, Uncle Tye. I'll feed it and brush it and give it nice warm baths.*

Warm baths. Hot water.

"Good, God!" he cried, shoving to his feet. "They've cooked the dog!"

Clare Donovan dabbed her handkerchief at her tearing eyes and wondered once again at the creative thinking behind her great-grandmother's recipe for the flavoring extract the Donovan Baking Company used to such success. In the family, the brew was called Magic, and its formula was a closely held secret.

Unlike her brothers, who had been given the recipe upon their eighteenth birthdays, Clare was forced to wait until she turned twenty-three before her parents entrusted her with the knowledge. Even then she'd suspected they'd misled her. Sugar and honey and lemon peel in the recipe, yes. But chopped cabbage, pickled beets, and cauliflower?

Her mother had only smiled and urged her to give it a try. Clare then made her first batch of Magic and, sure enough, the strange combination of thirty ingredients did indeed cook down to a syrup so extraordinarily delicious that a single spoonful added to a batter turned an appetizing cake into a Magical cake.

Magical cakes, in turn, had propelled a small family bakery into a prosperous business whose products were in demand all along the Gulf coast.

Of course, it had taken more than extra-special baked goods to make the Donovan Baking Company what it was today. It had taken Clare's brother Thomas and his advertisement idea. Thomas had been the one to parlay a notation from Great-grandmother Gertrude's journal into a legend. She had written that the marriages of those couples who'd served a Magical cake at their weddings proved blessed with a special happiness and joy over the course of a lifetime. Thomas had publicized that claim, and five years ago, the first of many articles about Donovan's Magical Wedding Cakes had appeared in the *Galveston Gazette*.

It proved to be the beginning of the end for Clare. "Oh, stop thinking about it," she grumbled to herself, her knife slicing emphatically through a head of cauliflower. She was in the midst of a new beginning—a new business in a new city, far away from her family or fiancés or talk about a not-so-Magical Wedding Cake. Besides, she needed to keep her mind on her work. It wouldn't do to make a mistake in the recipe. The ingredients for Magic were expensive, her money in short supply. The rent and renovations on the bakery shop space had used up more of her cash than she had anticipated. "That's another mistake I made," she muttered. If she'd known how much establishing a new life would cost, she'd have taken more than her jewelry with her when she fled Galveston.

Clare stirred the final ingredient into her mixture, checked to ensure it remained at a slow boil, and placed the lid on her tall soup pot. Flipping the timer, she paused as her gaze fixed on the sand trickling through the hourglass. Thirty more minutes of cooking, then an hour or two of bottling, and she'd be through with this chore for a good six months. Still, as much as she disliked making Magic, she'd be happy to repeat the task weekly if it meant the citizens of Fort Worth found The Confectionary's baked goods worthy of their support.

The Confectionary. Clare thought it a good name

for her bake shop. The name *Donovan* wasn't part of it anywhere.

Lining her knives, spoons, and measuring cups in precise washing order on her cutting board, she hummed an upbeat tune as she mentally inventoried her supplies. She needed to order more sugarhouse molasses, cloves, and gelatin from Mr. Hankins at Fort Worth City Mercantile. She likely had enough flour, pulverized sugar, and cinnamon. Better check on the carbonate of ammonia. She hoped to be settled in and open for business two weeks from today.

She'd finished washing and had picked up her dishtowel when she heard the first thud coming from the rooms above her. Alarmed, she glanced toward the ceiling. No one should be upstairs. When he'd leased her the business space four months ago, her landlord had refused to rent her the convenient apartment above her street-level shop because he kept it for use by visiting family members. But her landlord and his wife were currently out of the country on a belated honeymoon. What reason would any family have to be visiting?

Don't borrow trouble, Clare, she told herself. Despite the fact that Fort Worth had more murders per acre than anywhere west of the Mississippi, the sheriff kept that type of activity pretty much confined to the Acre. She'd never once felt less than safe here in this building. Well, except for when the sisters from the Catholic church across the street paid a call. That Sister Gonzaga was downright scary.

Still, when she heard a second noise above her—one that sounded suspiciously like a slamming door—she realized just how alone she was in the Rankin building this early in the day. The seamstress shop next door didn't open for hours yet. Unbidden, the memory of her brothers' constant warnings to keep her doors locked fluttered like a red flag in her mind.

Maybe it wouldn't hurt to heed some of their warnings now and again.

Setting down her dishcloth, Clare stepped into the public room and gave it a sweeping glance. Her shop was divided into two main sections, with her kitchen in the back portion. The front room contained a display for her baked goods, counter space, and five sets of small round tables and chairs for patrons who wished to consume their purchases in the shop. This portion of the building remained empty, thank goodness.

Her gaze drifted toward the unlocked front door that opened into a small vestibule rather than directly on to the street. Upon entering the Rankin building, customers faced three doors. The center opened to the staircase leading to the apartment above, and the right led to the dressmaker's shop next door. The bakery's entrance was to the left.

Clare took two steps forward until the footsteps pounding down the stairs brought her to a dead stop. She gasped softly when a shadow flickered in the frosted glass decorating the door. Whirling around, she fled back into her kitchen.

Door hinges creaked as Clare stepped quietly to her work table and picked up her paring knife. In her mind, she heard her brother Johnny say, "You're quick, Clare. A man gives you trouble, you go for the throat."

Good Lord, she didn't want to hurt anyone.

She glanced toward the door leading to the alley

and quickly debated whether to flee or hide. She chose the latter, thinking it best to stay out of the way of whatever trouble headed in her direction. Besides, she'd done enough fleeing from problems recently. She was finished with that. She dropped to her knees and prepared to crawl beneath the broad oak worktable when a near-naked man burst into her kitchen, hollering, "Girls, get the dog off the stove!"

Clare froze. He was tall and broad and wore only a pair of white cotton men's drawers, their legs hemmed indecently and unevenly short, halfway down his thighs. Red embroidered hearts adorned the cotton. Recognizing her landlord, Clare climbed to her feet. "Mr. McBride?"

He paused only long enough to give her a harried, curious look. "Who are you? Where are the girls?"

He rushed toward the stove, where her Magic bubbled. When he reached for the handles on the pot, Clare tore her gaze off the expanse of masculine bare chest and lunged forward. "What are you doing? Get away from my Magic!"

"Magic?" He yanked the soup pot off the fire, cursing beneath his breath and waving his hands. He hadn't bothered to grab hot pads. "His name was Sport."

"What?"

"The Blessings must have thought to give him a bath on the stove."

Clare couldn't remember ever being this flustered. The last time a man clad in nothing more than his underwear stood in her kitchen, she'd found herself engaged before sunset. But at least she wouldn't end up betrothed to Trace McBride; he was very much married.

And he was also aboard a Caribbean-bound ship with his wife, Jenny.

Clare gawked at the stranger's face. "Who *are* you?"

"Poor Sport," he groaned, his stare fastened on the soup pot. "I thought the girls were old enough to care for a pet. I should have left the pup at the whorehouse." Green eyes cut in her direction. "They are hiding, aren't they? The stink must have scared them off." He reached for the pot's lid. "I'll take care of this, but would you please go find my nieces?"

Still holding the knife, Clare lifted her hand. "Touch that kettle and I'll take your hand off. It ruins the recipe if you peek."

"Recipe!" The man's eyes rounded in horror. "You've cooked the puppy on purpose?"

"The puppy is under the table!"

"You've already removed the corpse?"

Clare pointed toward a basket beneath the table. "He's asleep, you imbecile. I didn't cook your dog. That's my Magic cooking on the stove."

"Magic. . . . Magic?" He strode toward work bench. "You cooked a cat?"

"Cat!" Even in her pique Clare couldn't help but notice the bunch of muscles in his thighs as he crouched down to peer beneath the table. After all, the red hearts embroidered around the hem naturally drew her gaze.

"Well, something died," he stated flatly, reaching a gentle hand toward the sleeping puppy, scratching him behind his floppy ears.

Clare slapped the knife down onto the cutting board, picked up her hot pads, and shifted the soup pot back onto the fire. Folding her arms, she said, "I killed a cabbage, sir, not a cat. A cauliflower, too."

For a long moment, he didn't reply. Then he twisted his head and grinned up at her, looking like an entirely different person than the man who'd barged into her kitchen a few confusing moments earlier. Wicked amusement danced in his eyes, and his smile . . . well, it made Clare's knees go a bit weak.

Lifting the puppy from its makeshift bed, a basket and blanket Clare had provided upon discovering the canine in her kitchen when she arrived at the shop that morning, he cuddled it against his broad, bare chest and slowly stood. "So you're the one the sheriff has been searching for."

"Pardon me?"

"I doubt it. Probably get ten years to life in Huntsville prison. Be a right shame, too, if you ask me. Your eyes are too pretty to be looking out from behind bars. Remind me of the Texas sky on a rain-washed spring morning. Too bad you had to turn out to be the one."

If Clare had been flustered before, now she was downright addled. "What one?"

"The vegetable killer, of course. Tell me, do you limit yourself to 'C' plants, or have you branched out, included a squash or tomato or two?" He eyed the soup pot suspiciously. "I wouldn't be surprised to learn you stalked broccoli, to tell you the truth."

The absurdity of the entire scene struck her, then, and she started to laugh. "Well, that takes care of me—I'm the vegetable killer. So who are you?" Feeling bold, she allowed her gaze to sweep his body deliberately. "A refugee from one of the sin parlors in the Acre?"

He glanced down and winced. "I was in a hurry to

save the mutt, here. Grabbed the first thing I came across. Emma gave these drawers to me yesterday. She's trying to teach herself to follow in her mama's footsteps."

"I hesitate even to wonder as to Emma's mother's occupation," Clare said dryly.

He muttered something beneath his breath, shoved the dog at her, and strode from the room. Five minutes later he was back, dressed in cotton-twill pants and buttoning a blue chambray shirt as he entered the kitchen. He rattled off his explanation in crisp, concise sentences. "I'm Thackery McBride, Trace's brother. Please call me Tye. The puppy is a gift for my nieces, one of whom is Emma. Her mother, Jenny, is a seamstress. My nieces have a tendency to tumble into trouble, so when I woke to find the pup missing from my room and a godawful smell coming from downstairs I naturally assumed they'd gotten into more mischief. But I checked and they're still in bed asleep. Now, that explains me. How about you?"

With his rapid recital, the situation fell into place for her. "You're the relative caring for the McBride Menaces while their parents honeymoon."

He frowned. "I know the reputation my nieces have here in town, but I prefer a different term—Blessings. They are the McBride Blessings, Miss . . . ?"

Clare felt a rush of warmth toward this strange man and she smiled. The girl who'd grown up to the moniker Catastrophic Clare appreciated his sentiment more than he could ever know. She wiped her hand on her apron, then extended it. "Clare. Clare Donovan. I rented this shop space shortly before your brother left on his trip."

He shook her hand, but his brows arched and his

tone held a doubtful note as he asked, "You're the baker?"

"Yes."

"You intend to make food and sell it from this shop?"

Her appreciation faded at the doubt she heard in his voice. She snatched her hand away from him. "You have a problem with that?"

He rubbed his palm across his jaw, then gestured toward the pot of Magic. "I've made the acquaintance of men who drove cattle from here to Wichita, never once washing their clothes. I have to tell you, ma'am, their socks had nothing on your brew, here, when it comes to perfume. I just hope the stuff tastes better than it smells, that's all."

Clare wasn't offended. The making of Magic was an odorous undertaking. Shrugging, she walked over to the large earthenware jar that sat on her worktable. Lifting the lid with one hand, she gestured with the other. "Molasses cookies. Help yourself."

"Is it safe?"

She challenged him with her smile.

He cocked his head and clicked his tongue. "I purely hate looking like a coward to a woman with hair the color of a West Texas sunset." He approached her, and standing close—too close—he reached a hand into the jar and drew out a sweet. His gaze never left hers as he took a small bite of the cookie. Immediately, his eyes widened. Then they drifted shut. He chewed slowly, swallowed, and dropped to one knee. "Miss Donovan." He took her hand. "Will you do me the honor of becoming my wife?"

A gasp, a squeal, and a screech sounded from behind her.

"This is wonderful!" a girl's voice exclaimed. "Just what we hoped for."

A different voice. "Yippie! Another family wedding! No animals this time, Uncle Tye. We promise!"

Clare whirled around just as a third girl spoke. "Wait a minute. We've made a mistake. The hair color fooled us!" She pointed dramatically toward Clare. "Look, sisters. That's not Loretta Davis!"

Look for
The Bad Luck
Wedding Cake
Wherever Paperback Books
Are Sold
Coming Soon
from Pocket Star Books.